# THE CITY OF NEW APHROS
## BOOK 2 OF ANDROMEDA'S ACCOUNT

L.B. BENSON

EMERALD MOON

# ALSO BY L.B. BENSON

*ANDROMEDA'S ACCOUNT*

*The Bartered Soul*
*The City of New Aphros*
*Andromeda's Vengeance*
*The Northman's Lullaby*

*THE WOLVES OF WOODBINE HOLLOW*

*Sunset Daydreams*
*Neon Elegies*

# THE CITY OF NEW APHROS
## BOOK 2 OF ANDROMEDA'S ACCOUNT

By
L.B. Benson

Cover design by Hampton Lamoureaux / TS95 Studios www. ts95studios.com

Illustration by Annika Weidner / Pitchblack Illustration www.pitchblackil lustration.com

Edited by Aimee Vance
www.aimeevancebooks.com

ISBNs
979-8-9861231-3-4 (eBook)
979-8-9861231-4-1 (Paperback)
979-8-9861231-5-8 (Hardback)

Published by Emerald Moon Press
https://lbtheauthor.com

*To anyone who has been dimming their glow.*
*It's time to step into your power.*
*xo, LB*

# CONTENT WARNING

*The City of New Aphros* is an adult fantasy/romance that contains content that might be upsetting for some readers. It is intended for readers over the age of 18.

To view detailed content/trigger warnings, please visit the author's website: https://lbtheauthor.com or scan the QR code below.

# PROLOGUE

*Two Months Ago*
*Grand Castle of Aphros, Selennia*

"**B**ring the new prisoner in," the Commander of the Guard barked to one of the two soldiers flanking the massive oak doors of the throne room.

Commander Charleston stood in his usual place, just to the side of the throne where King Dargan Blackwell sat, overseeing his men and the entirety of the throne room. One of the two guards gripped the iron handle to retrieve the prisoner from where he was being kept in the outer hallway, the creak of the hinges drawing the eyes of the guards lining the sides of the cavernous space, empty but for the throne in the center of the room. Cast in cool colors of white and grey, the chamber should have felt serene and light, but the dark man perched on the throne cast a shadow over the room and those within it.

King Dargan reclined on the stone bench wearing his usual dark tunic and breeches. Tired of listening to the endless prattling of his subjects, he picked at his tidy finger-nails with a small blade while the young guard dragged a bloodstained figure through the doors, over the grey and white marble tiles, and to the foot of the dais. Blood and dirt stains sullied the pale floors while Blackwell wrinkled his nose in distaste. He liked things pristine.

"Why are you bringing this creature before me, Commander?" Blackwell's deep voice echoed through the empty room. He raised his dark brows at the Commander at his side, impatience written clearly on his expression. Commander Charleston may have been his closest confidant — a friend, even — but today even *he* grated on the King's nerves. Charleston, of all people, knew Blackwell's standing order: criminals, rebels, and heretics were to be executed immediately.

No trial.

No appearance before the monarch.

This spectacle was a waste of time.

"This man was captured stealing outside the city, then fought against the guards in Athene when he was arrested. But the story he told will be of interest to you, Your Majesty," the Commander answered, bowing his head.

Blackwell's eyes lingered on the Commander as his brow creased in thought. Charleston was always clean-cut — his red and black armor polished to perfection, accenting the simple sword that hung at his side. He was handsome, save for the deep scar cutting from his temple to his chin, just missing his eye, that pulled his mouth into a constant grimace. A remnant from the takeover eight years ago, when he fought valiantly to protect the King as they defeated Adelaide's forces. Then Adelaide herself.

"Hurry up, then," the King demanded of the man slumped at the guard's feet as he tapped his fingers against the arm of the white throne he sat upon.

Even though Blackwell's griffin emblazoned the banners hung on the pale stone walls behind him, hiding the carvings from Adelaide's rule and the reigns of the queens before her, he never bothered to replace the throne that was once hers. Knowing the rage Adelaide would have felt at seeing him in her place upon the sacred moonstone seat of Selennia brought Blackwell great pleasure.

In response to the echoing tap, the prisoner whimpered, still curled on the floor. The young soldier who dragged him before the dais kicked his side in encouragement, causing the man to groan and pull his knees to his chest.

"I've already given you more attention than a criminal such as yourself deserves. Speak now, or be hanged for wasting my time," the King's voice held no inflection, his neutrality more frightening than anger.

"Tell your king the tale you spun for my men. Now." The Commander demanded, stepping off the dais to pull the prisoner to his feet.

Hanging limply in the Commander's grip, the man finally looked up at the King with pale eyes full of pain and fear. As if compelled by the force of Blackwell's dark gaze, words tumbled from the prisoner's mouth.

"When my brother didn't dock in Athene aboard the *Bartered Soul*, I panicked, Your Majesty," the prisoner began, his hand hovering over his injured side as he wheezed through what sounded like a broken rib. "I took to the taverns to ask the crewmen of his whereabouts. Most of them pushed me off, refusing to speak to me at all. But one finally took pity on me and whispered a shocking tale."

"Get on with it," the King urged, rolling his eyes. He shot a sideways glance at the Commander, his pursed lips a message that his friend would suffer consequences for this colossal waste of time just as much as the prisoner in his grip if he wasn't satisfied with the remainder of the tale. The Commander merely encouraged Blackwell to continue listening with a tilt of his chin.

"The sailor said my brother had been involved with an incident aboard the ship after leaving Artemisia. He disobeyed the captain and was thrown into the sea for it. All over the captain's whore," the prisoner spat the final words.

"Commander, explain to me why this man is still speaking. Why would I care about a pirate's whore or a criminal's missing brother?"

"She... she was a priestess, Your Majesty. One of the whores leftover from the temples!" the prisoner blurted before the Commander, or the vicious young guard still standing at his side, forced him to talk.

"A priestess?" Blackwell leaned forward on his throne, his curiosity piqued.

"Yes, my King." The prisoner nodded vigorously, his eyes expanding as he silently begged for mercy. "The crewman reverently said she was beautiful and vicious, almost like he was proud to have witnessed my brother's punishment. She must've put a spell on the captain — why else would he not let the rest of his crew lay with a whore? After he told me this tale, I made my way down to the docks and saw the bitch with Captain Lennox. He was carrying her back to the ship as if she had tried to escape."

"What did she look like?" Blackwell continued his questioning more softly, coaxing the information from the man, even as his eyes glistened with excitement.

"Black hair. Blue eyes. Skin as perfect as the inside of a seashell. A ghost of Queen Adelaide, herself." The prisoner clapped his mouth shut as soon as the words left it. Everyone in Selennia knew better than to mention the late queen to Blackwell. The memory of his savage takeover was still fresh in the minds of those who had survived it.

Blackwell's dark eyes grew wide as the man spoke, his fingers gripping the armrest of the throne. Hearing of a beautiful, vicious priestess in and of itself would have interested him. He enjoyed breaking beautiful things. But hearing of a woman who resembled Adelaide... This was something Blackwell could not ignore.

After eight years on the throne, Blackwell was no fool. He was fully aware that the majority of the population of Selennia disapproved of his rule, both because of the way he took power — sending soldiers to drag priestesses and villagers alike out to be slaughtered and tossed in mass graves, or hung in town squares to serve as examples while destroying temples and neighboring sacred groves along the way — and because of the continued violent persecution of those who dared to speak against his policies or the new religion he forced upon them. Many still worshipped the Goddess even though it was now illegal to do so, feigning adherence to the new religion while risking their lives to meet in whatever groves still stood under full moons. It was only by fear that he controlled them at all, kept the rebellion that simmered from boiling over, and kept the Old Ways hidden from plain sight.

When he disposed of Adelaide, he had sent men to all of the temples to crush the threat of the priestesses, the last ones who might stand in his way. But his troops were also supposed to search for, and bring back, any of the young women who resembled the late queen. He knew she had an heir hidden in the temples, but his spies hadn't been so gifted as to know where, or what the girl's name was.

Peasants still whispered about a lost heir, one who might return to save them, like a heroine from some fairy-tale. If she were to resurface now, his tenuous hold on the country could slip and he could lose power completely. But, if he could finally locate the woman and force her to stand at his side, if he could unite their rule with her as his captive queen, then he would secure his position perma-nently through her connection to Selennia and its people.

"Commander, it sounds like we need to send men to speak with the madames along the coastline. Especially in Artemisia and Athene. Investigate the brothels and find this woman. See it done. Immediately." Blackwell's orders were terse and Commander Charleston gave a sharp nod of his auburn head in understanding.

"What of this one, Your Majesty?" Charleston gestured toward the man still kneeling on the floor.

"What was he arrested for in the first place?" Blackwell asked.

"He was caught stealing in the market, mainly food-stuffs. When he was confronted, he put up a fight."

"Ah, a thief. And he consorts with pirates; he admitted as much. Brand his cheek to mark his crimes for the people to see. Then hang him from the gallows at the docks as an example," Blackwell calmly replied.

"What? No! Your Majesty, I beg of you!" the young man pleaded, his throat raw from the beating he had endured already. "I have a family, I didn't steal anything worth hanging for! I was just trying to provide for them!"

"A swift death is more than you deserve. Get him out of my sight." With a wave of dismissal and a cruel chuckle, the King dispensed his justice as the younger soldier dragged the sobbing prisoner back through the blood and dirt and out the oak door. Another soldier standing to the side looked disturbed at the struggle but rearranged his face before it was noted.

"Find the whore, Commander. And bring her to me."

"As you say, Your Majesty," the Commander agreed, then bowed and marched through the open oak door to dispense orders and ready his men.

# CHAPTER I

"Are you ready for tomorrow?" Lennox asks, stroking my hair while my head rests on his tattooed chest, the amber light from an oil lamp washing the room in a dim warmth. Our ship sways with the soothing waves of the gulf as we lay tangled together in the linen sheets of his bed, the orange sunset fading to twilight as we discuss our arrival in New Aphros tomorrow morning. The cabin of *Andromeda's Vengeance* is smaller than the one we shared on the *Bartered Soul*, but it has been a comfortable haven for us since leaving Delosia.

"I think so," I answer honestly, tilting my head up so I can look into his dark green eyes. "I hid my feelings and pretended to just be a whore for so many years, I'm sure I can fall back into the act."

"You just need to be prepared." He places a tender kiss on the top of my head. "I have to be the man you thought I was, the one you hated when we left Selennia."

"I know." The memory of the cocky rogue with his feet on Madame Celeste's desk at the House of Starlight ready to purchase my company rises to my mind, so at odds with the man holding me.

But now, two and a half months after that fateful night, I know the truth about Captain William Lennox — not just his hidden identity, but his honorable motives, as well. Just like he knows I'm not merely a priestess he fell in love with in the midsummer rites years ago or a prostitute trapped in a brothel on the shores of Selennia. A smile creeps across my face at the memory of how angry I was the night he procured Lyra and me, and then how relieved I was when I found he hadn't left me behind on the white sandy beaches of Delosia a week and a half ago.

"Remind me who Salome is again." I roll to my side and prop my head on my hand. We should reach New Aphros tomorrow, and I fight the drowsiness that threatens to pull me into sleep so I can hear his words. "And why we are staying in a brothel and not a boarding house."

"Salome was a friend of my mother's — another priestess. But she left Selennia years ago before Blackwell took power. I told you about joining Captain Jackson's crew after he took over the King's ship I was pressed on. The first time we docked in New Aphros, I found her. She's one of the wealthier madames in town and has helped find safe refuge for some of the women and girls I've brought across the sea over the years." He rolls to face me, aimlessly running his fingers through my loose hair.

"She's like family to me. But to the residents of New Aphros, I serve as a supplier of goods and women for her business. In exchange, she provides me lodging and diversion while I'm in the city. We need to uphold that image, my pretty priestess. I don't want anyone in New Aphros to think you might be a potential weakness to use against me. I won't risk you that way." His expression hardens, the muscles in his jaw tensing. "I have enemies everywhere — both uptight politicians who care more about tax dollars and think to catch me selling under the table and other pirate captains who wish to exploit any potential advantage over me. Even though New Aphros is a free city, run by the Merchant Council instead of a monarch or church, there are too many desperate people there for me to let down my guard."

"I understand. I can hide my feelings if you can."

My answer is far more confident than I feel. The emotions that began on our voyage from Selennia to Delosia, then thrived in the tropical heat, have only deepened during the short time it's taken to sail from the turquoise waters to the murky gulf. The cold facade I spent years building while I hid and worked in the House of Starlight has fully cracked, and I'm not certain I can hide the love I feel for the man at my side. I've never felt more vulnerable than I have in these past few weeks, sharing our stories and bodies in the amber lantern light, but I've also never felt closer to another person, more open with anyone. I feel safer with him than I have in a long time, even though I've decided to follow him into his life of piracy on the sea, where nothing is ever safe.

***

ANDROMEDA'S VENGEANCE, THE SLOOP TAKEN AT A HIGH COST on our trip from Selennia to Delosia, is anchored in the calm gulf. While the ship has been my home for our voyage from

Delosia, I'm still not certain its acquisition was worth the loss of six crew members, or the near-fatal wound Lennox took in the battle against the King's sailors who manned it, even if its capture does weaken our enemy's fleet.

Far in the distance, the bones of a new city are just visible from my vantage point at the bow of the ship, framing for new buildings and homes standing out against the wilder landscape beyond. I inspect the other vessels in the makeshift harbor, easily spotting the *Bartered Soul*, temporarily captained by Erik Varangr, its former quarter-master, for the short voyage from Delosia. The sounds of the crew preparing for the trip to shore is a familiar din, blending with the comforting slap of the waves against the hull. The pull of a now familiar presence drags my attention from the dark water, and when I turn I look up into Lennox's handsome face.

His naturally golden hair is masked with black walnut hulls again, making it a dark brown that appears black in the dim mist, obscuring his true appearance. Once again, he looks the part of a dangerous pirate, handsome and deadly, just like he did a few months ago when he pretended to buy my company. Today he wears all black, from his greatcoat to his linen shirt and breeches, while a dark tricornered hat tops his blackened hair. One of his pistols is visible at the front of his belt, while I know the other is tucked at his lower back, and his cutlass swings at his hip, all strategic choices contributing to his menacing aura.

Wrapping one of his arms around me, Lennox pulls me tight to his side. Together, we stand like dark sentinels on the deck as we prepare to meet the riverboat men who will take us to the free city of New Aphros, taking this moment to show our true affection once more before having to take on the roles of a pirate and his favored whore. Despite my perceived station, my company only adds to his fearsome appearance with the darkened sigil visible on my brow. The silvery upturned crescent mark remains clear after the full moon ceremony with Lyra and Siobhan on the sands of Delosia, no longer resembling a faded scar like it did when I left Selennia.

The city we are bound for is different from both the tropical island we recently left behind and the cool shores where I was born. Here, we can't anchor at the port, or row our boats straight to the town. First, we must take a small boat to the shore, then another flat-bottomed vessel will ferry us up a large river to the expanding city. During our layover, our ship's cargo will be transported aboard the riverboats to the city for sale and trade while we mingle with Lennox's contacts in the city.

I changed into a simple, dark grey dress for my intro-duction to the city, topped with a lightweight frock coat in deep indigo. Even though I've comfortably worn my dagger openly in the new sheath I had made in Delosia while on board, I know doing so in the streets of the city is at odds with the image of a pirate's whore. So instead, I tuck the plain blade away in a deep pocket like I have for so many years now, its presence comforting even if it remains a secret.

To occupy my time on the voyage from Delosia to the port of New Aphros, I worked with Lennox and Pike, the older man standing in as quartermaster in Erik's stead, to master the small weapon. Despite the hours of sweating and cursing, having my blade blocked or knocked from my grip by the older man with his affable grin, I made steady progress. I savored the sore muscles Lennox massaged for me in the evenings and the calluses that formed on my hands from those lessons. Each success brought me satisfaction that I was one step closer to being more capable of defending myself.

Now, I no longer depend on instinct alone to aim my blade, so the fear that I evoke in the sailors we encounter, here and elsewhere, will be more warranted than ever. Not just because of the superstitions the sigil delineating me as a priestess stirs, or the rumors that follow me describing my viciousness, but because there will be no hesitation to defend myself, and because my blade will strike true.

Double-checking that the dagger is in place one more time, I look out across the gulf. The late autumn air has a slight chill from the proximity to the water, but the mild temperature makes the linen coat I wear over my dress warm enough for the journey to shore and then up the river to the city. Keeping his arm around my shoulders, Lennox presses a final kiss to the top of my head before turning to his crew.

"Ready the boats!" Lennox shouts, and the crew springs into action, the order spreading through the crewmembers as they prepare several rowboats.

A deep breath steadies the nerves tingling under my skin, alight at the thought of the unknown that waits on shore. The time spent on Delosia was a pleasant surprise, and the calm days aboard the *Vengeance* have been a balm to my blemished soul, easing the pain I've held close for years. But the city we are entering is completely foreign to me. Uneasiness coils in my gut as I hope I remember how to don the careful facade I created when my old life was destroyed eight years ago.

Lennox helps me climb into one of the small boats before we are lowered down to the dark water below. The damp ropes creak under the strain of our weight and, despite the water being calm, the jolting splash when our boat hits the sea makes me grip the wood of the bench beneath me. Two of the crew members row our boat, while two additional vessels follow behind.

Adjusting to the gentle rocking, I turn to look at the other boats following us, inhaling the briny air heavy with morning mist. Erik sits in one of the boats from the *Bartered Soul* with a few members of his crew and a sampling of the cargo for trade. Erik's intimidating frame and distinct appearance — dark hair worn in a long braid with the sides shaved to reveal tattoos covering his scalp — make him unmistakable amongst the other men in the distance.

With a gentle bump, the row boats quickly come to rest at the edge of the murky water. I glance over the edge of the boat to find there is no pristine white sand to greet me here. Before I can contemplate how to get to shore without soiling my fresh clothing, Lennox hops out, his steps squelching slightly in the sludge, then lifts me to dry ground to save my skirts and boots from sliding in the thick, acrid mud.

A group of men stands on the shore between the gulf and the wide river lined with dark trees that empties to the sea. To their right waits a large, flat-bottomed boat, our transportation to the town in the distance. The men shuffle their feet and avert their eyes from Lennox and Erik as if they are wary of their presence, but when I turn toward them the waiting sailors openly inspect me. I can almost hear their jokes as they turn to one another with grins and laughter. I purse my lips and harden my gaze as I continue to observe the men, but their smiles disappear and they return quickly to work as Lennox steps to my side, grasping me firmly by my upper arm.

"I see your fearsome reputation *does* precede you here, Captain Lennox," I murmur to him, cutting my eyes to the side to see his lip twitching in a small smirk.

"As it should. New Aphros may be a melting pot of people and cultures, but violence is a universal language, and I am known to wield it freely. You should keep that in mind as well, my pretty priestess."

Nodding at his warning, I glance around once more at the shoreline and tall cypress trees standing beyond. The earthy scent of mud and silt is so different from the crisp air and rocky beaches of Selennia and the sparkling white sands of tropical Delosia. Memories of my friends on the sunny beach we left behind tug at my heart a bit, but I'm relieved to know they are both in a safe place, even if I work to press down my nervousness at the thought of the new city that awaits me. My fingers brush against my sigil, almost involuntarily as my mind drifts.

As if sensing the tenor of my thoughts Lennox leans close to me. "Don't worry about your sigil, there are plenty in the city who keep to the Old Ways. Keep your guard up, but don't fear Blackwell's men here," he whispers against the shell of my ear, his warm breath raising goosebumps along my skin.

I'm comforted knowing that the Old Ways are allowed in this city — how could they not be, having been named after Aphros, the capital city of Selennia, where the Central Temple and Grand Castle stand? My breath escapes in a sigh as I involuntarily lean toward his heat, but he huffs a laugh as he pulls away to guide me toward the waiting riverboat. With a wicked smile, he asks, "Ready to prowl the city of New Aphros, my she-wolf?" Without waiting for my response, he tugs me aboard.

As the flat-bottomed boat travels slowly up the massive muddy river toward our destination, propelled by grunts and long oars handled by the rough men from the shore, I perch on one of the crates of contraband staring into the churning water. A breeze from the gulf follows us, wafting the scent of rotting cypress needles and damp earth over me as I watch large white birds launch into the air from the shallows. The trees I saw standing on the shore continue lining the edges of the river as we make our way toward the town, their dark trunks wrapped in eerie mist as if ghosts lurk on the edges of the opaque water. Some are mere stumps sticking above the water line, while others loom high overhead with moss hanging from their branches, swaying in the cool breeze.

A shiver runs down my spine as excitement and wariness intertwine in my breast the closer we get to the port. Lennox leans against the rail of the boat, casually crossing his arms across his chest to face me, and to keep watch over the men who row and steer the boat up the river.

"Once we dock, Erik will handle the off-loading of the sample of goods. You and I will head to Salome's," he explains. "This week we'll be concerned with trade and sales so I can pay the crew for the season. Hopefully, we can dispense with the stock quickly and I can meet with my contacts on the Merchant Council for any interesting news they might have."

"And what am I to be concerned with, Captain?" I ask, giving him a sultry smile for the benefit of the strangers aboard, even if I *am* curious how I should expect to spend my time.

"Ah, you'll meet Salome and her girls, my pretty priestess. I'm sure between that and my needs you'll have plenty to do." His words seem crass, but I simply nod as he pushes away from the rail to lean over me where I sit, knowing prying eyes watch us. His breath is warm as he whispers against my ear, barely audible over the splash of the oars. "I'll have meetings throughout our stay, but I plan on showing you a grand time in this city, Nerissa. You needn't worry." I look forward to exploring a city with new sights and sounds that, from what Lennox has told me, are vastly different than what I experienced in Selennia, sending a ripple of excitement dancing over me.

"Of course, Captain," I answer as he pulls away, tipping my chin up with a finger to look into my eyes with a smirk. I avert my gaze, avoiding his burning stare as if he frightens me, the way I would have if I still feared him, the way the men on the shore did when he glared at them.

"Good girl," he chuckles roughly, before releasing me and stepping away.

---

WHEN WE DOCK AT THE PORT OF NEW APHROS, THE FAMILIAR cry of seagulls flying overhead greets us amongst the noise of sailors' shouts and oars smacking onto the wood deck. I wait between Lennox and Erik, dwarfed by their intimidating forms as the gangplank is dropped to the boards on the dock with a loud clap. Lennox steps down in front of me, boots striking a staccato rhythm as he straightens the front of his coat and swaggers onto the dock. Erik gestures for me to walk ahead of him so I'm protected from both sides. The cool breeze doesn't seem to bother him; his muscular biceps are on display in a short sleeve tunic, the same as they have been most of the time I have known the Northman.

My eyes grow wide as I step onto the worn planks of the crowded dock, surrounded by the cacophony of the busy street and the bustling port, to view New Aphros for the first time up close. Carriages and wagons line the street, both ornate and utilitarian varieties. Horses and mules resting in their traces snort and nicker to one another while goods are loaded and unloaded. Lining the far edge of the docks vendors selling food and drink hawk refreshments to the crowd, the scent of cider and seafood mingling with the odor of damp wood and men's sweat.

Although I lived in Artemisia and Athene, both port towns, they were small and quiet compared to the sight that greets me here. The clamor and activity assault my senses, my eyes darting from one new sight to another as goods and people are transported to and fro. New Aphros is one of the largest hubs for trade on the coast of the new continent, and business appears to move at a breakneck pace.

From the ship's deck, the city appeared small, despite what Lennox told me about it, but now that I stand ashore I can tell that the land dips and its true size was hidden from view. The center of town is far more developed and decorative than I expected, with a large central square across the street from the port, separated from the busy riverfront by a wrought iron fence and surrounded by neat rows of brick and multi-hued buildings. An ancient oak tree stands in the center of the square with a partially completed stone half-wall circling it. Multi-colored ribbons tied to its lower branches dance in the breeze. The construction I viewed from *Andromeda's Vengeance* lies on the outskirts of the city far in the distance, evidence of the growth of the elegant free city.

Men stand on scaffolding to work on the construction of a cathedral that faces the square and the docks, its clock-tower barely cresting the top of the oak tree to greet merchants and sailors as they step into the city or pass by on their errands. The clank of their hammers and the faint sound of them singing work songs and laughing to pass the time barely reach me over the rattle of carriages, clack of hooves, and grunts of men carrying heavy parcels to and from the boats tied at the dock.

I grit my teeth at the sight of the construction; it seems even here, the new religion so beloved by King Dargan is spreading and trying to take over the central life of the place, even though New Aphros was founded on freedom and answers to no king or deity. Although my sisters and I worshiped the Goddess, we never proselytized from our temples, merely opened our doors to help those who sought us out. No doubt priests will soon stand in front of the freshly completed steps to rant about the sins of a city that is founded on, and controlled by, commerce, both legal and illicit, if they don't already. It's how they operated before their feet stepped on Selennian soil, and how they have continued since Dargan Blackwell embraced their word and funded their spread.

Waiting on the dock, my eyes move beyond the cathedral, where streets run from the square into the other portions of the city. Foot traffic and carriages disappear from my view down different pathways between lines of buildings made from bricks and wrought iron. Vast numbers of plants hang on the balconies that line the streets and I'm reminded briefly of Delosia, where the tropical plants were as much part of the building as the wood and masonry, even if these look different than the ones that thrived in the bright island sunshine.

"That trunk and crate of liquor go with the Captain," Erik advises, instructing the men that rode up the river with us. Two of them lift the trunk with our belongings, grunting as they carry it to one of the waiting carriages, followed by a wooden crate that clinks from the glass bottles enclosed.

"Erik, we're off to Salome's. You'll be at your usual lodging?" Lennox confers with Erik for a moment while I wait, still standing in awe of the crowds that swirl around us, tucked close to the familiar warmth of the two men.

"Aye, Captain," Erik answers. "I will have the crew unload these, then meet with the tavern owners and see what they need."

"I'll meet you back here in the morning, then. Send word to the Den should any trouble arise." Lennox shakes Erik's hand, before turning his attention to me. The larger man nods once before returning to his task, his lilting accent bellowing over the cacophony of other seamen.

"Let's go," Lennox orders, roughly gripping my elbow to pull me toward him. For a moment, I start to pull away, startled at his grip, but catch myself and follow as expected. People scramble from our path and avoid eye contact with the Captain as we approach the waiting carriage, their behavior further confirming his fierce reputation in the city. Once we clear the main portion of the dock, the crowd thins and he releases his tight grip, pressing his hand possessively against my lower back to guide me a step ahead. He offers me a hand to climb into the carriage, where I arrange my skirt and sink into the padded cushion, watching the people pass by through the window.

"Take us to Salome's place," Lennox orders the driver, then follows me inside tapping once on the roof to indicate our readiness.

Once ensconced in the carriage, Lennox's hard expression dissolves, and his comforting presence, so unlike the man he seems to be in the street, radiates warmth next to me on the velvet seat. We sit with our hands entwined between us while I gape out the window to observe the city as it passes by. Snippets of music and laughter squeeze through the windows as we move away from the noisy din of the docks. This city is already so much livelier than Artemisia or Athene where I lived for so long, and the happy sounds make my heart feel lighter. Perhaps we will have a bit of fun in this new place, after all.

Sensing my happiness, Lennox caresses my hand with his thumb, sending shivers up my arm. He removes his hat before grazing my neck with light kisses as we bump along.

"I'll take you out to hear the music one night, maybe to the theater if you'd like," he whispers against my sensitive skin. I lean into him, enjoying the touch and pulling my eyes from the sights outside, but before we can pursue any other affection we come to a stop at a building just off the square.

"Here we go," I sigh, offering a smile to Lennox as he replaces his hat.

He answers with a quick kiss on my forehead and opens the door, jumping out into the damp street. I take his hand as he assists me out of the carriage, raising my eyes to the ornately painted sign over the door illuminated by oil lanterns hanging from the facade: *Den of Sinful Delights*.

The two-story brick building sits on the corner with a wide red double-door set at an angle offering access to both of the intersecting streets. An iron-railed balcony juts from the second story, wrapping around the entire building, accented with hanging ferns and flowers. Several women in slim-fitting sheer gowns recline on settees just inside the tall open doors leading into the second-floor rooms.

"Welcome back, Captain!" one of the women whoops from the balcony, and Lennox responds with a wicked grin as he glances up toward her. Her pouty lips and strawberry-blonde hair are on full display as she leans forward over the railing to better enhance the view of her nearly exposed breasts. Passersby on the street gawk at the beauty as she flirts, her companions giggling and waving down to the men on the sidewalk.

"Remember, it's all for show, my pretty priestess," Lennox whispers to me, his breath tickling the sensitive skin of my neck before he places his hand on my lower back once again to guide me toward the open door.

Music spills from the illuminated interior of the Den, the notes swirling on the breeze and into the cobbled streets. A broad-shouldered, ebony-skinned guard at the entrance dips his chin in a solemn welcome to Lennox as we approach, stepping aside for us to enter through the open bloodred door. Soft candlelight from candelabras strewn around the foyer cast a warm tone over the space, even though the day still has at least an hour of light left outside the front door. My eyes pause on a luminous crystal chandelier throwing rainbows of light around the space, reflecting the soft flickering of the flames.

The music grows louder as we approach a heavy velvet curtain in another variation of the deep red that surrounds us, the fabric separating the foyer from what I assume is a salon space. My heart beats faster, its rhythm hurrying to match the sultry notes. I expect to see men at tables with women fluttering around like I was used to at the House of Starlight, my home for so long before the pirate ship, but stepping through the velvet partition I immediately realize that New Aphros is an entirely different beast compared to anywhere in Selennia.

Nude women writhe on small stages in the corners, their hips moving to the music of a band tucked in the front of the salon on a larger raised stage that fills the entire front of the room. Their backs face the closed shutters lining the street, but the stage seems far too large for only the musical quartet, causing me to wonder what other kinds of shows are performed here. A small bar is set in the back of the space, while darkened booths line the walls, full of upholstered benches and tables. These booths are surrounded by more heavy velvet fabric to offer more or less privacy as the patrons prefer. Sounds of pleasure emanate from the dark spaces and I'm mildly surprised to see couples in various erotic positions in the shadows of the booths with curtains left open to the room. In Artemisia, there was no doubt about what was occurring in the brothels, but it was never on full display due to the puritanical ideals of the King's new religion.

While my eyes scan the salon, a small, curvaceous figure approaches from the bar. Several decades older than I am, her bronze complexion, berry-stained lips, and shining sable waves make her appear as decadent as the exquisitely decorated salon. Moving with easy grace, her sensuous curves are accentuated by the elegant, form-fitting burgundy gown she wears. Black lace adorns her bustline, as does a sparkling necklace of rubies. This woman is a living reflection of the luxurious and sensual room we stand in. As she nears, tension radiates off Lennox for a moment, tingling through his fingers on my lower back, but it disappears along with his touch as she approaches. Tilting his head arrogantly, he runs his eyes over the woman's form with a sly smile.

"My darling, William! You're finally back," the woman croons before pressing her lush mouth against Lennox's, rubbing against him in her low-cut gown. I tense when his hand snakes up to grip the back of her head, tangling in her dark waves as he returns the kiss.

*It's all for show. It's all for show,* I remind myself over and over, forcing breaths in and out of my chest to dispel the jealousy that rages through me, hoping that my expression remains indifferent.

When the woman breaks the kiss, she steps back to appraise me, taking in my sigil and my fists clenched at my sides. "My, my, William, who have you brought me this time? She's exquisite," she coos as she drags a long finger down my cheek and touches the hair that hangs over my shoulder.

"That she is, Salome, but I didn't bring her for you. This one is for my personal use, at least while I'm in town." Lennox smiles devilishly as he turns my face toward his and grips my chin, pulling my mouth to his for a rough kiss. "Isn't that right, love?"

"Yes, Captain," I reply, hiding my irritation by looking away from his hard gaze as if in submission. I knew this was what was expected, but it chafes when some of the patrons eye me surreptitiously, leering and whispering to one another. Especially after his lips were just touching this other woman's.

He strokes his hand down my arm, then wraps it possessively around my waist, gripping my backside for the men in the room to observe, before directing his words to the Madame. "Let's discuss the rest of our stay somewhere more private."

Salome turns and beckons for us to follow, glancing seductively over her shoulder as she leads us toward the back of the salon. Lennox grabs my arm at the elbow pulling me along with him, following Salome's swaying hips. As we pass through the room, patrons seated at the various tables take our measure, some appraising us openly, while others are far more guarded in their curiosity. The men are all well-dressed with fine clothing and flashy jewelry, which is unsurprising. Judging by Salome's attire and the finely appointed salon, it's obvious that this establishment caters to the higher classes in New Aphros.

Lennox follows Salome past the bar, leading me down a hallway and into a plush office where the sweet scent of burning herbs caresses me as I enter the room. A miniature version of the chandelier from the foyer hangs in the center of the ceiling, while a flickering fire anchors the back wall. Books fill a shelf behind a large desk, and the decor is completed by a couch and two plush armchairs in one corner. Before I can look around further, Lennox tugs me towards the couch, pulling me down onto the soft cushion next to him. Salome gracefully sits in the chair closest to me and pours a healthy drink for each of us from a decanter full of amber liquid into cut-crystal glasses waiting on the low table in front of us, handing the glasses around before sitting back to take a sip.

"So," Salome starts after swallowing a sip of her drink, "I see you found her, William." Her demeanor has changed from graceful seductress to relaxed confidante as she sinks into the seat, eyes softening as she looks between the two of us. I whip my head between the two of them and note the change in Lennox as well. He reclines against the back of the couch with his hat balanced on his crossed knee as he takes my hand in his, stroking his thumb over the back in soothing circles. The knot of jealousy eases in my chest at their friendly demeanor. Embarrassment tickles my senses; I knew the behavior was only an act, but the sight of her mouth on his was still an unsettling surprise.

"I did. Andromeda, this is Salome. She's the owner of the Den and a dear friend." He smiles conspiratorially with the older woman and she winks at him before turning her eyes to me. Their clear, light green color is striking against her tan complexion, and they shine with mischief and knowledge.

I continue to silently bounce my eyes between the two,

wondering why Lennox had not better prepared me for what to expect, but Salome draws me in. "Andromeda is not your true name, surely?" she asks, raising her dark brows over the edge of her drink.

"Is Salome yours?" I counter harshly, unwilling to share too much with this woman.

How am I having this same conversation with *another* older woman who seems to know so much more about me than I wish them to? Marie's questions on Delosia were an uncomfortable surprise, now Salome's knowing looks eat at me.

"Oh, I am known by many names, depending on who you ask." She smirks as she lowers her glass. "Madame Salome. The Witch Queen of New Aphros. My *favorite* is the new one the priests building their cathedral have decided on — Consort of the Devil and Mistress of Darkness." She laughs deeply at the statement, waving her hand nonchalantly. "They are so overly dramatic! As if I'm a succubus or some such nonsense. But once, I was known as High Priestess Salome of the Central Temple of Selennia." Her seafoam eyes focus on me as my own grow wide at the revelation.

# CHAPTER 2

My breath catches at the statement and my heart stumbles in my chest at her title. *The* High Priestess? The High Priestess of the Central Temple was the highest-ranking leader of all the priestesses; she was the most skilled, the most revered. The one sought by the Queen, herself, for guidance. But *Salome* isn't a name I recognize, as a high priestess or otherwise.

Selennia had four coastal temples, each led by a high priestess and her second, a priestess with the same advanced training and knowledge; someone who could step into the role should something happen to the leader. Those four temples answered to the fifth, the Central Temple in Aphros, which worked hand in hand with the queen. When a high priestess retired, she would pass along the title to her second in a private ceremony. No high priestesses left without passing on their power, at least none that I had heard of. How did *this* woman escape Blackwell's takeover? Had she left before he arrived? How was her name expunged from memory when she's barely older than Marie or the former queen herself?

"I don't understand," I say with a shake of my head. "When? Where were you?" Before I can rein in my emotions, my hands begin to tremble, clutching the thick crystal glass of liquor. "How could you abandon us?"

No matter how I try to maintain control of my cool expression, I feel it slip. I wasn't expecting this kind of news as soon as I set foot in a new place, in a strange town. Lennox places a hand on my leg but instead of comforting me, I slip my knee free, shooting him a sideways glare. Why did he not warn me about this woman when I asked about her?

Salome's eyes dart between Lennox and me, reading my anger. "Did you not tell her who she was meeting this evening, William?" Salome scolds, her dark brows knitting.

"I didn't know you were going to dive in immediately, Salome," he huffs back, his tone contrite and his jaw tense. "Forgive me for expecting a little respite after our journey when we arrived."

Salome glares at Lennox, pursing her lips in irritation, before turning to me with a small frown tugging at the corners of her full pout. "Well, my child, I see William did a terrible job of preparing you for your arrival. We have much to discuss, but from your reaction, I do believe I'll leave you two to enjoy yourselves this evening. You're safe here. Partake as you wish, with whomever you wish." She smiles seductively at both of us. "We should talk tomorrow. I think a sit down between the two of us would be easier once you have time to rest and clean up after your time at sea."

I start to protest, to demand answers to the growing number of questions racing through my mind, but internally acknowledge she's right and close my mouth. I'm not prepared to discuss this. I need a bath and to talk to Lennox about our plans before I listen to this elegant, enigmatic creature. Instead of replying, I simply incline my head and look to Lennox to guide me from here.

"William, shall I send up your favorite?" Salome questions. He nods his assent, taking me by the hand and standing. I place my glass down on the table and stand at his side, still watching Salome as she lounges and finishes her drink. She waves her hand toward the door in a dismissal, not rising, as if Lennox is so familiar with the brothel he can find his own way. "Your usual room is waiting for you both, enjoy your evening."

Lennox pulls me along behind him as his long strides eat up the hallway and past the bar. We retreat through the bustling salon, through the heavy curtains, and take the mahogany stairs to the second floor where Lennox opens a door at the end of the hall.

Our shared trunk already waits at the end of a four-poster bed, invitingly piled with luxurious bedding and pillows in matching jewel-toned brocades. The walls are covered in elegant damask wallpaper in deep red and burgundy. A door sits cracked open to my left, hinting at a private bathing chamber beyond. The back of the room has tall glass double doors covered in louvered shutters, to allow one onto the wrought-iron balconies overlooking the street below. Two chairs and a low table are tucked in the space between the bed and door, and a vanity with a full-length mirror sits across the room. Overall, the space is far bigger than I anticipated but as lavish as the room is, and as curious as I am about New Aphros, I'm still in turmoil at the announcement that Salome is the former High Priestess of Selennia, someone who likely had close contact with my aunt and her secrets. She is not merely a former priestess and friend of Lennox's mother's like he had explained, and my frustration at the fact that he did not give me any warning puts a damper on my excitement about the city.

"Nerissa, I'm sorry," he starts hesitantly at the sight of my tight expression, using my true name instead of the assumed one he gave to Salome. Draping his coat over the back of one of the chairs, he reaches out to take mine. "I didn't know she was going to divulge her title immediately. I thought I would have time to explain more once we were settled in." He strokes his long fingers across my cheekbone, cradling my cheek in his palm, and presses his forehead to mine. "And I didn't know she was going to put on a show as soon as we walked in the damn door."

"You should have told me before we got here, prepared me. I don't know how many more surprises I can handle, Billy."

For a moment I want to push him away, instinct telling me to begin building walls around myself again, but I remind myself that we are both learning how to navigate one another after such a long time pretending to be different people. Sighing, I turn my face into his hand and kiss his palm. As I start to rise to my toes to kiss him, accepting his apology, a small tap at the door freezes me in mid-motion.

"Hold that thought," he whispers as he rubs the pad of his thumb against my lower lip and turns to open the door.

Standing in the doorway is a beautiful young woman holding a tray of drinks and food. Her pale blonde hair falls in messy curls across nearly bare breasts covered in sheer rose-colored fabric. Wide eyes the grey of an oncoming storm twinkle as they lock on Lennox.

The frenetic energy of a squall surrounds her as she grins and squeals, "Lennox! You're back!"

# CHAPTER 3
## LENNOX

*Fuck. Me.*

*Dammit, Salome.*

Instead of immediately closing the door in Delphine's face, I can only look to the ceiling in exasperation, sending a prayer up in hope that the Goddess will intervene if Delphine and Nerissa go toe to toe. When I drag my eyes back level, it's clear that Nerissa's shock at the girl's squeal has been quickly replaced with guarded curiosity at my expression; her eyes narrow on me and one dark brow lifts slightly as she takes in the woman entering our quarters.

Delphine waltzes through the door, as if she's far too comfortable with being in my chambers, carrying a tray of delicacies. Her eyes flit over Nerissa as she bends to organize the plates of food on the table next to the chairs. My lips pull into a strained smile when I look over the young woman, her lithe form almost completely on display through the sheer fabric of her ensemble. The long skirt is slit up both sides, so glimpses of her bare legs peek through with each step as she gracefully moves through the room.

I know Delphine's history, so the sight of her legs isn't a shock, but a stifled gasp from Nerissa causes me to jerk my attention to where she stares at the newcomer. Nerissa fights to keep her expression neutral at the sight of the thick burn scars covering Delphine from her feet upwards to where they disappear under the thin fabric of her skirt. As I look between the women, Delphine's irritation at Nerissa's attention is plain. Her jaw clenches and her lips thin, while emotions war in her eyes when she meets Nerissa's empathetic gaze.

"So, you must be her then. Lennox's *Lost Priestess*," Delphine states with little emotion, all signs of excitement at my return dashed.

To her credit, Nerissa never flinches, rearranging her face into a neutral expression as she looks in my direction. It's impossible to keep myself from rolling my eyes once more before I release an irritated sigh, secure the door, and walk to stand between the two.

"Delphine, behave," I tell the girl sternly. "This is Andromeda. Andromeda, this is Delphine." I gesture between them in introduction, still using Nerissa's assumed name until she's ready to leave it behind, before taking a seat and pouring a glass of wine from the newly delivered decanter. Delphine purses her lips and finishes moving the food and wine from the tray, laying it out on the tabletop for ease of serving.

"It's nice to meet you, Delphine," Nerissa says in the low, gentle voice I've heard her take when speaking to wounded men. Thankfully, she seems to be taking the afternoon in stride, even if the women of the Den continue to try to sabotage me. I can't fathom why Delphine is acting like a jilted lover. Well, I can. She's always tough on new people, guarded and untrusting, but this is worse than usual.

"Are you in pain? From the scarring?" Nerissa's voice pulls me from my musings as she changes the subject. Her eyes drift from Del's legs to the trunk we brought ashore where I suspect she has some of her herbs stashed away for the many remedies and tonics she makes.

"No," Delphine snaps. "Salome takes care of me. I don't need your pity," she sneers, noting Nerissa's wandering eyes. Holding the tray under her arm, she examines Nerissa openly now, looking between the striking priestess and me. Nerissa stands straight and unflinching under Delphine's probing gaze — her sapphire eyes meeting the storm clouds boldly.

"Del," I start to scold the younger woman, but Delphine's expression softens as she cocks her head to the side, running her gaze over her as if finally seeing Nerissa instead of preparing her defensive retorts.

"She *is* beautiful, Captain. I can *definitely* see the appeal," Delphine remarks as she turns to me. She plants a quick peck on my cheek, then breezes from the room without a backward glance.

"Good Goddess. That girl is like a fucking hurricane," I mutter when the door clicks shut, leaving us in the room full of tension.

"A *favorite* of yours?" Nerissa once again lifts a dark brow, her full lips pursed. For a moment I wonder if she's jealous, but I hope she has realized Delphine is as good an actress as the rest of us.

"Not the way you probably think." I run a hand through my hair and take a piece of fruit from the tray, settling in for the conversation. "Come and sit. Eat. I'll tell you what I can; Salome or Delphine will need to fill in the gaps."

Nerissa gracefully takes the empty chair next to me, sinking into the plush velvet and accepting the glass of wine I hold out to her. A variety of fruit, cheeses, and cured meats sit on the tray for our dinner along with a loaf of crusty bread, and I catch myself watching her as she tries different items. Without further encouragement, she nibbles her meal. I continue to drink my wine, leaning my head back against the soft chair and closing my eyes for a moment to gather my thoughts. The memory of meeting Delphine is another that I wish I could bury. One I don't wish to burden Nerissa with.

"It's alright, Billy," Nerissa sighs, chewing a sweet fig and taking a deep swallow of the fine wine. "I'm not concerned about the women you've bedded in the past. I just wasn't expecting them to be paraded before me immediately. She's lovely, if a little... abrupt. We've both had other partners. I don't hold it against you for seeking comfort or pleasure in the arms of someone else these past years."

"No. It's nothing like that." I rub a hand over my face, although relief washes over me at her reaction. Some women might have responded quite differently to Delphine. "While I *have* bedded other women over the years, Delphine was never one of them. I helped save her from the priests. The memory of that night is... difficult." The words are quiet as I meet her deep blue eyes from my reclined position.

"The priests?" She pauses chewing and sits forward, angling toward me, and placing her food on the table. I don't blame her for losing her appetite with the mention of priests. The holy men of the King's favored religion can't *all* be evil, but the ones I've encountered certainly don't seem to practice the kindness and charity they preach. Especially not to women.

Sighing deeply, I lean forward, resting my elbows on my thighs and toying with the empty goblet between my fingers. "I've been coming to New Aphros since I led the mutiny and escaped the Royal Navy in favor of sailing with Captain Jackson. When I left the *Selkie's Tears* to captain the *Bartered Soul*, we came on a similar trip you just made with us — Selennia to Delosia to New Aphros. Salome knew my mother, and I introduced her to Jackson. So, between Jackson and myself, we'd been supplying her with goods regularly. I expected that trip to be like any other visit.

"When I arrived here, I knew something was wrong. Salome immediately dragged me into the office, no greeting like you saw, no sultry act. She told me one of her new girls — a former initiate from one of the temples in Selennia — hadn't returned from town, and she wasn't sure what to do. It isn't uncommon for women to leave working in the Houses, but for her not to say anything was alarming, especially since she was such a new arrival. I sent some of my men into the streets to see what they could find."

Nerissa takes a small sip of her wine, listening intently to the tale I wish I could forget. "Erik came back to report that some of the priests were heard talking about *Devil's whores* and *succubi* plaguing the city. New Aphros is known to be tolerant of all people, but some of the priests coming to convert new believers don't know the rules and get…

overzealous." I shudder at the word — the memories — then refill my goblet, drinking deeply before continuing.

"Erik told me the priests planned to light pyres near the river that evening, far down where it turns to swamps, so he and I decided to intervene. Salome insisted she come with us. Her House is targeted often by the priests because some of them know she used to be a priestess, not that she hides it, and that she shields former priestesses when she can. She isn't a forgiving woman. She refused to allow us to handle it on our own. By the time we found the right place, the fires were already burning. We were too late to stop some of the deaths."

I pause, looking up from where I grip the wine goblet with white knuckles, to find Nerissa's eyes shimmering with unshed tears in the lantern light. A tremor shows as she sips from her goblet, the wine sloshing slightly in the glass, more than likely revisiting the memories of the night her temple was invaded. I have to fight to push my own emotions down, thinking of how I found my mother after she met with the priests and King's men.

"Delphine's hair, so pale in the moonlight, caught Salome's eyes before I saw her. She was tied to a stake in the center of a pyre near the end of the line along the muddy bank. Salome moved so fast that I couldn't stop her. Up until that night, I'd never seen a priestess' *glow* used defensively before. She cut the men down with just a slice of her hand, but the one holding the torch had already lit the pyre before she got close enough to stop him, or the flames." The last words are almost a whisper and the hair on the back of my neck stands on end at the memory. I'll never forget watching Salome that night.

I look up from my glass into her eyes. "Have you ever seen it?"

Nerissa's jaw clenches slightly, but she shakes her head in response, saying, "No. It was something that was rumored to be possible by the high priestesses in the past, but no one ever showed us. It wasn't something included in our training." Her eyes search mine, their curiosity encouraging me to continue.

"Erik and I were able to get Delphine cut loose from the pyre, but as you saw, she didn't escape burning. After using so much of her power to cut down the priests, Salome didn't have enough to quickly put the fire out. She healed Del afterward, but the scarring remained. Delphine stayed with Salome, both to study the Old Ways and because they'd grown to be like family. She mainly works to support the other girls or gather secrets around town. So, yes. She and I have history, but not as lovers." I take a deep drink of the expensive wine, likely a bottle I left the last time we were in New Aphros, staring into the glass and savoring its taste at the end of the harrowing tale.

Scrubbing my hand over my jaw and then through my hair to grip the back of my neck, I give a wary glance toward Nerissa, trying to glean her thoughts through her pensive expression. No part of the day has gone to plan since we stepped out of the carriage, and it wouldn't surprise me if she's still vexed about the number of surprises that have greeted her since stepping through the Den's doors. Irritation simmers under my skin, mostly directed at myself for not being more forthright, but also at Salome. Delphine's moods are to be expected at this point, but Salome is usually more tactful. Thus far, this hasn't been the pleasant introduction to the lively city I'd planned.

As worries swirl through my thoughts, Nerissa quietly stands and places her glass on the table before taking the one out of my hand and doing the same, drawing my gaze up to her beautiful, solemn face. Then, she carefully sits across my lap, wrapping her arms around my neck as I encircle her waist in an embrace. She grasps my face in her cool fingers and gently presses her rose-colored lips to mine before resting her forehead against my brow.

"She survived. You helped her, just like you've helped so many others." Her words reassure and center me after rehashing the ghastly memory of the pyres on the riverbank and my misgivings over our arrival, as if she can sense the distress I've tried to hide. I reach up with one hand to stroke her smooth cheek before pulling her back for another kiss.

# CHAPTER 4

The sounds of hoofbeats and wagon wheels on the cobblestone streets outside our balcony pull me from my sleep the next morning. Lennox and I were both exhausted after the days of travel at sea and fell into the bed curled around one another after finishing the flagon of wine and plate of food last night. Delphine's horrifying tale haunted my thoughts until sleep pulled me under.

Stretching slowly, I savor the softness of the featherbed and smooth sheets around me before opening my eyes to the morning light. Already awake, Lennox is seated at the small table again, shirtless and relaxed, pouring us cups of steaming brown liquid from a pot. The aroma is different from the tea I expected, but the scent is vaguely familiar. He pours milk into the drink before noticing me watching him.

"Good morning." His smile spreads across his face as he rakes his gaze over my sheer shift and bare legs. "Coffee?" he asks, gesturing to the cup.

"They don't drink tea here?"

"They do, but most of the locals drink coffee. It's more

popular than tea, and is usually served with milk," he explains. "It goes wonderfully with these." He holds up a small rectangle of fried dough dusted white.

I crawl out of the bed and drift over to the strange breakfast items, white powder floating around as I lift one of the pastries from the silver platter. The moment it hits my tongue, the sweetness of the warm, doughy bread tells me the topping is some new form of sugar, and it puffs out in my breath. Lennox chuckles at my surprise, handing me a linen napkin to wipe my fingers. The hot, bitter coffee does pair wonderfully with the sweet pastry, and I sit in silence as I devour several of them and empty my cup. Lennox shares the food, then brushes the powdered sugar from his breeches before pulling a shirt over his head, tucking it in, and adding his belt.

"What are the plans for the day?" I finally ask, stuffed with fried dough and energized by the coffee. No matter how I try to wipe the sticky sweetness from my hands, it doesn't seem to come off, forcing me to resort to the ewer of water in the bathing chamber to resolve the issue.

"I need to make sure some of the deliveries from the ship are distributed. Would you like to come with me to see the city?" he asks when I walk back into the room, pulling on his boots and adding his cutlass to his belt. His pistols are stored in our trunk, but he leaves them where they are as he dons his black overcoat.

"Yes, I'd like that." I nod as I retrieve one of my gowns from the trunk and dress quickly. The dark blue wool will keep me comfortable without needing a coat or cloak, so I tuck my dagger into my pocket and don my sturdy boots. Knotting my hair at my neck completes my toilette, and I press a quick kiss to Lennox's mouth before we depart our room into the streets where we have to pretend to be a pirate and his prize once more.

Several closed doors stand between us and the wooden stairs in the elegantly papered hallway. More closed doors line the halls downstairs while the plush lounge from last night stands quiet and empty. The curtains are open, allowing soft sunlight to stream through the windows before it sinks into the velvet seating lining the room. For a moment, my thoughts drift across the sea to the House of Starlight — wondering how Celeste is faring without Lyra, and how the other women are surviving.

I glance past the bar toward the office where we spoke with Salome yesterday evening, curious if the older woman is behind the door, or in her own bedroom somewhere in the Den. I know a lengthy conversation awaits me when I see her again, but I push it to the back of my mind. Today I want to explore my new surroundings in peace.

Bright morning light greets us as we step outside, finding the city already wide awake and bustling. Horses and mules pull carriages and wagons full of people or goods, stopping to allow men to deliver casks of ale and cases of liquor and wine to the various Houses and taverns that line the row where the Den is situated. Everyone moves with purpose, traveling briskly down the sidewalks on whatever errands they are preoccupied with. As my eyes dart along the street, Lennox glances my way with a small smile, lifting his brow in a silent question, as if he can feel my nervousness. Exhaling a deep breath, I straighten my shoulders before he clasps my hand, guiding me in the direction of the square I saw yesterday.

"The opera house," Lennox points out as we pass a large theater. "It's smaller than the ones on the continent, but it attracts some talented singers. My favorite is down the row though, the smaller venues are more intimate, the energy more intense. This district holds all of the entertainment and pleasure one might seek on leave, whether it be music, theater, cabaret, drinking, or flesh," he explains, mentioning which establishments he prefers and why, as we walk through the district. "New Aphros has made a name for itself for its excellent food, art, and entertainment, even if it's still growing."

I take in the information as I soak in the sights, sounds, and colors of the district's buildings and its residents, so different than anywhere I have ever been before.

"On the other side of the square is the Merchant District," he continues, his hand still in mine. I glance down at our intertwined fingers as he speaks, hoping we don't stand out since we appear far more intimate than a man and his property should, but then, this is a different city, a different country altogether — perhaps men often keep courtesans or mistresses and parade them in public. Trusting Lennox, I don't pull away, savoring the rare feeling of normalcy as he continues to guide me along through the streets.

"Some of the businesses begin on the edge of the square, closest to the docks, to lure new arrivals and their coin right away," he adds as we near the entry of the square. "Which is helpful for when we want to offload goods as well, so they don't have to be transported as far."

My focus is pulled away from his soothing commentary when I hear another man's voice raised over the lull of the crowd. The pleasant feeling building in my chest is suddenly doused. His fiery voice grows louder as we approach the central portion of the square where the cathedral is under construction along the back edge. As the crowd thins around us, a priest is visible on the steps in front of the construction. My fingers tighten around Lennox's at the sight of him in his black habit. Memories claw to the forefront of my mind, making my throat tighten with fear. Images of sneering men dressed in the black robes of the King's new religion encouraging the soldiers to destroy our temple flash through my disordered thoughts and slow my steps.

"Renounce the Old Ways of the harlots! Repent your sinfulness and join your brothers under the true God!" the priest shouts over the early morning crowd. "The Council ruling this city is replete with sinners. They only care about how much money they can make off your vices! King Dargan and the true God can bring you the only real prosperity and grace."

Other priests stand amongst the crowd and mingle with the people passing by. My pulse soars as I catch myself wanting to retreat, tugging against Lennox's firm grip, my palm sticky with panic. It feels as if the sigil on my brow is a beacon that will draw them to me. My heart races, as if it's trying to escape my chest like I wish to escape the square.

Most of the passersby ignore the priest's words, but the lack of a crowd gathering below his pulpit doesn't seem to lessen his fervor. The priests mingling in the crowd are no less aggressive in their faith, brazenly approaching townspeople who seem to grow more agitated with their presence. "Repent of your wickedness," one cries, "Women will lead to your downfall. They are the origin of sin," from another. "Cast out the harlots that plague your streets!"

"Get away from me!" one man grumbles as he passes through, roughly pushing past a young priest. "No one in New Aphros cares about your king across the sea!"

I glance around the square, searching for a way for Lennox and me to get to the docks without nearing the crowd, but can't see a way around it. I grip Lennox's hand even harder as he pulls me closer, running his long fingers down my back to soothe me. "You have nothing to fear. These men do not run this town," he whispers. "There is no law against the Goddess here, no matter what they preach."

I know he speaks the truth, but it's hard to shake my instinctual fear of the priests, and I fight the urge to hide even with Lennox at my side. Clenching my jaw, I will my expression to calm, hoping it becomes unreadable. As I exhale, I bury my emotions deep, just as I've practiced for years, and lift my chin, prepared to continue on my way. Before I take another step, water splashes along my side as an angry voice shouts, "Devil's whore! Be cleansed with the holy water of the true God."

My anger sparks as I wipe the water from my cheek, burning away all fear as I turn to face the middle-aged priest standing far too close to me, an empty vial in his hand. Lennox pulls me toward him, pushing me slightly behind his intimidating form. His cutlass is already in his hand as he steps toward the priest in a clear threat. I grip my dagger as well, but keep it hidden for now.

"You forget yourself, priest," Lennox snarls.

The priest in his foolishness stands his ground, sneering at both my brow and the surly pirate in front of him. "I know that you both will burn in the fires if you don't repent. Her mere presence is sinful and *you* continue to provide these objects of vice to this city," he retorts at us, jabbing a bony finger toward Lennox.

Before I can think about my actions, my dagger flashes in the sunlight as I step past Lennox. Holding the blade at the priest's throat, my other hand grips the front of his black habit viciously as I bare my teeth. The training Pike and Lennox gave me on the ship proves valuable; the blade feels like an extension of my body as calm fury washes over me, erasing the fear that surged earlier.

"I am no mere *object*. And I'd love to see you try to force your penance on me, priest. I've survived this long, despite your *God's* best efforts. A pathetic creature preaching women's wickedness will not be the end of me." I barely recognize my voice as I hiss at the man.

It would only take a quick push of the dagger to watch his life seep from his body. Gasps from the crowd reach my ears as people stop to watch the commotion, but I care little about anyone else's reaction. Lennox's warmth is a steady presence at my back as he offers his support.

"Remember what happened to your brothers the last time you crossed one of these women? Don't doubt their ability to end all of you," Lennox warns, chuckling darkly. The words meant to remind the man of Salome's power, and the ease with which she dispatched the men trying to hurt Delphine on the river years ago.

Lennox's statement does its job. At this threat, the priest finally blanches and averts his eyes from mine. Disgusted, I push him away, a small bead of blood leaking from his throat as he stumbles to the stones of the square. Taking a steadying breath, I back away until I bump into Lennox's solid form. He wraps one arm around my waist and, in the comfort of his embrace, I allow my eyes to roam over the crowd standing in the square. Many people have already continued with their business, ignoring the disturbance, but a few openly appraise me. Some even nod in respect. I meet their eyes, keeping my chin high and gripping my dagger. I'm so tired of hiding.

Slipping his arm from me, Lennox squeezes my empty hand once, then steps to where the priest still kneels on the stones, holding his throat. He forces the man's chin up using the flat of his cutlass, the same movement I watched him make on an enemy's deck only weeks ago.

"Watch yourself, priest. And tell your brothers: if you accost any women, regardless of their beliefs or standing in this city, you'll find yourselves missing your tongues. Or worse." His whispered promise is too soft for the crowd to hear, but the priest shudders at the dark words and the chill of metal on his skin.

Challenge delivered, Lennox turns to meet the eyes of the other priests in the crowd, his blade still hovering at the man's throat. Even the one on the steps remains silent, although he eyes us with unconcealed malice. As Lennox locks eyes with the older priest he lifts a booted foot, pressing it to the still-kneeling priest's chest. With a hard shove, he pushes the priest over, not even bothering to glance down as the man crumples to the ground.

Returning to my side, Lennox places his hand on my lower back and leads me through the throngs of people in the square. Those we pass avert their eyes and step quickly out of our way. Neither of us sheath our weapons until we reach the next street where we turn from the square to head to the docks, only another few blocks away.

Forcing myself to shift my focus, I scan the buildings with their iron balconies and hanging plants, noticing the bright colors even in winter. It's beautiful, and my breaths become steadier, the tension from the square dissipating with each step toward the riverfront. Suddenly, a tug on my arm surprises me as Lennox hauls me into one of the alleyways. In an instant, he presses me against the building, his mouth crashing into mine as a rough hand grips the back of my head. Sinking into the searing kiss, I wrap my arms around his broad shoulders and pull him closer. Moments pass as I allow myself this reprieve, feeling my heart race in my chest once more for entirely different reasons than minutes ago.

With a gasp, we break apart, chests heaving as he nuzzles his nose against my neck, trailing kisses along my bare skin. His hands drift down, sliding over my shoulders and to my waist and hips, pulling me tighter against him. Even with the air cool and damp from the nearby river, my skin feels hot from his attention as his hands roam lower, pulling my skirt up on one side so he can run his palm up the side of my leg as he slants his mouth against mine once more.

"How long will this errand take?" I ask breathlessly when he pulls away, my skin burning where he touched me moments before while I wonder why we left the comfort of our room instead of staying wrapped around one another in the first place.

"Not long, my she-wolf. I just need to check in with Erik and Pike to make sure we have everything ready for delivery and to ensure there aren't any questions. Then we can return to Salome's." He cups my cheek with his warm palm and runs his thumb gently across my lower lip, now swollen from his kisses. "That's *not* how I wanted the morning to go. I'm not doing a very good job of introducing you to New Aphros, am I?" he says quietly, adjusting my skirt so it falls to cover my bare leg again as I catch my breath.

"It's alright. I'm fine." I offer a small smile, but the trembling I managed to hide in the square overtakes me and I briefly press my cheek against his chest in an attempt to steady myself. "It's best I earn a reputation of being someone to fear if I'm going to be at your side from now on." With a nod, Lennox wraps me in a strong embrace for a moment while we stand in the privacy of the quiet alley, kissing the top of my head firmly before we step back out into the light of the street.

# CHAPTER 5

"Captain," Erik greets us as we step onto the docks. "Mistress."

"Good morning, Erik." I smile at the Northman as Lennox clasps the man's hand in greeting.

"Ah, good morning!" Pike says in his deep timbre as he walks up from the barrel he was inspecting. The older man smiles a bright smile, his dark skin creasing at the corners of his deep brown eyes. "How do you like the fair city so far?"

Lennox leans past me, also shaking his hand. "Would have been more pleasant without the black rats in the square, but it seems we can't escape them."

"But what is a rat to a pack of wolves? They shouldn't bother us," Pike jokes, but continues in a more somber tone. "They do seem to be spreading worse than before though, don't they?" The older man glances at me as if inspecting me for my reaction, but I avoid his gaze by looking around the dock.

With a grunt of agreement, Erik nods. "I noticed them

yesterday evening, harassing patrons leaving one of the taverns while I dined. What has become of the city since we left last time?"

"I'm not sure." Lennox shakes his head, lip curled in distaste. "I'll ask around more now that we are settled in. Jean Alexandre might have news for me."

The men nod in understanding, a weighted silence hanging in the air between them, as heavy as the mist from the river. The men turn their attention to a ledger that Erik holds, while I watch the people moving past, acknowledging those I know as I wait patiently for their business to conclude. It's comforting to be in their familiar presence instead of surrounded by strangers in the Den, but I know I have to return and face my meeting with Salome eventually.

I sit on one of the rough wooden crates waiting to be loaded on one of the wagons, while Lennox focuses on Pike and Erik, letting the cool mist chill my cheeks as I watch the sailors and dock workers move about their work. But sooner than I'd anticipated, they call me back to where they huddle.

"Good," Lennox says, handing the ledger back to Erik as I reach his side. "It sounds like most of the goods the *Bartered Soul* and *Andromeda's Vengeance* carried have already been promised or parceled out," he murmurs to me.

"The entire hold has been claimed already?" I ask, shocked at how quickly the goods were handled. "We only arrived yesterday! How is that possible?"

"The people of New Aphros are familiar with me and my crew. They aren't scrupulous enough to pass up goods, whether they're legally obtained or not," Lennox explains with a wink and an arrogant laugh.

The men say their goodbyes, and Lennox pulls me along away from the docks. This time, we travel along the riverfront instead of passing through the square, the stroll peaceful and uneventful. The warmth from the sun battles with the cool river breeze as we pass storefronts and public houses. Ambling through the streets, I notice the wide variety of people inhabiting New Aphros; the city truly is the melting pot Lennox described. A rainbow of colors swishes by, the attire of the townspeople as varied as the pretty buildings that line the streets. The different styles and fabrics catch my eye, such a change from the more neutral, earthy hues seen on the streets in Selennia. A woman wearing a violet linen wrap dress, similar to those worn in Delosia, snags my eye, the bright color contrasting beautifully with the rich gold silk waistcoat worn by the man at her side.

Two young ladies walk arm in arm, both in tones of sapphire and garnet silk so rich I could be looking into a jewelry box. As they pass, the one closest to me glances over, eyes widening as she takes in my sigil. She pauses, placing her hand over her chest, and dips her head in respect. Her action halts my feet in stunned surprise, and when she moves her hand I see she wears a small silver crescent on a delicate chain around her neck. Lennox, unaware that I stopped, turns quickly when my arm holds him in place.

When the girl notes my companion, she dips the smallest curtsey and hurries off with her friend, glancing over her shoulder once as I continue to stare. "I told you the

Old Ways were still honored here. Even if some of the ceremonies are different, people still believe." Lennox presses his hand over mine.

"I believed you, but it's still a surprise after this long. To know we haven't been forgotten," I answer, finally taking a step forward.

Continuing on our way back to the Den, several people bow their heads in respect when they note my sigil in passing, and it almost feels like a welcoming to the city, warming my heart and putting me at ease after the encounter in the square. Now that I'm paying attention, I note symbols and evidence of other forms of worship from across the world, too, happily confirming Lennox's words that no one deity rules this place.

Although the Goddess is revered in many lands, She appears in different forms. Thick amulets of polished moonstone adorn some women's necks, and men have tattoos like Lennox of moon phases and constellations. Even Erik and the men and women of the northern isles show their faith with symbols decorating the torcs they wear or the ink piercing their scalps, cheeks, and necks. Some worshippers wear crow feathers and bones in their hair or as necklaces to honor the darker sides of the Great Mother, but no one looks askance at their neighbor or steps away from the darkness here. No one frets or cowers, no one hides their unique cultures, and I allow myself to relax further as we blend with the crowd wandering through a row of restaurants and taverns. It gives me hope that the priests won't be able to subdue the bright city as easily as they think.

"That is my favorite place to get freshly caught

seafood," Lennox points to a white building with a sign bearing a crab hanging from the awning. "And over there is the finest bakery; their pastries and breads are better than any you will find back home. They delivered the beignets this morning."

Voices speak over each other in various accents of the common tongue, mixed in with languages I don't recognize, giving the city its own pleasant hum of life. Everywhere we turn, eyes watch us, noting Lennox's openly carried weapon, but people respectfully step out of our way, not bothering to accost us as we continue back to the Entertainment District.

The district is quiet with the sun high in the sky, and the front door of the Den is closed tight instead of standing open and inviting like when we arrived in the evening yesterday. The guard from yesterday is gone, but before I can wonder how we'll get to our room, Lennox pulls a key from his pocket and unlocks the door, entering the building like he owns it. I follow close behind, inhaling the smell of sweet smoke as we cross the threshold. I close my eyes, letting the scent wash over me, carrying me back to my time spent in the temple so many years ago.

"A cleansing...," I murmur, standing still in the foyer, relishing in the scent of the burning herbs.

"Good afternoon," a sultry voice greets us as Salome steps from the salon holding a small dish with smoke wafting from its brim. Noticing my attention, she holds up the dish. "I do a cleansing at least once a week. More often if we have a problematic evening. It keeps the space feeling fresh and reminds me of home. Did you have a good first day visiting the city?"

"It was fine once we got past the cathedral," Lennox replies, irritation coloring his words.

"The priests?" Salome questions, raising a brow and raking her gaze over the both of us, looking for signs of a fight.

"Yes. When did they become so bold within the city limits?" Lennox asks, his voice dripping with disgust.

"A new wave of them arrived about a month ago." Salome turns, resuming her walk around the space as the fragrant smoke wafts around her. "From the sounds of it, Blackwell has been encouraging them to *spread the Holy word* and is sending them to all of the major port cities. They tried standing outside our doors for a day, but that didn't end well for any of them." Salome stops, turning back to us with pursed lips, eyes glittering with glee.

"They met Andromeda today. They won't be bothering her again from the looks on their faces." His hand rubs down my back, his approval radiating through the fabric of my dress and tingling along my skin.

"Yes, *Andromeda*," Salome states as she moves once more, her voice mocking as it caresses my name. "I would like to get to know you better myself. Do you have time to have tea with me now? Or do you and the Captain have *other plans* for the afternoon?" She winks at me, one side of her pout turning up in a knowing smirk.

Before I can rethink my answer, I swallow my rising anxiety and offer her a calm smile. This talk needs to happen, and my nervous curiosity about this woman and her connection to my homeland demands answers. "I have time. Unless you need assistance, Captain?"

His heated gaze lingers on mine, fingers tangling in the

fabric at the back of my dress, telling me that, like myself, he'd rather be stripping my clothing off at this very moment to continue what we started in the alleyway near the dock.

Sighing, he releases the fabric of my dress, smoothing it as he replies, "Please. Enjoy your tea. I'm going across the way for a meal and will see you back in the room afterward." He kisses my knuckles and smiles up at me like a dark prince. Dropping my hand, he turns to Salome with a stern look, an unspoken conversation happening between them, before departing through the front door that still stands open.

With a click, the door closes behind Lennox, and I turn to Salome, my heart pounding with my nerves. The smoke rising around her casts an ethereal air over the woman in the dimly lit space. Now that I know her former rank in Selennia, there is no mistaking what she truly is, her poise and grace are so similar to my former high priestess; radiating command and demanding respect with just a glance, even if her sigil is missing from her brow. She smiles at me through the smoke, her seafoam eyes striking against her warm, tawny skin and dark hair.

"Come along, Andromeda."

Smoke wafts behind her as she leads me back through the salon and into her office, wrapping around me in her wake. Pushing the door aside, she leaves the still-smoking juniper in its dish on a table by the entry and sweeps her hand to encourage my entry. Dressed much more modestly in the daylight hours, Delphine is bent over a table, setting up a tea spread. I admire her simple dress of blue and white vertically striped wool topped with an embroidered waistcoat. A thick leather belt circles her slim waist, and her pale blonde hair is tied back tightly to control the wild curls. Noticing my lingering gaze, she offers me a stiff smile, her eyes inspecting me from head to toe, before slipping out the door to leave us to our discussion.

Wiping my sweaty palms on my skirts, I select the same seat I occupied yesterday, watching as Salome pulls her chair closer to sit across from me. Silence lingers as she pours a cup of steaming dark tea and offers me milk and sugar cubes. I decline both with a shake of my head, preferring to savor the fine tea as is to offset the array of cakes and sweet breads on the tray. Though I know I'm unlikely to touch the delicacies as my stomach twists in anticipation of this dreaded conversation. Unbothered, Salome pours tea for herself, stirring in several sugar cubes and a splash of milk before sitting back in her chair. She watches me while she enjoys a few sips, head cocked slightly as her bright eyes take my measure.

*Here we go again*, I think, forcing my hands to remain steady as I remember my conversation with Marie on Delosia. While part of me is eager to know more of Salome and Lennox's story, I remain guarded concerning my own tale.

"First thing's first, my dear," Salome begins, placing her teacup on the delicate matching saucer, the lantern light glinting on the gold edge, and sitting back in her chair. Like Delphine, she's dressed more modestly today, her full figure covered from high at her neck all the way to her wrists and ankles in a printed chintz day dress. "Let's drop the false name, at least in private. Nerissa Faelan, I would know you even if I didn't remember you as a child."

Involuntarily, I suck in a sharp breath and my cup

rattles lightly as I place it on its saucer. No one besides Lennox has called me *Nerissa* since I stumbled upon Priestess Amaya in the alleyway in Athene. And *no one* has used my full name in over a decade. Priestesses never used surnames; I was simply *Initiate*, then, *Priestess Nerissa*. Before Blackwell arrived with his new religion, surnames were passed through the matrilineal lines, so I shared the Faelan name with both my mother and her sister, Queen Adelaide.

With a smile, Salome reaches forward to pat my knee, but I pull away, eyes roving her face for an explanation. "Don't look so shocked, child. I told you I was the High Priestess over all of Selennia. You surely know that responsibility came with privilege and knowledge. *And* a close relationship with Queen Adelaide. I didn't think you would remember me; you were very small when I last saw you, but I remember *you* clearly. Always a tiny replica of my dear Adelaide." Salome's voice softens, the bold and boastful madame reduced to a friend remembering someone they've lost. "Now, you look just like she did when she was in her prime."

Surprise wars with panic as I struggle to keep my hands from fidgeting in my lap while I cast through memories of my time at the Queen's palace, trying to find Salome in the recesses of my mind. Visits from before my mother's death, times I stole glimpses of court life before I was old enough to participate, then my mind snags on the memory of a dark priestess in midnight robes trimmed with metallic threads. Her sigil shone clear and bright on her brow when I caught a glimpse of her luminous face as she walked with my aunt. I vaguely remember heated words and my aunt's laughter, clearly dismissing whatever hushed warnings the other woman shared.

"I do remember you," I whisper.

Salome smiles sadly. "I wasn't sure if you would. I know you were a little thing, hiding in dark corners without anyone to play with. The last time I saw you, you were hiding behind a tapestry when I warned Adelaide what would happen if she didn't rid Selennia of Dargan Blackwell and the poisonous beliefs he brought with him. She wanted to hear none of it. That day, or any other." A deep sigh punctuates her words as if the memory of my aunt is as painful for her as it is for me. "Adelaide was stubborn. She had faith in the Goddess, and confidence in her country's loyalty and love. She didn't want to face the truth that many of the men were tired of listening to weakened priestesses and a gentle queen.

"Those men wanted conquest, glory, and riches. When she repeatedly rejected Blackwell's proposal to be her consort, I knew it wouldn't be long before her reign would end. I'm just sorry to see you weren't better protected from my predictions." Salome's eyes shine with tears, but, with a gesture I am all too familiar with, she takes a deep breath and straightens her shoulders, swallowing her sadness back down.

"What do you mean, you warned her?" I ask, my voice sharper than I intend it to be. I dig my fingernails into my palms as I fight from spilling all the questions that bubble to my lips.

"I met Blackwell during one of his quests to claim her hand, years before I renounced my position and left Selennia. He was charming and handsome as many young men are, but there was something *off* about him. Something cruel lurked under the pleasant facade. Although he seemed like he was enjoying the chase and attempted courtship, it became apparent to me that his pride was more than wounded when Adelaide never considered his offer. She shrugged off my warnings, insisting that she never took *any* of her suitors seriously.

"But the acid in his expression when she formally refused his proposal wasn't a normal scorned lover's reaction. Blackwell was a powerful man politically, even if he was a younger son of one of the great families across the sea — he had wormed his way into the minds of many of the other politicians during his years visiting Selennia, and rumors swirled of gathering discontent. I warned Adelaide that she needed to increase the army, to encourage the temples to teach defensive tactics once again, but she waved me off. It wasn't long afterward that I decided to come to New Aphros. I couldn't continue to sit idly by and watch as she and my homeland were destroyed. I was too frustrated to fight harder when no one would listen. It's one of my biggest regrets, leaving her without my support." Salome looks down at her hands, hiding a look of shame.

Taking the time to absorb Salome's tale, I take a sip of my tea, wishing the astringent taste could cleanse my bitter feelings, both toward the help we didn't receive, and the man who caused so much pain for my people. Salome's eyes glance up to find me, and I finally break the silence by saying, "I miss her terribly. Being her ward for those few years was the happiest time of my life. After I left for the temple, I only saw Adelaide once. My early education felt like a whirlwind, and once I was past that phase, things had already worsened with Blackwell. There was no safe way to see her. Then, before I knew it, she was gone."

I never admitted it to anyone, but deep down, I had always felt closer to Adelaide than my mother. When she took me in as her ward after my mother's death, it had felt *right*, and part of me still harbors guilt for cherishing my time with her more than my own mother. Memories of my aunt walking with me through the hothouses at the palace and teaching me the newest court dances threaten to pull me under as sadness hollows my chest. I can barely remember my mother's face, but memories of Adelaide are clear in my mind.

As a young girl living in the palace, I missed out on most of the news and gossip that swirled around the Queen and her various suitors. I knew Blackwell was one of them; he had proposed to her numerous times over the years and I heard rumors swirl about him even before I left the castle at fourteen, headed for the temple in Athene. But in all of my memories, never did I remember Adelaide speaking with any emotion about him, one way or another. She held the throne as a solitary queen until her untimely death, never accepting *any* of the proposals from potential consorts. Many assumed she preferred the company of other women, but I'd never seen evidence of that, either. She never paraded any lovers through the castle while I was in residence.

"Her ward?" Salome pulls me from my memories, her head snapping up sharply from her teacup with her question, dark brows drawing down. "What do you mean?"

"I was only eight when my mother passed. I knew I was destined for the temple and had dreamed of it since I was little, but I was far too young still. Aunt Adelaide took me in as her ward until I was fourteen. That's why I was at the castle when you visited," I explain. My brow furrows in confusion as I wonder, *If Salome knew my aunt, knew the secrets of Selennia as she claims, why does she look shocked?*

"Oh, my darling girl." Salome's words are a whisper on her full lips, her head tilting as her eyes soften. "She never told you."

"Never told me *what*?" I ask warily, my eyes searching her face for an answer as my heart beats in an erratic rhythm, nervousness skittering across my skin.

Her expression turns pained as she leans forward and starts to reach out a hand for mine, but thinks better of it, resting her soft palm on my knee instead. "Queen Adelaide wasn't your aunt, Nerissa. She was your mother."

# CHAPTER 6

My ears ring with the dull pounding of my racing heart as I blink rapidly, trying to absorb this new information from Salome.

My mother.

*Adelaide* was my mother.

I grip the soft arm of the sofa intending to stand as my emotions flood me. I need to get out of this room, away from this woman.

I can't breathe.

I can't think.

Panic seizes me as I try to stand, knocking over the teacup and saucer perched on the edge of the table at my knees.

"Nerissa!" Salome reaches out to grip my hand to prevent my flight, but I pull away and stumble to the door, my vision tunneling on the brass knob. But where can I go?

Tears gather in my eyes, burning as I fight to hold them back. I've been running and hiding since I fled the temple, pushing down any secret that might out me for what I truly am. I thought I might finally find some respite across the sea. But here I am, faced with the biggest truth of all, and it splinters my already bruised heart with the force of the knowledge.

Queen Adelaide was my *mother*.

The woman I always looked so much like. Who indulged me and laughed easily. Who showed me so much love and comfort when I came to live with her. Was my mother.

My heart aches at the betrayal, worse than I thought possible even after everything I have experienced. Painful thoughts flood my mind, each like a dagger to my tender heart — *Was she ashamed of me? Who was my father? Does he live? Did she not love me enough to tell me I was hers? How could she not have told me?*

"I don't think she knew how, Nerissa. She wanted to keep you safe." Salome's voice is full of sympathy as she stands behind me.

I blink at her from where I stand, still gripping the knob of the door with white knuckles, finally comprehending that I spoke the final question out loud.

"Please, come sit back down. I understand your desire to flee, but you have been running a very long time, child. It's time you learn the truth."

I shiver at the idea of there being more secrets, even as the warmth from the fireplace surrounds me, but find myself slowly floating back to the chair. It's as if my body understands the older woman is right, even if my mind still races, encouraging me to run once more. The teacup and saucer have been picked up and placed back on the table, and a tea towel soaks up the amber liquid from the rug. Salome walks to her desk and returns with a decanter.

"Take a few breaths, Nerissa," she soothes, giving me space before returning to her chair. I do as she says, closing my eyes as I fight to find the indifferent calm I used to don so easily. The clink of the stopper pulling free of the glass decanter brings me back to the present.

"Now, I believe something stronger than tea is required for the remainder of the afternoon, don't you?" She raises her brows in question, and I nod numbly, watching as she neatly pours a couple of fingers of the liquid into my empty teacup and hands it to me.

The smoky scent of the whiskey burns my nose when I raise it to my lips and take a delicate sip, savoring the sting as it heats my chest and refocuses my thoughts. After the second sip, I will my hand to unclench from where it twists in the fabric of my skirt, and finally meet Salome's eyes as she watches me from across the table, countenance full of concern.

Delphine's angry statement when I looked at her burns rises to the forefront of my thoughts, and I have to fight the words from escaping my mouth — *I don't need your pity.*

"I don't pity you, Nerissa. I miss my friend," Salome states.

*Can she read my thoughts?* My eyes widen at the idea. *How powerful is this woman?*

"Your thoughts are written across your face, child," she answers my unasked question with a sad smile. "And I've had many years to learn how to read people."

Gripping my teacup between both hands, I rest it on my lap and heave a heavy sigh. "So, tell me the truth then. The real truth. All of it." My voice is hard. Unfamiliar. The curiosity that simmered in my mind earlier is deadened and replaced with anger and hurt, but I *need* to hear more.

Salome sighs and her mask fully drops, sadness overtaking all of the cocksure posturing she had shown up until this afternoon. Now I can tell that she must be at least the same age as Lyra's grandmother Marie, the small creases at the corners of her eyes and lips more evident in her distress than when she wears her smiling guise for the public.

With a deep drink of her whiskey, she slouches in her chair, resigned to her sad tale. "This might take a while, but it's time you know everything. I met Adelaide when she was preparing to take the throne. We were close in age, and I was a high priestess from the west awaiting my ascension to the Central Temple. I was younger than most of the former high priestesses to take that title, but my power far exceeded theirs, and I had proven myself more than capable of the position.

"Adelaide was like a beam of sunshine." Salome warmly smiles at the memory, her eyes drifting over me as if weighing my scowl against the memory of her friend. "She was always smiling, always joking, and everyone adored her. I was no different. We became close friends, and once we both settled into our new roles I became her most trusted advisor. While it was tradition for Queen and High Priestess to work in tandem, our bond was different. More like best friends or sisters, and it became clear that some didn't approve of how closely we worked."

My brow draws down in confusion at her words, but I remain silent. Once again reading my expression, Salome lets out a bitter laugh. "Some of the courtiers felt I was too radical." She waves her glass in the air before taking another sip. "I immersed myself in researching the ancient ways of the priestesses. In doing so, I encouraged Adelaide to look into her lineage as well and we spent hours pouring over texts. I made it known that I felt like some of the Old Ways needed to return — defensive use of the *glow*, training new priestesses to learn and explore *all* their potential talents, not just focusing on a single strength. We priestesses used to be able to defend our country and its people. I wanted to know why that stopped, how we could return to that level of power." She leans forward in her chair, her elbows resting on her knees as her expression shutters.

"I also spoke out about protecting our people from the men who had just started creeping into Selennia. Rumors reached me that these priests were preaching a new religion with a male God. They spoke out against women in power and encouraged violence to overthrow what they saw as an abomination in Selennia. No matter how relevant my concerns were, or how vocal I was, the others thought I was foolish to heed the priests' ranting, brushing it off as a passing nuisance. Each time I presented reasons to make changes, a small battle ensued, until I was exhausted."

I say nothing, absorbing this new information, but take another sip of my whiskey when she does the same.

"I eventually told Adelaide she needed to choose a consort. Not because I felt there *had* to be a man at her side, but because I knew she needed an heir. I repeatedly heard disturbing rumors from the villages and other temples. Some of the priests had infiltrated the minds of our coun-trymen. They began to complain about being under the rule of a beautiful queen and the priestesses, insisting that our beliefs were suppressing their ability to make money and find glory." Salome pauses for a moment, tipping the last of the whiskey in her cup into her mouth.

"I'm sure you understand that royal marriages are often just alliances dressed up as love." Her words are full of bitterness, either for the tradition or the responsibility forced onto her friend, or maybe for her own choices in the past. "I thought that if perhaps she could ally with a royal house from the continent it would alleviate the influx of priests since they seemed to be streaming from across the channel. She could have whatever lovers she wanted once the marriage was complete and an heir was conceived, the way things have always been. But Adelaide wanted none of it, and the subject became a bit of a wedge between us. She had fallen in love with one of her personal guards and wouldn't entertain the idea of bedding another man, or having anyone but him at her side. You can probably guess what happened next." Salome smiles sadly at me, and I know.

Of course, I do.

"I happened," I breathe.

"You did." Salome nods solemnly. "On one of her regular visits to see me, I knew before she could say the words. She glowed, and not in the way we priestesses did. She was so happy and excited about the babe blossoming within her. But she was also terrified. She wanted to marry Gareth, her guard. But she knew it would cause an uproar in Selennia. Gareth was from a peasant family, had no connection to any nobility, and offered no great alliance for power with the continent. She feared that announcing their relationship would widen the rift between her and her opposition and further weaken her rule. For the sake of Selennia, she felt she had to hide their love, and you, until the time was right and she had regained the control she needed over the country.

"So, instead, she announced she would be spending time visiting the temples, leaving her trusted council elders in charge to rule in her stead while she was out of sight for the late stages of her pregnancy. Your Aunt Iris and I brought you into the world at the temple in Cybele on Beltane. For a few months, Adelaide and Gareth had a period of happiness, hidden away from all prying eyes. The other priestesses residing there weren't even aware that the Queen was in residence. For once, they were just a man and woman with their child, hidden in the forests at the foot of the mountains, with none of the pressures of ruling on her shoulders while she recovered from the birth."

Salome lifts the cup to her mouth, forgetting she had drained it moments ago, then pours another. Her pale green eyes glisten silver with unshed tears as she traverses her memories of Adelaide. After a brief moment, she continues the story as I sit in silence, absorbing the tale of my birth.

"Unfortunately, their happiness was short-lived. Adelaide was brokenhearted when she decided to have her sister raise you as her own. Iris was kind and fair, but she was a stern woman. I worried for you, but I knew she would be a safe haven for you and a way for Adelaide to see you easily without raising suspicion. Iris had spent the months at the temple with Adelaide, so no one would look askance at her coming home with a baby. As you know, it wasn't unusual for unwed women to raise their children alone after seeking assistance in the birth at the temple, so she took you with her back to her manor outside Cybele. Adelaide prepared to return to the palace, Gareth at her side. On the way back, they were both distracted, sad about their goodbyes to you. That lack of focus allowed a surprise attack to slip past the guards' notice. The wagon train was ambushed as it neared Aphros and many of the guards were killed protecting Adelaide, including Gareth." Salome looks down at her hands, a tear escaping down her cheek.

"Adelaide never knew who ordered the attack. I had my suspicions but was never able to prove any of them. I immediately went to her side once I heard, but she was changed. She showed no true emotion. She maintained a constant farce of a carefree, laughing creature, even in private. Although she had always been positive, this was a brittle shell; a false happiness I was certain everyone could see through. But the longer I was around her, the more I realized I was the only one who cared, who understood what losses she had truly suffered. She buried all of her pain deeply and remained that way until the end of her days. She never took another lover that I know of and refused all potential suitors. The only time she expressed anything was when she was able to see you."

Another tear slips free from Salome's eye, trailing down her cheek and dripping onto her lap. I fight to hold back my own, remembering the happiness I felt with Adelaide. "Her joy when you came to live at the palace was real, even though she mourned her sister's passing. When I told her I was leaving Selennia was the first time I ever saw her angry. She told me she wouldn't stop me, but that she would never forgive me for abandoning her. Those words still haunt me."

Words are lost to me. Emotions swirl through the haze of the whiskey and are too numerous to process properly — sadness, anger, betrayal, loss. All are familiar to me, but the weight of them compounding with the truth of my parentage threatens to drown me, as surely as if I had lept from the deck of the *Bartered Soul* in the middle of the ocean.

Once I finish the cup of whiskey, I immediately hold it out for more. Salome's lips tighten into a line, but she obliges with another heavy pour. I have as many questions as I do emotions, but I need to decide which is the best to ask first. The memory of my aunt — no, my *mother* — is even more painful to me now that I know the truth. My chest aches with this new layer of loss added to the weight I already carry.

"Did he know? When he brought me here?" I ask Salome, breaking my silence while looking into the teacup as if I can see the truth in the amber liquor. "Did he know what he was bringing me to learn? Who he was rescuing?"

"He?" she asks, a line forming between her brows in confusion. "You mean William?"

I nod in response. First, Marie. Now, Salome. Had this all been a ploy to pull me back into this world, this role? Lennox never fully explained whether he knew my true identity, and now it's clear to me that he has known Salome for years. I can't stop myself from assuming the worst. Perhaps convincing me to fall in love with him was just a convenient way to lure me here. Fury crashes over me like the waves against the cliffs of Selennia, threatening to break my heart entirely if that is the case. Anger at my naivety burns so hot it almost overtakes the ache in my chest caused by the thought of him deceiving me. I cannot withstand another betrayal.

"No," Salome says with a shake of her head, bringing me back from my maelstrom of thoughts as she reassures me of Lennox's honesty. "At least not that I know of. No one knew Adelaide's true story except me, her, Gareth, your Aunt Iris, and now you. I've known William even longer than I've known you. His mother, Anise, was one of the priestesses that trained alongside me. She was the High Priestess at the Western Temple until I gave her permission to marry William's father. It's rare to see such a deep love as I saw between the two of them." She cuts her eyes to me, but continues, "William found me here once he started sailing with Captain Jackson and told me the sad tale of his mother's death." She sighs deeply, shuddering at the memory, and my heart aches for all those we lost in those terrible days. "I never feel old until I count the number of those I've lost."

Before she resumes her story, my mind snags on something. "His mother was a *high* priestess?" I question. Memories surface of Siobhan telling me on Delosia that Lennox's mother had been a priestess who left her post to marry his father, but she never mentioned she was one who held any rank.

"Didn't he tell you?" She cocks her head. "I assumed he would have given you her robe by now. He told me Celeste kept Anise's raiment waiting for you," Salome states, appearing to be just as confused as I am. My eyes widen at the revelation — I never put the pieces together that the robe and jewelry were his mother's. When I asked him about them before, he had only said he had connections, never what those might be.

"I knew through letters from Anise that he had gone through the rites when he was eighteen. She said she worried for him because he seemed to be enamored with the girl he joined with that night. She, of all people, knew what difficulties one would face trying to nurture love between a priestess and a partner outside of the temple. I see now why he loved you. And I can see when you're together that his love hasn't dimmed. If anything, it seems to be even stronger. Even if you're trying to convince the world otherwise. I was relieved that he'd found you at last. I confess, between his description of you, and the things I've *seen,* I suspected who he pined after. But I never disclosed who you might be."

Though I still tremble with my warring emotions, I push down the despair and indignation. This changes nothing; why am I letting the truth twist my insides and break my heart so badly all over again? I left Selennia with no family and the weight of a hidden title on my shoulders. These revelations only serve to remind me that I'm still adrift except for my recent attachment to Lennox.

Although the whiskey has finally begun to dull my senses, I study Salome's face before asking, "If you were a priestess, what were your talents? Lennox told me you can use the *glow* for defense, but that hasn't been done in centuries. It's all but a myth." My voice slurs slightly, and although my thoughts are mildly muddled, I push on before she can answer me. "And where is your sigil?" I point to my brow, indicating the darkened silvery mark of the Goddess. Salome's brow is smooth and clear, only marked by a few of the normal lines of aging. Nothing visible indicates her dedication to the Old Ways or our Goddess.

"I forget how much they failed to teach you at the temples once I departed. I was the High Priestess over all of Selennia. I had access to ancient texts and studied them voraciously. I trained in *all* the arts, but divination was always one of my strongest talents. That's how I knew Lennox would find you again, even if he started to think I was only humoring him in my insistence." She gives a half-hearted smile at the admission. "As for my sigil, I cloak it. Just like I've taught Delphine and others who have passed through these halls to cloak theirs. One can't be too careful. Plus, the surprise on people's faces when our powers are revealed is exhilarating." A flicker of fury shines behind her pale green eyes at the chilling admission.

"I tried to convince Adelaide to make it mandatory for all priestesses to learn defense, to be trained across the disciplines, but she refused. She was weary of my pessimism and the pushback from her council who felt that it would make those who worship the Goddess more threatening to outsiders. I regret not staying and taking matters into my own hands after all that has happened."

"If I was her true heir, with no expectation to marry or make another, why didn't she make it known? Why did she let me train as a priestess?" I'm still confused by all of the information pouring into my head and sway slightly in my seat. I should stop drinking, but I take another small sip against my better judgment.

"In ancient times, the queen was also the highest-ranked priestess. She possessed the full knowledge and power of the Goddess, to rule while protecting and caring for the land and its people. She trained the lower priestesses to act as protectors as well. Adelaide thought it a concession to me that she would allow you to train as a high priestess, so you would be prepared like the queens of old when you took the throne, even if we hadn't determined why she and her recent ancestors had no power of their own. I don't know why she never told you, or when she planned to. I never got the chance to ask her."

"Can you teach me?" I mumble, my mind too fuzzy to fully comprehend her any longer.

"Teach you?"

"Yes, teach me. How to do… what you do?" I wave my hand toward her, much more clumsily than I anticipate. "How to protect myself?"

"Oh, sweet girl, it would be my honor." Salome touches her chest, hand lingering over her heart as her eyes rake over my face. "Although, from what I can tell, you have done a fine job of it yourself so far." She reaches across the table and gently takes the cup from my shaking hands. I want to laugh at her thinking I'm a *sweet girl*. If she knew what I'd done these past years, she wouldn't think I was nearly as endearing as she seems to, but my eyelids droop from the strong drink and lack of food, my stomach churning slightly, so I keep my mouth shut. I haven't touched any of the tiny pastries or other items on the elaborate tray and regret the oversight as my head spins.

"Let me get William to help you," Salome murmurs as I clench my eyes closed to help steady myself.

# CHAPTER 7
## LENNOX

The tavern across from the Den is already relatively quiet at this hour, but a hush descends on the few tables and the men drinking at the bar when I walk through the open front door and stand on the stained planks of the shabby barroom. In New Aphros, as with so many other cities along our trade routes, my name is one to incite fear, just the way I like. I have spent years violently defending my reputation and the reputation of my crew through these streets, whether it be enforcing for Salome or taking someone to task for trying to take what is ours. No one has been bold enough to attempt to poach my clients, raid my ship, or touch one of my crewmembers in years.

I was honest with Nerissa when I told her the city is full of desperate people and those who would take advantage of them. I will never be either of those things. The helpless young man who was dragged aboard the King's naval vessel years ago to suffer under the lash died at sea. The man who rose from the waves in his place would rather perish than kneel to one of Blackwell's minions, or any man, again. Chairs scratch across the floor as patrons move out of my way, watching as I saunter through the room. My eyes scan the occupants as I approach the bar, taking in faces both new and familiar. Even those brave enough to meet my eye aren't granted a smile. The young barmaid dips her blonde head when I reach the edge of the counter, lifting her pale lashes to gaze up at me as she asks, "What can I get you, Captain Lennox?"

"Ale. What's on the menu today?"

"Cook's made some roast pork with root vegetables, sir," she answers, placing an almost overflowing tankard on the bartop. Foam sloshes from the side as she trembles, her eyes downcast to avoid my gaze.

"I'll take that as well. Bring it to my table." I toss a couple of coins on the wet surface and make my way across the stained floorboards to the most private table near a window, sitting with my back to the wall so I can see those who enter.

My mind wanders to the women across the street as I wait for my meal to arrive. The encounter with the priests in the square was unexpected. Had I known they were out confronting people in the streets, I would have avoided walking past them in the first place. I never intended for Nerissa to be shaken like that, especially so quickly following her encounter with Salome last night. When I imagined bringing her here, I wanted her to have time to relax and get to know Salome and Delphine, to learn from them, and discover the latent power I am certain she possesses.

Thinking about the priestesses' powers, I'm almost over-whelmed by the memories of my mother that suddenly flood my mind. For a moment, my chest aches at how badly I miss her and my father. How happy they were together. But this is neither the time nor place for me to let my emotions get the best of me, and I tuck those thoughts back into the recesses of my mind. I know that I need to share more with Nerissa about Mother, but the time never feels right. Discussing your late mother isn't exactly pillow talk.

Once she has time to talk to Salome about what she can teach her, once we have a moment of respite from secrets and surprises and the stress of being at sea, I'll commit to telling her everything. To lay it all out on the table. Discuss our future.

The past week and a half at sea between Delosia and New Aphros have been flush with discussions of adventures and places we could go, all while laying tangled in each other's arms. I don't know if I will ever tire of the way she tastes, the hint of herbs she carries on her skin, the way her silky hair tickles when it brushes against me in her sleep, but we haven't solidified any sort of true plans for what we want our future to look like.

The dagger training Nerissa did with Pike and me was valuable, as she proved this morning with the priests, the memory of which makes me want to torch their cathedral in rage. Nerissa continues to prove she is just as vicious as I am when needed, honoring me by choosing to stand by my side. Watching her at her fiercest, wielding that blade like it's a part of her, makes my chest swell with pride, and my cock...

Well, the things I want to do to her when I see her with that blade are indecent.

I'm lost in contemplation when the young barmaid

interrupts, holding a plate of steaming meat and vegetables alongside a fresh baguette. Clearing my throat, I shift in my chair at her approach, trying to stifle the desire that coursed through me at the thought of Nerissa.

"Anything else, Captain?" she asks, stepping away from me quickly as if I would grope her or pull her onto my lap, misreading the lust on my face as a want for her.

"No," I huff dismissively, taking a deep drink of the ale and digging into the meal. Without waiting to be waved away, the girl hurries back to her place behind the bar. This tavern always has excellent food and drink, even if I'm unable to truly relax within its walls.

Leaning back in my chair, I push my empty plate across the table and hold up my tankard to the barmaid, indicating she should bring another. She obliges with haste, and I hold back a smirk when she rushes to the tableside, wondering which story they told her about the fearsome Captain Lennox to make her rush about so quickly.

Possibly the tale of me beating a man to death with only my fists right here in this very tavern for insulting Salome during my first visit to the city. I've managed to gain better control over my temper with age; it was harder to rein in after the mutiny and subsequent months on Captain Jackson's ship, but I can keep it locked away now.

Then there's the story about me keelhauling a crewman for disobeying orders, dragging him below the ship until his body was shredded beyond recognition. This one is false. While I've heard rumors of keelhauling, it isn't a practice I've ever desired to explore. Although reflecting on it now, it would have been a suitable punishment for Crewes after trying to rape Nerissa on the voyage from Selennia.

Once again, her choice of justice was poetic, but I would have preferred his pain to have been drawn out as her suffering has been over the years.

Perhaps it's merely my reputation as a trader of women that has the girl on edge and keeping her distance from me. Whatever the reason, I don't mind. If these stories keep my enemies in line, I'm willing to accept the blame for all their fictional villainy.

I'm pulled from my musings when a familiar head of light blonde curls pops through the doors, drawing my eye. Delphine makes her way to my table, pulling out a chair and plopping down next to me in a most unladylike manner.

"Delphine," I greet her, my voice flat, lips tight.

"Lennox," she mutters back with squinted eyes, just as emotionless. She casts her gaze around, making sure no one is close enough to listen in before continuing, lips spreading into a mischievous smile. "Well, you found her finally." Her brows lift in a teasing manner as she reaches across and takes a swig from my tankard. "Shouldn't you be shouting from the rooftops with glee instead of glowering over a tankard in this hovel?"

Mistaking my lack of a response as an invitation to go on, Delphine continues with a glimmer in her eyes. "Unless there's already trouble in paradise. Any chance you need assistance handling her?"

I lean forward, snagging my drink back from her as a smile tugs on my lips. "You are something, Del. Was that bitter performance last night your attempt at flirting? If so, you have a lot of learning to do about how to woo women," I scold with a slight shake of my head. "I thought you didn't bed men if you could help it. Why would you offer assistance in mine?"

"Not for *you*. But for *her*, I'd be willing to try anything." She winks one stormy eye and raises her brows to punctuate her offer. "Maybe if she thought you'd been bedding me, she would have to seek comfort *elsewhere*. And believe me, Captain — I have no trouble wooing anyone," she teases, dropping her voice to a sultry tone.

I huff a laugh at the young woman's confidence. "Well, lucky for me, she didn't hold you against me. But, I prefer dark-haired women. I don't know if I'd want you spoiling things." I take another deep drink of the ale, allowing my mind to stray to what it might be like to see Nerissa with Delphine wrapped in the soft sheets of the Den. I wouldn't deny Nerissa that pleasure if she wanted to participate; I'm confident in who her heart belongs to. I blink away the thought, adjusting my posture in the booth, and push away the last of the ale before this conversation gets away from me.

"Do you want the rest of my ale, Del? Or something for yourself? Otherwise, I'm going to go back across the way to wait for her to finish talking to Salome." I offer the half-empty tankard to Delphine, who tips it back for a deeper swallow and sits back in her chair.

"So, is it true?" she asks, placing the tankard on the rough tabletop. Her words have me scanning the space, but the tavern has cleared even more since I arrived; only a few men sit staggered at the bar, and the other tables are empty and wiped clean.

"That depends on what you're asking." I hedge my statement.

"Is she so good in bed that she captured your heart after a single night, or are you just pathetically romantic?" she teases, not asking what I had anticipated at all.

Before I can offer any response beyond a sigh and a roll of my eyes, the door pushes open, creaking loudly on its hinges as light streams in from the street. Salome stands in the doorframe, glancing around the room momentarily, before locking eyes on me.

"Lennox, I need your assistance. Now, please." Salome has already spun on her heeled slipper and is back out the door again before Delphine and I can react. We both hastily rise from the table to follow her out into the bright afternoon.

"What's happened? Is she all right?" I hurry to catch Salome, grabbing her upper arm to stop her while I palm the hilt of my cutlass in the opposite hand. If someone has harmed Nerissa, I will kill them.

"She's fine. We could just use a bit of help getting her to your room," Salome calmly replies, removing my grip with a soft tug of her slim tan fingers. Relief fills me but is immediately replaced with confusion at her statement.

"Wait. Why can't she—" Delphine starts to ask, echoing my own thoughts, before Salome interjects.

"Just come with me now, the both of you, and stop asking inane questions," Salome answers before turning in a rustle of skirts and the irritated click of her slippers on the cobblestones.

Delphine stays at the bar while I follow Salome down the hallway, only a step behind her as she quietly opens the door to her office and slips inside. Dark hair peeks over the back of one of the chairs, and I hurry to Nerissa's side, watching as she rests against the soft upholstery, eyes closed against the flickering lamplight. The sound of the door snicking shut causes her breathing to stutter, pulling her from her doze as I scoop her up and cradle her against me. My heart warms as she nuzzles against my chest where it rests under her flushed cheek.

"What *happened*?" I whisper harshly to Salome.

"She's fine. Just didn't eat, and had a bit too much of the good whiskey. Take her to lie down, and make sure she eats when she wakes up." Salome gives the motherly advice in a soft tone, then brushes a gentle touch against Nerissa's hair and cups her cheek. "She's taken in a lot of unexpected information today. Be gentle with her."

I huff in frustration, but rather than ask any more questions, I carry Nerissa's limp form out the door Salome holds open and up the mahogany staircase to our room.

# CHAPTER 8

It takes several blinks to clear the sleep from my eyes, glancing around the unfamiliar room, and running my fingers across the burgundy sheets on the soft bed. The fog clears from my mind when I see Lennox sitting in the armchair across the room, rifling through papers in his lap as he relaxes in just his shirt and breeches. For a brief moment, I wonder if the exchange with Salome was all a dream. However, the throbbing in my head and nausea that churns in my belly confirm that I did indeed drink far too much liquor on an empty stomach. If that was real, then the conversation was, too.

The sounds of the lively city drifting on the river breeze pulls my attention to the open window, framing the twilight sky. The part of me that has been running for so long wants to pack up our trunk and take one of the flat-bottomed riverboats back to the ship tonight. That part trembles at the thought of embracing the full truth Salome has told me, wishing to vanish into the darkness like the sun dipping below the horizon instead. But another part of me — one that has lain dormant under a blanket of fear until it was coaxed awake by Marie's words and the ceremony on the beach of Delosia — tells me to pause. This part of me is what gave me the courage to stay with Lennox instead of disappearing alone again, and is ready to fully shed the false identities I've embodied for so long. To finally figure out, and embrace, who I really am.

How much longer can I run, truly? If nothing else, my curiosity about my past and potential power anchors me here, urging me to stay and learn more from Salome. More about my heritage, more about her powers, just… *more*.

With a resolute sigh, I push off the soft mattress, prepared to sit up and speak with Lennox, but my spinning head has other plans for me. A groan escapes me before I can contain it as I plop back on the soft pillows.

The sound of my pain draws Lennox's attention, looking up from his paperwork as he stifles a laugh at my predicament. A wry smile pulls on his lips as his emerald eyes dance in the lantern light. "Salome should have warned you about the good stuff," he chuckles. "I already had them bring up bread and butter, as well as some water for you. Would you like anything else? Broth?"

"Yes, to all of it," I mumble into my arm draped across my face, remembering why I don't drink like this. With a soft chuckle, Lennox stands, walking to the door to ring a small bell to call a servant for the broth before bringing me a hunk of bread slathered in rich, creamy butter and a cup of cool water.

"Did she tell you what we discussed?" I ask through small bites, still reclining on the pillows. The bread is hearty and brown, tasting of honey and salted butter, and its comforting aroma is surprisingly soothing to my griping stomach.

"She told me you took in a lot of information about your past, but that's all," he says, sitting on the mattress next to me. He searches my face intently but allows me a moment as I sip the water. "I know Salome can be overwhelming. She usually means well, though."

"Marie was wrong," I say slowly. His brow furrows as he observes me, but I continue, "About me."

"How so?" Lennox cocks his head, running a hand through his darkened hair in confusion. Messy strands already hang across his forehead, as if this isn't the first time he's run his fingers through it while waiting for me to wake.

"Adelaide wasn't my aunt." I sigh before continuing, the sadness I covered with anger earlier rising to the surface. "She was my mother." The confession feels heavy on my shoulders as I look down at my hands clutching the bread and cup.

"I see." His words are serious as he sits back to study my face for a moment before entwining his fingers with mine. "Does that mean I have to start calling you *princess* now, my pretty priestess?"

The hint of teasing in his voice has my eyes jerking up to his face, where I'm greeted with a devastating grin. The tension in my chest eases a fraction and I can't hold back an eye roll, smacking him on the shoulder with the heel of the bread. Lennox snatches my hand before I can pull it back, his tattooed forearm flexing as he draws me toward him. Clasping my hand tighter, his gaze turns serious again.

"This changes nothing, Nerissa. Not anything that

matters. I can tell you're distressed; it's written all over your face. But you are your own woman. If you want to leave the past in the past, you still can. You don't owe anything to anyone. You still have a choice. Even if this news *does* mean you have all the more reason to return to Selennia to seek justice and claim your birthright, you can still walk away, just as you could this morning as the Queen's niece, not her daughter."

My breath is shallow as I look into his eyes. The knowledge that he would support my decision if I decided to forget it all is staggering. For a moment I'm almost ashamed for thinking he might have tricked me into loving him, that his love could be feigned or false, and my chest tightens with a wave of affection as I study his face.

With a sarcastic sigh, I ask, "You're telling me that you'd be content with me desiring to merely be a pirate's wench from now on? Just forget about everything else?"

"Well, I'd hope you'd be *my* wench," he chuckles, pulling me close. "But I'll honor your choice, Nerissa. I always will. Even if we both know what Blackwell really deserves." His last words turn serious once again, bitterness winning out over the playful banter, but I know he speaks true and my heart stumbles knowing he won't pressure me as I decide what to do next.

"I honestly don't know what I want," I confess. "This journey was supposed to be my escape, my chance for freedom, and to start a new life with you. An opportunity to discover who I am now. Who I want to be. Yet I keep getting pulled back into the past, no matter how far away from Selennia I get. It's like the universe won't let me go." Silence stretches between us, but Lennox's warm hand brushing across my arm is a soothing reminder that no matter how lost I am in my own mind, he is a balefire to guide me back home.

"Do you trust Salome?" I ask as I search his face for the answer.

"I do," he nods, offering me a reassuring smile. "I've known her since I was born. She loved my family, and has offered a safe place for me to escape to in the years since their deaths." He runs his thumb in soothing circles on the back of the hand he still holds in his. "She may have a formidable reputation, but deep down she cares about the women who work here, the townspeople, the people she left behind. She's a good woman."

"I'm so tired of running, Billy. I'm tired of hiding. And I'm so tired of being afraid. I want her to teach me what she can do with our power. I only learned how to scratch the surface when I was in the temple." Frustration bubbles up when I think about how useless lessons in rites and rituals were when I should have learned how to manage elemental powers and defense. "Whatever I decide to do, wherever we go from here, I want to know what she does. I want to be able to protect myself, protect others, protect you." I squeeze his hand in mine and meet his eyes.

"There's my she-wolf." He smiles and cups my cheek, tracing his fingers over the curve of my cheekbone before pulling me to him and pressing his mouth against mine, causing my pulse to leap and my head to spin for reasons beyond the lingering whiskey.

A knock at the door interrupts us, and Lennox stands to return to the door, thanking the servant as he takes the tray. Steam rises from the bowl as he walks back to the bed, carrying broth with a savory scent that makes my mouth water. I sip at it slowly, happy that my stomach has settled. Draining the last of it, I stand, circling the bed to join Lennox in the armchairs where he has resumed sorting through his papers.

A sideways glance tells me that these are receipts for the deliveries and trades the crew has taken care of since arriving in the city. We sit in companionable silence while the night sounds drift in and the twilight darkens to full night, wrapped in the amber lamplight of our quarters. The laughter of pedestrians mingles with the clack of hooves pulling carriages and the music that seems to permeate all portions of the city so far, lulling me into a peaceful reprieve from my emotional day, and soothing my residual headache.

"Are you feeling well enough to dine in the salon tonight?" Lennox murmurs, still looking through the parchment, matching figures to those in a ledger open on the low table in front of him. "Or do you wish to have a real meal brought up?"

"We can go down. I think I'm feeling well enough, and if we stay in the Den I can always come back up if I need to."

He nods, sorting through the last of the pages.

A burning question from earlier, momentarily forgotten as I nursed my aching head and stomach, softly slips from my lips, "Why didn't you tell me the robe and jewelry you gave me were your mother's?" Twisting my hands in the dark blue fabric of my skirt, I glance out of the corner of my eye when the rustle of paper is suddenly silenced, finding Lennox tightly gripping the slips of parchment.

"I see Salome has shared *my* family history, too," he replies just as softly in return, looking up at me through the dark hair hanging across his brow. He doesn't look angry, but there is a wariness in his eyes I don't quite understand.

"I'm sorry if it brings you pain to speak of your mother. I just don't understand why you would keep that detail from me." With a sideways glance, I look to the chest at the foot of the bed where I know the robe and jewelry are packed. Knowing the items were his mother's, whom he loved so much, adds a layer of intimacy to them.

"It's not that," Lennox says with a shake of his head, shuffling the papers and tapping them on the table before he sets them down. His full attention is on me as he continues, grabbing my hand. "I mean, there *is* pain when I think of what happened to her. But I remember her as she was — fierce and beautiful. She loved Celeste and me so much. When my father died, she never broke; never let us see the hardship or heartbreak she endured. She bowed to no one and commanded respect from everyone she met. I only wish you could have known her. She would have loved you and the two of you would have been formidable side by side." He smiles sadly, memories heavy on his mind.

"Celeste took Mother's robe and ceremonial jewelry when she and Lyra fled to the city. Mother insisted that she have them, to hide them away until it was safe for them to be worn openly again. Celeste told me when you showed up at the House that she knew they were meant for you. She made sure they were packed in your trunk before we left."

The revelation that Celeste cared enough to give me the last piece she had of their mother touches something in my heart. I was never sure of the meaning behind the strange rapport we shared, but now I understand that she was always challenging me, pushing me, out of a place of respect instead of antagonism. The memory of her bright red hair and reproving glances coaxes a smile from my lips. "What did she look like?" I wonder aloud.

"Mother?" Lennox asks.

"Yes, did she look like Celeste?" I compare Lennox and his sister in my mind. I never saw her without the red hair color, but even without that difference, they've never struck me as looking similar enough for their relationship to be obvious. Lennox is so overtly masculine with his hard planes and angles, while Celeste was always the epitome of feminine curves and softness. The only similarity I can connect is the pout of their full lips.

"Well, both Mother and Father were fair-haired, as are Celeste and I naturally. But Celeste took more after our father. I always favored Mother more; she was tall and slim, and I have her eyes. I remember my father being a large man, with a thick beard and hands that were as big and strong as his laugh. But then, I guess we all think our fathers are big when we are small. He died when I was six and Celeste was nine."

"I never knew mine," I reply sadly. "I was told he'd died when I was a baby, which I suppose was the truth, but Salome told me that he was one of Adelaide's personal guards." I never put much thought into who my father was. I made peace with the fact that he passed into the Afterlife years ago. But now I wonder what Gareth looked like. Was he honorable? Gentle? Brave? Am I like him at all? Once again, bitterness toward Adelaide reigns over my emotions, if she'd only been honest with me I could have asked her.

Lennox stands, placing the papers from his lap onto the table, then kneels before me so our eyes are almost level, taking my hands in his. His eyes are gentle as they rake over my expression as if he can read me as easily as the papers on the table. "I'm sorry you were never able to know him, and that I didn't tell you the truth about the robe and jewelry upfront. I just wasn't sure if you would accept them."

I lean forward so our foreheads touch as I whisper my gratitude to him. "Thank you. For sharing her with me. For giving me her things. I truly do cherish them."

"You're welcome, Nerissa," he whispers before kissing me on my forehead. "She would have loved you as much I do."

# CHAPTER 9

"Ready?" Lennox asks me as he shrugs into a black frock coat, more formal tonight than his usual greatcoat.

Pinning my coronet braid in place, I nod before standing to join him. *Or, as ready as I can be,* I think, hoping I can maintain the cool exterior I hid beneath so easily in the House of Starlight. The dark blue of my dress contrasts sharply with the paleness of my complexion, but accents my eye color perfectly, and the touch of silver embroidery at my hem and sleeves adds just enough elegance to make this gown stand out from my usual, more muted, choices. The selection is deliberate to demonstrate Lennox's wealth since the patrons below need to believe I belong to him.

A touch of rouge on my cheeks and heavy kohl around my eyes helps to hide the fact that only a few hours ago I was distressed from Salome's words and recovering from the whiskey I tried to drown them in. My attire and makeup will help me play the part of Lennox's plaything when we descend to the salon. Lennox cracks open the door as I turn to him, and music drifts up from the salon below. Although it's quite late to be having dinner, the district stays up until dawn, and I'm eager to get a glimpse of the dancers Lennox told me will be on the stage tonight.

With a final glance in the mirror, I smooth my skirts. Gone is the haunted woman who learned painful secrets about her past; the untamed priestess lurking underneath has returned to the surface to walk arm-in-arm with the notorious Captain Lennox. The door clicks shut behind us, sealing in my true identity as my spine straightens. We prowl down the mahogany stairs, and I note the glint of cruelty in Lennox's eyes. Hopefully, my own expression has flattened to become unreadable to those who don't know me.

The sound of a violin, horns, and percussion greets us in the foyer before we pass through the velvet curtain of the salon, the beat urging me to get lost in the rhythm. As we step through the soft barrier, my eyes adjust to the dim atmosphere. Oil sconces dot the walls and sweet-smelling beeswax candles sit on the tables, working in tandem to wrap patrons and workers alike in flattering warm hues. Most of the men sit at the small tables, but some stand near the bar, propped against the edge as they watch the girls move throughout the close space. Once again, I can't help but compare the Den to the House of Starlight, the heady pulse of the band here is louder and more lively than the single piano that accompanied the nights there.

Scanning the crowd, my eyes find Madame Salome, and my pulse increases momentarily at the memory of our earlier conversation. Her lush curves are wrapped in luxurious silks, the deep eggplant color flattering her bronze skin and making her pale green eyes even more striking than usual. A smile ghosts across her richly colored lips when she sees us. She inclines her head in acknowledgment before taking a deep drag on a cigarette she holds in a silver quellazaire, elegant and scandalous. Inexplicably, her presence soothes me, and my nerves calm while Lennox walks ahead of me to a darkened corner booth.

Both employees and clients note our presence as I trail behind the Captain, some openly, others with guarded glances. Their attention is brief, quickly refocusing on the woman dancing on the stage in the front of the room, peeling her sparkling ensemble from her body piece by piece. Lennox pauses in front of the booth, motioning for me to sit, then takes a seat next to me and pulls the curtains almost closed against prying eyes, leaving just enough of a strategically placed gap that small glimpses can be seen both by those inside and outside the fabric divider.

Hardly a moment of privacy elapses before Delphine appears at the curtain opening. Her pale hair is pulled away from her lovely face but is left to drape across her full bosom and cascade down her back. Tonight, she's wrapped in sheer panels of blue, and I can't help but notice her curves on display through the material.

"Salome advised me to care for you both tonight. What can I bring you?" Her curt tone from yesterday has vanished and she's much more amenable this evening. I study her, searching for the meaning of the change as she stands before us waiting on Lennox's request.

"Water and wine for the table, and whatever tonight's special is," Lennox demands. His harsh tone snags my attention away from Delphine, but I remind myself that *this* is who he is to those who don't know him. Who I thought he was when he visited the House of Starlight. With a lingering glance towards him, Delphine nods and quickly disappears into the back of the salon.

Relaxing into the plush cushions of the booth the scent of vanilla and cinnamon wafting from the candle on our table soothes me, reminding me of decadent desserts and expensive perfumes. The warm scent, combined with the sight of the alluring woman on stage swaying her hips to the music, distracts me from my earlier concerns. My eyes eagerly flit over the room, soaking in the hedonistic scene through the crack in our velvet cocoon. The stoic expression I've maintained thus far is threatened when the band begins to play a more upbeat tune, my toe involuntarily tapping as a smile tickles the edge of my lips, all remnants of queasiness forgotten in the erotic haze of the salon.

Lennox leans over and whispers in my ear, drawing my eyes to his devilish smirk. "Time to act the part, my pretty priestess." He grazes his lips down my neck and sucks at the tender skin where it meets my shoulder, igniting appetites beyond those our meal will satisfy. Trembling under his touch, I lean my head away from him so he has more access to my neck.

"Of course," I whisper back, biting my lip seductively as he pulls away from me. I don't have to feign my lust for him, even if I am supposed to be playing like I'm just with him for coin. My fingers tangle in his hair as he licks along my sensitive skin, but I can't resist the urge to keep my eyes open to take in the activities in the salon. A tendril of desire wraps around my core as I absorb the sensuality surrounding us in the room, almost as if it has enchanted me as much as the women do the Den's patrons.

The women who work for Salome are undeniably beautiful as they seduce the clientele with their eyes and bodies. Each is unique in some way, some with full figures and soft curves, others bearing colorful tattoos etched on their smooth skin. All are graceful and elegant, swaying to the music or reclining on patrons' laps. Whether they remain covered in the sheer fabrics Delphine wears, or are completely nude, these women hold the control in the room, with customers practically begging for their attention. Now that I know Salome's true nature, and see the way her clients treat the women who work for her, I know they are well-protected and cared for.

Lennox's magnetism pulls me closer, longing to feel his heat at my side, and I run my hand up his thigh earning a sultry smirk when he cuts his eyes to the side in surprise. "Mmm… is this for appearances or do we need to go back to our room?" he murmurs, that dangerous smile still playing on his full lips.

"Oh, I would very much like to return to our room, but first we should give the locals something to talk about. Don't you think?" I whisper, rotating so I can breathe the words against the tan skin of his neck before grazing my lips up the side. He shudders slightly, unable to hide his desire from me. But only I can see the movement since we are hidden in the darkened space, and it fuels the pulsing warmth in my belly as I pull his face to mine so our mouths slant against one another. I have to restrain myself from climbing onto his lap as our kisses deepen and he winds one calloused hand through the loose strands of my hair, tugging lightly as he makes a low rumble in the back of his throat.

A derisive snort at my back drags me back to our surroundings. I pull away from him languidly at the sound, cutting my gaze toward the interruption, remembering to maintain my air of indifference to an audience. Lennox's eyes are hooded with desire, and he maintains contact, rubbing my loose hair between his thumb and forefinger. Sighing with irritation, he slings his other arm across the back of the booth in a casual pose as I remain tucked against him.

Delphine stands alongside Madame Salome at the curtain, both holding in their smiles even though their eyes dance with merriment at having caught us so distracted. "I see you're feeling better, Andromeda," Salome croons. "It looks like you're both enjoying the mood of the salon."

Delphine's eyes linger on my swollen lips for a moment before drifting down the portion of my body visible above the table, an unreadable expression clouding her eyes briefly as her cheeks pink. Without a word, she places the bottle of wine and pitcher of water on the table along with the two goblets she holds between her fingers, then spins to return to the bar.

Salome lingers for a few more moments, leaning casually against the table. "Are you ready to begin tomorrow, my dear?" Salome murmurs as Lennox pours dark red wine into our goblets. My stomach flips at the sight of the alcohol, but I say nothing to stop him.

"Begin?" I ask in a sultry tone. It doesn't escape my notice that the question has been worded in a way to deceive curious ears in the room, as if they might hear over the band, but my breath hitches at the insinuation. Anyone eavesdropping would think I'll be joining the ranks of the other women in the brothel, and my stomach sinks at the thought of returning to this life.

"Yes, darling girl." She blows a cloud of sweet-scented smoke from her full lips and smiles seductively. "Your *training*."

"I would be delighted to begin tomorrow, Madame. If, of course, my Captain can spare me." I run my hand down Lennox's chest, toying with the brass buttons of his coat as I meet her eyes, but nod slightly. The older woman lifts one side of her lip in quiet acknowledgment.

"You may, Andromeda. I can share with the Madame if I have to," Lennox growls possessively, sighing as he takes a deep drink of the wine as if my absence will be an inconvenience.

"Then I will leave you to it tonight and will see you in the morning. I hope the two of you enjoy your evening. Don't tire her out too much, Captain."

Salome pushes off the table and strolls through the salon, swaying her full hips on her way to stop at other tables to converse with her customers. The move reminds me so much of Celeste doing the same in the House of Starlight, ensuring her guests are pleased with their choices as she seemingly did at our alcove.

Before I can be dragged down by my memories, Delphine pulls back the curtains once more, tray in hand. The smell of roast beef with vegetables and a loaf of dark bread rises from the tray, and I find I'm hungrier than I realized. She adds another bottle of wine to our table without Lennox's prompting.

"I'm told I'll be getting to know you more closely, Andromeda. I'm very much looking forward to it," Delphine whispers to me as she places my plate in front of me. Her slim fingers graze mine as she steps back, and I look up quickly to see a flirtatious smile on her lips as she turns away, sheer fabric drifting behind her. When I snap my head to Lennox, he wears a wry smile of his own at the sight of my mouth slightly ajar from Delphine's sudden shift in attitude.

"She seems much friendlier tonight," I observe with suspicion. Lennox huffs a laugh in response, finishing his wine and pouring another glass. When he raises a brow at my glass, still untouched, I shake my head. I might be up for visiting the salon, but I'm not ready for more to drink tonight.

"Delphine is a conundrum," he says, leaning back lazily against the cushion of the booth, arm draped behind my back. "Despite her alluding to a past between us when you first met her, she prefers the company of beautiful women over men any day. She mentioned earlier today that she thinks *you're* beautiful. Salome must have told her you spoke today, so she has…*warmed*…to you even more."

He raises his brows as his hand drifts across my shoulders and down my arm closest to him, curling around my fingers under the table as I process his words. I've been with women in the past, but usually find myself with male bedmates. But the thought sits at the forefront of my mind as my eyes search the crowd for the capricious woman.

Delphine has undeniable appeal as she sashays confidently through the men of the salon, brushing off their advances without a second glance until she seats herself firmly in the lap of a sandy-haired man with a thick beard and sculpted mustache. She smiles broadly as she wraps her arms around his neck and whispers in his ear, then pulls him to his feet and out the door.

"*That* didn't look like a beautiful woman, Captain." I nod toward the hallway where the two disappeared.

"Remember that not everything is as it appears here at Salome's, my pretty priestess. Intrigued?" he teases, nipping at my ear lobe. I press against him and run my hand down his stomach, stopping to toy with the top of his breeches.

The sensual atmosphere of the salon pulses in my veins, urging me to touch and tease the man at my side. "Are you suggesting that you want me to go to bed with Delphine, Captain? Are you planning to join us, or just watch?" My face flushes at the thought, but I *am* intrigued by the idea, even though I feel the ugly grip of jealousy in my stomach at the idea of sharing him with someone else.

"I'm suggesting you are free to do whatever you wish, if she, or any of the other girls, interest you. I'm happy to participate in any way you desire," he mutters against my neck while he kisses the sensitive skin, running his hand over the fabric covering my thigh. Then, he pulls back and wraps his hand around my throat, tilting my chin up as he pulls me closer to capture my mouth with his in a rough kiss. Too quickly, he pulls away to whisper, "But make no mistake, my pretty priestess. You're the only woman I want. Don't waste even one moment worrying about that."

His touch is rougher than I've become accustomed to but reminds me of our first kiss aboard the *Bartered Soul,* when I confronted him about the women and girls I thought he was trading before I knew his true motives. The memory of how my body wanted him even before I understood why, and how his kiss burned against me before he dismissed me that night, sends heat surging through my core as our lips remain close, breath mingling in the dim booth.

"My only worry tonight is how quickly you can take me back to our room, Captain," I huskily reply, running my hand up his leg to grip his hard length through his pants. "If *this* tells me anything, I'm not concerned about you wanting anyone else but me."

Growling low in his throat, he draws my mouth to his once more before pulling me from the booth. Indicating to one of the serving girls to bring our meal to our room, he guides me back to the stairway with a tight grip on my upper arm toward our waiting chambers above.

# CHAPTER 10

L ennox releases his grip when we reach the top of the stairs, pulling me along by the hand as we briskly walk down the hallway to our room. I can't help but smirk at his impatience as we pass customers sneaking from doors and couples entering other rooms along the way, enjoying the exhilarating, sensual energy that pulses through the entire brothel.

Lennox and I stumble through the door to our room, wrestling with our clothing — peeling off piece by piece between kisses, dropping it where it falls, until only my thin cotton shift and his pants remain. My mood grows lighter as I melt against the warm planes of his body, all other distractions dissolving when I'm in his arms.

Trailing hot kisses down my neck, he nips at the tender spot where my shoulder and neck meet, and I can't hold in a breathy gasp at the sensation. His lips curl in a smile at my response and he lifts me easily to carry me to our bed, my legs wrapped around his waist, fingers gripping his shoulders as I nip at his neck. He briefly squeezes my behind before laying me across the bed with a gentleness that belies his need, trailing his tongue down my bared throat.

A light tap at the door draws our attention, followed by a female voice. "Captain, I've brought your meals as requested."

Sighing, Lennox stands while I stifle a giggle as he adjusts himself before answering the door. "How about a hot bath tonight, my pretty priestess?" he asks me before turning the knob.

Despite having a private bathing chamber, we were too exhausted last night to indulge in more than a quick wipe-down before we collapsed in bed. A real bath sounds divine, and I nod quickly in assent. He instructs the young brunette woman to place the tray of food on the table and requests water for our bath before she escapes back into the hallway, keeping her eyes downcast. Shortly after, three servants arrive carrying full buckets of heated water to fill the copper tub in our bathing chamber, then discreetly let themselves back out of the room, noticing the heated gaze passing between Lennox and me.

As the door clicks shut, Lennox slowly pulls my shift over my head, trailing a finger over my bare flesh as he strips it from me, raising goosebumps. I return the gesture and slide his breeches off before pulling him into the adjacent room. Steam fills the small chamber, wafting from the surface of the luxurious copper tub, the large centerpiece serving as proof of Salome's wealth and prosperity. The water is scented with oils and herbs and the comforting scent of lemon balm and lavender surrounds us.

Dipping my fingers into the hot water, I can't help the

groan that escapes my lips at the anticipation. We had no such luxury on the ship, and I'm eager to sink beneath the relaxing warmth. Lennox presses against my back and nuzzles at my nape before I feel his hands in my hair, pulling the pins free that hold my braid in place. He drags his fingers through the loosened strands and trails them along my lower back when he's finished, wrapping his arms around me. I check the temperature of the water again before tentatively dipping my foot in. My skin flushes pink as I step fully into the water, sinking into the soothing liquid and closing my eyes in contentment.

A light splash sounds as Lennox climbs in to join me, and I crack my lids to see him across from me, smiling hungrily at me through the steam. Under the water, our limbs tangle together while he gently strokes his fingers down my calf and foot. His touch makes my belly tighten and my heart flutter. I want nothing more than to curl around him and be lost in his kisses, to banish the swirling thoughts in my mind forever. But before I can act on my wishes, he grabs a bar of soap and forms a lather between his hands, tattooed forearms flexing as the soap adds its pleasant clean scent to the fragranced water we lounge in.

"Come here," he orders with a wicked smile.

My breasts peek above the water, nipples hardening in the cooler air of the room as I crawl toward him. He inhales sharply and sucks his lower lip between his teeth, watching my every movement, but indicates with a twirl of his index finger that I should turn to face away from him. Obediently, I comply, leaning my back against his solid chest. The evidence of his desire presses against my backside, but instead of acting on our shared need, he merely begins to run his soapy hands against my body, bathing me gently and exploring my slick skin. The foam leaves bubbles on top of the water, hiding our forms beneath the surface as he works his calloused hands over my breasts and down my stomach, heat to match the temperature of the water boiling within me. I lean back farther against him, baring my neck as he continues to trace my form, inching slowly to the ache between my thighs. A small groan escapes my lips as he slips one finger into my core and my body arches against him. He caresses the sensitive spot at the apex of my thighs with his thumb and wraps his other arm around my chest, caressing my breasts and pressing me against his heated skin.

"I want to hear you come for me, Nerissa," he whispers into my ear as water splashes from the edge of the tub and onto the tile floors with our movements. I move my hips in rhythm with his hand, and his voice, thick with desire, almost sends me over the edge right then. The feel of his cock, firm at my back, drives me to distraction and I pull away from him, the gentle movement causing him to release me so I can turn to face him. His lust-darkened eyes show confusion for just a moment until I turn fully toward him and take his face in my hands. Leaning in to capture his mouth, I gently brush my lips against his before rising out of the water to straddle him. I suck his lower lip into my mouth, coaxing a breathy moan from him as he grips my hips.

"Together, Billy," I breathe against his neck before sliding myself onto his swollen length. His gasp of pleasure and tightening fingers are a heady reward as I take him fully into me, pausing for a moment to study his face before kissing him deeply once more. Taking it for the invitation it is, he pulls me closer, pressing one hand against my lower back and grasping the back of my neck with his other, our kisses becoming needier as I rock against him. My release coils as we move together, the sound of water splashing around us mixing with our heavy breaths in the steamy room.

"I love you," he murmurs against my chest before taking a rosy nipple into his mouth, sucking and nipping at the pink tip. His words send me over the precipice. I grip the edge of the tub to steady myself as pleasure ripples through my body, and an incoherent whimper leaves my lips. I move my hips faster, riding my release and bringing him to his own climax after. His moan is decadent, and I capture it with my mouth as he wraps his arms around my body. We stay joined for a few moments, breathless in the warm tub, surrounded by the scent of herbs and soap.

"I love you, too," I whisper to him, smiling at the warmth spreading through my chest at the words. Even though we have said the simple phrase to one another many times in the past few weeks, it still catches in my throat, the emotion one I never thought to truly feel.

Our love is the most powerful anchor I have; canceling out the fear that has chased me for the past eight years, even surpassing the wrath I feel toward King Dargan Blackwell all the way across the sea.

Once we have separated, Lennox quickly scrubs himself with the bar of soap he cleansed me with earlier, and we both climb out of the cooling water to wrap in linen towels. My skin is flushed from the heat, and I catch his eyes following me as I dry myself.

"May I help you, Captain?" I give a coy smile, my eyes glittering in the candlelight of our room as I notice his arousal through the thin towel.

"You are the most beautiful creature I've ever seen, Nerissa. If I could stay in bed with you for the rest of our lives, I would die happy."

The guileless expression on his face reminds me of the young man he was in the firelight of the rites all those years ago, even if I was unable to fully see his face beneath the mask he wore then. The memory makes my chest ache for the years we missed out on together, and the life we could have built. I drop the towel, damp linen landing at my feet to soak into the puddles we made with our splashing, and stand bared to him with my long hair in waves over my breasts. My eyes stay locked on his while I back out of the bathing chamber, taking small, languid steps until my knees hit the edge of the plush feather bed.

"Well, I don't want you to die any time soon, but I think I can certainly make you happy." I hold my hand out to him as I perch on the mattress, running my tongue over my lips. "Come here."

His sweet smile, the unguarded one he only shows to me, lights his face as he drops his towel and strides to me, covering my body with his and trailing kisses along my neck as he presses me into the cool linens. I allow myself to return his smile, basking in our happiness before we blow the candle out for the night.

# CHAPTER 11

The early street sounds drift through the closed shutters the next morning, mingling with Lennox's breathing to tease me into consciousness. His warmth at my side is a comfort I've grown accustomed to these past few weeks, and I never wish to go back to a time when I woke alone. A few months ago I would have been terrified at that admission, but now I welcome the vulnerability these feelings create as I slowly dismantle the armor I've built around my heart.

Studying his sleeping form in the dimness of the dawn light I wonder, *do I dare allow myself to think of the future with this man?* I know our feelings are mutual, but I haven't dreamt of what our days ahead might look like, where this will all end. He stirs, and as his green eyes blink open, I bury my thoughts away, masking any worries as he pulls me closer and holds me against him.

"Good morning, my pretty priestess," he greets me, voice raspy with sleep as he kisses me on my sigil.

"Good morning, Captain." My chest warms as I snuggle

against him. Smiling to myself, I aimlessly trace a fingertip over the moon phases and constellations tattooed on his chest.

A light tap at the door pulls us both from our embrace, and Lennox rises from the bed to answer. He grabs one of the discarded towels from our bath and wraps it around his lean hips before opening the door. Delphine walks in, fresh and alert despite the early hour, carrying a tray of coffee, milk, and breakfast dishes. I blink at her in her muted grey dress with her hair carefully coiffed, wondering if I look like a wild creature in comparison, my own hair in disarray from drying in my sleep.

"Good morning," she greets us as she sets the tray on the table, then turns to me. "Salome told me you would begin training with us today. Eat first, and then I'm happy to assist you to dress whenever you're ready. Just ring the bell."

"Thank you. I can manage to dress myself, but I'll be down within the hour, Delphine," I reply, rubbing my eyes with the hope that my confusion at her unpredictable moods is hidden. I'm not sure what Salome has told her about me, or her expectations, but I'm relieved that the young woman seems to have stopped resenting me, if only for now.

She leaves without another word, and I slip from the bed, grabbing the other towel from the night before. Lennox drops into a chair next to the food, and I follow suit as he opens the covered dishes for breakfast. Inside is porridge with cream and brown sugar and a few rashers of bacon for us to share, the savory scent of the meat mixing with the sweet sugar to make my stomach growl as it clenches with hunger. I'm ravenous, even though we ate part of our cold dinner the night before after several hours of other activities, and I have to remind myself to slow down before I embarrass myself. Lennox pours me coffee in the local fashion, with milk, and we eat peacefully as the sun seeps through the shutters and the city fully awakens outside.

"Are you nervous?" Lennox asks between sips of his coffee.

"Should I be?" I glance up at him between bites, skirting the question.

"So that's a *yes*, then," he chuckles. "Salome will teach you everything you need to know. You have nothing to fear."

"What if I can't do it?" I whisper into my cup, breathing in the coffee's comforting aroma.

His cup clinks against the tray as he sets it down, fully focused on me. "You are magnificent, Nerissa. You can do anything. Don't let your mind trick you into failure."

While I hear his words and feel his support, part of me can't help but fear failure while we tread these uncharted waters. There's no way to know whether I'll be able to learn the skills it has taken Salome a lifetime to perfect. Even if I just want to protect myself and those I love, I feel enormous pressure to succeed at these lessons. The thought that I might be able to truly save myself from the horrors I've lived before, to keep those atrocities from happening again to others, is a driving force behind my desire to learn. I can't bear to think about what will happen if it's too late for me to master the task.

"How can you be so certain?"

"I know what I saw my mother do, even though she was

no longer an active priestess. I know you can do the same and more," he answers, then stands and kisses the top of my head before moving to the trunk and pulling out fresh clothing for the day.

He dresses quickly while I finish my breakfast and coffee, then helps me button the back of my simple, dark blue dress. I braid my hair back in its entirety, trying to tidy its wild tangles as much as possible before we descend together to the main salon. Hand in hand, we walk to Salome's office.

In the silent hallway, Lennox presses a kiss against my brow. "I'll be out for part of the day, but should be back when you're done," Lennox whispers as he squeezes my hand one last time. I nod to him as my heart races in my chest, fighting to control my nerves even if my placid expression doesn't show it.

Lennox raps a knock on the door and pushes it open when Salome's voice answers, "Come in!" With a glance up to meet his eyes, I give a tight smile and pass through the open door.

"Good morning, my dear," Salome greets me from behind her desk when I enter the room, the latch clicking closed behind me. An exaggerated slurp alerts me to Delphine's presence as she sits in one of the chairs across from the desk. "Please sit. May I offer you coffee?"

I nod my assent, even though I already had more than enough upstairs and my hands still tremble, although I'm not certain whether it's from the coffee or my nerves. Taking the seat next to Delphine, she pours me a cup and offers milk, adding it when I accept. I momentarily get lost in the swirl of the cream in the dark liquid as I stare into my cup, just as ornate as the other fixtures in Salome's office. Blinking away my nerves, I take a small sip before placing it on the coordinating saucer that rests on Salome's desk.

"Now, where should we start?" Salome muses, picking up her cup. "Delphine, what do you think the most important lesson you've learned is? Perhaps we will begin there."

"Cloaking, Madame. But, that might be more difficult for her than it was for me since I had only just gotten my sigil when I learned." She turns to look me full in the face before continuing, "*Why* is your sigil so dark if you've been away from the temple for so long?"

"Delosia," I answer simply, meeting her questioning gaze. "We held a ceremony there during the full moon with another priestess and Lennox's niece. Mine and Siobhan's sigils darkened when we were wrapped in the *glow*."

"So there is another practicing priestess near?" Salome asks, eyes alight with excitement. "That is heartening news. Why did she not join you on the journey here?"

"She's the apothecary on the island. She seems content in her home there, so there was no reason for her to join us," I explain, smiling at the thought of my gentle, fiery-haired friend. "From my understanding, she hadn't participated in a formal ceremony in quite some time; just marked the phases on her own." My heart warms at the memory of sharing herbal tea with Siobhan and Lyra in the cozy kitchen of the apothecary shop. Siobhan felt like a kindred soul, even though we were only able to spend a short time together. I miss her dearly as I stare into the cup of coffee, wishing it was one of her soothing teas boosting my confidence instead of the bitter liquid.

"I'm pleased to hear she can practice her skills in peace

there, even if she does so quietly." Salome smiles. "So few of us are left. Now, to proceed. I think Delphine is right, we need to teach you to cloak your sigil, if only for convenience. Then, we can move along to more complicated tasks."

She places her empty cup on the tray, and Delphine dutifully removes it to clear the space. For once, Delphine's eyes are soft as she looks at the Madame with reverence in her gaze. I wonder about their relationship, even while I should be focusing on the task at hand.

Salome steps from behind her desk, and her stunning cream and burgundy floral day dress draws my eye, admiring its elegance and expense. Standing in front of the carved edge, Salome creates a triangle between herself and the two of us sitting in the chairs. She holds her hands out to both of us and I rise when Delphine stands.

When our hands meet, creating a united group of three, the familiar heat builds in my chest. As it moves through me, bright white illumination begins in our hands and spreads slowly up our arms. I can't help but hold my breath, watching as both Delphine and Salome are quickly and completely enveloped by the *glow*. Tension I didn't realize I held in my shoulders eases as it spreads to me, wrapping me in a peace that feels long-forgotten.

Salome begins to chant words in the ancient tongue, and a shiver of power tickles my skin as both women reveal silvery-white upturned crescent sigils glowing at their brows to match mine. Even though I knew they were cloaking their sigils, disbelief wars with a burning desire to know how to cloak my own. All of my emotions are soon eclipsed by the joy spreading through me as our power merges to wrap us in a warm embrace. Just like on the beach of Delosia, when Siobhan and I shone for the first time in ages, I'm overwhelmed with emotions. Happiness that I've found new sisters, and that my *glow* has returned, is mixed with sorrow for the friends and time I've lost. Salome finishes the words, the *glow* fades, and their sigils disappear with it. I touch my brow with my fingertips, wondering if it's still marked, breathing rapidly at the feelings I hold close.

"It's still there," Delphine mutters as if I'm a child asking a tedious question. I frown as I cut my eyes to her.

"That was just to test your power, my dear," Salome adds, patting my hand in a reassuring gesture. "Now the real work begins." She smiles, transforming into a gentle teacher instead of the bold brothel owner.

We spend hours locked away in Salome's office as she and Delphine explain different methods to access the Goddess, and how to mask our nature to those around us. By the time we take a break for lunch, my stomach is tight with hunger, and my head aches at the effort put in throughout the morning. Regardless of the exhaustion weighing heavily on me, I'm overjoyed that my sigil is finally cloaked when I walk from the office.

I climb the stairs to my shared room, hoping Lennox is waiting for me there, but find the space empty. Although I'm disappointed that he's not back yet, I'm relieved to find that our laundry has been seen to, my dress and his coat are brushed and hung, while my soiled shift is presumably being laundered. In the bathing chamber, the tub is empty and polished to a high shine, and the bed has been made up with fresh linens. The tidy space offers comfort after the draining morning, and I'm pleased that I don't have to worry about being interrupted while I rest.

After ringing the small bell to call for refreshments, exhaustion pulls at me, and I lay on the bed while I wait for the servant to show. I catch myself touching my brow lightly with my fingertips as if there should be an ache or other indicator that my sigil is missing, but it feels smooth as it should. The motion is one that I barely realize I'm doing, a movement I catch myself making often as though I need my sigil to remind me who and what I am, even though I've been devoted for over a decade. Without it though, I almost feel like more of a stranger to myself than I did working in the House of Starlight.

A soft knock on the door snaps me back to attention, and I quickly rise to answer it, glancing once more in the mirror as I pass to confirm the sigil is hidden.

Standing in the doorway is the same girl who delivered my broth yesterday, her brown hair neatly plaited, wearing a simple dress with a burgundy pinafore. "Hello, Mistress," she greets me with a shy smile as I step from the opening to allow her into the room. Placing the tray of fruit, cheeses, and a half loaf of a crusty baguette alongside a pitcher of water on the low table, she turns to hurry back toward the door.

"Wait a moment." I stop her, pulling a coin from my purse. "Here, this is for you. Thank you."

She hesitates for a moment before accepting the coin, pocketing it in the pinafore. "Thank you, Mistress." She dips her head, averting her eyes as she makes for the door again.

"You don't have to be afraid of me," I say, halting the girl's retreat once again.

"Oh! No, Mistress. I'm not afraid of you," she replies quickly. "It's just I didn't know if Captain Lennox would be back soon. I didn't want to disturb the two of you." Her cheeks pink at the mention as she involuntarily cuts her eyes from me to the bed, and I almost laugh. Instead, I smile and give a small nod of understanding.

"I don't think he will be back soon. What's your name?"

"Constance," she answers, shifting her weight between her feet.

"How long have you worked here, Constance? Are you from New Aphros?" I question, taking a seat on one of the chairs.

"For about six months." She clasps her hands in front of her as she answers, finally looking at me instead of her feet. "I'm from outside the city, I needed work and I was told Madame Salome was one of the nicer ones to work for. She said I'm too young to be one of her girls, but she pays me to work in the kitchen and clean. I send money back home for my mama and baby brother. My papa died, you see."

"Ah," I answer, sorrow for the girl rising in my chest. "And have you found the Madame to be as they said?"

"Oh yes, Mistress. She's so kind to us, but…" Constance trails off, looking at her feet again. "But, I'm afraid of Captain Lennox, Mistress. I've heard he's a brute. Even… even if he is handsome." The blush that faded earlier has returned in earnest now as the girl looks up at me, stumbling over her words.

"I've heard the same thing, Constance. But don't fear, he won't harm you," I reply softly, giving her a wink. "I'm glad to hear Salome is kind to you, thank you for bringing me my meal."

"Of course, do you need anything else?"

"No, you may go." Constance gives a small curtsey, then quietly closes the door behind her, leaving me to my meal and smiling to myself at the reputation Lennox has earned for himself, even frightening the kitchen maids.

I sit curled on the bed with the meal spread before me and sip cool water while I leisurely pop the different foods into my mouth, reflecting on the morning's lesson. I worry over the fact that it took all morning to learn only this one thing. How long will it take before I can wield my power like Salome? What does that power even look like now? Do we have that long? I certainly had no plans to stay in New Aphros for an extended period, nor will I stay here without Lennox at my side if he sets sail.

The thought of Lennox leaving snags in my mind, and my jaw stills mid-chew as the panic I felt when I thought he'd left me behind on Delosia resurfaces. The memory of racing down the street to catch him making my chest tight with dread. While I know we stopped in New Aphros to trade the goods in our holds, I now realize that I was so preoccupied with the novelty of freedom and romance that I foolishly failed to ask how long we would be staying here. New stress over this uncertainty now combines with the tension of my cloaking lesson, drawing a deep sigh from my lips.

Lennox briefly mentioned that storms tend to kick up quickly this time of year when he told me about the time they weathered one on the *Bartered Soul,* but we haven't discussed our plan for the winter storm season. If the goods have already been distributed as he says, I can't imagine we will be here for an extended period. But then, I'm not eager to sail into a storm, especially after seeing him shudder at the memory of the violent squall. Surely we will find safe lodging — either here, somewhere along the coast, or could we possibly return to Delosia so soon? I brighten at the idea of returning to the warm island. If it were up to me we would spend our winter there. I already miss Siobhan and Lyra more than I expected, and the opportunity to pass along what I learn from Salome would be beneficial for Siobhan to know, too.

Questions continue to flood my mind as I pick at the food in front of me, weighing me down along with the hollowness left over from my lesson this morning. But, despite my roving thoughts, I struggle to keep my eyes open. Soon the sounds from the street curl around me, acting as a lullaby from the city to guide me to rest.

# CHAPTER 12
## LENNOX

After leaving Nerissa safely in Salome's office, I head out into the familiar streets of New Aphros. Slipping into the persona that earned me my reputation, I swagger through the streets, flipping a silver coin high into the air and catching it as I walk. Mid-morning, the Entertainment District where the Den is situated is quiet, missing the usual sounds that accompany the raucous lifestyle that draws in so many of my fellow pirates. Cooks and maids bustle through the street running errands for their bosses to prepare for the inevitable late nights, and wagons deliver supplies to several of the brothels and taverns that line the streets.

Even though most of our goods have been distributed to their usual destinations, the finer quality liquors and other luxury items are saved for a specific merchant, whom I intentionally save for myself.

Passing through the warren of streets behind the square, I snag a crusty pastry filled with beef from a vendor's cart without missing a stride, listening as an angry shout follows me down the street.

"*Thief!*" the vendor shouts, and guilt eats at me internally for my actions.

"That's Captain Lennox!" another voice answers in a hushed tone. "Don't you know who he is? One pasty doesn't matter."

At hearing my name, several other pedestrians hop out of my way, and my lips tick up in a smirk. A small boy huddles on the edge of a dirty alleyway, hat in hand as he waits for generosity he won't find. Noticing the way his clothes hang from his thin frame, the hand holding the pasty pauses midway to my mouth. With a quick look around, I duck down, removing my tricorne as I lean in close.

"See that man?" I point back towards the vendor I stole the beef pasty from. The boy glances behind me, then nods, but his eyes remain fixed on the food in my hand. I take a bite, then hold it out to him, his dirty palms closing around it instantly. I also hold out the silver coin in my hand. "Take this coin back to him, and buy another, but do not take the change."

The boy's eyes expand at the promise of not one, but two, pasties and he nods excitedly.

"Good lad," I say as I pat his head, rising back to my feet and donning my hat once more. Before I can even step away, the boy shoves the pasty in his mouth and runs from the alley. I watch momentarily to make sure he returns to the vendor, but duck through the alleyway before he can turn back to where I paused, and step into the high-class portion of the city.

The pristine streets here are filled with a mixture of opulent shops, fine dining restaurants, and palatial residences — a stark contrast to the flashy Entertainment District only a few streets over. The mild weather this morning seems to have drawn out several well-dressed ladies who stroll the streets with their maids, pushing prams holding small children. While some of the bolder servants openly eye me, most of the residents here dart away from my presence. Some may recognize me, but the rest note my heavy black overcoat and the cutlass openly carried at my side as reason enough to steer well clear of me. I tip my hat to a few of them, winking at the ladies to raise a blush, before turning and climbing the steps to the residence I seek.

Despite the early hour, I knock loudly on the plum door, the brass lion head knocker clanging through the quiet street. A well-dressed butler in livery that matches the door promptly answers, his face registering distaste at my presence momentarily before dropping back into the suitably bland expression most servants in this area have mastered.

"Captain Lennox," the man drones, far less hospitable than would be acceptable if I was a resident on these streets.

I *tsk* at him. "Now, Georges, is that any way to welcome a guest? Has old age wiped away all your graciousness?" I needle the grey-haired man, knowing full well he, and his employer, tolerate me for what I can provide, not my company.

"Good morning, Captain. How may I assist you so early in the day?" he asks, still standing in the doorway with a frown.

"Tell Alexandre I'm here to see him." As I step forward,

he moves back with one eye on the cutlass swinging at my hip, and I push past him into the foyer. The entry has a grand chandelier hanging above a carved mahogany table where an exotic vase holds an arrangement of sweet fragranced flowers. Plucking a pink and white lily from the arrangement, I smell it before calling over my shoulder, "I'll be in his office."

I toss the flower on the table and turn down the hall to the right, boots digging into the freshly beaten rugs as I wind through the floral-papered hallway lined with golden oil lamps until I reach the oak door to the merchant's office. Georges' irritation tickles my back, and I smile at his annoyance as I push into Jean Alexandre's private office.

As I wait for the merchant to arrive, I study the familiar room. Alexandre conducts the majority of his business in his storefront in downtown New Aphros, but this isn't the first time we've met in his home office. His love of money drips from the oiled wood beadboard, the crystal decanters lining a shelf, the gold leaf trim on all the furniture. An oil painting of Jean Alexandre and his young wife stares at me from behind his desk as I peruse the books that line one wall. Steps in the hallway draw my attention and I remove my hat, tossing it on the desk. It knocks a quill from its stand, but I leave it, assuming my arrogant air again, making my way to the decanters before the door swings open.

"Lennox." Alexandre greets me from the doorway as I lean against the counter of a hutch to face him, the most expensive bottle of liquor hanging casually from my finger-tips. His eyes narrow as they move from the bottle in my hand to the hat on his desk, to the quill on the floor, but his lips only purse into a thin line.

"The hospitality in your home is grossly lacking today, Jean. First Georges, now you. '*Good morning, Captain! How was your voyage, Captain? Have you brought me more goods to sell to line my pockets and keep my pretty wife amused with me, Captain?*'" I chide and level my gaze at the portly gentleman still standing in the doorway. "Very disappointing." Never breaking eye contact, I reach over to pull one of the crystal glasses from the shelf, filling it halfway before replacing the bottle.

"Apologies, *Captain*. I knew to expect you after I heard of your arrival, just didn't know our meeting would be today. In my home," Alexandre states in his heavily accented voice, a bit more bluntly than most of the other merchants in town, but this is why I like him.

He closes the door behind him, then rounds the desk to sit, eyeing me warily while I continue to browse his office. "How *was* your journey? I heard talk of *two* ships arriving in the bay. I had hoped this meant we have business together once more."

Ignoring his prying question, my fingers pause as I reach his cigar collection. I snap the box open and rein in my urge to smile when he visibly cringes in my peripheral vision. Taking a long sip of my brandy, I run my fingers over the tightly rolled contents, pulling the most expensive one from the case and smelling it. I usually don't smoke them, but I can't resist reminding the man that, without me, he wouldn't have nearly as much to fill his coffers.

"Mmm… this is a fine one, Jean."

"It is, Captain. I received a fresh shipment a month ago

from Captain Trevino. I assume you saw him if you stopped by Delosia on the way here?" Alexandre straightens his brocade waistcoat and smooths a hand over his pomaded, thinning brown hair as he sits in the leather chair.

"If I didn't know better, I would say these were from Halasea. Last I checked, trade with Halasea is illegal here, according to the Merchant Council," I reply, rolling the cigar between my fingers before slipping it into an inside pocket, enjoying the grimace the man fights to hide. "Something about piracy and stolen goods. Can't quite put my finger on the law, but I'm sure you know it."

"Halasea does have the finest tobacco." Alexandre tilts his head to the side, appraising me. "But you are mistaken. Those are from Delosia."

"Ah, yes. My mistake." I draw another sip of brandy, letting the silence linger on as Alexandre shifts his weight in his chair. I circle the room again, running my finger across the wooden shelves full of golden trinkets as I turn my back to the man. "So, old friend. How is business?" I glance over my shoulder, but still don't take the seat across from him; my constant movement keeps him on edge, just as I intend.

Our relationship is built on power plays, but, despite my teasing, it's also vital. *I* know Alexandre has the money to buy the most valuable items I can bring into port, and *he* knows I will offer a fair deal in exchange for news, gossip, and political insights to the city. Even though Salome is well-connected, her information is usually related to the underbelly of the city and the Entertainment District. Alexandre, on the other hand, sits in one of the highest seats of the Merchant Council, the leaders of the free city.

The goods I've brought to him over the years have helped build his empire just as much as his own political shrewdness, making me his most important supplier.

"Business has been steady, Lennox," he replies, his eyes following me as I casually peruse the books on his shelves. "Though shipments have grown scarce. Have you brought me something new?"

"I have some bolts of lace, handwoven like the ladies prefer for their unmentionables on the continent. I thought of your sweet wife immediately when I saw them in the merchant's hold. Particularly a red one. Very bold. Would look delightful on her, or the floor." Alexandre's face reddens as my eyes flick to the painting of his wife. The woman, a girl really, is beautiful and barely in her twenties, while Alexandre is old enough to be her father. "I also have some silks and velvets I thought you might be interested in, bottles of brandy, if you need them, and a few cases of rare spices I set aside for you to inspect first. There also *might* be a spare case of munitions from Selennia, should the market look promising."

Clearing his throat, Alexandre nods, his eyes lingering on me, a glint of avarice hidden in their brown depths. "Very good. But, are you certain the lace is something you should part with? I heard a romantic rumor about you recently."

My heart races in my chest at his words, but I still my expression, only raising a brow as Jean pours himself a glass of brandy. "I'm sure many rumors follow me. What fairytale was spun for you, Jean?"

"Only that you brought a new beauty with you when you arrived, and that you've been seen with her several times now. Can it be that the notorious Captain has finally settled on a lady? And a priestess at that."

I have to fight the urge to snap my head toward the man, instead barking a laugh as I take a sip from my glass.

"Jean, my old friend. Are you starting to believe in romance in your old age, or has your wife been reading to you from some of those scandalous novels that have become popular?" I scoff, but worry rises in the back of my mind. Have Nerissa and I been so obvious with our true affection in public? "She certainly serves as entertainment for me, but we both know I'm only interested in how well she can take my cock."

Alexandre chokes on the sip, glass still raised to his lips, sent into a coughing fit before he settles once more. "Well, if you leave her here when you ship out, and she is what they say — marked by the Goddess — at least tell the poor girl to steer clear of the cathedral. The priests have grown bolder since you and your crew were here last." His tone is sincere but laced with a hint of bitterness, drawing me closer to the desk so that I finally sit in the overstuffed leather chair facing him.

I cross my booted foot across my knee and lean back, casually swirling my brandy, feigning indifference, but the man now has my full attention. "Yes, I noticed that. We had a run-in with them after we arrived. How is it that the Merchant Council hasn't curbed them yet? Men shouting in front of your store can't be good for business."

"Unfortunately, you are correct," he pauses, sipping at his brandy once more. "At least for those who have shops near the square, and even for some places in the Entertainment District. It's causing quite a few ruffled feathers across the city. I'm not sure how much Salome has told you while you've been staying at the Den," he casually mentions, showing he follows me just as closely as I follow him. "But a ship from Selennia landed a while back full of priests. More than we'd ever seen arrive at once before, and far more aggressive than the ones already residing here.

"Caldwell, one of the newer merchants on the council — new money, you know — has bought into this religion. He has some connection to King Dargan and Selennia, and has helped fund the new cathedral, encouraging the priests to come and spread the word." Alexandre scoffs, and I pretend to take another sip, but no more alcohol crosses my lips.

The news of so many new arrivals and support of the King here in New Aphros is information I'd sought but wasn't prepared to hear. My heart sinks at what this will mean for the women in my life, and for the vibrant city that's a regular home for us on our long visits.

Fortunately, Alexandre doesn't seem to pick up on the unease rolling through me as he continues, "Nonsense, all of it. You know as well as I that the only *god* in New Aphros is coin, regardless of whose altar someone prays to. Adding these zealots to the square will only drive away commerce." Surprisingly, Alexandre downs his brandy, loudly clapping the glass on the desktop.

"I see. And how do the other merchants on the council feel about Caldwell's conversion?"

"Most think he is a fool. They're hoping he will end up donating all his wealth to the cause, and then he can be removed as a player from the board. However, I think it might be more serious. Some of the people in the city are listening to the priests' words, and if too many fall under the sway of this new religion, that gives an opening for Blackwell to come calling. I don't want to be ruled by a king across the ocean. I know most here would agree with me, at least those of us with monetary interests in the city."

"I'm sure the owners of the bars and brothels would agree with you, Jean. As do I," I concede. It's no secret that I have animosity toward the ruler of my homeland, but no one knows my true story, only that of a pirate fighting against the rule of any but the sea. Placing the glass of brandy on his desk, I stand and straighten my coat. "Any other news I should know about?"

"I'll let you know if anything else reaches me. How long are you docked?"

"Until after Solstice, at least. I'll send the goods to your shop tomorrow. Is there anything else you're looking for?"

"Not specifically. Between Trevino and di Micios, I have most of my usual goods, but I know I can count on you for the more exotic items to get us through the winter. The lace and fabrics will be welcome in the shops and the brandy is always a good addition. Beatrix will probably want the spices. I'm sure one of my contacts will be very interested in any munitions you have to spare."

"Very well," I snatch my hat from the desktop, but as I turn toward the door, the merchant's voice stops me.

"Lennox?"

Turning to face the older man, still seated at the large desk, I answer, "Yes?"

"Tell Salome to watch out for herself and her girls. I know what happened to some of them a few years back with the priests, and that was just an early wave. These men are different. I don't want harm to come to any business owners. Salome is a good woman and contributes a lot of money to this city. I know she listens to you."

"I'm touched, Jean. Is there something I should know about you and the Madame?" I raise my brows in curiosity, hoping the look masks the concern that builds at his warning.

"We're done here, I think." Jean Alexandre's voice is stern, his face reddening, but I merely chuckle at his reaction.

I smirk, donning my tricorne once more. "Always a pleasure, Jean."

Breezing back down the hallway and past Georges before he can open the front door, I turn the knob and hop down the front steps into the cool air of the street. Turning toward the docks where I'm due to meet with Erik, I look back at Jean Alexandre's house once, hoping the merchant's fears are unfounded, but dread settles in my heart at his concern for Salome and the city itself.

<hr />

MY MEETING WITH ERIK AND THE CREW IS QUICK, AND THE sinking feeling that has followed me since Alexandre's parting words propel me through the busy streets, anxious to return to the Den. Entering the office, I find Salome with her slippers kicked off, resting on the couch with her legs tucked under her skirt, smoking one of her herbal cigarettes and sipping a dram of whiskey. In the warm glow of the oil lamps, surrounded by luxe fabrics, she looks every bit the part of an elegant madame without a care in the world.

"Where's Nerissa?" I ask softly, stepping through the doorway at her gesture and quietly pushing the door shut behind me.

"She retreated to your chambers a few hours ago. If I were to hazard a guess, I'd assume she is sleeping after her lesson this morning," Salome replies, taking a deep drag and letting the sweet smoke wrap around her. "It was trying for her, but she will learn."

"Did things go well? Did Del behave herself?" I ask, taking a seat in one of the armchairs and removing my hat.

Salome purses her lips as she raises her dark brows, pale green eyes twinkling. "Does Del ever truly behave herself?"

I huff a laugh in commiseration because no, Delphine usually does what she wants.

"All in all though, yes. Delphine was on good behavior. It just seems as though Nerissa has some kind of...," the older woman trails off, considering her words while she takes another drag. A cloud of smoke lingers around her as she exhales, then continues, "...block. Like she won't allow a wall to come down, won't allow herself to really *feel*."

"That sounds correct," I admit with a small smile, thinking of Nerissa's regulated emotions bubbling over on our voyage from Selennia to Delosia. How she held back from admitting her feelings until the night she thought I was about to leave. But then, I did the same thing, so I can't condemn her for it. She and I both war internally between the people we really are, and the ones we have to be, but don't most people?

"How were the docks? Is Jackson back in town?" Salome changes the subject, asking about my former captain and ally.

"Missing the old man, Salome?" I tease. Ever since I introduced Captain Jackson and Salome years ago, the two have maintained a casual, yet passionate, affair. Both of them are like family to me, like an aunt and uncle that never wed but can't seem to avoid the pull toward one another. It warms my heart that I was the catalyst for their meeting and that I could contribute to their happiness when they have each pulled me from despair at one time or another.

"Oh, stop that, William," she scolds, laughing at my waggling brows.

"Yes, he's back. He spent a few days on the *Selkie's Tears* when he reached the gulf, but he was at the docks with his men when I met with Erik. I'm sure it won't be long before he comes calling."

"Well, I will welcome him with open arms." She adjusts her full bosom before giving me a look from under her lashes and winking, still as flirtatious as she was years ago. Rolling my eyes, I smile before she asks, "Any news coming through that I should be aware of?"

The smile fades from my lips as I sit forward in my chair, resting my elbows on my knees and twisting the ring on my right index finger. "Jean Alexandre passed on similar information to what you had heard about the influx of priests. He mentioned them disrupting business in the Merchant District and near the square, and made a comment about you and the girls being safe." Frustrated, I run my fingers through my hair. "Surely Blackwell doesn't think his reach from Selennia can encroach on these shores? Not without a fight?" I study Salome as I speak, trying to glean anything from her expression, to see if there is more that she hasn't shared with me.

The coquettish bravado from earlier in the conversation falls from Salome's face at my words as a heavy sigh escapes her, cigarette seemingly forgotten where it dangles from her fingers. "I don't know, William. I would think not, but then, some people are so easily lured by promises of salvation, whether it be spiritual or economic, that they just might believe their ravings in the square." Her brow creases as she stares into the fire blazing in her small fireplace. I follow her gaze, almost expecting a dark cloud of soot to be hovering over the hearth as it does this conversation. Dread wraps around my heart as she says, "I think we need to be prepared for violence, but I'm not sure how likely it will be. I'll see if Delphine can garner any news from Danny and her other contacts and keep you informed."

Stubbing out her cigarette, Salome rises to slide her slippers back on her feet. I take this as my cue to excuse myself, standing and kissing her on the cheek before retreating to my quarters to check on Nerissa.

PUSHING THE DOOR OPEN ON SILENT HINGES, SOME OF MY unease from earlier leaves me at the sight of Nerissa curled on her side in the middle of the plush bed, her dark hair like spilled ink on the pillow. A tray of half-eaten food is pushed toward the edge of the mattress, forgotten in her slumber. I take a moment to admire her features from where I stand in the doorway, savoring the sight of her expression softened in sleep, illuminated by the soft sunlight coming through the open shutters.

With her brow relaxed, the usual furrow is nowhere to be seen, and her full rose-colored lips are parted slightly as if begging to be kissed. My breath catches for a moment at the bare skin where her sigil usually rests. The sigil that's now missing — evidently she *did* master at least one part of her powers today. I don't wish to disturb her if her lesson was as draining as Salome made it seem, so I shut the door as quietly as possible, drape my coat and hat across the vanity stool, then grab a book from the desk and rest in one of the armchairs, propping my boots on the low table.

Still, I can't seem to pry my eyes from her, so different, and yet the same as the girl from so many years ago. Nerissa's beauty struck me the first night I saw her, her black hair shining in the firelight against skin the color of moonlight. The graceful way she danced around the fire captured my attention, and the foolishness of youth told me it was love. But knowing her heart, and seeing her fierceness these past months, has solidified and expanded those feelings to far more than a skin-deep attraction. I thought I knew what love was, but I never imagined the emotions this dark siren could ignite in me, or that she would be an equal match to me in ferocity and desire.

For years, Celeste teased me saying I was a foolish, hopeless romantic. But how could I not be when it seems like Nerissa and I were written in the stars? She is the moon to my tide, always drawing me back to her. What I feel for her now is almost painful, as though she has reached in and grasped my heart in her hands — I'll do anything she asks of me as long as she continues to hold it so.

Silently, I thank the Goddess again for bringing us back together, and for giving us time to rest before whatever comes next. Content, I sit back and open the pages.

About an hour passes before the smallest rustle reaches me from the bed and I feel the tingle of being watched. After a moment, I can't help but tease, "I know you're awake, my pretty priestess. Are you enjoying the view?" A wry smile twitches at my lips, but my eyes never leave the page.

"I don't know what you're speaking of, Captain," Nerissa's throaty whisper responds as she uncurls from her side and stands, drawing my gaze. She walks over to me and casually slides into my lap, upsetting the book still lying open across my legs.

"Now you've made me lose my place," I sigh as the book falls to the floor.

"Mmm," she breathes against my ear, causing my stomach to flutter and my breeches to feel a bit too tight. "Perhaps you will have to punish me for my misdeeds."

"Perhaps I will," I retort, gripping her chin firmly and pulling her mouth to mine. She melts against me, lips parting to allow my tongue to explore. It's an invitation for more, but I pull away and study her face, tapping a finger on her forehead where her sigil has seemingly vanished. I've always associated the mark with her and can't stop myself from gently running my thumb across the skin before pressing my lips to it in reverence. "I see you were successful with Salome and Delphine today, then?"

"Somewhat. But it took all morning and wore me out. Clearly." She sweeps a hand toward the bed as if to explain why she was sleeping in the middle of the afternoon. "I'm not sure how much I can learn before we leave again." She looks crestfallen, almost as if she's ashamed of not achieving more in one day.

I quickly realize yet another of my follies, closing my eyes in frustration at another mistake on my part — she doesn't realize we are here for a much longer duration than we were on the island of Delosia. I've spent so much time these past years keeping secrets and plans close to my chest, that I forget they're safe with her. Even if sharing doesn't come easily to me.

"You'll have time. We won't be leaving until after the Winter Solstice," I reassure her, explaining further at the look of confusion on her face. "The water will be too rough to sail the routes between here and Selennia earlier than that, perhaps for even a month or so after the holiday. I won't risk your safety more than it already is." I gently caress her dark hair and run my fingers along her cheekbone, unable to keep myself from soothing her. At that, she presses her cheek into my palm, bringing her hand up to rest on mine.

"What of your crew? Will they be content with that? Solstice isn't for another…," she pauses, calculating the time in her mind. "…Five weeks? Should we not have stayed on Delosia for Erik to be with Siobhan?"

I'm surprised at her concern for the crew, but it only endears her to me further, that she would be worried about their happiness instead of focusing on her own.

"Don't fret, this isn't solely about you and training. It's more to do with the timing in general. It isn't unusual for us to rest in one place to wait out the winter, and New Aphros is prime for trade to fill the crew's pockets. They have their usual haunts and it's a favorite port, especially for the Winter Solstice celebration. But," I warn, "We may need to be more convincing in public with regard to the nature of our relationship. Somehow word of me possibly *settling down* made it to one of my contacts on the Merchant Council."

"Hmm… are they not convinced that your charms are enough to have me falling on my knees for you, Captain Lennox? I'll have to do a better job at resisting you, I suppose," she teases, grinding against my lap.

I run my thumb across her lower lip, replying, "You on your knees doesn't sound like such a bad idea, my pretty priestess." Before I can finish the stroke, she sucks the digit between her lips and into her hot mouth. A breathy groan escapes me at the sensation and Nerissa leans forward to kiss me, drowning out all other thoughts besides one another.

# CHAPTER 13

After another lesson to practice cloaking my sigil, I master the task. Even with distractions and Delphine prodding me, I can now proudly manage to keep my true nature hidden with minimal concentration. I expect my next lesson to move forward with a focus on elemental gifts, those which some of our teachers in the temples flirted with, but rarely made use of. But when I enter the office Salome has several seemingly ancient books on her desk, transporting me back to my time as an initiate in the temple. The old language springs from their creased spines as I curiously inspect their faded covers and rough edges on my way to the chair next to Delphine.

"Is today a scholarly lesson?" I ask, tilting my head toward the books with a raised brow.

"To a degree. What did Adelaide tell you about the relationship between past queens and high priestesses before you left for the temple?" Salome asks while Delphine pours tea for us.

"Only that they shared a close relationship. I saw her

meet with the High Priestess often when I was older, and with you when I was young, even though I didn't realize who you were at the time. I'm beginning to think she left out some details if these texts are any indication," I reply, bitterness coating my words as I gesture toward the stacks. While I still remember Adelaide fondly, I feel betrayed by the fact she failed to tell me the truth about my heritage before I left for the temple. I always knew I was considered her heir, but so much was lost because of her secrets. So much has changed.

"Did she ever tell you the story of the Goddess and her consort?" Salome asks, sipping her sweetened tea. "Or of the legend of how the queens of Selennia came to be?"

"I know the tale. All children learn that as a bedtime story," I reply, vaguely recalling stories through the years. Those fairytales were pushed to the back of my mind as I began to train as an initiate, learning the ancient language, then turning my attention to herblore and more intimate forms of rites and worship as a novice priestess. Of course, all of my studies came to a crashing halt with the invasion. "What do bedtime stories have to do with my training?"

"If you're to be queen, quite a lot I would think, *Nerissa*," Delphine grumbles with a roll of her eyes.

My gaze snaps to Del's then to Salome. "What have you told her?" I grit through my teeth, reining in my frustration.

"What she needs to know to be the most helpful," Salome replies, relaxing in her chair, unruffled at my irritation. "Delphine is my most trusted confidante; don't worry about her selling your secrets. She probably knows more about the residents of this city than even I do." Salome waves her hand dismissively as if she can wipe the indignant look off my face.

Delphine smirks over her teacup, looking as satisfied as a cat with a bowl of fresh cream. Tension fizzes through my blood, but I swallow back a retort, instead offering, "Fine. I would prefer any other information about my own life to come from me in the future." I turn to Delphine to explain, "And I would prefer you *not* call me Nerissa in public."

Delphine merely gives a little dip of her chin in acknowledgment, then returns to sipping her tea. Exhaling, I push down my annoyance and ask Salome, "What is it I need to know about these legends?"

Salome flips open one of the books and slides it forward. I can't help but lean close to see the writing and accompanying drawings as it rests on the edge of her carved desk. My eyes scan the page, trying to ascertain the meaning of this lesson, but I fail to see the connection. A man and woman stand hand in hand, both crowned, but the woman bears the crescent sigil of a priestess. A snarling wolf with a matching sigil stands at the woman's side as if ready to defend the two from danger. A small huff is all I allow to acknowledge the image.

"Have you seen this before?" Salome asks as she leans back in her chair.

"No. I just think it's an interesting coincidence that wolves keep popping up in my life these past few months. Lennox's flag, my nickname, the new figurehead on the *Vengeance*, now this."

"Nickname?" Delphine questions, her brow furrowing in amusement.

"Um… well, yes." I blush, feeling as if I'm exposing intimate knowledge of my relationship with Lennox by admitting this. But there's no use hiding it now since it seems all our secrets are fair game. "He calls me '*she-wolf*' from time to time."

Salome chuckles, somehow sounding sultry instead of mirthful. "That makes sense considering the story of the Goddess and her consort was one of Anise's favorite legends. I'm sure he grew up hearing some version of it."

"And we all know he's a romantic fool," Delphine adds, rolling her grey eyes as if romance is a shameful thing. I can't judge her too harshly for her reaction — had you asked me my opinion a few months ago, I would have likely had the same response.

Ignoring Delphine's jab, I request, "Remind me of the legend." I hate how ignorant I sound, but I'm humble enough to admit when I don't know something, adding, "I knew there was a tale of the Goddess taking a human lover, but I don't understand the full implication, or what it has to do with the queens of Selennia."

Salome studies my face momentarily before speaking, but what she seeks escapes me. "Legend tells that on the night of a full moon, the Goddess came down from the sky to wander a forest she had admired each night from her home in the sky. While she was there, she met and fell in love with a mortal man who ruled over the beautiful island covered with snowy mountains and lush forests. She decided to stay with him on his island, married him, and became his queen. After their union, the land grew stronger and more fertile, and the people were prosperous and happy from the Goddess' blessing." She pauses, taking another sip of tea as an inexplicable chill washes over me, raising the hairs along the back of my neck.

"But, a rival king couldn't bear to allow the island to thrive above and beyond his own holdings across the sea, especially knowing his enemy had an unearthly beauty at his side. Bitter jealousy drove him to launch an attack to take the island and the Goddess for his own. She fought against the rival army at her husband's side, despite being in the early days of pregnancy with their first child. Wielding what we now think of as the glow, she fought fiercely against the invaders. But her power couldn't hold out forever without rest. As it began to wane, the enemy landed a mortal blow against her husband. The Goddess fell to her knees in grief, unable to bear the idea of returning to a lonely life amongst the stars without her lover at her side. In her agony, she used the remainder of her power to transform into a wolf, one of the animals who worshipped her in the night sky, and ripped the rival king's throat out, saving the island from the usurper."

I hold my breath as Salome recounts the tale; some parts are familiar — that the moon goddess fell in love with a human man — but others are new twists that were omitted from the fairytale I grew up with. How had I never heard of her becoming a queen, or going into battle before now? I catch myself perching on the edge of my chair leaning toward her as she speaks, biting back the questions that ebb and flow in my thoughts.

"After that, the Goddess resumed her human form and stayed to rule over the island herself until her heir came of age. From that time forward, Selennia, the island of mountains and forests that she loved so much, worshipped the Goddess of the moon as their own. The Queen gave birth to a daughter who became the first High Priestess-Queen, as did each first-born daughter of the queens who followed. It's why you bear the name Faelan; it means *wolf* in the ancient tongue."

Salome watches me as I fight to keep my reactions contained, to keep my fingers from tracing over the image of the Goddess and her wolf on the page in front of me. I knew the meaning of my surname in the ancient tongue. I had always thought it was merely a name passed down like any other though, its meaning fading through the generations, and that Lennox's endearment was a coincidence that corresponded with my viciousness on our trip to Delosia.

She continues, her voice distant as if she's been transported back to our homeland as she speaks, the same way her words transport me. "The union of the King and Queen was thought to be what strengthened the island, what granted fertility. It's the basis for the rites and why we welcome the opportunity to embrace our sexuality, and that of the people, in our temples. Our ceremonies were held under full moons in the groves in memory of the Goddess and her love of the forests, even if her power to shift into one of the beasts who roam through the wild spaces has been long forgotten. The Goddess herself guided the first priestesses through their lessons, gifted them the *glow,* and in return, they swore they would support future queens and protect Selennia and its people from that time on."

While questions simmer in my mind, I continue to stare at the open book and the snarling wolf inked there. Words to express my thoughts escape me as I absorb this new version of the fairytale I knew. The parallels between the legend and what has happened with Blackwell in recent history are not lost on me as I take in the full story.

"But, why did the queen and high priestesses split powers?" Delphine asks a question I also ponder, and my eyes drift up to Salome, seeking her answer.

"And why did no one ever tell me that the Goddess was our first queen? Or of this battle?" I add, pointing to the drawing.

Never in my years spent living in the castle had I ever seen any sign of power in Adelaide. She consulted regularly with a high priestess, never mentioning to me that the two most powerful positions in Selennia were once one and the same, or that the queens were supposedly descendants of the Goddess. If, of course, any of it was to be believed as anything other than fantasy.

"No one knows for certain," Salome replies with a deep sigh, pouring more tea into her now empty cup. "But everything I've found shows the division around five generations ago. That's when our power began to weaken and the legends started to die. The queens no longer led as priestesses, and only the priestesses in the temples trained in the use of the *glow*. From then forward, ruling became a partnership between the two roles, with the queens consulting on certain topics with the High Priestess of the Central Temple. I have scoured these texts for years, and those left behind before I came to New Aphros, but I'm still trying to decipher the reason for the split. Although Adelaide agreed to search as well, I never found out if she discovered anything more once I left. It was our researching together early on that caused concern from the other members of her council and the other, older high priestesses."

"So, these are from home?" I ask, delicately tracing a

finger over the edge of the thin and brittle pages, fearing that even the barest touch might damage them.

Salome nods, her eyes following the movement of my hand on the books. "I managed to take some of the oldest texts from the temple when I left. I knew if Blackwell succeeded in his conquest they would be destroyed, so I determined the risk of discovery would be worth it. I was already fleeing without full approval. What was one more rule broken?" She shrugs with a smirk, her tan skin creasing at the corners of her eyes with mischief.

Memories of being dragged through the temple where texts burned in the center of the room flash in my mind at her words. The recollection is so at odds with her smile and sends a ripple of unease over my skin. "I've found draw-ings and texts describing close bonds between ancient queens and priestesses who had unique abilities beyond elemental powers or the *glow* we share, but the queens always had power and high priestess status, too. I've not found what caused the division of power, but I'm still scouring the texts, even if the translations slow me a bit." Salome sips the rest of her tea, pouring a bit of brandy into the empty cup when she's finished.

"May I?" I ask, reaching for the open book.

Salome waves her hand in permission, sitting back once more while I study the words and admire the drawings. The desire to touch the pages became almost overwhelming as she recounted the legend, and I have to restrain myself from snatching the text from her desk. It's heavier than I expect, with thick leather binding still in excellent shape for something so old.

"Did no one tell you these things? Didn't they know

who you were at the Western Temple?" Delphine breaks the silence with her incredulity.

"They knew. Or at least my High Priestess did. The other two initiates training alongside me were near mirrors of me — dark hair, fair skin — decoys in case of danger. I assume the others knew I was someone of import, but we never discussed my relationship to the Queen." My eyes flicker to Salome. "We never delved deep into the ancient legends, focusing more on rituals and ceremonies. The elemental powers were rarely mentioned and, to be honest, I'm not sure which older priestesses still worked with them. I've never seen power or control like you both have," I say sincerely.

"So they were basically training you to be a sweet, obedient princess to follow in the Queen's footsteps with hardly any knowledge of your true power or heritage?" Delphine's words cut deep, rubbing salt into the gaping wound in my heart that I've been struggling to stitch shut. Each new secret, betrayal, or omission that I uncover keeps it from healing. Though I want to snap at her, to defend the priestesses who trained me and the mother I didn't truly know, I bite my tongue so hard I almost draw blood.

"*Delphine*," Salome scolds with a glare. "That's not helpful at the moment. But I won't deny that your observation is somewhat accurate." Del merely shrugs, sipping from her tea. Salome rolls her eyes toward the sky as she shakes her head with a deep sigh. "What stubborn women. They wouldn't have wanted to challenge the current status quo. Why would they want a future queen to know *she* should hold the power they possessed? When I began to delve deeper, to work on expanding and honing the powers we could use, I was consistently advised by the elders to cease my search, even though my position outranked them all. It seems I was right to continue, though."

"What did you mean you left without full approval?" I change the subject, my thoughts still mulling over her earlier words while I try to ignore my frustration with Delphine's pointed observations. My eyes drift over the pages of the tome, hopefully hiding my feelings while catching on a few familiar words here and there.

"Adelaide didn't grant me leave to go. I didn't perform the succession ritual to pass on most of my power to the priestess who followed in my place the way others who left the temples would have."

"I, for one, am glad you didn't," Delphine mutters, watching her mentor. Had Salome followed the rules, it's unlikely Delphine would have survived the pyre years ago.

"What happened to the Goddess when her daughter took over ruling?" I ask, still thinking over all the details Salome's version of the legend held compared to that which I had learned in my youth.

"No one knows. Some versions say she returned to the heavens, others say she gave up her immortality to be with her lover in the Afterlife. I'm not sure anyone will ever know for sure." Salome answers with a small smile. "Now, to get to our lesson," Salome begins, clearing her throat and moving to stand. But, before she can do so, a light tap at the door interrupts, and all three of us spin to face the door.

"You may enter," Salome calls.

Moments later the door opens and the pretty woman with strawberry-blonde hair that greeted us upon our arrival to the Den steps into the room. "Madame, I'm sorry to interrupt. I wouldn't have, but a girl from the Midnight Magnolia is here. She said Lili is in labor and is struggling with the birth. She asked if you might be able to come help?"

The name Lili immediately makes my pulse increase as I remember the young woman with the same name that I helped recover from a miscarriage at the House of Starlight in the weeks before I left on the *Bartered Soul*.

"Ah! Of course, Juliet. It's a bit early, but I knew her time was near. I'll need a moment to pack up a few things and change. Tell the girl she can return to the Magnolia, and that I'll be there soon." Salome stands and immediately pulls a soft-sided bag from behind her desk. Juliet gives a nod and closes the door with a tight smile.

"I'd like to help," I say, standing and smoothing my skirts. It would be a relief for me to assist with something as familiar as a birth, to focus my thoughts and be of service after so many disquieting revelations and the feeling of incompetence. Perhaps I can show my lack of knowledge doesn't extend to healing. Delphine gives me an inquisitive look, as if she's shocked I would offer, but stays quiet as she begins to clean up.

"Of course," Salome replies. "You can gather whatever you need and change clothes. I'll meet you back here in fifteen minutes."

# CHAPTER 14

"It's only a few blocks down from here," Salome advises as we hustle down the cobbled sidewalk of the Entertainment District. While Salome prepared her bag, I rushed to my room to change into a plain dark dress since I'm not sure what stage of birth we might be attending. Most stages are messy, but this should hide any stains that might result. It seems Salome thought the same as she wears a black skirt with a linen blouse tucked in at the waist, sleeves already rolled high to her elbows, topped by a black pinafore.

When I called on some of the women I helped in Artemisia, I would have entered at the rear of the building, but Salome doesn't hide our destination. Instead, she bursts through the black front door of the Midnight Magnolia as though she runs it, immediately taking the stairs to the rooms that wait above. Several women wearing worried expressions stand outside one of the rooms as we sweep through the halls, the guttural sounds of childbirth reaching me through the closed door.

"Oh, thank the Goddess you're here, Madame!" one of the women gasps, reaching out for Salome's arm to lead her to the room.

"It will be all right. You did right calling for me," Salome soothes as she turns the knob to the room. I follow behind, ignoring the curious gazes that sweep over me. A tiny room lies beyond, taken up by a small bed holding a young woman stripped to her bloody shift. Another woman holds her hand and pats her forehead with a damp cloth while whispering soothing words, but when we enter the attendant looks at us with terror in her eyes.

"How are you, Lili?" Salome asks, her calm demeanor never faltering as she stops at the side of the bed.

"I think I'm dying, Madame." Lili's voice trembles as she grits her teeth, her body preparing to bear down again with labor.

"All women think that when they birth babies," I answer, taking the young woman's free hand. "Squeeze my hand through the pain, and don't forget to breathe." Dark brown eyes meet mine as she grunts, and the contraction takes control.

"Unless you wish for Sally to stay, Andromeda and I should be able to care for you, Lili. She's newly arrived from my homeland and is just as skilled as I am," Salome says once Lili has collapsed back against the flattened pillow behind her. With an exhausted nod to her friend, Lili excuses the other woman who flees the room as though death waits in the corner.

"Now," Salome says, patting Lili's other hand. "Let's see where things stand, shall we?" Lili nods again, and Salome expertly lifts the edge of the soiled shift to examine her. Salome's brow furrows as she removes bloody fingers, looking at me from the side of her eye. Next, she palpates Lili's belly, feeling for the baby's body with a grim expression.

"Lili. It seems like the baby isn't turned quite right for birth at the moment."

The younger woman's eyes fly open wide, all exhaustion vanishing with the surge of fear evident in them.

"It will be all right, I just need to adjust some things. I want you to hold Andromeda's hand until I'm done. I know it's very difficult, but please try not to push harder than you have to until I'm finished."

I squeeze Lili's hand in mine, laying my other one over top, hoping the contact will offer comfort. Birth is painful and dangerous enough under the best circumstances without the added fear and pain an extended labor with a baby in the wrong position brings.

"Prepare yourself," Salome says, looking up at me while addressing Lili. She nods her head quickly while I hold her hand and begin to ask questions to distract her from the pain of Salome's fingers pressing against her abdomen as she tries to move the child into the correct position.

"Where are you from, Lili?"

"Not far from here, out in the dark forest," Lili replies, trying to steady her breathing as Salome works, her face screwed into a grimace.

"Do you still have family there?"

"No," she shakes her head, eyes clenched shut. My heart breaks at the sight of her pain, but I continue to let her speak. "I've been on my own since I was fifteen. I started working here two years later and have never made it out."

"Is this your first baby?" I ask, both hoping it isn't, so her labor will hopefully progress quickly after the baby is turned, and that it is, since I didn't see any children hiding in corners or on the stairs we walked up like one often finds in brothels.

"I lost one a year ago. I should have known better this time. Madame Salome gives us the tea we need to prevent them, but I ran out, and Rolfe wouldn't let me go to her to get more in time."

"I see." Fury burns in my chest at this unknown man who should be providing the preventative to the women of the House instead of making them seek it out.

Lili's words die as she grinds her teeth through another contraction. I search Salome's eyes as she works to maneuver the baby, panic beginning to seep into me at the possibility that the baby may not turn, or that it and its mother might not make it.

"Done." Salome finally says after what seems like an eternity while my fingers go numb in Lili's tight grip. "The baby is positioned correctly now, Lili. Time to get to work."

The labor progresses quickly after Salome's adjustments, and Lili gives birth to a healthy, screaming baby boy. I lay him on Lili's bare chest and smile as he begins to root immediately for nourishment.

"That's a good sign," I whisper, wiping her brow with a cool cloth. After Lili passes the afterbirth completely, Salome and I work silently to clean her, making sure her bleeding slows before changing her shift and the sheets on the featherbed, moving her gently from one side to the other to allow her to stay reclined with her child.

"One of us will come to check on you each day of your recovery," Salome recites as she wipes her hands clean while I pour a cup of herbal tea and place it on the side table within reach of the new mother. "I'll make sure someone here knows what to look for in case they need to come get me. Remember," she stops, making sure she has the woman's full attention before continuing, "you need to eat and sleep. And no *work* for at least six weeks or more."

"If Rolfe gives me that long," Lili whispers, more to the babe than to either of us.

"He will," I reply, earning a surprised, but approving, look from Salome at my boldness. My conscience can't allow these injustices to stand if I can do anything about it, even in a strange city. "And I'll be sure that you and the others have the tea you need."

As we leave the room, Salome pulls Sally aside to give her instructions while I stand looking around the brothel. The Midnight Magnolia isn't as luxuriously appointed as the Den; only candles in sconces light the halls here, whereas Salome has installed oil lamps. No additional decor, like framed paintings or vases of flowers, accent any of the spaces, and only closed doors line the hallway. Since I can't see in the other living quarters, I assume the rooms match Lili's, cramped and austere. I paid no attention to the entertaining salon when we entered, if one even exists in the smaller building. Unease claws at me as I wait for Salome to finish her conversation, made worse when a lanky man with a dark expression starts up the stairs. He scowls when he finds me at the top of the landing, looking over my slightly soiled gown and then studying my face.

"You aren't one of mine," the man sneers, pushing past me. "You'd best let yourself out before I put you to work."

I whirl to follow him with my eyes and find him frozen in place when he catches sight of Salome. Her expression is one that could turn a man's bowels to water as she strides toward him.

"Salome, what are you doing here?" he asks, trying to hide the tremble in his tone.

"Taking care of one of your girls, Rolfe," she spits back, disdain written in her every expression. "Since *you're* incapable of doing so. Lili would have died if someone hadn't snuck out to find me."

"Women give birth to babies all the time. It's nothing to get worked up over."

The rage in my chest threatens to overthrow any control I've worked to maintain. I have to concentrate and blink rapidly to quell its burn, hoping my sigil stays hidden. After a deep breath, I calmly reach into my pocket and pull my dagger from its place, silently stepping behind the man as he looms over Salome, standing far closer than necessary for conversation as he challenges her presence in the House.

"It won't be long before you kill one of them," Salome murmurs, the ice in her tone cold enough to extinguish my boiling blood. "And when that happens, I'll be waiting for you."

The man takes a step back from Salome, directly into me where my dagger presses gently against his back.

"As will I," I whisper in his ear as he tries to turn his head to face me.

"Salome, come on now," he sputters, arching his back away from the blade in my hand. "You know I don't mean them any harm. They just have to earn their keep."

"Then allow them the time they need to care for themselves, to purchase what they need to prevent babies since you are too miserly to provide it as a decent establishment owner should. Your behavior is a blight on this district." Disgust drips from Salome's curled lip as she reprimands the man.

At the insult, the man's neck reddens with anger. "Don't act like you're better than me, *witch*. Just because you're in bed with that pirate, you get all the choice whores and goods from him. You're no better than one of these girls working on their back," the man retorts, receiving a deeper poke from my blade.

"You speak of your girls as though they should be ashamed. You're the one who does nothing to earn his coin. Fucking coward," Salome replies calmly, stepping around him and placing her small hand on my arm to pull me away. "One of us will be back to check on her and the others. Don't get any ideas about stopping it from happening. Andromeda," she pats my arm, and the blood pounding in my ears ceases momentarily as I refocus on her, "He's not worth you sullying your blade. Let's go."

***

"WILL SHE BE ALL RIGHT THERE?" I ASK SALOME AS WE TRAVEL back down the road toward the Den. The streets are quiet in the early afternoon, but I know in a few hours they will be bustling with foot traffic and carriages going to the theaters, brothels, and taverns that line the lively Entertainment District. Men and women wave or nod their heads toward Salome as we pass, respectfully acknowledging her and curiously studying me.

"She should be. Rolfe isn't truly evil, he just has no consideration for what his employees put themselves through. I don't think he would intentionally harm one of them, but his ignorance does. He doesn't take proper care of them either, and is too stupid and prideful to ask for help."

"Do you visit them often? The other Houses?" I ask, curious to know how the Houses work together here in the district. Until today, I hadn't seen Salome outside the Den, and find myself eager to better understand her place in the city. "Aren't there physicians and midwives to help?"

"I do. Especially when someone is giving birth or having other health issues. Unfortunately, the physicians don't rush to the aid of this district as quickly as they should; they answer to whoever has the most coin first. Most of the midwives who would normally tend to them have been driven out by the physicians or the priests. So I use my knowledge to help them instead. They know to come to me first, and that there won't be a fee."

"I used to do the same," I reply, remembering visits to neighboring Houses in Artemisia, sneaking through back alleys to deliver babies and help the other women and girls if a customer had been too rough, or they fell ill.

"I assumed as much with how you acted in there. I'm glad your teachers trained you well in that respect, at least." Pride pinks my cheeks at her words as if I'm a child earning praise from a favorite teacher.

We reach the Den and enter through the front door where one of the guards sits with a bored expression.

"Brighten up, Joe." Salome teases, poking him in the shoulder as we pass. "In a few hours, you'll be a busy man. Don't look so put out with a bit of silence."

The guard, Joe, chuckles at the small woman, a smile gracing his face as he shakes his head at her. "As you say, Madame. You're right."

The foyer is dim compared to the afternoon sun, but my eyes adjust easily to the darker space as I follow behind her. "You're done for the day, Andromeda." Salome waves me off, not bothering to glance behind her. "We can continue our discussion another time. Feel free to have a drink with the girls before it gets busy." She flicks her hand towards the bar as she passes, and I notice a dark-haired woman with skin the same bronze as Salome's sitting at the bar enjoying a mug of something that's surely alcoholic. Next to her lounges Juliet — the one who came to retrieve Salome earlier, and who hung over the balcony to greet Lennox when I arrived the first day.

"Juliet, I don't think you've been formally introduced to Andromeda yet. Get her a drink and make her feel at home," Salome says to the strawberry-blonde beauty before disappearing down the hallway toward her office and living quarters.

"Welcome, love!" Juliet greets me with an easy smile, her green eyes sparkling. She steps around the bar, not bothering to ask the bartender for help as he tidies bottles along the back wall, and pours whiskey into a cup for me, sliding it across the polished surface.

"Thank you," I reply with a small smile.

"Of course! This here is Bonnie," she says indicating the other woman she sits with. The brunette gives a small nod in greeting, holding her cup up in welcome.

"Long day? Are Lili and her baby all right?" Juliet asks, returning to her stool between Bonnie and me. Her dress is a flimsy fabric the women wear for their shifts, her full bosom peeking from the sheer material.

"They are. Hopefully, they remain that way."

"Glad to hear it, poor thing." Juliet's eyes flicker down to the gold bracelet that circles my wrist, branded with the name of Lennox's ship and engraved with waves and sea creatures. "So, you and Lennox, hmm?" she asks over the edge of her cup, her eyebrows raised in a conspiratorial gesture. Bonnie giggles into her drink, but doesn't speak.

"Hmm?" I hum as I fiddle with the bracelet. It once marked me as his property and, although it still might make onlookers view me as such, I now wear it willingly.

"I saw you when you arrived with him. We all know you're staying in his chambers, you lucky thing."

Swirling the whiskey in my glass, I pause before answering. "He purchased me for the trip from Selennia. When he left Delosia I accepted his offer to come to New Aphros with him." Not entirely a lie, but not the whole truth either. No matter how much Salome and Delphine know of my story, I feel safe in the confines of the office with them. Outside of those walls, or the privacy of Lennox's and my room though, I'm supposed to keep up the ruse that I'm no one of import to Lennox.

"Mmm hmm... I'm familiar with that trip on his ship," Juliet confides with a sultry smirk, her long hair falling over one eye. I take a long drink, letting the heat of the whiskey distract me from the woman's words and the jealousy I fight to tamp down.

"Only, when he brought *me*, he was saving me from rough handling in the House I was working at in Athene. One of the shittier ones. I offered him *compensation* several times, but the funny thing is, he and his men never did take the bait."

My eyes flicker up, then over her pretty face and lush curves.

"I guess maybe I wasn't his type," she says, returning my inquisitive look. I sip at my whiskey again to give myself somewhere else to look, but she leans into me, her breasts brushing against my arm as she continues, "I have to know — does he fuck as good as I imagine? Good Goddess, the things I'd let him do to me for free." She leans back and fans herself in jest, letting out a cackle of laughter at my blank expression. Bonnie joins in, clinking her glass against Juliet's in agreement.

"He's a fine-looking one, indeed. But that temper of his always makes me keep my distance." Bonnie finally speaks, her voice gentle as she finishes her drink.

"Might make him even better, if you get my meaning," Juliet replies to her friend with a wink, then turns her attention back to me. "So, you won't give me *anything*? Fine," she sighs with an exaggerated huff when I remain silent. "I guess I'll have to get you drunk on something stronger next time and pull it out of you."

I smile over my drink, relief washing over me at the fact she gave up so easily, and at the casual teasing I remember from the women I used to work with. Some of my tension flows out of me, and I find myself relaxing in the women's company.

"But really, he's not as bad as everyone makes him out to be. I'm sure you could've been snatched up by worse if you were still living in Selennia," Juliet remarks, all teasing vanishing from her tone.

"Why did you decide to stay here after he saved you?" I ask, curious about the Den and its inhabitants aside from Salome and Delphine.

"Salome is one of the good ones. She makes sure we are all well cared for and is scrupulous about her patrons. Honestly, she's more like a mother to most of us than a boss. I'm thankful this is where Lennox brought me." She downs the remainder of her cup before holding it out for more, tossing a coin on the bar.

The bartender pushes off of the back bar, scooping up his coin as he refills her drink. His dark eyes are friendly as he tips his head to Juliet. He gives me a small smile as well, his teeth glinting in the light of the oil lamps from under a dark mustache. "It really was good of you to go help Lili today." The change in subject is jarring, but Juliet's expression is sincere.

"Of course. I did the same for the women and girls on the row where I lived back home."

"We had a healer who would come visit where I worked in Athene, but one day she disappeared and never came back," Juliet says, her smile fading with a shudder. "Midnight Magnolia is a rough one. The owner doesn't beat them, but he doesn't take good care of them either. Be careful if you go around there by yourself."

"Especially with these priests running around these

days," Bonnie adds, making a disgusted sound in her throat. "Seems like we can't catch a break." With those words, she stands and downs the rest of her drink as she prepares to start her night. "It's good to know there's someone else who will care for us, though. We need more people who give a shit without expecting anything in return."

I give a small nod in thanks before she leaves, and my gaze follows her as she makes her way back toward the curtained foyer.

"I have to get ready for the night, too, " Juliet says as she stands, gathering her fresh drink and winking at me. "I'll see you around, Andi."

"Nice to meet you," I reply as she follows her friend through the curtain.

I want to get back to my room before patrons fill the space, so I ask the bartender to have the kitchen make a small tray of food for the room.

"Here you go," he says, passing the tray to me over the bar. "I'm Jim, by the way. Since Juliet didn't see fit to introduce me," he jests, smiling broadly. "I'm new here, too."

I haven't eaten since my breakfast and my stomach growls with reproach as the scent of roasted chicken wafts through the air. "It's nice to meet you, Jim. I'm Andromeda. I'm here with—"

"Lennox. Yes, I know," Jim interrupts. "Don't worry, I won't get you into any trouble with the Captain." He winks, giving me another friendly grin. Returning his smile I dip my head to the kind man, balancing the tray of roasted chicken, fruit, brown bread, and a bottle of wine in my hands to head upstairs.

A smile creeps across my face as I reflect on the day. After nearly a week, I almost feel like I've found my footing — proving my worth to Salome at the birth and then being wrapped in the comforting familiarity of the conversation and gentle teasing from Juliet and Bonnie. Even the warmth from Jim was more welcoming than Delphine's biting words have been, and I find myself relaxing as I stroll down the carpeted hallway to my room.

# CHAPTER 15

## LENNOX

"All right, Erik. Everything looks in order, we should be able to start distributing the crew's pay," I advise, handing the ledgers for both the *Bartered Soul* and *Andromeda's Vengeance* to Erik. "Pike!" I call, drawing the older man over to where we stand on the edge of the dock.

"Aye, Captain?" he answers, strolling away from the two women he converses with.

"Make sure you pass along word to the crew staying at your lodging to meet with Erik for their pay." Pike nods his understanding as I inspect the women he left waiting. "Is that Hadley?" I ask loudly, directing my question both to Pike and the sandy-haired woman.

"It is, Captain! Don't you recognize me?" The woman answers with a laugh, approaching us as she pulls her companion behind her.

"I confess, I did not. You're usually in roughspun breeches and a knit cap, sailor," I answer with a smile. Hadley is about the same age as Nerissa and has sailed on the *Bartered Soul* for nearly three years. It's unusual to see her on land, let alone dressed in a floral skirt and cinched bodice like she dons today. "What brings you to the docks on leave? Seeking your coin already?"

"No, I wish it was that simple. Tell him, Caity." Hadley gestures for the woman standing just behind her to step forward to speak. The younger of the two, Caity dips her light brown head, uneasiness radiating from her as she inspects the three of us staring back. "Go on, the Captain won't harm you."

"You see, sir. I work at one of the Houses, The Scarlet Rose, it's just down from Madame Salome's. I do the washing and help in the kitchen and such," Caity's voice trembles slightly as she looks up at me.

Silently I nod my understanding to encourage her to continue.

"Well," she starts, wringing her small hands. "I was returning from my errands yesterday and one of those new priests grabbed me as I turned onto the row. He started shouting at me and demanding I repent from my sins. He frightened me terribly and I don't know what he would have done if Hadley hadn't been waiting for me in front of the Rose."

"The bastard knocked her basket from her hands and was shouting so loudly it's a wonder the entire street didn't turn out," Hadley hisses, wrapping her arm around Caity's delicate shoulders. "He screamed in my face while he was at it, but I told the fucker where he could stick it and he backed down. I just thought you might want to know since you and Salome practically run the row."

Gritting my teeth I look toward Erik and Pike, nostrils flaring with anger at the priest's behavior. "Thank you for finding me, Hadley. I'll keep an eye on the situation, but watch yourselves. These priests seem to be getting braver than expected."

The two women nod their understanding, Hadley replying softly, "Yes, Captain. I thought your lady might wish to know, too," before retreating from the docks and blending back into the crowds milling through the street.

"It is getting worse," Erik murmurs as we stand watching the two women.

"It would seem so," I respond. "I'm going back to the Den unless the two of you need me for anything else?"

Both Pike and Erik shake their heads, all of us becoming quiet as Caity's story sinks in. With a dip of my chin, I turn and stalk back through the square toward Salome's. The shops near the square all have their doors closed, presumably to block out the hammering of the construction at the cathedral site. While I don't run into any of the ranting priests, I do take note that the usual chatter of the public space is muted. People now rush past the central oak with its colorful ribbons, trying to avoid being stopped by any of the black-robed newcomers who reside in the cathedral. Few people stop to make offerings or tie their wishes to the tree's limbs now that the beady eyes of the cathedral watch over the square.

Swallowing down my irritation at these subtle changes that are crushing the soul of the city I have always found joy in, I turn the corner to the row, hopeful that a reunion with Nerissa will calm my agitation. Entering the building, I take the stairs two at a time and stride through the door to our quarters.

"Welcome home, Captain," Nerissa greets me from

where she sits at the low table. Looking up from her spread of refreshments, her broad smile immediately elevates my dismal mood. It's an expression I could only have hoped to receive from her a few months ago.

"Hello, my pretty priestess. How was your day?" I kiss her cheek and return her smile before hanging my coat and hat on the peg by the door. Then, sitting at her side, I pour a glass of wine. In her company, I unclench my jaw and drop my shoulders, the troubles of the town disappearing as I relax in her company. While I wish we were somewhere we could call home, where we could be our true selves all the time, I savor these moments spent together in the confines of our chambers.

"Tiresome and messy. Salome told me a pretty story for our lesson until we were interrupted. Then I helped her deliver a baby down the road."

"Where?" Tearing a piece of bread from the loaf I sit back and cross one booted foot over my knee.

"The Midnight Magnolia. The owner is a delightful man." Nerissa's eyes turn hard at her words, lips thinning into a line of irritation.

"Ah, yes. Rolfe. Not the worst, but certainly not a prize. Did he give you trouble?"

"Nothing Salome and I couldn't handle," she replies with a gleam in her eye. I know that look, and intrigue has me leaning forward in my seat, curious how my she-wolf reacted to Rolfe for her to say such a thing. "I also had chat with Juliet. I hear you are *acquainted*."

My jaw drops open as I fumble for words, but she stops me with an upheld hand and a throaty laugh. "Don't worry, she only asked if you were as good in bed as she imagined.

Apparently, she's still very sad you never let her pay for her passage from Selennia."

With a shake of my head, I laugh, sipping my wine. "She's a feisty one, that's for sure. I hope you let her keep her impression of my talents intact." Reading between the lines, I'm relieved that Nerissa is getting to know some of the other women in the house — Delphine is difficult with even her closest friends, except for Salome, of course, and, I've worried that Nerissa misses Lyra's constant companionship.

Guilt washes over me knowing I'm the reason she parted ways with my niece and the budding friendship she formed with Siobhan, but like a wave cresting on the shore, the feeling doesn't linger long. Nerissa made her own choice. It's why I neither stopped her from staying nor encouraged her to come with me, just to be certain she wouldn't have any regrets.

Plucking a dried fig from the bowl, I toss it into my mouth. "So what story did Salome share this morning?"

"The legend of the Goddess and her consort. Did you know —"

The loud pounding of boots on the stairs echoes through the hallway outside our room, interrupting her speech and drawing our eyes to each other, then the closed door.

The steps continue, getting louder as they approach this side of the Den, and my pulse spikes as I hop to my feet when they stop outside our door. A fist slams against the wood as a deep voice yells, "Captain!"

Nerissa quickly stands, a look of fear briefly flashing in her eyes, but I push her behind me as I draw the blade from my boot, and wrench the door open.

"Tom?" I ask, recognizing one of the crewmen from the *Vengeance*, fist held up ready to pound on the door again. The man's breaths come in heavy pants as a dark flush stains his tan cheeks from his rapid approach. Pulling his knit cap from his head, he twists it in his hands as his dark curls stand on end, damp from either exertion or the humidity in the city, eyes wild with his flight.

"What is it, Tom?" I demand, re-sheathing my blade. In my periphery, Nerissa also hides her dagger away and pulls her boots on, sensing the same urgency as I do.

"Erik sent me to retrieve you, Captain." Tom looks between us, still breathing heavily. "There's word from the rivermen who just landed on the docks that a woman has arrived by ship asking for you. She didn't give a name but said it was urgent. She should be on one of the next boats coming up the river. I have a carriage waiting if you please."

Uneasiness runs through me; who could be looking for me with such urgency? Glancing behind me at Nerissa, I consider whether this is a situation I should heed with haste, or whether I should order the mystery woman to come to me. I don't want to risk guiding an enemy straight to our door, especially if they don't know Nerissa is with me. I clap my hat on my head as we start to leave the room, pulling my coat on as we walk.

"I want you to wait here with Salome," I tell her when she reaches for her own coat.

"What? Why?" she asks, uncertainty clouding her eyes. She draws her brows together in irritation as her fingers tighten in the navy fabric.

"I don't know who's looking for me, or whether they

know about you. I can't risk your safety." Pleading with my eyes, if not my voice, that she will heed me on this, I press a quick kiss to her brow, explaining, "I'll meet this stranger at the docks, in case it's some kind of ploy. Salome can keep you safe and I can take care of myself."

"Fine." She agrees, even though her lips flatten into a line and I can tell that she disagrees with my request. She drops her coat back across one of the chairs and crosses her arms waiting for my next instructions.

Apprehension coats me as we all storm down the stairs. I hate leaving her behind, but I don't want to risk leading her into trouble if I can help it. Pausing at the curtain in the foyer, I brush a kiss against Nerissa's lips before she silently enters the salon, heading toward Salome's office to relay Tom's message, then I follow Tom out into the street. With a last glance behind me, I climb into the waiting carriage while Tom takes a seat with the driver. A moment later, the reins crack and the horses pull us swiftly down the road toward the docks.

I can't relax into the velvet seat as we rattle through the street. My racing thoughts pass through my mind as rapidly as the hooves on the cobblestones, bouncing in my head as often as I do in the confines of the carriage. I have no inkling as to who might seek me out. The only ones who know where we are are those we left behind on Delosia, but surely one of the crewmembers would have identified Siobhan or Lyra, or they would have announced themselves in their message. How has it been less than a full week since our arrival, and we already have urgent mysteries dragging us from one another? I'm used to danger and the unknown, but I would love nothing more than to offer some peace to

Nerissa while we are docked for the season. After the life she's fled, I want to share her burdens and ease her sorrows, to protect her and care for her; not drag her into more trouble.

Life at sea is dangerous, even in the best of times, but after searching for her for so long and then finally having her at my side, I foolishly pushed that reality aside. When she came to the docks on Delosia I knew I couldn't part from her again if she chose to come with me. It would be like cleaving my chest open, even if the smartest choice would have been to sail away and leave her safe with Siobhan and Lyra. Now, seeing the changes in the city and already facing possible danger, I could kick myself for acting like the naive romantic both Celeste and Delphine have always accused me of being.

The carriage makes quick work of the trip, and soon I step into the bustle of the riverfront. People mill through the stacks of barrels and crates. I scan the crowd, studying faces and looking for a sign of the mysterious woman. My eyes snag on Erik where he looms on the docks, easily spotted since he stands at least half a head taller than those around him. The gentle expression on his face as he speaks to the person in front of him has me moving faster; my solemn second usually reserves such expressions for private encounters with friends. Recognition sparks in me as I rush through the crowd, people stumble to escape me as I try to reach the small figure in the dark cloak talking to Erik. Golden hair peeks from the hood that hides her face, and I break into a run. Hearing the protests of those I push through on the dock, the woman turns, lowering her hood in time for me to fold her into my arms.

"Celeste," I breathe her name, barely hiding the tremor of fear lacing through me at seeing my sister here on the docks of New Aphros. The embrace lasts mere moments before she pushes me away gently.

"Billy," she says, her usual soft tone breathless with relief.

I study her face, worry building in my chest as I try to reason through her presence. "What are you doing here?"

"I... I —" She blinks her hazel eyes a few times before they roll back and she swoons, falling against my chest as I hold her up from the wood of the dock underfoot. Panic seizes me, and for a moment I forget all facades I might wear. I tremble, gasping my sister's name as I lift her limp frame and carry her through the crowd.

"Get the fuck out of the way!" I snarl as I retreat to the carriage that still waits. Sailors and pedestrians alike avert their eyes and step quickly out of the way of both me and Erik, who strides behind me. Leaving Tom on the dock to oversee the tasks he was supervising, Erik vaults into the seat next to the driver while I deposit Celeste on one of the soft cushioned benches. With a rough tap on the roof to signal to the driver that we are ready, the horses trot back to Salome's.

By the time we reach the Den of Sinful Delights, Celeste has revived, but her face is wan and I struggle to hide my shock at how weak she seems. The sight of her hair its natural blonde instead of brilliant auburn is unsettling, drawing me back to a darker time in our lives. She's thinner than I remember, her cheeks hollowed, and, in the dark cloak and plain dress she wears, she's a shadow of the bold woman she transformed into years ago.

Sitting quietly, clutching my hand in hers like she used to when we were children, she watches the city pass by until the horses slow and then stop at the rear of the brothel. Each silent moment that ticks by ratchets my nerves until I can barely sit still in the carriage. Erik opens the door and helps Celeste down, then we dart into the Den and shut the back door to block out any curious glances before slipping through the hallway to Salome's office. A too-loud tap on the door is answered almost immediately, the older woman appearing with Delphine at her side. Nerissa pauses near the fireplace as if she's been pacing in my absence.

"Celeste!" Salome gasps as she holds open the office door. "My darling girl." Salome grips Celeste in an embrace, which Celeste returns. They fiercely cling to one another for a moment before Salome guides Celeste to the low settee, sitting close by her side to offer comfort as she asks, "What's happened?"

Tension clouds the space as we all wait for Celeste to gather her bearings and explain her sudden presence. Silently, Delphine presses a glass of brandy into Celeste's hands and steps back into the shadowy corner of the room, dipping her chin in response when I smile at her in thanks.

Leaning against the door frame, I will my body to still, to not let the anxious energy rule me as I watch Celeste take a tentative sip. She hasn't spoken a word since she fainted. I haven't encouraged her to do so, afraid she might swoon again. That same concern seeps through me as I stand with Erik, both of us with arms crossed over our chests. Nerissa steps to my other side and meets my eyes briefly before turning toward her former employer, worry etched on her face as well.

It seems as if the room holds its breath in anticipation of Celeste's explanation. She continues to look at her hands wrapped around the brandy glass, a shade of the older sister I grew up with. Unable to take it anymore, I step forward, sinking to my knees in front of her to place one hand on her knee. Her eyes meet mine, unshed tears lining them as she takes another sip. A heavy sigh passes her lips, and her eyes close, while my pulse thrums with impatience. Just as I'm about to break the silence, Celeste opens her eyes and looks directly over my shoulder at Nerissa.

"They came to Artemisia. For *you*."

# CHAPTER 16

Silence spreads over the room like the mist on the river, and a chill runs down my spine as everyone turns to me after Celeste's pronouncement.

"What do you mean they came for her? Who came?" Lennox asks, but everyone already knows what Celeste means. I swallow my fear before taking the chair next to her as she sets her glass carefully on the side table.

"Blackwell's men. Somehow they heard a former priestess was living in one of the brothels along the western coast. Something about her bewitching men. Why they care after so long, and how they had any idea who she was, I don't know. But they came with priests and soldiers. They turned all the women out for inspection and kept the madames for… questioning," she pauses, clenching her hands tightly and steadying her voice before continuing. "I kept my word, Billy, I never told them. My other girls kept silent, too. But someone… *someone* told them. They burned it down." She raises her eyes to look at her brother, and I am unable to look away from her red-rimmed gaze. "The House of Starlight is gone."

Rage burns in my chest as I clench my jaw, grinding my teeth together until my muscles ache. The women I lived with and healed, some I would have even considered friends if I had allowed myself to have them, are now adrift because of me.

*No.*

Not because of *me* — because of a hateful man who desires power over everything else.

When I look at my companions they all inspect me warily. My anger quickly fades to confusion as Lennox asks for what must be the second time, "Are you all right?"

His mossy eyes raise to my brow as his forehead creases with concern. My fingers follow his eyes, drifting over my sigil.

"Well, all that work on cloaking didn't amount to much," Delphine snidely murmurs from her place in the corner, earning a harsh glance from Lennox.

Even though it doesn't feel any different, my sigil must have returned with the anger that surged through my veins. I brush my fingertips across my brow once again in frustration, then turn to Celeste.

"Hush, Delphine," Salome admonishes, but when I look over, mild disappointment is evident as her eyes flicker over my brow.

"Celeste, I am so sorry. I never wanted anyone to be hurt," I say gently. I'm unsure how to behave toward the quiet woman at my side. She was my employer for so many years. Even if I pressed against her rules and made demands of my own while living in her establishment, in the end, I answered to her whims. But the Celeste at my side seems small and frightened, and my instinct to shield and protect her is screaming at me to do something to soothe the hurt radiating from her.

"It's not your fault, Andromeda. I knew the risk I was taking harboring a former priestess, but I became complacent. After this many years, I thought they would have stopped searching, stopped caring. Enough of them passed through the doors as customers without incident that I no longer worried. I don't understand why anyone would be concerned about you working as a whore in a port," she replies, expressing the same thoughts that run through my mind.

"Are you injured?" I ask quietly, my eyes raking over her frame, still huddled under the cloak.

"No, they didn't hurt me. Not physically, at least. I am *not* well suited to life at sea, though. I haven't felt well for weeks. I was lucky to abscond with a stash of money from the wall of my office before they lit the building on fire, and made for the docks, seeking passage on one of the departing vessels with an open cabin. I wasn't sure if I should go to Marie directly or come here. I didn't think you would linger long on Delosia, so I opted for the five weeks it took to get here, rather than the longer route there, just in case," she says to Lennox. When she turns her focus back to me, she narrows her eyes. "I didn't expect you two to still be together, though. I thought *you* would have stayed with Lyra." Her hazel eyes shift between me and her brother, full of curiosity.

Lennox takes my hand in his, squeezing it tightly while he still kneels on the carpet in front of Celeste. "Where one of us goes, the other will be. I won't be parted from her again."

"Nor will I," I reply, looking into his eyes as my chest tightens with emotion.

"*Finally,*" Celeste exhales, a small smile pulling up the corners of her mouth for the first time since she arrived. "Maybe you will be more amenable now, Andromeda; and he will finally stop being a lovesick fool." Lennox and I both purse our lips at her jest, but the tension in the room lifts, and it feels like a collective breath is drawn.

"Delphine, take Celeste to a clean room on the second floor and help her in any way she needs. Tell one of the servants to bring her water for a bath, and have the kitchen send up food and drink for her," Salome directs the younger woman and gives Celeste a tight hug. "Celeste, my darling, if you need anything please let Delphine know. I assume if you have any belongings they were brought to the dock?"

"Thank you, Salome. I had a small trunk that was deposited on the riverbank. I believe someone with the crew took care of retrieving it," Celeste explains before following Delphine to the door. "Billy, please come see me when you have some time."

Lennox nods in agreement, then the door snicks shut behind the women.

Pushing to his feet, Lennox takes the seat next to me and gestures for Erik to join us in one of the armchairs. Salome sits at her desk and takes a hand-rolled cigarette from a silver box on her desk, inserting it into the silver holder before lighting it.

"Well, it sounds like you retrieved her just in time if they were sniffing about so soon after you left." Salome takes a deep drag and nods toward Erik. "Does your quartermaster know everything?"

"I know enough, Mistress," Eriks states simply, his eyes briefly skirting over me. "I know that this woman is a friend to me and a sister to my love. I know she is fierce, and a brave warrior with the power of the Goddess in her. I know my captain loves her and will protect her with his life. I will do the same."

His words touch me, the honesty ringing true, and my heart lifts to know I have so many on my side. "Thank you, Erik. But there is a bit more to it than that," I start to explain.

"I know who you are. I knew as soon as Marie spoke about the heir at dinner. Your ancestry does not matter to me, you are a good woman," he says in his warm, lilting voice. "Regardless of your status or rank, I will protect you, however I can. Siobhan would be ashamed of me if I needed more reason than that. No soldiers or priests will have you as long as I stand."

"Thank you, Erik," I whisper. Lennox nods to his second in approval, a grim expression on his face.

"Do you think Blackwell's men will follow Celeste across the sea? Do they have communication from the priests at the cathedral?" I ask nervously. Even though I'm tired of running, I can't deny the shiver of fear that ripples over me. I can't be caught unaware by these men again. If I am to face them, I will be prepared this time.

"I don't know," Lennox states. "I would assume they'd be hindered by the storms, but Blackwell doesn't seem to care who he harms. I don't know if the threat of death or damage would stop him from sending a ship so late in the season." The only sign of his agitation is the number of times he's run his hands through his hair; it's a tousled mess and longer strands hang across his forehead.

"I worry for Siobhan and Lyra," I confess, my chest burning with anxiety. If the King sends a ship here, we might be able to stay hidden, but Delosia is a small island, with only one town and a few settlements dotted across it. The town might not be able to save Siobhan, marked as she is. Lyra doesn't bear the sigil, though, and since she's Marie's granddaughter, she might be safe.

"I will go to them." Erik stands abruptly. Although he's stoic as ever, worry creases his brow as he looks at his captain. "It is a risk, but if we end up having to stay there for the season, at least we know the island is safe."

"It actually might be helpful to have the healer here if you can return," Salome says, then turns to me. "Since her power aligned with yours on the island, it's possible she could help you focus," Salome reasons, taking a drag from her cigarette. "We can extend her training as well. It sounds like we might need all the help we can get if Blackwell is indeed looking for you."

"You have my permission to captain the *Vengeance* and return to Delosia, Erik. Take a small crew and move as quickly as you can. I'll send a letter for Marie with you. Set sail at first light," Lennox says, standing and grasping the Northman's forearm, as Erik does the same. Before releasing his captain, Erik claps Lennox on the back once and a look of understanding passes between the men. Recognition of the violence that may await Erik. That may await all of us. Erik bows his head to Salome and me before exiting to arrange his crew. I watch him as he leaves, worry settling deep in my bones.

"I don't understand." I look between my remaining companions. "I'm not a threat — I don't want anyone harmed because of me. Can't we just leave?" I want the King to pay for his crimes against my family and friends, but, more than that, I don't want to be the cause of any more deaths.

"You know if Blackwell thinks there is any truth to the rumors of Adelaide's heir being alive that he won't rest. He cannot risk the people's rebellion. Without fear gripping them and keeping them in line, he is vulnerable. Many still remember our ways and honor the Goddess," Salome states simply, betraying pride for the people she left behind.

Truthfully, I never heeded the whispered rumors, never thought of the fact that my bold presence at the House of Starlight might be a beacon. Not after all these years in hiding. But now, I can't help but realize that I was so preoccupied with my own misery and survival that I grew complacent.

I still can't fathom what has sparked the King's search after so much time has passed. Is his reign really in such jeopardy that he needs to destroy me? But then I think about the nods from the pirates when I stepped onto the *Bartered Soul*, the warning from the elderly shopkeep in the apothecary in Athene, Marie's promise of support from Delosia should I need it, and even the people watching in the square here in New Aphros after I stood up to the mouthy priest. Dread seeps through me at the thought of formally making myself known. But, that bit of fire I've kept burning inside warms my heart — I am not alone any longer.

"I will not risk losing you," Lennox's voice is soft, a promise to me and a threat to anyone who might seek me out.

"We need to train harder, then. I won't have anyone risk their lives for me without being able to help," I reply, meeting Salome's seafoam gaze. Steeling myself for the work ahead, the dangers we may face, and the memories of what I experienced before, I take a steadying breath.

This time I will not be helpless.

# CHAPTER 17

*The city of Artemisia is dirty, the streets smell of fish from the docks and night soil. Everywhere I look, I can't help but notice the filth, so different from Athene's clean streets. Or the crisp air of the mountains and forests surrounding the temple I left. Or the earthy villages I've hidden in these past few years. Even when sleeping in barns or storage sheds, the dirt and manure smelled cleaner than this place. From what I know, Artemisia was once as pristine and respected as Athene. But that was before it was torn and tainted by the patrols in the streets and the fear of impoverished souls hiding here. I wonder if the scent of fear is still ripe on me or if it has been so long that no one will notice anymore. If it's just my smell now.*

*I don't know what day it is. What month. How long it has truly been since I've merely existed instead of lived.*

*The first few weeks were the worst — after I escaped the temple grounds and made it through Athene, I stole clothing from a line that had not yet been burned or destroyed and hid trembling in the remains of a smoldering farm until I heard the King's men file through.*

*On their way to the next victims.*

*With no way to hide the sigil still silvery bright on my brow, I had no idea who would turn me in or kill me outright to protect themselves. As I kept to the outskirts of the villages and the edge of the forest, hunger and exhaustion beat out the fear that ravaged me, forcing me to risk approaching homes that still secretly bore symbols of the Goddess. A few threw caution to the wind and fed me, allowing me to stay for a night or two, but never any longer.*

*Sheer spite propelled me through the mountains, freezing winds tearing at the worn clothing I clutched as I dragged myself through the passes between the territory where Athene was centered, north to Artemisia. At least the cold consumed my thoughts, temporarily relieving me of the constant despair that had taken root in my soul. But, by the time I reached the other side, the sorrow and fear returned, and by then I was so thin and broken that I wasn't sure there was a point in continuing.*

*An elderly woman, only answering to Móraí, found me and healed me, keeping me cloistered in her cozy hut at the base of the mountains. Her white hair shone as bright as the full moon, and I swore she was the Goddess Herself the first time I set eyes on her wrinkled face. When satisfied I was sturdy enough to go on, Móraí released me, giving me a cloak with a hood to help me hide my sigil, thick-soled boots to keep my feet warm, and a bag of dried fruit and meat.*

*Artemisia was never my intended destination. I didn't truly have one. I considered taking passage on a ship, but I had no currency except the small container of gold dust I smuggled out of the temple. No protection except the dagger I kept tight in my grip almost constantly. And when I lurked in the shadows near the docks the fear of the men I saw there was overwhelming. There was no way I could bear any amount of time on a ship with no escape from that terror.*

*I lost count of how many weeks I spent huddled in alleys in this reeking city before I saw the red-haired woman. I had exchanged myself for food and warmth a few times already, choking back my vomit at the touch of a man's hands on me again, an act that was once sacred now sullied. But as I walked aimlessly through the streets near the row of brothels, I saw her.*

*She was a well-dressed beauty, with smooth skin and ample curves, a permanent smirk upon her mouth, and the boldest red hair I had ever seen. I knew she must be one of the women from the Houses. No ordinary female would dare be so showy any longer. So I followed her. Trailed her through the streets for a day, then two, until a week had passed. I saw the House she came from, the respect the other whores showed her on the streets, even that the men exhibited, and I knew she was one of the madames. And somehow, despite the fact that she might turn me in to protect herself from punishment for harboring a priestess, instinct told me that she would protect me.*

———

*Without knowing her name, or what I might look like, I make the decision that tonight is when I will throw myself at her mercy on the doorstep of the House of Starlight. It's early evening, the lantern lights shine bright in the street, and a large, dark-skinned man looms at her side as she returns from her errands in the filthy city. Like a flame in the darkness, her brilliant red hair shines, complimented by the green velvet of her dress. When I see her approaching the House, I dash from the shadow of the alley. I kneel at her feet, pushing the hood of my cloak down to expose my face, even if I'm looking at the ground and only my dirty, matted hair is visible to her. I hope it reveals that I'm not a threat. The large man takes a step forward but is halted by the woman's extended arm.*

*"What do you want, girl?" she asks tartly.*

*"Please." It has been so long since I've truly spoken that my voice is a rasp, all the pride I once possessed crushed under the weight of the past months and years. "Please. Help me."*

*I look up into her eyes, my sapphire ones meeting the warm hazel of her own. This is the moment of truth.*

*At the sight of my brow, she gasps and looks around, shock flickering across her face. Almost instantly, she resumes her haughty demeanor, though. I expect her to rebuff me now that she sees what I am… what I was. But her next words surprise me.*

*"Jacob, help her immediately. Take her to a spare room. I will be there shortly." She crouches in front of me, whispering so low only I can hear. "You are safe here, priestess."*

*Relief washes over me and I sway on my knees. Instead of cowering from the man she called Jacob, I welcome his strength. He lifts me to my feet, then scoops me carefully against his chest to carry me inside.*

---

JOLTING AWAKE, I GASP FOR AIR AS I SIT UP FROM MY PILLOWS. The room is dark and my cheeks and pillow are damp from the tears I've shed in my sleep. As I try to calm my breathing, tremors run through me from the memories that haunted my dream. My nights have been free of nightmares for the past few weeks, lost in Lennox's embrace and distracted by my lessons with Salome. But Celeste's arrival, and the news she brings, causes the past to torment my dreams once more.

"Nerissa? Are you all right?" Lennox's voice is thick with sleep as he rolls toward me, surely feeling the trembling coursing through me.

"I… it was a dream," I whisper. "When I met Celeste, the months before then…," I trail off, unable to articulate the memories, even to Lennox who holds so many of my other secrets.

I've never spoken to anyone about that time, not even Celeste after I first showed up at the House. She never asked me for details or expected answers, just gave me a room and allowed me to nurse my bruised spirit until I was ready to join her other girls. Warm fingers brush my shoulder, but I flinch involuntarily away, memories of harsh hands still fresh in my mind.

The mattress shifts under us as Lennox sits up. "I won't hurt you," he whispers at my back. "I'll never harm you. You're safe."

"I know… I know," I answer, wrapping my arms across my chest to try to settle the residual fear surging through me. "I'm sorry."

"You have nothing to be sorry for." His words are as soft as his hand against my arm, where he presses the barest of touches on my pebbled skin after my earlier recoil. I turn to face him, his eyes gentle as he observes me in the faint light of the slim crescent moon seeping through the shuttered windows.

Lennox's patience never ceases to surprise me. Even though he often reminds me that my choices matter, I still have difficulty believing him. How can someone be so encouraging when I struggle to even reassure myself? We both fight the demons from our past, but together it seems like the battle is not as harrowing as when we struggled alone. Taking a few breaths to remind myself that I'm safe, I sink back into the soft sheets to seek solace in the refuge of his arms.

# CHAPTER 18

By the time the sun crests the horizon the next day, the memories that haunted my dreams seem part of my distant past once more. Dressed warmly, I join Lennox at the dock to see Erik and his crew off. I made sure to send supplies with him from my stock: pre-cut linen for bandages, tonics and tinctures for wounds, and teas for illnesses. Ensuring they have what they need in case of injuries, while still keeping my hopes high that our worries are unfounded. Perhaps Blackwell's men will give up until the winter season has ended, or will avoid Delosia altogether. The men and women of the crew finish loading supplies onto the flat-bottomed boat and stand together, waiting on their captain to join them.

"Be careful, Erik," I say, surprising the large man with a tight hug before I leave him and Lennox to speak. "Tell Siobhan and Lyra that I miss them."

"Of course, Mistress," he smiles back through his dark beard. When he turns to Lennox though, his mouth returns to a serious slash. "Captain, we will return as soon as possible. I will ensure Lyra and Marie's safety before coming back."

"I know you will, my friend. I wish you smooth sailing," Lennox answers. The two men clasp forearms, then embrace quickly, giving rough pats on the back before Erik strides to his waiting crew.

Lennox and I stand close together at the edge of the dock until the riverboat has disappeared toward the salty gulf. The breeze off the river is chilly as the season grows colder and I shudder through my heavy cloak, even though I pull the fox fur-lined hood up to protect me. I don't know if the breeze or my worries are to blame for the movement. Lennox tucks me into his side, kissing me firmly on the top of my head in reassurance before pulling me toward the bustling street to merge with the crowd, the stress of the recent news seeming to distract him from the ruse of our relationship only being for pay.

We pass through the Art District, where colorful paintings and crafts stand on display in all of the small shop windows. The bright storefronts are interspersed with bustling public houses serving warm meals and drinks to break the fasts of merchants and townsfolk alike, and the sight of so many people smiling and chatting lifts my dark mood. Sensing my attention lingering on a cafe with a purple-striped awning and small tables on the sidewalk, Lennox tugs on my hand, pulling me inside.

We hide away in a back alcove to sip coffee and share a late breakfast in the privacy of the shadows, but our view still looks out on the picturesque street. For a moment in time, no one gives us wary glances or scoots away from us as though we are predators roaming the streets. Here, we can have a moment to relax and simply be.

Warmth spreads in my chest with each small touch of Lennox's hand against mine, the feel of our thighs pressed together under the table, the way his eyes flick down to my lips as I lick away the residual powdered sugar from the pastries we share. My heart flutters and my belly tightens watching him, the hard planes and sharp angles of his face softened in the watery morning light. How could I have ever believed that this man was the cruel beast he portrayed? That he *still* portrays to those who don't know him well.

*Will this desire I feel for him ever abate?* I wonder, lost in my daydreams until he catches me staring at him and pulls me tight against him, pressing a kiss to my temple. *I hope it doesn't*, I decide, as I melt into his side while we finish our coffees.

SEVERAL DAYS PASS, ONE BLEEDING INTO THE NEXT AS WE GO through the motions of existence and ignore our worries over Erik and the *Vengeance*. On the third morning after Erik's departure, Lennox returns to our chambers after delivering a breakfast tray to Celeste. I'm finishing my morning routine when he pushes through the door, cinching my hair into a tight chignon at my neck and smoothing the deep green wool of my skirts. The color reminds me of the forests in Selennia and a pang of homesickness aches in my breast as I pick at a bobble on the fabric.

"How is she?" I ask, spotting his glum expression in the mirror.

He's made it a point to stop by Celeste's room at each meal since she arrived, trying to coax her to eat, but, each time, she's only pushed things around her plate. The barely touched trays I've noted outside her door are evidence of the same; she hasn't been eating nearly enough to recover her strength from the rough sea voyage.

"She seems better. At least she remembers Salome from when we were younger, so she has that anchor here. Surprisingly, she and Delphine are getting along thus far. I think Del is close enough in age to Lyra that Celeste feels like she can mother her."

He gives a tight smile, but I can sense the worry radiating off of him, and I can't blame him. Between Celeste's well-being, Erik's departure, and the threat of storms while his crew is at sea, unease sits heavy in my chest as well.

Lennox continues, interrupting my worries. "She's been visiting more with Salome, helping with some of the book-keeping and other administrative tasks for the Den. Things that are familiar to her from running the House of Starlight. She mentioned that she might even start helping more downstairs in the evenings now that she's settled in."

Guilt niggles my mind over Celeste as I watch Lennox in the mirror. Since her arrival, we haven't spoken except for a few passing pleasantries. My shame at being the cause of her having to run from her home runs through my mind each time I see her, but that is no excuse for my self-absorption and failure to comfort her. Even though I'm not certain she will welcome my company, knowing that she protected me for all these years, even after I departed the House with Lennox, makes me willing to try. The least I can do is offer her support now.

"I'm going to go speak with her," I blurt, more to myself than to him, standing from the vanity. "Do you think she'll answer?"

"I have no doubt that she will, my pretty priestess. I think that would be good… for the both of you," Lennox replies with a sideways smile.

I rummage through our trunk before departing, pulling out various herbs to mix a calming tea blend for Celeste before taking my leave; perhaps I can at least offer her something to soothe her nerves, even if she won't speak with me. I mix rosehips, chamomile, lemon balm, and peppermint in a small pouch, a blend I've made many times for myself. As I pour in the last of my peppermint, I glance over the rest of my herbs and make a mental note to find an apothecary soon to replenish them, along with herbs for my personal supply of contraceptive tea.

Stopping to kiss Lennox's cheek on the way to the door, I step out into the hallway, determination winning out over my nerves. Celeste's room is closer to the stairs than our suite, so I pass several closed doors along the way. The Den is larger than the House of Starlight, with rooms both upstairs and down for the girls and guests. I haven't wandered around the living quarters of the lower halls, but upstairs there are fifteen rooms including the one I share with Lennox. A mahogany banister overlooks the grand foyer with its glittering chandelier, while the walls are covered in red damask paper above dark wood wain-scoting.

I count the doors, breathing deeply with each one I pass, trailing my fingers over the banister as I will my emotions to settle. Pausing in front of Celeste's door, I take one more deep breath, knock lightly, and wait, half expecting the summons to be ignored. But soft steps creak on the hard-wood beyond and the door opens a crack as my heart beats rapidly in my chest.

As Celeste pauses in the opening, I drop my eyes in nervousness, instead focusing on her simple grey-blue wool dress and the way her hair hangs loose around her shoul-ders. The natural golden shade is so similar to Lennox's that their kinship is unmistakable to my eyes now. But, more than anything, I notice that she's barefoot even though her dress covers her feet, something I've never seen the woman do before. At the House of Starlight, I was rarely shod and she was always dressed in finery, down to her heeled slippers, so that I always looked into her eyes instead of having to glance down as I do now. The change in her is startling. Even if her hair was still colored the bright titian I am so used to, her entire demeanor is dulled down to her toes.

"Did you come to stare?" Celeste asks, and I finally lift my eyes from her dress to meet her own.

"May I come in?" I ask, a blush rising to my cheeks. Silence lingers as she appraises me, and I fight to not shuffle my weight on my feet. After several moments, she steps aside and allows me to cross the threshold into the small comfortable space, closing the door quietly behind her.

"Billy said he brought you breakfast. Do you need anything else?"

"He did. There's still some tea if you'd like. It came with two cups, but he didn't drink any, not that it would matter if he had, I suppose." She pauses with a small sigh, her soft voice strained and wistful. "It's strange to hear you speak so casually, to see you so vibrant. To hear someone call him Billy again." Celeste's hazel eyes are haunted as they inspect me. This has to be a reflection of more than the rigors of life at sea for the past five weeks. Guilt knots my stomach, even if it may be unwarranted. Were it not for me Celeste would still be the vibrant one with her daughter at her side, comfortably ensconced in the House of Starlight.

"Have I not always spoken to you openly and honestly, even when it got me into trouble?" I ask, studying her face before looking around the room to mask the remorse I struggle with. Her quarters aren't as large as mine and Lennox's and are cast in a more neutral color palette, almost like a boarding suite instead of a luxurious brothel. I can see a private bathing chamber through an open door, but the tub isn't gaudy copper like ours and the space isn't as airy. A two-seat wooden table and a settee at the end of the bed are the only seating aside from the bed itself. There is no vanity, only a mirror mounted to the wall where one can pull a chair from the table to sit and prepare for the day. The entire space, while comfortable, is a far cry from the ornate office Celeste prowled in the House of Starlight, and another twinge of guilt aches in my heart at her dramatic change in station.

Celeste sighs, the sound so plaintive that it draws my attention back to her. She waves her hand toward the small table where a teapot and set of cups wait, indicating I should choose a seat. "You have. Even if I made every effort to hold you at arm's length. You always felt more like a sister than any of the other girls." Her eyes linger on me momentarily before she sits in the chair across from me. "I hated seeing you working in the House of Starlight, especially in the beginning when you were so hollow. I knew your life was so different before and always worried that you wouldn't come back from the entire ordeal. Once you started working you were always so self-contained, so detached from the other girls, even when you were helping them. I wasn't sure you wanted to feel anything again. I'm pleased to see you do now."

I let her words sink in as I pour tea into my cup before speaking, remembering my own darkness once more, how I remained aloof to save myself from the pain of more loss. My voice comes out barely above a whisper as I say, "You did more for me than anyone else did at that time, Celeste." Hating the emotion I betray, I pause, sipping at my tea to regroup. "I knew what I was doing when I came to the Houses on the row. I'm not ashamed of how I survived. You offered me somewhere safe. My only regret is that that safety has been rewarded with a need to flee your home. *Again.*"

Guilt floods me as I recall Lennox explaining how Celeste and young Lyra had to run when Blackwell's men started to comb the country, rooting out followers of the Goddess who refused to convert to the new religion. The House of Starlight had been a safe place for her to keep her anonymity and protect her child. Now, it stands in ruins, and Celeste is once again adrift. This time in a strange place across the ocean without her daughter, all because she shielded me.

"I know. There was no shame in how you lived, how we have all lived. At least in the House, I could protect the girls in some small way. I know Billy wanted to take you sooner; he raged about it when he would visit and see you in the salon. But there were so many complications, and I truly didn't think you would accept his offer if I couldn't send Lyra as a compelling reason," she explains, a guilty smile playing on the edge of her lips. "It was partially my own selfishness. I couldn't bear to be without her any earlier."

Hearing her words, remembering those days in the House, brings about a sadness I don't wish to acknowledge, and I glance out the window in search of a distraction, wishing I could see all the way to the sea instead of only viewing the building across the way. I can only hope that Erik can bring Lyra back with him from Delosia; I, too, miss the young girl who brightened so many of my days on our journey together. Perhaps Lyra's presence will offer Celeste comfort that neither Lennox nor I can.

When I turn back to Celeste, her eyes shimmer with unshed tears, and instinctually, I reach across the table to take one of her hands in mine, squeezing it gently.

"Celeste, we have all been surviving in the best way we know how. You offered me choices and a place to heal. I never shared what I endured for those years before I made it to Artemisia. What I had at the House of Starlight was paradise compared to what happened after the temple fell." I sigh, repressing a shudder as the memories wash over me against my will.

"You treated us all well. You didn't allow the customers

to treat us poorly. You didn't beat me for my sigil, or for sneaking out to help the other women on the row. And, without you, I wouldn't have made it back to Billy, even if I didn't know what we'd have with each other when the initial deal was made." More than anything, I want her to know I harbor no ill feelings toward her. She wasn't my captor; she never forced me to do anything.

"I don't even know your true name, Andromeda. You never told me, and I never asked. I know who you are now, of course, between the way Blackwell's men hunted you, and the way Billy and Salome guard you." Her hazel eyes bore into my own as if she can pull the truth from me without me speaking the words.

My eyes flutter shut briefly as I inhale and release a deep breath before responding. When I open them, I confess, "Billy didn't know it when he was looking for me. He knew me from the rites, but he didn't know who I truly was until Delosia and Marie. Even then I didn't fully understand the truth until Salome told me everything. I'm...," I pause for a moment, then state on an exhale, "My true name is Nerissa Faelan. Queen Adelaide was my mother."

The admission lifts a weight from my chest as soon as the words leave my lips. This is the first time I have spoken the truth to anyone besides Lennox, and the power of the words is stronger than I anticipated. Accepting my identity is frightening, even if I don't wish to claim the throne, and I tremble slightly while Celeste wraps her hand around mine. She squeezes it firmly as I allow a tear to run down my cheek.

"Well, who would have thought my brother would end up with a princess?" she jokes, a warm smile spreading across her face. "But, it doesn't matter to me if you're royalty or a pauper. You protected Lyra. Billy told me you stayed by her side the entire voyage, and that you took care of her like she was your own blood. My brother loves you — that's obvious. No matter how hard you are both trying to hide it, Salome told me you can barely keep your eyes, or hands, off one another." She gives me a smirk, in response to my wide eyes, a hint of her former self finally peeking through. I bite the inside of my cheek in response; this isn't the first time someone has made mention of our feelings toward one another. I fear we are still doing a poor job of pretending for the locals.

"You cared for the girls in the House without hesitation, even the ones who feared you or treated you unfairly. You have proven you're a good person. Now, you are a sister to me, and I thank you for bringing my family back together even if you didn't know you were doing so," Celeste says, her emotions finally escaping for the first time since her arrival as a tear slips down her cheek, followed by many more. When she releases my hands to dab her cheeks, I step around the table and wrap my arms around her soft body, crouching beside the chair. Returning the embrace, Celeste cries into my loose hair until she has no tears left.

"I'm sorry for what happened to the House, for anything they did to you because of me," I whisper to her as she sniffles.

"We all made it out. The other girls divided into other Houses before I left. Mine and the one next door are the only two they fully destroyed. We are all right, you have nothing to be sorry for," she whispers, hugging me tighter again for a mere moment before pushing back to look me in the eyes. "Never apologize for things done by that bastard on the throne again."

Celeste takes a cleansing breath, then refreshes the tea in both of our cups, the scent of bergamot rising on the steam while I rise and move back to my chair, sitting back to enjoy the comforting warmth of the liquid and newfound sisterhood.

# CHAPTER 19

Light flickers around the room, and I marvel as it dances across the ceiling. But it doesn't come from the candles in the sconces or the dying embers in the fire. It comes from me and moves at my bidding. With each passing lesson alongside Salome and Delphine, my *glow* grows stronger, and I continue to be astounded by these women's ability to control the elements around us, in addition to their bright white *glow*.

Each time Salome uses her power to rustle papers on phantom winds, ignite or extinguish the flames in the small fireplace in her office, ripple the wine in a goblet, or make the earth beneath us shudder, I can't help but be in awe.

"All basic tasks," she casually explained one morning to my chagrin. But nothing she has shown me is as impressive as what Lennox described her doing on the riverside, and I yearn to see her do more.

Delphine exhibits similar abilities but she's not quite as powerful as Salome. While her running commentary is sarcastic and cutting, she's surprisingly reserved when it comes to demonstrating her own powers, going through the motions when asked, but not offering anything more. I sense there's something she hides behind her irritable facade, her pretty face so at odds with the everchanging moods beneath. I anticipated her wanting to show off and upstage me whenever she could, but instead, she usually sits back and watches as I work with Salome.

In the years I spent living and studying at the temple, I was taught that the energy of the Goddess unites all things. That we are all one with it, and with the universe. But while there were old tales of priestesses who controlled the elements, it was never explained that this connection could afford us the ability to manipulate the world around us quite like these women do. How the priestesses I trained with and lived alongside hid these abilities, or were ignorant of them altogether, alarms me. How much more do I not know? How naive was I in my youth?

"Oh, look! Your brow is burning again," Delphine mocks in a singsong voice as I unsuccessfully try to light the candle in front of me with my mind. She places a fresh pitcher of water on the table before starting to clear away our tea dishes, and part of me wants to throw the ewer in her face for her jest.

"Del, give it a rest," Salome murmurs from behind her desk. Sighing, she plucks a new rolled herbal cigarette from the silver box she stores them in, placing it in her elegant holder.

"Yes, Del. Give it a rest." I glare at the young woman as I sit back against the cushion of my seat, frustration simmering under my skin. I hate being baited and know I shouldn't respond, but Delphine is a curious frustration to me. I have yet to capture a read on her this afternoon — one moment she's sharp and cruel with words that cut; the next she's coy and soft, offering a drink or stepping close so that our hands graze each other, sending tingles through my skin. It's grating on my already frazzled nerves more than usual.

"Well, you'd think if she was so adamant about being able to help, she'd focus harder," Del pushes, speaking to Salome like I'm not in the room as she rolls her dark grey eyes and purses her lips.

"I'm. *Focused.*" The words slip through my gritted teeth as I glare at the blonde woman.

Exhaustion tickles my senses after the long session, and I am in no mood for more of her ridicule. Anger courses through me, and before I can think about it, I throw all my usual caution and restraint out the window, aiming my fury at Delphine. Every candle in the room ignites, and the fire in the hearth makes a great *whoosh* as the flames leap toward the flue.

Delphine's face drains of all color, and the tray she carries with our dirty dishes clatters to the floor as she vaults away from the fire. As soon as she moves, I realize my mistake and the flames flicker back to normal.

"Delphine!" I cry, rising to my feet. "I'm so sorry, I didn't mean—"

"It's fine. I'm fine." Delphine stands on the opposite side of the room, pressed against the wall in the darkest corner of the office. Her chest rises with shallow, short pants as she stares toward the hearth, delicate hands fisted in her pale blue skirts to hide their trembling. I hadn't considered where exactly my power was aimed, or what elements might get swept up for its usage. I never meant for the flames to react, especially not toward someone who has suffered their burning embrace before.

"It's *not* fine," I say as I approach Delphine, remorse gnawing at me. "I apologize. I should never have allowed my anger to take control of me. I know better."

"I believe that therein lies the rub, my darling," Salome speaks from behind her desk where she quietly observed my outburst. She leans forward to light her cigarette with one of the candles on her desk that I ignited a moment ago, then reclines back into the cushions of the chair. Somehow, she remains as calm as before I almost lit her sarcastic protégé on fire.

"What do you mean?" I ask, pausing my steps to look at the Madame.

"The fact that you control your emotions so thoroughly. That you keep them locked inside, crying to be released. Those emotions have energy. *Use* them," Salome commands, a smile playing on her lips as her green eyes sparkle in the bright candlelight. "Don't let them rule you; otherwise, things like that will happen more frequently. You must step into your power."

"See, I knew being an ass would be helpful in the end," Delphine gloats, but her eyes remain glassy and her words lack any force as she remains in the corner of the room.

I throw my hands in the air, annoyance resurging with my apprehension about what Salome is asking of me. "I think I'm done for the day." I turn my gaze to the woman in the corner. "Delphine, may I speak with you, please?"

Delphine eyes me warily, glancing sideways at Salome

briefly, but nods and follows me toward the exit. "I'll be back to clean up the mess," she says passing Salome.

"No need, Del. I'll take care of it," Salome answers.

"Good evening, Salome," I murmur as we slip through the door. Salome remains like a queen on a throne behind her desk, waving her cigarette in dismissal as the door clicks closed.

Delphine trails behind me as I walk past the bar into the salon. The room is empty, save for Jim and a serving girl who set up for the evening. I drag Delphine into one of the curtained booths and pull the fabric closed around us to offer a hint of privacy before turning my gaze back to her. My anger abates as I spy the way she adjusts her skirts when she sits, knowing what scars hide beneath. "You have to know I didn't mean to do that, Del. I'm sincere in my apology."

"I know," she replies, but keeps her eyes downcast, not meeting my gaze. "I shouldn't have reacted as I did, it was just a surprise. I'm really all right."

"Lennox told me what happened to you. I know you are *not* all right. None of us are. But, despite you being a pain in my ass—" Delphine huffs a laugh, glancing up to meet my eyes momentarily, and I attempt a smile as I continue, "I'd like to consider you a friend, Del. I know you said Salome takes care of you, of the physical pain, but if you ever need to talk, please know you can speak with me."

The silence of the booth surrounds us when she doesn't respond immediately, the only interruption is the clink of glasses from behind the bar and the sound of chair legs hitting the wooden flooring as the serving girl sits them upright for customers.

"Thank you, Andromeda," she says after a while. For once, there is no hint of sarcasm or bravado. "I knew Lennox would tell you how we met. What the priests tried to do to me when I was still just a girl. I don't need to elaborate on what that was like, but it changed me." She looks down at her hands, twisting in the fabric of her skirt.

"I know I can be *difficult*," she continues, glancing my way with a raised brow and a wry smile. "I've always had a sharp tongue and few friends. It took several months before I even let Salome in after she took me in off the streets once I arrived in the city. She's been like a mother to me ever since she healed me after the pyre. I think...," Delphine trails off, glancing around the booth as if she will find the words she seeks nestled in the velvet.

Slowly, I reach my hand out to place it atop hers where it rests curled in her lap, hoping to soothe her frayed nerves as she revisits her past. When my fingers touch her she jerks her head up to meet my stare, then twists her hand so our palms touch, entwining her fingers with mine.

"I think you're very similar to Salome, ready to help others when they need it, even if they push you away," she says to our hands, swallowing thickly. "You're both far better than I am." Her words make my chest ache with the sadness they hold. I sense Delphine covers her emotion with her harsh words just as I push mine down under my mask of indifference.

"That's not true. You don't know me, Delphine. Not really," I reply, the guilt of my past returning. The way I left my sisters behind at our temple when I ran to save myself. The way Celeste was punished because of my presence. The fact that I've killed men, even if they deserved worse deaths than I gave them.

"No. Not really. Not yet," she replies softly, looking up at me through her lashes and brushing her thumb against my wrist gently — once, twice. My stomach flutters at the soft caress, but as quickly as it happened, she pulls her hand away from mine, scooting to the edge of the curtain and away from me. As she opens the curtain, she looks back to say, "You're lucky you found one another."

"What?"

"You and William. And I'm glad to call you friends." With those words as a farewell, she lets the curtain drop behind her and I'm enveloped in the solitude of the booth.

# CHAPTER 20
## LENNOX

My steps are brisk as I walk back to Salome's, hoping to outrun the squall that rumbles in the distance over the gulf. Dark clouds roll and the wind whips my black coat around my legs, promising one of the first rains of the, so far mild, winter storm season. The weather reflects my piss poor mood as my concern for Erik and the crew of the *Vengeance*, Marie, Lyra, and Siobhan on Delosia, and Celeste, hidden away in her room mourning yet another life upended, all vie for my attention. I had hoped that sparring with the crew would quell the constant tension in my muscles, but it hasn't seemed to help. Staring up at the wide red doors of the Den, I roll my shoulders back to try to erase some of the stress before seeing Nerissa.

One of the newer doormen sits inside, safe from the impending storm. "Captain," he greets me with a dip of his chin as I remove my hat and run my fingers through my hair. I return the gesture as I pass, eyes focused on the waiting stairwell beyond the salon.

I plan on finding Nerissa to see if she wants to dine in

our room tonight; we both are in desperate need of a distraction between worrying, her frustration with her powers, and the impending foul weather. At just the thought of her, my mind shifts from food to her body, far more enticing than the cook's fare.

Need fills me as I glance between the salon curtain and the stairwell to our rooms, weighing where I think she's most likely to be. Her lessons in Salome's office have been lengthy lately, leading me to check there first. Deciding that I can always swipe a bottle from the bar if it turns out she's upstairs, I push the soft red curtain from my path and step into the partially empty space.

Most of the evening girls are on display, a rainbow of sheer fabrics floating around them as they absentmindedly sway to the beat of the music the band plays. Fewer customers fill the seats than normal at this hour, the weather will most likely keep all but the most lonely away tonight, so the girls gather together to gossip with one another until they're beckoned to offer company to one of the men. Sipping drinks and smiling, the women's laughter punctuates the air, a sharp contrast to the rumble of thunder creeping closer outside. Juliet, forever a flirt, winks at me when I look over at them, and I return the gesture with a smirk. She tips her chin to the back of the room before turning back to chat with one of the women I don't know.

The men who do sit around the tables are mostly regulars, ones I easily recognize, and they either give nods of respect or avert their eyes entirely when my gaze travels over them. As I step through the curtain completely, letting it fall behind me, I spy Nerissa sitting at the bar, quietly sipping a mug of ale, exactly where Juliet indicated.

My worry deepens to another level at the sight. Things must not have gone well in her lessons today for her to be drinking in the open salon.

Jim, the bartender, catches my eye and murmurs something to her as he wipes the bar top with a linen towel. She turns in her seat, eyes meeting mine across the room as she gives me a tight smile. Turning back to the bartender, she says a few words, then stands and begins to weave through the tables toward me.

Before she reaches me, one of the men sitting at the table nearest the bar takes note of her as she moves. Stout and drunk, he reaches out and pulls Nerissa toward him, almost onto his lap, as if she is some common whore to grope. She jerks her hand away, stumbling back slightly only for the bastard to grab her again, releasing a booming laugh as he pulls her down onto his lap.

"Oh a fighter, this one! One of the boys told me about you arriving, but I didn't believe them when they said such a beauty was here! Salome must be making a fortune off you!" The man's slurring words echo through the salon as the music stops and mugs land loudly on the wooden table tops.

I see red. This asshole is *not* a regular. If he were, he would know that even if Nerissa *was* one of Salome's girls, Salome would never tolerate someone treating them in such a manner.

"Get the fuck off of me," Nerissa snarls, struggling in the tight grip holding her down on his lap.

In any normal circumstance, she would already have her

dagger in hand, but the man's arms pin hers at her sides, preventing her from reaching into the pocket where she keeps it hidden from view. I drop my hat on the planks of the floor as I storm through the tables. Patrons push back from their chairs and move away as I approach, none wishing to impede my steps. Those who have been to Salome's for years know who I am, and have seen how I earned my reputation.

"Let her go." I don't raise my voice; I don't need to in the silence that has fallen on the salon.

"Piss off, I saw this one first," the man mutters, his back to me as he tries to paw at Nerissa, pulling at the neckline of her bodice as she leans farther away. "You can wait til I'm done with her."

"I think you're mistaken. She's mine, asshole."

"I said fuck off. I'm a paying customer, just like you — wait your turn. I'm sure she'll still have some fight in her when I'm done," he laughs, still not looking at me as I stride closer, too preoccupied with holding her against him to notice who speaks to him. In the brief moment it takes me to reach them, she struggles enough to slip a hand free, slapping him hard across the whiskered cheek as the words leave his mouth.

*There's my she-wolf,* I think, pride swelling in my chest even if it pisses me off that she's still in his grasp. But the smack of her palm against his cheek transformed the bastard's expression from that of a drunken fool to one of anger, and the world around us fades as I focus on him.

"This one's already paid for, you sorry fuck. That's the proof on her wrist," my cold voice cuts through the silence. Light from the oil lanterns glints off the gold bracelet wrapped around Nerissa's wrist, almost as if the gleam is trying to warn the man of his error.

It only takes an additional step for me to wrench the smaller man's hand off Nerissa, freeing her from his grasp so she can throw herself back toward the bar. When my grip tightens, the man looks up at me, finally realizing to whom he has been speaking so boldly.

"Oh, shit. Lennox. I... I didn't realize..." The drunk searches for words, holding his hands up as if I ever offer quarter to anyone.

"I don't give a fuck."

Rage floods me as I grasp the back of his head and slam it into the top of the table where he still sits. His companions have retreated, not wanting to risk joining in this confrontation. As blood trickles from a cut over his eye, I wrench his head back and slam it down once, twice, three times, knocking the tankards of beer from the surface to spill on the wooden floor.

His lack of fight pisses me off more than if he would take a swing back at me. The bastard would dare offer me a challenge with my woman trapped against him, but be a fucking coward when it comes down to it? The prick doesn't even try to defend himself.

Pulling him from the chair by the collar of his coat, I throw him to the floor at my feet, where he lands in the puddle of spilled beer. My boot cracks ribs with each kick I land while the man groans, trying to protect himself as he curls into a ball. A voice inside tells me this is enough, my point is made, but the fury in my blood will not allow me to stop. It never does.

Over the past few years, my reputation has made it so

that I'm rarely challenged directly anymore, but anger and frustration have been my constant companions for so long that they sometimes take over. Seeing this man handle Nerissa like she is chattel, nothing more than a pretty plaything for his pleasure has sent me past the point of no return.

Nerissa belongs to *no one* but herself, no matter that she wears my emblem on her golden bangle.

Dropping to my knee, I slam my fist into his face enough times that my knuckles split on his teeth as he tries to speak through the blood leaking from his broken nose and cut brow, finally going limp under the blows.

"Captain Lennox!" Salome's voice slices through the silence, stopping me as I reach for the knife in my boot. Chest heaving, I drag my eyes away from the unconscious, bloody form on the floor to find Salome standing over me. Her hands rest on her full hips as she glares down at me. "If you spill any more blood in this salon tonight, I may be forced to revoke your welcome. I don't care how many beautiful women you have brought me over the years."

Her words are stern; she's serious about kicking me out, but I also know she's maintaining our ruse of madame and procurer, not the familial relationship we have. Sufficiently chastised, I slip the knife back into my boot and sit back on my heels.

"Who brought this man here?" Salome asks, looking around the crowd.

"I... I did, Madame," a dark-haired gentleman steps from the side of the room, looking toward his feet instead of at the diminutive madame.

"Nathaniel, never bring a disrespectful prick to my

establishment again. You are a good customer, but make no mistake, I will happily flay you, and any of your friends, for treating one of my girls improperly," Salome threatens, then looks down with disgust at the man crumpled on the floor. "Get this creature out of here."

The gentleman and two others rush toward their friend, not making eye contact with me as I stand to move out of the way. They grip their wounded companion under the arms and drag his limp body from the salon, blood dripping in places to mark their exit.

"What a fucking mess. Jim, please clean this up," Salome mutters under her breath to the bartender. Turning to me, she shakes her head and grumbles, "Captain, go to your chambers and don't make another appearance tonight. I'm in no mood to deal with *whatever* this is." She gestures toward me with her hand, lips downturned in irritation.

Salome turns toward her office, and Nerissa rushes to my side from where she was watching. She looks me over, studying my face and gently inspecting my hand where my knuckles ooze. The rings I wear on the swelling fingers won't be coming off anytime soon.

"Let's go up, " she whispers, grabbing a bottle of whiskey from Jim before dragging me from the salon. "I'll come back down for food later."

Delphine stands near the curtain to the foyer as we exit with a smug smile on her lips. At some point during the fight, she retrieved my tricorne from where I dropped it and stands with it dangling on one finger while her other hand rests on her hip. Wrapped in sheer grey fabric as if a shadow hugs her curves, she's outfitted to flirt in the salon even if she rarely offers much else to the men there.

"Well, I see why you two are so well suited. Temper, temper," she chaffs, clucking her tongue and earning a reproachful glare from Nerissa. Nerissa snatches the hat from Del's finger and pulls me past, Delphine's chuckle chasing us up the stairs as we climb.

When we reach our room, I shuck my coat and collapse into one of the armchairs. The rush I felt during the fight — if one could call something so one-sided a fight — has almost faded, and, while anger still simmers, I force myself to rein it in. Running my fingers through my hair, I glimpse the gore that coats them, blood from my knuckles and from the asshole's face blending together to make a mess of my white shirt and now my hair.

Disgusted with myself and the mess, I call out, "Nerissa, could you —" But, she's already returning from the bathing chamber with a cloth and water to clean my wounds.

"I am fairly certain that any idea of us just being a pirate and his prize has now been dashed," she remarks, stepping close to me.

With a sigh, I hang my head. "I'm sorry."

"Sorry for what?" she asks, kneeling in front of me, taking my damaged hand, and sponging away the blood. It's sore, and will likely hurt something fierce in the morning, but I've endured much worse. She looks up through her dark lashes, making my cock twitch at memories of her like this in much more pleasurable instances over the past months.

"For him thinking he could touch you. For that spectacle. It's one thing for you to see me lose my temper like that in a battle, but I just couldn't control it," I try to explain, looking toward the ceiling as she wraps a linen strip around my stinging knuckles, mistaking her silence for fear.

"I liked it."

Her throaty words make me snap my eyes to hers where she still kneels between my knees. But instead of timidity or fear, her gaze is bold. Desirous. My belly clenches and my breeches strain against my arousal as she smiles up at me. She flicks her tongue out to wet her lips, drawing my eyes down to them, then farther down as she rises on her knees, running her palms up my thighs and leaning forward.

"Oh, did you?" I ask, my voice raspy with need as she presses her breasts against my legs.

"I did. Would you like to see how much?" she replies, running a finger between my waistband and stomach over the fabric of my shirt.

A shaky exhale passes my lips as she pulls my shirt from my pants, pushing it upwards to reveal the planes of my stomach. I take her motion as an invitation, so I lean forward and reach behind me to grab the collar, pulling the shirt from my body and tossing it to the floor. She pushes me back against the chair, dragging her nails across the muscles of my abdomen before trailing kisses along the skin above my waistband, teasing me until I can barely think straight. As she starts to unbutton my pants, she continues to torment me, licking and sucking along my stomach until she pulls my cock free. I groan as she takes me in her hand, running it up and down my length, all the while teasing me with kisses.

When she runs her tongue up the bottom of my shaft, I tilt my head back. My breaths come more quickly as she flicks her tongue over the tip, then slides her hot mouth around me. She slides me deep into her throat, following her motions with her hand as she sucks me in and out of her lips. I run my fingers in her hair, tangling my bandaged knuckles in the dark strands as I cradle the back of her head, letting her choose the tempo for now. A low moan deep in her throat is almost my undoing as I watch her rose-colored lips wrapped around me. She increases her speed, gripping my hip with one hand while the other still works my cock.

"*Nerissa,*" I gasp, my voice ragged. I'm not sure if I can hold back much longer, but she pushes her hand against my abdomen, glancing up to meet my eyes and holding me in place as she continues. Another little moan from her is all it takes for me to come undone, gripping her hair as my hips jerk with my release. She hums in satisfaction, sliding me in and out of her mouth while she swallows, making sure I'm finished before giving me a salacious grin as she sits on her knees in front of me.

"All better, Captain?" she teases, starting to rise to her feet, but I quickly snag her wrist in my uninjured palm, pulling her toward me and onto my lap.

"Uh-uh, my pretty priestess. I'm not done with you," I whisper against the shell of her ear, running my palm over her breast and down her stomach as I press my lips against the column of her throat. Goosebumps rise on her skin as she shivers and sighs under my touch, and I grin with plea-sure as I take her mouth with mine.

# CHAPTER 21

Dawn greets me the next morning with rumbling thunder and skies as dark as the emotions that fueled both my lesson and Lennox's outburst in the salon yesterday. Laying next to him, I listen to the patter of rain as the thunderstorm rolls in from the riverfront, brooding over my continued struggles to master control over my *glow* and elemental powers, as well as Delphine's taunts about Lennox's and my well-matched tempers.

A bright streak of lightning sears the skies outside our shutters, illuminating the slats, followed by a booming clap of thunder that jolts Lennox from his dreams. Restless energy has radiated off him in the days since Erik set sail, emotions simmering under his skin even if he strives to project a cool exterior. He's spent his days checking in with the crew and training with them, returning to the Den with scrapes and bruises from sparring, both with fists and blades, that I tend with salves and caresses at the end of the day. When he isn't at the docks, he keeps Celeste company while I'm secluded behind Salome's door. It's really no surprise that he reacted the way he did last night after nearly a week of bottling up his worries.

"Good morning," I mumble as he sits upright, glancing around the dim room, the coverlet pooling around his bare waist. "The storm finally reached the shore."

"Apparently. Has it been raining long?" he asks, reclining against the pillows. I watch as he flexes his fingers, working to test how sore they are from the fight last night.

I shake my head. "The rain just started. But the thunder has been going on for a while now."

"Are you all right? Did you not sleep well because of it?" He studies my face, stroking his thumb across my cheek, probably noting dark circles that I can only assume have taken up residence due to my lack of rest. I'm convinced he can sleep through anything at this point since he rarely seems troubled when he closes his eyes at my side. "Or is something else bothering you?"

"I didn't sleep well, but not just because of the storm." Exhaling a frustrated sigh, I finally explain what happened with my flaring temper and the fire in Salome's office. "Delphine keeps pushing me, keeps making snide remarks about me not trying. But I *am* trying, Billy. I don't understand why I can't master things more easily, or why I let her words get to me. I finally lashed out yesterday and nearly set the damn building on fire, including poor Delphine."

Between enjoying one another's bodies, eating a quiet dinner, and falling asleep from pure exhaustion, I avoided the subject easily last night. But each clap of the unrelenting thunder seemed to urge me to wallow in my thoughts instead of sleeping through the night.

"I don't know if I would say *'poor Delphine'*," he replies with a tight smile. "If she's been needling you, she had to know she would get a rise from you sooner or later. I doubt she realized how much anger you have buried, though. Is *that* why you were drinking in the salon last night?"

I glance sideways at him, both hating and loving that he knows me so well. "Yes. After I spoke with her privately to apologize, I stayed in the salon. Juliet kept me company for a bit before customers started filling in but then left to talk with the other girls. I can't figure out why it's so difficult for me to get a grasp on this power. Even if I missed out on lessons in the temple, surely this is something I should be able to master?"

"I don't know, Nerissa. But I do know that Delphine is exceedingly talented at pissing people off. Perhaps you need to work with Salome alone." He chuckles, then kisses my forehead and retreats to the bathing chamber. "She may just be distracting you too much for you to get the basics?" His voice drifts from the small room to where I still snuggle into the warm sheets and downy comforter.

"Perhaps you're right," I admit, eventually emerging from my cozy nest.

Sitting on the edge of the bed, I stretch, then stand and open the shutters to peek at the storm outside our window. Plants along the street are being blown about as the strong winds and heavy rains pummel them. The edges of the cobbled streets run like small creeks. The sidewalks are empty, and most of the adjacent buildings are shuttered against the torrent. As I gaze out the window, Lennox approaches from behind me, wrapping his inked arms around my waist and pulling me against his warm chest.

Relaxing against him, I smile and lean my head to the side so he can kiss down the column of my throat.

"Remember," he murmurs between kisses. "Don't let your mind stand in the way of your power. You can do anything, my she-wolf." My eyes flutter to match my heart at his confidence in my skills, even if I doubt them heavily at this point. I turn to face him, pressing my mouth against his as I determine to seek out Salome today for a private lesson.

---

"COME IN!" SALOME'S SULTRY VOICE SOUNDS THROUGH THE carved wood of her office door. I push the door open and peek inside, finding her reclining on the plush sofa, her dainty-heeled slippers kicked off, and a glass of brandy in her hand. Several books are spread around her, some litter the small table in front of her, others are open on the floor, and one lays in her silk-covered lap.

"Am I interrupting?" I ask, my eyes flitting over the tomes as I shut the door behind me.

"No, no. Of course not, just refreshing my memory on a few things." Salome slips a scrap of paper in between the pages of the book in her lap and tucks it between the cushion and the arm of the sofa. She gestures to one of the armchairs at her side, and I sit as requested. "What can I help you with, Nerissa darling?"

"Well..." I don't know why I'm nervous to ask her for additional help, whether it's shame at having lost control yesterday or my embarrassment at my recent struggles, but I exhale deeply and continue, "I was wondering if you might be able to help me with my lessons. Alone? Lennox seems to think Delphine might be a bit too good at goading me, and perhaps it would help me to work only with you for a few tries?"

"He always was a clever boy, so much like his mother," she replies with a wistful sigh, absentmindedly running a hand over her dark hair as if to tidy any loose strands that may have escaped from her chignon. "And he may be right. Delphine can be a bit too enthusiastic with her barbs, but I'm not sure she is entirely to blame for your lack of focus. I do think the two of us working together, alone, might be a good thing, though." Another clap of thunder punctuates her statement, rattling the crystal chandelier and sconces on the walls. I start at the sound, unused to the violence of the storms here, so different from the ones in Selennia.

"It's all right, Nerissa. The storm will pass soon. Let me call for tea and we can get started." Salome stands and pads out of the room, still barefooted, leaving me clutching my skirt as another rumble of thunder echoes through the Den.

After nibbling a few biscuits and drinking more than a few cups of tea to fortify my nerves, I begin my private lesson.

"You mean to tell me that they ceased *all* instruction when Blackwell began his assault?" Salome stood dumbfounded when I explained that our high priestess had stopped training on everything except healing and herblore once Blackwell's first fleet from the continent hit the shores.

"She thought it prudent we focused on skills that would benefit the refugees who sought our help. Beyond the ceremonies and rites, I never learned more than those healing skills, a few languages, and the study of the sacred texts," I explain, hanging my head as if it's my fault my instructor failed me. "We ran out of time."

"Fools!" she exclaims, shaking her head in exasperation. "They should have immediately begun to teach... Nevermind." She takes a breath, then more calmly orders, "The past is in the past. Show me your cloaking again. Then the elemental phases." She slips behind her desk to perch in her chair to observe.

I inhale deeply, closing my eyes and concentrating on the warmth that begins in my hands and spreads to my chest along with the silver *glow*. Salome murmurs a small sound of encouragement, so I move on to the elemental control portion — earth, air, fire, and water.

Earth is the most difficult to access within a cobbled and bricked city, so Salome keeps small potted plants around the room for us to use. Approaching a lovely vining ivy, I place my hand on its pot, willing my energy into the soil it lives in. Working with plants always brings Siobhan and her peaceful garden in Delosia to the forefront of my mind. I can almost smell the sweet flowers she grows and hear her joyful laugh. The pot shudders under my touch as I keep my eyes shut tight, before a cool, gentle caress presses against the back of my hand. Opening my eyes, I'm pleased to find the vine has lengthened, wrapping part of itself delicately around my wrist as if in introduction. Seeing the small progress brings a smile to my lips, and Salome returns it with a nod and a matching expression.

"Good job, Nerissa. Excellent focus this time. But as we have discussed, earth is one of the easier elements. Let's move along to water."

My jaw tightens slightly in response, knowing she is

right. The energy needed to manipulate and strengthen the earth is significant, but not nearly as much as the amount needed when working with water.

Approaching the pitcher of water Salome brought in for this purpose, I go through the same steps as with earth, placing my hand on the pitcher instead of the flower pot. As I concentrate, the pitcher quivers, and the sound of water sloshing begins to crowd my ears, drowning out any ambient noises from the girls lounging in the salon down the hallway. I continue to concentrate, thinking of the soothing waves as we sailed across the sea, the crystal waters off the coast of Delosia, the lap of the water on the hull as I laid in Lennox's arms on the *Vengeance* while we drifted into the gulf.

"Open your eyes, child," Salome whispers.

When I comply, I stifle a gasp. Water from the pitcher undulates in front of me, creating its own small ocean above its former prison. This is more control than I have shown for water since we began our training, and I fear that if I lose concentration, I'll soak the rugs and furniture. As I begin to doubt myself, the waves cease, and the water wobbles in the air.

"Put it back. Will it back before you lose it," Salome instructs calmly.

Anxiety prickles along my skin and sweat begins to seep under my arms as I try to concentrate, barely getting the droplets back into the pitcher.

"What happened, Nerissa? What caused you to lose concentration?"

"I... I don't know," I lie. My panic over the failure distracted me, but I can't bear to admit it.

"Hmmmph," Salome snorts. "Air, next."

My fingers drift to my brow for a moment, tracing where my sigil rests with a slight tremble. When I glance at Salome she gives a small incline of her chin to tell me I'm at least still cloaking the sigil, even as I struggle to maintain my other control.

"Remember what I told you yesterday, Nerissa. Use your emotions. Channel them, don't fight with them." Salome nods her encouragement as I drop my hand. I cut my eyes to her, but don't respond, determined to control both my emotions and my power.

Once again I close my eyes, willing the warmth of the *glow* to surround me. As I begin to channel my energy into the air around the office, my hair whips around me, tickling my cheeks. The breeze cools my warm skin and dries the nervous sweat that dotted my body after my work with the water. Pages from Salome's books rustle in the soothing breeze. I focus in on the energy I expel, thinking of the sails of the ships, the currents under the wings of a gull, the soft breath of a lover.

"Excellent, Nerissa," Salome's voice carries on the gusts of air to reach me, telling me I can release the control and allow the wind to stop.

When the room is still, I open my eyes and stifle a giggle; Salome's dark hair is fluffed from the breeze and her books are in disarray, but she grins, pride shining in her pale green eyes.

"All right, so far things have gone well. Are you ready to try fire?" she asks, her voice more serious than before.

Swallowing my nerves, I nod.

"Very well," she replies. "Move to the fireplace. Light

the candles in front of it." Salome gestures to the candelabra she placed on the hearth, safely away from the flammable rugs and books in her office.

Sweat prickles along my spine as I step slowly toward the candles. The memory of my loss of control yesterday, of my anger, floods me, making my chest tighten and my breathing shallow. *Don't let your mind get in the way. Control it,* I think to myself as I steel my body near the hearth. My hands tremble, but I squeeze them into fists, digging my nails into my palms as I close my eyes and will the *glow* to spread over me.

This time, no pleasant memories float to my mind to fuel the element. No scent of fresh leaves, no gentle waves, no lover's gasp. This time, fear coats my skin as the scent of smoke from burning texts, burning trees, and burning flesh rises to the surface. Trembling takes hold as I try to push the memories down, gritting my teeth. I try to use any other emotion to light the candles, but all I can think of is the memory of the night our temple was destroyed, the night that my old life ended and this journey began. When I think the fear will overwhelm me, another emotion presses against my chest. One I've fought with just as much as my fear. One that was recently kindled by Celeste's arrival and the memories of the injustices from which we've all fled — *anger.*

The sound of crackling flames presses down on me, and, in the distance, I think I hear a woman's voice. I can't focus on the words as I sink deeper into the anger that grips me, fury burning through my veins. Through the red haze, hands grip my shoulders, shaking me.

"Nerissa! *Nerissa! Stop!*"

The words finally sink in, and I open my eyes, glancing down to find Salome's eyes wild as they stare up at me. Her fingers grip my upper arms so hard that her normally tan knuckles are white. I still tremble, but when I look away from Salome to the hearth, a gasp escapes me. The candelabra has melted. Not just the wax of the candles, but the metal itself pools on the bricks of the hearth, running down the front onto the hardwood below. The logs in the fireplace, solid and fresh when I began, are fully consumed and lay in orange, smoldering embers. The exterior brick is covered in soot as if the fire escaped its confines, and the scent of smoke permeates the hazy air.

"What have I done?" I choke, pulling away from Salome's grip. "Salome, I'm… I'm sorry." I take two steps backward before turning and bolting to the door. Tears spill over my cheeks as I tug on the knob, trying to flee from the destruction I almost caused, from the memories that made me lose control so badly. The door is either locked, or being held closed by Salome's power, and no matter how much I scrabble with it, I can't wrench it open. Sobs take over and I sink to the ground, holding my arms around myself as I rest my forehead against the door. "Please let me leave, Salome. Please."

"Not until you calm down and speak with me, Nerissa." Her voice is calm, soothing even, as if I deserve to be comforted when I almost set her entire building ablaze. "What happened? What caused that reaction?"

After a few moments, my tears slow and my breathing finally evens out enough for me to speak. "I lost control. I'm sorry."

"There you go speaking about *control* again. What emotion overtook you? What happened?"

"Fear." The small word is barely audible as I stay huddled on the ground. It seems so silly that such a tiny word can cause so much damage, but the evidence of it is visible just across the room.

"And?"

I clench my jaw, raising my eyes to meet hers as I release a deep breath. "Rage."

# CHAPTER 22

Salome crouches down, arranging her claret-toned body-skimming skirts around her, before pulling me against her lush figure in a tight embrace. I cling to her, my tears dripping onto her shoulder as she strokes my hair and murmurs gentle words to me.

"How long have you been holding these feelings in, child? Have you not shared them with anyone since everything collapsed?" she finally asks when I sit back against the door.

"Who would I have shared with? Who would have cared?"

"The girls you worked with? William, perhaps?"

"He knows more than most, but I don't wish to burden him. I know so many have suffered. *He's* suffered. I'm not unique. My plight isn't more important than anyone else's. Why can I not control this?" I blurt, holding my hands out, frustrated with my foolishness.

"Nerissa." Salome grips my chin, tilting my face up to hers so I note her serious countenance. "You're no more or less important than anyone else. You are allowed to have feelings and to express them. I see what's happening now. Pushing these memories and emotions down for so long has stifled your abilities. If you don't face these things, you'll forever be controlled by them, even if you think you are the one in control."

I clench my jaw at her words. When I reflect on the number of times I've been unable to fight the overwhelming terror crushing me, I wonder if she's right. Would sharing help me? Cutting my eyes to Salome, I sniffle and force out the words, "Could I… could I tell *you*?"

"Of course, you can, darling." Salome smooths my hair back from my tear-streaked face. She gracefully stands and retrieves her decanter beckoning with it for me to take a seat. Curling on the couch across from her, glass in hand, I begin to share the story of how I fled the temple that night, ended up in Celeste's brothel, and finally came to be in her office.

Partway through my rambling, Salome moved to sit beside me on the couch, holding me as if I were a child as I recounted the misery, guilt, and grief that has haunted me for so many years. She never spoke, only soothed me when needed and refilled my glass when requested, holding space for my emotions to pour from me and sift through the office.

After several drinks and countless tears, I finish my tale, my chest feeling lighter and my heart freer than it has in quite some time. Wiping my eyes and nose on one of the linen handkerchiefs Salome offered, I embrace the older woman once more in gratitude for her solace.

"Now," she says once I am collected. "Show me what you can truly do."

For a moment I hesitate, my brow furrowing as I look to where her hand points at the fireplace. I jerk my head back to her, only to find her gathering another batch of candles to place on the scorched bricks.

"Salome, are you certain?"

"Yes. *Use* your emotions, don't fear them, don't repress them. Let that energy help you," she encourages.

Taking several breaths, I stand from the sofa and approach the hearth. I close my eyes and the familiar warmth spreads over me more quickly, as if the haze of grief that held it back no longer smothers it. Then, I allow my fury to wash through me and outward, no longer falling into the fear I felt before.

"Open your eyes, Nerissa." Salome's voice is a pleasant whisper.

When I open them, the candles are all lit, flickering cheerfully along the hearth without threatening the boundaries. A gleeful giggle escapes me as I engulf Salome in a tight embrace.

---

ONCE I HAVE PRACTICED EACH ELEMENT A FEW MORE TIMES, Salome and I deem our lesson complete for the day. The challenge will now be whether I can maintain my control in the presence of other people, mainly Delphine and her sharp tongue, but I practically skip out of Salome's office and through the near-empty salon. While I should be exhausted, I'm somehow more alert and energized than I was when I woke this morning, a sense of contentment blooming in my breast.

Passing the front door, I find the usual watchman is in place, but the door is securely closed against the rain. Outside, the storm continues to rage and it doesn't seem as if anyone will be coming in to enjoy the company of the Den's ladies tonight. As I hurry up the stairs, the sound of the angry thunder no longer makes me nervous. Instead, energy skips along my skin as if the lightning has passed through the walls and surrounded me with its excitement. I'm eager to see Lennox and to share with him how my lesson went.

When I burst through the door of our room, Lennox straightens in his chair. He has the shutters thrown open, the dark skies looming beyond as the heavy rain pelts the wavy glass overlooking the balcony. A book and a glass of wine are balanced on the small end table, while a tray of food sits to the side, untouched.

"You look like you had a good day." He smiles, looking me over as he stands from his seat to wrap me in a welcoming caress.

"I did. You were right," I reply, pressing against him and capturing his mouth with mine. He makes a low sound in his throat and deepens the kiss, tangling his fingers in my hair as he holds the back of my neck.

When we break apart, his eyes flutter open as he breathes, "Evidently. I was right about what?"

"Working with Salome one-on-one. It helped immense-ly," I explain. I don't share that spilling my secrets to

242

Salome has also lifted a burden from my shoulders. I'm exhilarated from the day, and now all I can concentrate on are his lips on mine and the touch of his skin.

Slipping from his grasp, I skip lightly across the room, smiling wickedly at him. He purses his lips and cocks his head to the side at my playfulness, a noted change from my usual somber mood.

"What have you been up to while I was working with Salome?" I ask as I edge closer to the trunk stored in the corner, watching him from the side of my eye.

"Mainly fending off boredom due to this foul weather since I wasn't able to make it to my meeting with Jean Alexandre. I dined with Celeste for lunch. Very exciting day," he replies, his green gaze watching my every step with curiosity. "What are you up to, my pretty priestess? Is working with Salome all it takes to put you in such a pleasant mood on such a gloomy day?"

"Learning new things can always brighten one's mood. Tell me, Captain… would you like to erase your boredom? Perhaps a lesson of your own?" I reply coyly, raising the lid of the trunk and searching through it for the leather thongs I spied once in his cabin aboard the *Bartered Soul*. Eventually, my fingers find the soft, supple leather. I glance up through my lashes and suck my lower lip between my teeth as I grab hold of the strips, running the pliant length through my fingers.

"I expect I am," Lennox replies huskily when he sees what's in my hand, lust clouding his eyes.

"And pray tell, are these for me, or for *you*?"

At my question, he exhales and says in a rough voice, "They're for whatever you want. Surprise me."

Grinning with delight at his response, I stride back to him, brushing a light kiss against his lips. I tug his shirt from his trousers and he lifts his arms so I can pull it off his body. I can't help but run my hands over his bare chest, tracing the moon phases and constellations I find there, following the patterns down his shoulders and arms. Satisfaction burns in my chest when he trembles under my touch and leans closer to me.

I gently graze the dark pink scar on his side, a remnant of the slash he took capturing the sloop we now call *Andromeda's Vengeance*, before I slide my touch downward over his lean stomach to grip him through the fabric of his pants. He's already hard in anticipation, and I ache with my own desire for him. Looking up through my lashes, I push him steadily toward the bed until he's forced to sit. When he leans forward to wrap his ink-covered arms around me, I step out of reach, gripping two of the leather pieces.

"*Tsk-tsk*, Captain." I grin, then command sweetly, "Lay down on the bed. Please."

He does as requested, and I situate myself astride him over his pants, still fully clothed. Pushing each arm over his head, I wrap his wrists with the leather, loose enough to not hurt, but tight enough to bind him, then tie the loose ends to the bedposts.

"Let's agree that if you want this to stop you will say a special word. What should it be?"

"Mermaid," he replies quickly with a smile. I bite my lip, but can't contain a giggle at the mythical woman he names.

"Mermaid it is. You had that one ready awfully quickly.

Have you done this before, Captain?" I look shocked but smirk at him as he bucks lightly under me.

"Are we really going to discuss that right now?" he replies, arching his hips again under me to remind me of his need. And my own.

"Do you trust me?"

"Yes, always," he says, his eyes honest as he looks me in the face.

"Then let's play."

Smiling seductively, I slide off the bed to stand before him as he angles his head to the side to watch me, that devilish grin tipping up the corners of his lips. Removing my dress, my underskirt is the only thing still covering me. I turn my back to him, glancing over my shoulder as I untie the bow at my lower back painfully slow. Pleasure wraps in my belly when I hear him suck in a breath as I grip the waistband and bend over at the waist to remove it, fully exposing myself to him. He curses under his breath at the sight of me bent before him, earning a smile when I meet his glittering eyes. Then, I stand to step out of the fabric piled at my feet.

Prowling to the bedside, I crawl up to straddle him again, leaning forward and pressing my mouth against his neck. Trailing my tongue along his collarbone and down his chest, I nip gently, then harder on his nipple causing him to gasp and arch his back, pulling against his bindings. Lean muscles tense under his skin as I rake my fingernails over his chest and abdomen. Smiling up at him, I continue to tease down his stomach with my tongue to the edge of his pants. As he arches his hips off the bed, trying to seek the relief friction would offer, I return my attention to his chest, throat, and lips, sliding my body against him until my knees press his arms into the mattress, pinning him just as much as the bindings do.

Staring down at him, I sit back on my heels. "Are you certain you want me to do this? Without your hands, you won't be able to tell me to stop. Your mouth will be too occupied to even think of a mermaid and I don't want to smother you." I taunt and bite my lip.

"I can't think of a more pleasant way to die, my pretty priestess," Lennox replies, his voice husky and his eyes hooded as they rake over my nakedness.

With a breathy laugh, I grip the headboard, tilting forward until the apex of my thighs is aligned with his mouth, then lower myself down to seek the pleasure he offers. Grinding against him, I chase my release as he tastes and teases me. As my muscles tense and I tumble over the edge, he lets out a low rumble of male satisfaction, instinctively flexing at the leather that keeps his hands from touching me. Sitting back, I catch my breath, my eyes studying his grin.

"Is that all you've got for me, my pretty priestess?" he challenges, his eyes glistening in the low light. In answer, I run my tongue along the seam of his lips, tasting my arousal there before dragging my attention lower.

I rub my breasts against him, trailing my tongue down the groove of his abdomen before slowly unbuttoning his breeches. Yanking his pants from his hips, I free his cock and drag a moan from his lips as I continue to tease him, licking along his thigh and hip without touching him directly where he craves it.

"*Nerissa,*" he gasps when I finally slide my hot mouth

over him, taking him all the way to the back of my throat. His muscles tense once again at his bindings, wanting to cradle the back of my head, to grab my hair, setting me alight once again with his desire.

After running my mouth over him a few times, I turn my back to him and straddle his waist, leaning forward a bit to give him a view before raising up over him and slowly sliding him into me. He releases a breathy groan as I lift myself and slide down over him again, knowing he can see our joining in the dim light of our room. I rub myself at the apex of my thighs, my muscles tensing as I edge toward my climax, little noises escaping my lips.

"Oh, *fuck*," the Captain growls as I increase the tempo of my hips, bringing him closer to his release. I come again hard as I continue to grind against him, my core pulsing with waves of pleasure.

"Holy fuck, Nerissa," Lennox moans as he follows me over the edge. Rocking a few more times until he is finished, I slide off of him and crawl up to untie the leather bindings. As soon as his arms are freed, he brings me into a tight embrace, slanting his mouth over mine as I open my mouth to return his kiss just as fervently.

---

We lay curled in one another's arms, the leather thongs tossed aside, as the rain continues to pelt the windows. Between the late hour, and the storm clouds, our room grows darker by the moment. Finally, Lennox pulls away from me, murmuring, "Let me light one of the candles; we can dress and go down for food if you want."

"Wait," I respond, grabbing his arm to stop him from standing. "Let me show you."

He reclines back against the headboard, the sheet covering his legs and trim hips. I can almost see his brow furrowing in confusion in the shadows, but he doesn't speak as he waits expectantly.

I sit up, crisscrossing my legs under the coverlet, and push my loose hair back from my face. Taking a deep breath, I close my eyes and concentrate, just like I did in Salome's office. The tingle of warmth ignites and surrounds me quickly as I recall memories of the great fire at the rites Lennox and I shared years ago, heat washing over my skin as I picture the masked boy's eyes landing on me. Then, I direct that warmth outward toward the table where our candle rests. Lennox's sharp intake of breath makes me pop my eyes open, faint worry creasing my brow in case I failed again. But, the candle is lit, the flickering flame casting friendly shadows around our chamber, and my worry transforms into a broad grin.

"You're magnificent, Nerissa," Lennox whispers, eyes flickering between the candle and me. When he turns to face me, he matches my smile, then cups my cheek and pulls me in for a deep kiss.

"Fire was the most difficult, and arguably the most dangerous, but I was successful with water, air, and earth, too. I can show you those soon, but they're harder to demonstrate in this room."

With his hand tangled in my hair, he pulls me closer, pressing a firm kiss against my sigil, which I've ceased cloaking for now. Pride swells in my chest as we finally stand to dress for dinner.

# CHAPTER 23

The next few days pass in a haze as thick as Salome's sweet-scented smoke. The closer we edge to the night of the full moon, the easier it is for me to draw on my power. The *glow* travels quickly over my skin during our sessions, tingling with energy each time I reach for it. I'm delighted that I no longer struggle to cloak my sigil, and have proven my ability to manipulate the other elements reliably after my private lesson with Salome, finding it easier to focus my emotions to work *with* the elemental energy, even in Delphine's derisive company. This development seems to have made her warm to me more fully, and I catch her eyes lingering on me often as we gather in Salome's office each day. We haven't spoken again about my loss of control, both seemingly content to leave it in the past.

We have spent hours practicing the ability to call the Goddess' power at will, pushing the power of the *glow* itself outward instead of focusing on manipulating the individual elements, and I'm hopeful Salome will show me how she's wielded it for defense in the past. Even though I did relatively well during the session, tension and worry still cling to me as I count the days Erik has been gone. Although I'm looking forward to the full moon ceremony tomorrow evening, I could use another distraction to keep my mind occupied.

As if reading my mind, Delphine rises, fixing her skirts, and looks to Salome. "I'm taking Celeste out to a few shops in a little while. Do you need me to pick up anything else?" She pauses, raising a brow, as she asks, "Any other *errands*?"

I perk up at the mention of leaving the Den; a trip into the city would be welcome, especially since Lennox and I have spent more time hidden away than we'd planned.

"No, I think the list I gave you yesterday should be enough. Be sure to take Celeste by the seamstress to see if she needs any new clothing." Salome takes her place behind her desk, pulling a ledger from one of the locked drawers.

"Is there an apothecary on your way? I'd like to come," I interrupt before Delphine can finish tidying the tray of refreshments from the table and leave the office. Delphine's hands still for a moment as she looks up at me, but she resumes her cleaning quickly. I would like to try to get to know Delphine outside of our lessons and spend more time with Celeste, plus my supply of herbs and tonics is dwindling, so a trip to the apothecary *is* necessary. "I could stop by to check on Lili while we are out, too," I suggest, hoping that will make Delphine amenable to the suggestion.

"That's a good idea," Salome agrees, and Delphine shoots her a wary glance.

250

"Just be sure you don't draw too much attention," Delphine replies, looking at her hands instead of me.

"When do I ever?" I counter curiously.

Delphine looks up at me where I sit in the armchair, still bending to pick up the final dish from the table, her eyes raking over me before she rolls them with a little huff of laughter. "Oh, you always manage to stand out," she murmurs, straightening to her full height and picking up the tray.

"So, the ceremony tomorrow is by invite only?" I ask Salome, changing the subject and looking away from Delphine, hoping the warmth in my cheeks is not obvious in the muted light of the office.

"It is. Only those trusted patrons I have selected personally will enter the salon tomorrow evening for the ceremony," Salome replies. "We used to hold it near the river in the light of the moon, but with the influx of priests over the past few years, we've withdrawn here instead. The energy isn't quite the same as under the full moon, and it's certainly no comparison to what it was like at the temples or in the groves, but we will be left to celebrate in peace. I don't want to ruin the mood by killing anyone, do I?"

A smile quirks the corner of my lip before I understand there is no humor in her statement. Delphine meets my eyes and winks once. "See you in an hour. Meet us in the foyer," she says, then retreats from the room with a swish of her striped skirt. I can't help but admire her graceful figure as she departs, my eyes following her until she is out the door. I'm still unsure how to interpret her mixed signals since our last conversation, but they no longer feel remotely antagonistic.

"William would share you with her if you wished, especially tomorrow," Salome drawls, lighting another cigarette and looking pointedly between me and the door that has closed behind Delphine.

My head whips in her direction as I narrow my eyes to look at her sharply. Delphine is a mystery to me — one moment bitter and sharp, the next sultry and soft. Once Lennox pointed them out, I find myself flattered by her longing glances and shy smiles, even if they are offset by biting words. As frustrating as she is, Delphine is undeniably alluring, but I'm not certain that my physical attraction to her is equal to wanting her in my bed.

"I'm not saying you have to, I'm just saying he wouldn't be jealous. The full moon is known to incite all kinds of urges, as you well know." Salome smiles at my blush, her words reminding me of moonlit nights in the temple grove back in Athene. I roll my eyes and give a small curtsey before moving to exit her plush office without taking her bait, even if I can't hide my flush at the suggestion.

Lennox reclines in a wooden chair with his booted feet propped on the tabletop in the vacant salon. He has taken to standing guard in the salon throughout the day when he isn't checking on the news at the docks or negotiating with merchants and other captains. It isn't obvious that he's waiting for *me* since most people in New Aphros know he stays at the Den while he's in town, but even so, we have given up on trying to hide our affections in public.

An open book rests in his rough hands, the binding worn and cracked as though it's a frequent favorite; a goblet of wine sits on the floor next to him within arm's reach. I stop for a moment in the hallway, leaning against the frame of the entryway, to admire his profile — a study of contrasts with sharp angles and soft lips, strong shoulders and broad chest, long fingers covered in scars yet elegant in mannerism.

The warmth in my chest spreads watching him read, my heart fluttering with emotions until he leans down for his wine and notices me observing him. No one else is in the room at this hour and he smiles broadly at me, the harsh pirate cast aside for the moment. Just for me. I return with a matching grin and stride across the hardwood planks toward him while he lowers his feet, the chair scraping loudly in the quiet salon, and places his book on the table. Since I'm wearing my trousers and shirt instead of a dress, I don't hesitate before easily swinging one leg over his lap and straddling him at the table.

His hands rest on my hips, thumbs making circles through the light wool of my pants as I lean down to press a soft kiss to his mouth. He tastes like wine when I run my tongue against his lips, grinding against him as I deepen our kiss and cup his face in my hands. When I sit back to look at him, he smiles at me once more before asking, "So, how was your lesson today?"

"It was fine. Although, Salome made an interesting statement." I smirk as he tilts his head in curiosity.

"Oh? And what did she say now?"

"Just that she seems to think you would be happy to *share me* with Delphine tomorrow night." I raise a brow while a devilish smile creeps across my lips. "It seems everyone in the Den knows about her little crush."

Lennox chuckles in response, gripping my hips as he presses against me. "Oh, I think the mutual attraction between the two of you is obvious. But Salome didn't tell you anything you didn't already know."

Rolling my eyes, I change the subject, not wanting to face the truth — I *am* attracted to Delphine, even if it is on a purely physical level. For a moment, my mind drifts to what it might feel like to have her mouth on my skin alongside Lennox's warm hands, but I shake my head once to clear the distraction.

"Speaking of Del, I'm going into the city in a bit with her and Celeste. How was your day?" I ask, rubbing myself against his growing arousal, my body responding with heat building in my core, both from his proximity and my daydreaming. I let out a husky sigh as he runs his lips down my throat, trailing his fingers through my loose waves.

"I spoke with Jackson briefly at the docks," he says against my throat, sitting back before continuing his statement. "His men finally finished distributing their cargo and are ready to celebrate the season now that their pockets are full. They will remain here until Solstice, too. A few other new ships just anchored with news that the waters are beginning to get rough to the east. I can only hope Erik returns soon."

His words are sobering, but I'm pleased to know Captain Jackson is firmly in place in the city. He's proven to be a decent man thus far, especially knowing he played a large part in Lennox escaping his naval servitude so many years ago. I can only hope that if things worsen with the King that he will remain an ally. Pirates are not known for working together, but if it comes down to a choice between siding with us or Blackwell, I am fairly certain the pirates will stand with their own kind.

"I hope they make it back soon, too," I whisper.

I refuse to allow myself to even entertain the idea that they might not return, or that I somehow brought this down upon them. Siobhan's vision still haunts me — her vague description of blood and a dagger and a crown — and I send up a silent prayer to the Goddess once again, willing it to be about the past and not foretelling a violent future. Siobhan herself couldn't determine the vision's true meaning, even though divination is where her talents lie, so I feel hopeless trying to puzzle it out even though it plagues my mind often.

"Captain Jackson will be attending the festivities tomorrow," Salome's voice jerks us from our quiet moment as she strolls down the hallway. Startled out of my musings, I sit back quickly. Lennox keeps his grip on my waist though, holding me tight against him as the Madame walks slowly around to the back of the bar. She dips herself a mug of ale and raises her brows toward us in question, but we both shake our heads at her offer. She replaces the dipper before coming to join us at the table.

"Do you think Celeste will join us for the ceremony?" she asks Lennox. "I haven't broached the topic with her yet."

"I'm not sure," Lennox answers, releasing his grip on my waist so I can turn myself to sit on his lap facing Salome. "She's still been very quiet, but I take it as a good sign she's spending more time out of her room now."

"She's been very helpful with the ledgers and accounts."

Salome nods, taking a sip of her ale. "I can tell she was shrewd and successful in Selennia."

Memories of how smoothly she operated the House of Starlight come to mind, and, now removed from the situation, I can't help but agree with Salome's assessment of Celeste. Determined to help her if I can, I say, "I'll talk to her while we're out later and see if I can convince her to come. Perhaps it will brighten her spirits."

I lean in to press a kiss to Lennox's lips before standing, but he pulls me tighter, kissing me deeply. Breathlessly, I break from him and stand, straightening my attire while Salome smiles wickedly at me. I return her smile with pursed lips and a narrow-eyed glance.

"Be careful, my she-wolf. Even if you and Del can handle yourselves, the streets are tense. Keep your wits," Lennox murmurs, touching my hand once more before I leave the salon.

"I always do, Captain," I whisper in response, turning to retreat from the salon and up the stairs to ready for our trip into the city.

# CHAPTER 24

Taking Delphine's words to avoid standing out to heart, I choose a charcoal dress in place of my breeches and shirt and pull all my hair into a simple, elegant style instead of wearing any of it loose like I'm most comfortable with. I tap on Celeste's door on my way to the stairs as I head to the foyer. When she answers, she's dressed in the same muted blue dress she has worn often since her arrival, and Salome's instructions for Delphine to take her by the seamstress shop suddenly make more sense. I never saw her wear anything as subdued as this in Selennia, and I wonder if a new dress might help brighten her mood and make her feel more like herself.

"Did you need something?" Celeste asks, cocking her head to the side.

"I'm coming with you and Del. Are you ready?"

"Oh!" Celeste seems surprised, but not displeased. "Of course." She turns to pocket a small purse, then pulls the door shut behind her.

We walk side by side into the foyer where Delphine

meets us, dressed demurely in her striped wool dress. A thick leather belt cinches her narrow waist and a purse hangs from it, bouncing against the curve of her hip as she moves. Without a word, she guides us toward the back entrance and into the narrow alley that travels behind the buildings.

Our first stop is the Midnight Magnolia. Rolfe is nowhere to be seen when I enter, leaving Delphine and Celeste out front while I sneak up the stairs to Lili's room. As I pass the doors along the hallway, a few women chatting through the open doors nod in greeting. Their rooms are all sparse, holding only a bed and wash basin, and I grimace at the lack of personal effects or comforts. At least in the House of Starlight, I had my small collection of jewelry and a few other gifted pieces. Even if they never really soothed the true wounds in my soul, they still helped me hold onto a piece of who I was. Sally steps from Lilli's door as I approach, relief lighting her face as I near.

"Oh, Mistress! I'm so glad you came by!" Sally exclaims clutching my hand.

"What's happened? Is Lili all right? The baby?" Panic surges in my chest at the thought that something has happened without Salome or myself being notified.

"The baby is fine. He seems to be nursing well and is growing, but Lili isn't herself at all. I don't know how to make her better, and it's worrying me so," Sally says, her eyes lined with silver.

"It's not uncommon for women to struggle after birth. Let me check on her." I try to soothe the younger woman, but worry eats at me knowing that some women have a harder time than others. Living in these austere conditions without proper support, even if the other women are doing their best to help, can't make it any easier for her.

I tap gently at the door before opening it. "Lili?" I say softly into the dim space. The curtains are drawn and only a candle burns to illuminate the room.

"Yes?" a weak voice answers from the bed. Lili lays on her side facing the window, her back to me while the baby lies cooing in a basket nearby.

"It's me. Andromeda. I came to check on you," I say in a soft voice, hoping my visit will be welcome. She doesn't answer, but I close the door behind me, rounding the bed. Light flickers over her face and tears stain her cheeks as she stares at the candle flame.

"How are you feeling, Lili? Sally mentioned you haven't quite been yourself?" I perch on the bed, feeling her forehead for fever and smoothing her lank hair from her face.

"I…," she begins, lip trembling as she looks anywhere but at me. "I feel empty. I don't know what to do. I just want to run away, but I don't have anywhere to go, or anyone to leave him with." Tears begin to fall in earnest now as she curls into a ball. The baby begins to cry, surely sensing his mother's flood of despair. Torn between comforting mother and child, I stand to pick up the small bundle from the basket and hold him close as I return to Lili's side.

"I know things seem hopeless sometimes, Lili. But, this isn't uncommon. Perhaps I could send someone to help you? Is there anything you need? Anything I could bring you?" I've never been one to fawn over babies, and I was rarely around children at all outside of healing them, so having a distressed mother and screaming baby vying for my attention begins to scatter my thoughts. A few minutes pass while both mother and child cry before the door cracks open, and Celeste steps through.

"Celeste? What are you doing?" I ask, surprised she left Delphine to come inside the unfamiliar House. "Is everything all right?"

"Delphine is just outside the door. Perhaps I could help with the baby?" she says softly, reaching out for the tiny bundle and expertly cradling him to her bosom. "Hello, darling. Do you have a name yet?" she coos and smiles as he grizzles and nestles against her ample chest.

"Not yet," Lili sniffles, watching Celeste sway, comforting the infant in her embrace. Within moments, Lili seems to calm down as well so we are able to discuss her condition more thoroughly. Together we decide that I will send some special teas for her to hopefully alleviate some of her sadness and aid with her healing, as well as the contraceptive tea for all the women of the house since Rolfe has still not provided it. As we finish up our chat, Delphine's sharp voice sounds through the door, followed by the gruff tones of a man I recognize immediately as Rolfe. Celeste settles the baby, tucking him against his mother's chest to nurse, then turns to me as I pull my dagger from my pocket.

"What the fuck are you doing here? Get out of my House!" Rolfe snarls at Delphine.

"I'm here with my acquaintances to assist your girls. Fuck off," Delphine answers as I reach the door, her voice showing no sign of fear.

"Who does Salome think she is, sending anyone she wants in here?"

"She didn't send us." I step from the room, Celeste hovering behind me.

His eyes turn to slits as he stares me down. "Of course it's *you*, meddling where you're not welcome. Get out, and leave that bitch alone so she gets her mind right and back to work."

"We told you she can't work for at least six weeks. Perhaps if you offered some kindness or proper care for her, her condition would improve more rapidly," I answer coldly. Rolfe scans me, eyes flickering over the dagger and then to Celeste.

"Is this another one of Lennox's whores he's brought to Salome? Where the hell does he find such prime pieces as you two? Maybe I need to start sending someone to scour Selennia, too." Foolishly, he reaches out as if to touch Celeste, and instinct takes over, my dagger slicing through his forearm as it nears me. "You stupid, bitch!" he shrieks, blood dripping from his arm onto the bare floorboards of the upper hallway.

"Careful of your next actions, Rolfe," I advise, holding the tremor from my voice. "You'd do well to be wary of the women from Selennia. One of us will be back with supplies for Lili and the other women. I'd prefer to not see you when I return. Now, get out of our way and let us pass."

In the first intelligent move I've seen him make, Rolfe steps aside, his bleeding forearm wrapped in his shirt tail as Celeste slips past me. Delphine guides her down the stairs while I trail behind, keeping my eyes on Rolfe until we are out the front door.

As we stroll down the sidewalk toward the apothecary,

Delphine cuts her grey eyes toward me. She lets out a little huff, smiling and shaking her head as I turn to look at her.

"What?" I snap.

"So much for you not standing out, hmm?"

Before I can answer with a sarcastic remark, Celeste interjects, "You don't think he will harm the girl, do you? Punish her for our actions?" Worry creases her brow, and she glances behind us toward the Midnight Magnolia until we turn the corner toward the adjacent district.

"No. He barely has enough girls to fill his House, as it is. He might bitch and rage, but he knows he will have to answer to Salome… or Lennox since he's in town. He's too much of a coward to do anything more than bluster," Delphine replies, laying a hand on Celeste's arm in a rare display of comfort.

I only hope her words are true.

***

Delphine leads us through town, weaving between streets I have traversed with Lennox and some new to me until we arrive at a seamstress' shop. Celeste proceeds straight to the counter, seeming more herself after the interaction with Lili and the baby, and I can't help but be pleased about the change in her. While she orders a few new items, I find myself running my fingers over each fine fabric, admiring the bright colors and varied patterns.

But nothing holds my interest as much as the apothecary next door. Run by a middle-aged woman, the shop is tidy and pristine, resting just on the edge of what Delphine refers to as the Merchant's District. Herbs and dried flowers in dark containers line the back wall, while blended teas and medicinals are packaged for quick purchase alongside bottles of tonic and tinctures. These must sell quickly for the proprietor to mix so many ahead of time, indicating her popularity in the large city.

"Hello, Delphine. Who are your new companions?" the older woman greets us as we peruse the shelves. She wears a pair of spectacles and her greying hair is in a neat bun at the top of her head.

"Good afternoon, Mistress Beatrix. This is Celeste and Andromeda, both newly arrived from Selennia." Delphine is surprisingly cordial, if not overly friendly to the woman as she points us out.

"Welcome, ladies! Please don't hesitate to ask for assistance."

Celeste browses the small selection of perfumes and cosmetics in the corner while I select a few parcels of tea blends. Watching her, I wonder if Celeste will resume coloring her hair the bold auburn I was so accustomed to in the House of Starlight, but step to the counter to speak with the apothecary instead of pestering.

"Can I help you, dear?" Mistress Beatrix asks, studying my face.

"I need a large quantity of *preventative* herbs. Do you have that available?" I ask quietly.

She tilts her head in confusion at my request. "Of course! But, Salome should have a supply already; I sent her order last week."

"It's not for Salome. I'm providing it to a different House." I pull several gold coins from my pocket, part of the earnings I brought from the chest Lennox gave me on Delosia.

"I see. Give me one moment and I will have it ready for you. Delphine, why don't you come back here to help me?" She steps behind the curtain at her back, waving the younger woman through first before the sound of rustling emanates from where she works. Quiet whispers punctuate the opening and closing of bags and jars, but I am unable to make out the words the women speak.

I return to Celeste's side where she smells different fragrances, toying with a bottle of rosewater. "Find anything you like?"

"It all seems so frivolous now. The perfumes, the hair dyes." Celeste's melancholy mood has seemingly returned, which is not surprising even though I thought the visit to town had brightened her spirits. "Especially seeing how that poor girl and her child were living."

"You can't punish yourself, Celeste. We can still help her. We *are* helping her."

"Oh, like you haven't been punishing yourself for things that happened in the past for years now?" Celeste's words surprise me, the flinty madame I once knew peeking out from her more plain facade.

Ignoring her words, I ask, "Is there one you'd like? I have extra coin with me."

"No, thank you. It's not the cost, I'm just not sure I'm quite ready for any of it yet." As she answers, her eyes drift out the front glass and a small gasp escapes her lips. I track her gaze and spot two priests walking down the street with a small group of followers. As they pass different shops, they shout at people on the sidewalk —

some shoppers step aside while others angrily shout back.

"Delphine!" I call out. Moments later Del is at my side, peeking through the lettering on the glass, too.

"*Shit*. I had heard they were starting to cause problems for businesses but hadn't seen it yet. We need to go."

Before I can respond, Mistress Beatrix joins us, peering into the street. "Out the back, darlings. These fools have been causing problems all week, and I don't want you three stuck in the middle." She hands me a large bag filled with herbs and I press two of the gold coins into her hand. "Best of luck! Now out you go!"

She ushers us through the curtain behind the counter before returning to the front of the shop. Delphine guides the way through a packed storeroom and kitchen before we slip into the back alleyway. I hold onto Celeste's hand as we scurry down the alley behind Delphine, not wanting her to be separated from us. She breathes heavily at my back, likely from nerves more than exertion, and I fear this trip has now had the opposite effect than intended.

"I can't believe the Merchant Council hasn't put a stop to this shit," Delphine hisses as she peers around the corner of the alley. The priests are still several shops down, almost to Beatrix's apothecary, but the crowd on the street seems to be growing as business owners and patrons spill from the buildings to shout their frustration back at the priests.

"Are there no laws against such behavior? Where are the patrols to stop them from harassing the businesses?" Celeste asks, and I, too, remember the near-constant presence of the so-called peacekeeping patrols that roamed the streets in Selennia after Blackwell's takeover.

"If there was a law against men being idiots, there would be no men left in the streets. There's no law against acting like a fool," Delphine replies, her disdain clear. "We need to get across to the other side, then we can get back to the Den. Otherwise, it will take forever to get around the other side of the district." Delphine's words are punctuated by a low rumble of thunder, another storm brewing in the sky to match the one in the streets.

With a quick glance to the sky, Delphine's face settles into a grave expression. "All right, stay calm and follow me. Hopefully, they won't take note of us. Come on."

Her skirts swish around her legs as she steps out onto the sidewalk, and I follow her, hoping she's right.

"Get out of our district, you fanatics!" a man's voice shouts over the crowd toward the priests and their followers. "You're ruining business!"

"Your avarice is a sin! You will fall under the weight of your greed!" a priest shouts back. "Look at the sinful wares you sell!"

As I follow Delphine winding through bodies in the crowd, Celeste clinging to my hand behind me, I cut my eyes to see where the men are shouting. The storefront appears to be a bookseller. How can books be sinful? We make it to the other side of the street and head in the opposite direction, trying to return to the Entertainment District, but the crowd has grown larger and their agitation has increased in the few minutes it has taken us to squeeze through.

Someone begins throwing objects, empty bottles and trash sailing through the air toward the priests. The men who travel with the priests lash out in return, throwing rocks or using staffs to push people back from their circle.

As the crowd presses against us, panic surges in my chest. Celeste's nails dig into my hand as Delphine tries to push through the people. She reaches behind her and grabs my other hand, pulling us both along with a strong grip. Even though Delphine stands several inches shorter than me, she is somehow able to maneuver through the people with far more ease than I can, not pausing before forcibly shoving bodies from our path. Finally, she drags me into one of the smaller spaces between buildings, Celeste on my heels.

"Del, we need to keep going. What are you doing?" I hiss, fearing what will happen if we are trapped here with nowhere to run.

"Be quiet and come here," she grits through her teeth, pulling Celeste farther into the alley, then presses me up against the bricks at my back. The crowd continues to move as people are caught in the crowd, pushing them through the streets in front of the alleyway and effectively blocking us in.

"Del, what are you —"

"I said *be quiet*," she commands, her eyes flashing furiously as her face lingers mere inches from mine. Just then, her eyes close, and a wave of power drifts over me, the alley darkening further. Glancing at the sky above, I realize quickly that the dark storm clouds overhead are not the source of the darkness. Shadows soundlessly coalesce around us while Del takes deep breaths, her chest still pressed close to mine. "I can keep us safe, we just have to stay silent and wait," she whispers, her breath tickling the loose strands of hair that have escaped their pins at my neck.

My breath catches as I realize the darkness is coming from *her*. How foolish I've been to not realize that Delphine has been hiding her true powers from me this entire time. Although rare, and something I have never seen, it was said that some priestesses were granted darker gifts from the Goddess. Gifts that allowed them to manipulate shadows, to pierce the veil and commune between worlds, and to channel the energy of others. Briefly, I wonder if Delphine's link to the realm of death was always present, or if the connection formed after she escaped from its clutches on the pyre.

Del leans in further, her breath tickling my sensitive neck as I try to calm my racing heart. Now, however, I can't tell if it thunders from our flight from the mob, or from the proximity to the woman pressed against me. I realize that she still grips my hand and I squeeze it once, hoping it offers comfort, but half expecting her to pull away from me. Instead, my breath catches as she strokes her thumb across the back of my hand, leaning just slightly closer, sending heat to my core and sparks along my skin where her touch grazes.

"Del...," I murmur breathlessly, running my tongue over my lower lip.

"I think they've passed us by," Celeste's soft voice pulls me from my thoughts. "And I think it's going to start raining soon."

"Let's give it a few more moments, then we can head back," Delphine whispers. She releases my hand but doesn't step away, stroking her fingers down my side to rest

at my hip. My mind returns to Salome's words earlier —
that Lennox would share me with Delphine — sending my
heart into a quicker rhythym again as I breathe in her
jasmine perfume.

"All right, we should be safe now," Delphine finally
says, looking up into my eyes for a moment before she
turns to walk away from both me and Celeste.

"Del, wait." I grab her forearm as she turns, pulling her
back to me. "When were you going to tell me you could do
that?"

Delphine looks down at my hand on her arm, then gives
a sarcastic grin, replying, "Oh, there are plenty of things I
can do that I haven't shown you yet." She gently tugs her
arm free, proceeding to the alley entrance to peer into the
street.

Celeste gives me a sideways look, her golden brows
raising in an expression similar to one her brother has given
me before, yet another glimpse of her former self peeking
out. All I can do is roll my eyes and exhale in response.
"Let's go."

<hr>

WE SLIP IN THROUGH THE REAR ENTRANCE OF THE DEN WHEN
we reach it, having snuck through alleys the entire trip
back, both to avoid the crowds and to try to stay out of the
rain that has started falling. Damp and haggard, we drag
ourselves into the foyer to part ways.

"Celeste, I meant to ask you," I say as we ascend the
stairs to our respective rooms, having left Delphine to fill

Salome in and change in her downstairs bed chamber. "Will you attend the ceremony tomorrow night?"

She pauses on the stairs while I continue to climb, forcing me to stop and look down at her. For a moment, she chews the inside of her cheek with hesitation in her eyes. "I haven't attended a proper full moon ceremony in a very, very long time," she says, still looking unsure. "But, yes. I think I shall. I have to start building my life here, and today was the start. I think the ceremony will do me good. Thank you for the invitation."

"Of course. I'm glad to hear that," I reply, offering her a small smile before she slips into her room.

My door at the end of the hall beckons as I drag my tense body down the carpeted walkway on sore feet. Pushing the door open, my tired gaze settles on Lennox dressed in only his breeches, his linen shirt and coat each laying out to dry.

"Well, at least I'm not the only one who looks like a drowned rat," I announce as I push the door shut behind me. "Where did you go out to?"

"Ah, but a lovely sight nonetheless," he flirts as I place my packages on the table and start to remove my damp dress. "I visited Jean Alexandre again, the merchant I mentioned before. We were finalizing a few things, and then some excitement with the priests ensued in the streets."

"We witnessed that too. We were at the apothecary shop in the Merchant District when they came through. Thanks to Delphine we slipped away without much trouble, but it makes me uneasy."

"Things are vastly different than the last time we were

here, that's for sure. The priests have never been this vocal before. Jean Alexandre is just as perturbed as we are."

"I also had a disagreement with the owner of the Midnight Magnolia, but I think Celeste may have found something to keep her preoccupied."

"Oh?" he asks, helping me out of my dress and laying it across the remaining chair.

"She seemed to take to the new baby Salome and I delivered. The mother is struggling, but perhaps Celeste could help her to get through it. If we can just keep Rolfe in line." I turn to wrap my arms around his waist now that I'm somewhat dry.

"She always did have a soft spot for babies. I'm sure it makes her think of Lyra. But you may be right, I'll see what I can do about Rolfe."

"She agreed to attend the ceremony tomorrow, too." I lay my cheek against his tattooed chest, letting his warmth seep into me. "She seems like she might be starting to feel a bit more normal."

"That's wonderful news," he replies, kissing the top of my head as we hold one another.

# CHAPTER 25

Residual nervousness from the run-in with Rolfe and our flight from the angry mob in the Merchant District clings to me all through the following day as I try to prepare for the full moon ceremony. This evening, I sit with one of the linen towels wrapped around me, bare from the waist up as I apply shimmering gold dust across my shoulders, collarbones, and chest while my hair dries after my bath. The scent of the sweet oils and herbs Salome sent up with the serving girls cocoons me along with the notes of music that drift in from the Entertainment District outside. Sounds of laughter and revelry punctuate the music, filtering through the half-open shutters overlooking the balcony, and I smile at the joyful city that always seems to be celebrating just outside these walls.

Lennox is half-dressed, his black trousers hanging low on his hips as he walks up behind me. I track his movements in the tall mirror mounted to the wall as he approaches my back and shiver as he runs a hand down the side of my bare breast and waist. Gooseflesh rises on my

273

skin and my nipples peak at the pleasant sensation. Reveling in the feeling, I lean my head back against his stomach and look up at him, biting my lip as he smiles seductively at me, eyes hooded with arousal.

"We will never make it downstairs if you don't stop trying to seduce me, Captain," I tease, my voice husky.

In actuality, I wouldn't be upset if I spent the night tangled with him in our plush bed instead of in the room below, but I know the importance of tonight's full moon ceremony and I'm curious as to how Salome hosts it here in the Den of Sinful Delights. Lennox rewards me by running his hand back up the center of my stomach, then grips my chin as he leans over me to kiss me firmly, sucking my lower lip into his mouth and drawing a whimper from me, before he releases my chin.

"We will have to make up for it tonight, then," he breathes against my lips when he pulls away. His words are a dark promise that sends another bout of shivers over me and warms my core simultaneously. Squeezing my thighs together, I cut my eyes to him. He quirks his lip and raises his brows once before turning to pull a clean shirt from the trunk to finish dressing. With a deep exhale, I shake off the lingering desire, even as my cheeks burn with my imagination, and begin my toilette.

Wrapped in the silver robe I now know belonged to Anise Lennox, with my jewelry and circlet arranged properly, I turn from the mirror to view the Captain in his finery. My gaze skates over his well-cut dark green frock coat and black pants tucked into his tall boots, before returning to his handsome face where mossy eyes sparkle with mischief. He rakes his hungry eyes over me in turn, circling me for a full inspection of my ensemble.

"Beautiful as ever, my pretty priestess," his words caress me as his hand grazes the small of my back. I inhale sharply at the tingle his touch leaves behind and arch my body in response.

"Thank you, Captain. Shall we?" I ask shakily, even though I would prefer him to pull the robe back off me to touch my bare skin.

Taking my hand in his, he pulls me in for another deep, but all too brief kiss. "We shall."

A hush envelops the salon as we descend the stairs, a bubble of reverence and respect enclosing the usually raucous space. The red front doors are firmly shut, and Joe stands on the interior to open the lock and check each patron before allowing entry. Lennox peels the velvet curtain back to reveal that the tables have all been moved to the edges of the room, some even resting on the stage usually reserved for dancers or other entertainment. The curtains usually draped in front of the booths are held open wide and the floor has chalk markings written upon its normally plain surface. Some of the tables have guests already seated at them, I recognize a few as regulars in the salon, but there are several new faces as well. Everyone is dressed in finery, each wearing some symbol of the Goddess — moonstone jewelry, a splash of silver clothing, a crescent moon sigil, or a celestial token.

Standing in the back of the space, Salome has propped herself against the bar. She wears midnight blue robes edged in metallic symbols representing all of the different arts. A gold circlet similar to mine rests on her brow. She looks every bit the part of the former High Priestess. Delphine stands at her side in black robes edged with golden serpents. After her use of shadows in the alley yesterday, her natural gifts explain her dark moods and rapidly changing emotions. Now, seeing her in her black robe seals that assumption.

No one wore the dark robes at the temple in Athene when I was younger. They were reserved for those with the rare ability to work with, and within, the shadows and to pierce the veil. The wearer's power to channel the energy of others, whether for good or nefarious purposes, caused them to be looked on with suspicion and fear since some assumed they would try to steal or manipulate others' power for their own gain.

As my thoughts whirl, my eyes drift over the dark fabric and back to Del's pretty face. She raises a pale brow and her full lips turn up in a smug smile, but whether it's in pleasure at my admiration or a challenge to any negativity the black robe might elicit, I don't know.

My robe shines in the candlelight. The cloth of silver ripples like moonlight on the ocean as the flames reflect off it, and the gold at my throat, waist, and wrist as I approach the other women, watching as Lennox takes his place at a table nearby. As I pass, I cast my gaze over the other man who is already seated, surprised to find it's the usually flamboyant Captain Jackson. Tonight he looks more elegant than I've ever seen, his hair styled in a tight club and wearing a brocade jacket of navy blue, vastly different than the multi-hued and textured coat he usually preens in.

Stepping up to Salome's side, I turn to view the room in its entirety as Celeste enters through the curtains. Her eyes linger on her mother's robe before rising to meet my gaze. I hold my breath, waiting for her reaction, and feel my heart soar when she smiles. Like everyone here, she looks lovely in her finery. Her golden hair is tied in a neat knot at her neck, and her dress is a simple style in a dark color that is hard to distinguish in the candlelight.

Before Celeste can take a seat between her brother and Captain Jackson, Lennox stands and meets her, guiding her over to a neighboring table. I watch as he introduces her to a portly man with thinning brown hair seated next to a pretty woman, young enough to be his daughter. Celeste looks confused for a brief moment, but I see her smile and take the man's hand. The three of them speak for a moment, the young woman curiously inspecting the room around her, before Lennox and Celeste return to the table with Jackson.

"You look lovely, Nerissa," Salome whispers to me when I return my attention to her. I have taken up my space at her left side, and Delphine stands to her right. Del gives me a small nod with a flicker of a smile as she appraises me, and I incline my head to her in return.

"Thank you, Salome. You both look beautiful," I whisper back, my eyes scanning the symbols covering her robes in shining threads of silver and gold.

"Only a few more moments before we begin," she says to both of us, turning to retrieve a bottle of wine from the counter behind her. Handing a crystal goblet to me and then one to Delphine before clasping one for herself, she pours the bloodred liquid from the bottle for each of us.

Constance, the young woman who has brought my trays and bath water to my room numerous times, carries candles from behind the bar, placing them in the center of the room amongst the sigils and chalk on the floor, then steps back quickly and retreats into a darkened corner. The other candles and lamps in the room dim, surrounded by wisps of shadows, while, with a sweep of her hand, Salome lights the ones on the floor. My eyes widen, and a flutter of surprise runs over my skin at the power used so openly with others in the room. My skin tingles with excitement, the feeling more potent than any other time I've participated in a ceremony.

The salon grows silent in anticipation as energy pulses around the patrons, zipping along my skin and raising the hair on my arms, making it abundantly clear why the priests fear the women in this House. They call them witches and other vile things because the power that resides here is that of ancient legends, *proof* of the Goddess among us. My own power surges within my breast, demanding to join them and threatening to do as it wills if I don't allow it, as Delphine and I link hands and walk toward the center of the room, trailing behind Salome.

Standing in the center of the chalk sigils, Salome pours a small amount of her wine on the floor. Delphine and I mimic her actions before sipping the liquid and placing the goblets on the ground at our feet. The three of us clasp hands, and immediately the *glow* illuminates where we touch, warmth and light spreading quickly up our arms. Salome begins the full moon chant, Delphine and I echoing her words accompanied by those who fill the room. I close my eyes and allow myself to be swept into the words like I used to when I was at the temple. Everything else falls away until only the warmth of the *glow* remains in my mind, surrounding me and my sisters with comfort as if the Goddess has reached down to wrap us in a loving embrace.

As we begin to sing in honor of the full moon, I open my eyes to see that Delphine and Salome have allowed their sigils to show on their brows. I release the control over my own, letting it shine in the celebratory atmosphere as smiles form on all our lips.

The song comes to an end, and power pulses beneath my skin as we step away from the candles. A reminder of what lies just under the surface waiting for me to call on it. Salome raises her hands in an invitation, and some of the guests step toward the circle and candles, dropping small offerings or crouching to burn slips of paper that likely have intentions, things to release, wishes, or prayers inked on them; visitors at the temple would often do the same thing when they came for ceremonies.

When everyone has returned to their seats, the candles continue to burn, but the shadows recede as Salome raises the lights in the room to a comfortable level, subtle yet bright enough to see one another.

"That was exhilarating," I confess to Salome quietly, still basking in the retreating *glow*. While the heat of power fades in my breast, it still hums over my skin, teasing me with the promise of more. "I've never felt anything that strong before."

She waves her hand and the musicians begin playing, while Jim begins to pour drinks for the guests at the bar, then pulls me aside. "*That* is the power that you should have been trained to use. We were once channels for the magic of the Goddess, not just obedient nursemaids and scholars like they taught you to be. Can you feel all that you've been holding back? All that still waits for you to tap into?"

I nod in response, my mind swimming with the desire to learn more as my skin tingles in anticipation. But before I can say anything else, Salome's lips curve into a smile as she places two mugs of ale in my hands, and directs me toward the table where Lennox sits. She takes two mugs in her hands as well and follows, gracefully melting into the empty seat next to Captain Jackson, placing her second mug in front of him. Draped across Lennox's lap, I hand him my spare. Delphine offers Celeste a glass of wine as she passes our table, but Celeste declines with a shake of her head, sitting quietly and observing the space.

Although the House of Starlight was equally luxurious, the dark paint and cold celestial theme was a stark contrast to the deep-bloodred paint, warm wood, and fiery gold that engulf us here at the Den of Sinful Delights. The House always had a sense of refinement and restraint, even if it was a brothel, while the Den throbs with life and celebration. The band changes to an upbeat tune, and the salon fills with the chatter and laughter of the intimate group as everyone emerges from the reverence of the ceremony.

"Is it like this every full moon?" I ask no one in particular, sipping from my mug while taking in the lively atmosphere. Seductive energy seems to permeate the space yet again, tendrils of lust wrapping around as I press into Lennox's warmth. It doesn't only affect me — couples start to pair up and slink away into dark corners, or drift toward the foyer and the comfortable rooms beyond.

"It's often more subdued since we are usually just a duet. Having three priestesses makes it more powerful, even if we are forced to keep the festivities indoors," Salome breaks from her conversation with Jackson and Celeste to explain.

She sits close to the older man, her knee peeking from the high slit in her robe, casually touching his thigh. Jackson's striking blue eyes rake over her figure approvingly, her full bosom highlighted by her low-cut bodice. But Salome acts as though she's unaware of the attention. My eyes flick between the two; this must be a game they play since it's clear to me she desires him as much as he does her. I quirk a brow at Lennox, cutting my eyes to the couple, but he merely winks at me and takes a long drink of his ale before sliding a hand up my bare thigh as I lean my shoulder against his chest.

"Let's dance." He leans forward to whisper, finishing his drink and kissing me quickly on the curve of my neck. I take another sip before placing my cup on the table and rising to my feet. Once standing, Lennox takes my hand and pulls me against him, leading me to the floor.

He spins me, turning me to face him as I rest one hand on his shoulder, the other wrapped in his. "Who is the man you introduced Celeste to?"

Briefly, his eyes scan over my shoulder, taking in the other patrons. "Jean Alexandre, of the Merchant Council. He decided to venture to the exciting side of town with his wife to see what the fuss was about."

"He seems very interested in *us*," I whisper, noting the man watching us from his table.

"He's trying to determine if you've truly gotten to me. I insisted you were just a passing fancy when he asked me about us," Lennox replies, turning us so he faces the man. A wolfish grin spreads across his face as his hand slips lower on my backside.

The center of the salon remains clear as the candles burn, their hot wax leaking down the sides like tears into the wine we spilled on the floor in offering. Couples dance outside the chalk to the music of the band, bodies pressed close even though the music isn't a slow melody. I sink into Lennox's embrace as he circles my waist with his arms, pulling me tight against him. His darkened hair, a light chestnut now, falls across his forehead and brushes my cheek as he leans forward to press breathy kisses against my throat, earning a shuddering sigh.

From the corner of my eye, a shadow appears at the edge of the bar, and I know before I focus on her that it's Delphine. Her cornsilk hair is braided in a coronet like my own with the rest loose and curling wildly around her shoulders. She casually holds a full glass of dark wine between her delicate fingers as she watches the crowd, not joining in to dance or chat with anyone. As we turn to the music, her eyes meet mine, and she smiles before averting her gaze down into her glass. From this distance, it's hard to be certain, but her pale cheeks seem to have darkened in the flickering candlelight.

"Delphine has a crush on you, my pretty priestess," Lennox whispers against my ear, grinning wickedly at me with twinkling green eyes. "Look how flustered she is."

"So you have mentioned before, Captain. Are you suggesting I do something about it tonight?" I tease, rolling my lip between my teeth and cocking my head with curiosity. "Perhaps you *are* as depraved as I feared when we first met."

He runs his long fingers down one of my bare arms and retorts, "I've told you before — you may be mine, but I will not deny you whatever pleasure you might seek. You need only tell me what you want."

A shiver runs over me as I glance again at the beautiful woman still staring at us. She bites her full lower lip when I meet her eyes, then quickly averts her gaze once more. Chewing on the inside of my cheek, I observe her from the corner of my eye as Lennox guides us around the floor to the slowing music. I don't want my intentions to be misinterpreted. Delphine is already a mercurial being and I don't want to risk her moods becoming more volatile over a bruised heart. I have no interest in a romantic entanglement with the woman, but if she agreed that it was only to sate our mutual attraction and not because of deeper feelings, I am open to the offer.

"She *is* beautiful, but I don't want her to misunderstand. I've seen firsthand what happens when a woman is scorned in a place like this. Women can be unbelievably cruel to one another," I murmur seriously, dragging my eyes from her to focus on Lennox once again.

"Oh, I think she would be more than happy for it to be just a night. She's desired you since you arrived. She makes it clear to me at any chance she gets." He huffs a laugh. "She knows who your heart belongs to, but I understand your concern." His eyes are hooded with desire when I rise on my toes to brush a kiss against his lips. "If you don't want her, I'm happy to satisfy your needs on my own, my pretty priestess."

"Let me speak with her. Tonight, I don't think I would be opposed to testing your theory," I whisper against his mouth, the idea of sharing myself with both Lennox and Delphine causing my pulse to quicken as heat spreads across my skin.

I could use a pleasant distraction from my lessons with Salome, from the worry that grips my heart when I think about Erik and the women of Delosia he has gone to protect. Lennox pauses, holding me at arm's length to inspect my face with a questioning look in his emerald gaze. I let a flirtatious gleam glint in my eye as I turn up the side of my lips, raising an eyebrow as another question to him.

"Losing your nerve, Captain?" I tease.

He looks across the room to Delphine and twirls me in his arms toward her.

"Never, my pretty priestess," he murmurs against my ear, pressing a kiss against my neck before giving me a slight nudge toward Delphine.

# CHAPTER 26

As I prowl through the revelers, Delphine's grey gaze follows my movements before latching on mine. A flicker of confusion clouds her face as I get closer, and I smirk when she glances at Lennox over my shoulder, waiting near the curtained entry to the salon. I face the bar when I reach her side, but she remains focused on the crowd. Leaning my elbows against the polished surface, I glance over at her, running my eyes over her figure before meeting her heated stare.

"Delphine."

"Andromeda."

I can't hold back a smile as her eyes focus on my lips. "I have a question for you."

"Yes?" Her voice catches slightly as she studies my face, leaning closer and biting her lower lip.

"Would you care to join Lennox and me this evening? Perhaps we might make an additional offering to the Goddess?"

Her eyes focus on mine, reading my intention with a coy

smile. I turn to face her, leaning into her and coiling one of her unruly curls around my finger, making sure she understands exactly what I mean.

"I wish to join *you*, Andromeda. If William is part of the package, I don't mind," she whispers, turning to face me as she trails a finger down my arm. "I've been with men before, and he's more handsome than most."

"You know I love him, don't you?" I ask seriously, making myself clear.

"Everyone knows that," she replies, furrowing her brow in confusion.

"I don't wish to mislead you. If you come to my room tonight, can you promise you won't think it means anything more than the fact that I think you're beautiful? For us to enjoy one another and celebrate the full moon?" I will not have her heart broken, nor do I want her to think she could come between Lennox and me.

Delphine leans closer and my pulse quickens in response to her nearness. Her sweet jasmine perfume tickles my senses as she brushes her lips near my ear. "I don't love you," she whispers. "I just want to taste you." She runs her soft hand down the side of my arm once more, lightly brushing my fingers as she looks at me for my answer.

My stomach tightens in response. "Then come with me."

Taking her palm in mine, sparks tingling where our fingers entwine, I pull Delphine behind me toward where Lennox stands with wide eyes. Apparently, he didn't expect the conversation to take the turn it has. But as we approach, he holds the curtain open for us to walk through, a smug smile on his lips, then follows in our wake.

Our steps are hurried as we climb the darkened stairs, reaching the door to our room more quickly than I anticipated. I have no reason to be nervous; this is not the first time I've been with multiple partners over the years, and yet my heart tumbles shyly when Delphine presses me against the wall while Lennox unlocks the door. She runs a hand over the side of my waist and hip, so similar to how she did in the alley when she hid us from danger, and gazes up at me with a soft smile.

Once we are in our room, Lennox pours a glass of whiskey, then takes a seat in the armchair after shedding his coat. He looks between the two of us with hooded eyes, as if awaiting instructions. Delphine steps away from me, inching toward the plush bed behind her as she studies us, waiting for me to take the lead.

"So, tell me, Delphine. What should we do first?" I ask, my voice more sultry than I expected as I watch her. She sucks her bottom lip between her teeth as she pauses, taking a step back toward me, then another, until she's close enough to trace her delicate fingers down my arm. The touch sends shivers over my skin, and heat coils in my belly when she glances up at me through her lashes. I close the gap between us to press my lips against hers, pulling her closer and burying my hand in her soft curls. A sigh escapes her plush mouth as she opens it to deepen our kiss, the taste of wine still on her tongue.

Delphine clutches me to her as if I might pull away, cupping my face as she sucks my lower lip into her mouth. When we break apart, my eyes flicker to Lennox, still reclining in the chair, knees casually apart as he rests one arm lazily over the armrest. He holds the glass of whiskey in his long fingers, his eyes hungry as he watches us together. But he doesn't make a move to join us, merely traces his thumb across his lips as he observes. I lean down to kiss Delphine again and push her gently toward the bed as our caresses become more urgent, hands roaming over one another through the silky fabric of our robes.

When the backs of her thighs hit the mattress, Delphine spins me so I sit on the bed. She steps between my legs, rucking my robe up to expose my pale skin. Slowly, she pushes the shoulders of her robe off to reveal one full breast, then the other, allowing the dark fabric to drape around her waist. I run my hands over her smooth, perfumed skin, cupping one breast and skimming my thumb over her peaked nipple. A gasp escapes Delphine's parted lips as I draw her hardened nipple into my mouth. Her fingers twine through my hair with pleasure.

"Goddess." Her breathy voice pulls my attention upward to see her staring down at me, eyes dark with need. Sliding my hands down her slim waist, I slip her black robe from her hips so she stands before me bared completely. The creamy skin of her body is a stark contrast to the horrific reddened burn scars that mar her to mid-thigh. She swallows thickly, hesitancy flashing briefly in her eyes.

"You're lovely," I whisper, running my fingers over her stomach and the curve of her hip. Looking up to meet her gaze, my hand skates lightly over her scars and up her inner thigh to slide against the wetness building between her legs. She closes her eyes and tips her head back, all hesitation vanishing as I slip against her and press kisses to her stomach and chest.

"Kiss me," I murmur, as I scoot back on the bed and

drag her mouth to mine, pulling her over me. Our limbs entwine as we explore, then Delphine sits back, straddling my waist to pull my robe from my shoulders, revealing the shimmering gold that I dusted across my breasts and collarbones. She trails kisses down my neck, pressing her soft curves, so different from the hard planes of Lennox's muscular physique, flush against me as she grinds her hips in rhythm with mine. I can't keep the little noises of pleasure from escaping my lips as she cups my breast and kisses me deeply, sliding her free hand up the slit in my robe to explore the nakedness underneath my skirt.

Slipping to the side to pull my robe off completely, Delphine looks over her shoulder to Lennox, still just an observer. "Aren't you going to join us?" she asks, her voice low. She reminds me of a statue of a siren curled on her knees at my side, long curly hair covering her breasts as she flutters her lashes at Lennox.

When I raise up on my elbows to observe him, he takes a sip from his glass and smiles. His voice is ragged when he leans his elbows on his knees and answers, "I wouldn't want to be in the way." He knows Delphine doesn't want to bed him and won't join us just to seek his pleasure.

"You're being so patient, Captain. Surely you deserve *some* relief," I drawl, running my hand over Delphine's soft skin now shimmering with gold powder from where our bodies touched, noting the outline of his arousal pressing through his breeches.

"Oh, my pretty priestess, I plan on getting relief soon enough," he replies with a rough voice, stroking a hand over himself as his eyes linger on our bodies in the candlelight. I give a half smile in return, heat pooling in my belly at both the sight of him and at the feel of Delphine at my side.

Pulling Delphine's lush mouth back to mine, I roll atop her, running my hands down her stomach until I reach the apex of her thighs. She moans when I circle the sensitive bundle of nerves and suck on her neck, nipping the delicate skin. As she arches into me, I slip one finger into her warmth, pleased at how wet she is in response to my touch. Curling my finger against the spot I know will be pleasurable, I press the heel of my hand against her, wringing a pleasure-filled gasp from her lips. Continuing to slide against her, I whisper into the shell of her ear, "Is this what you like, Del?"

"Oh, Goddess. Yes," she sighs under my touch, gripping the sheets and whimpering. As she rides my hand, nearing her release, her muscles contract around my finger.

"I want to hear you come for me," I murmur wickedly against her ear before running my lips over her bared throat as her head tips against the pillow, her back arching from the mattress. Trailing kisses over her breasts and belly, my mouth reaches the apex of her thighs, my tongue joining my fingers in caressing her.

"Oh, *fuck*," she pants, gripping my hair in her fist as she presses against my mouth. I savor every stroke, her taste sweet on my tongue. After a few more moments, she cries out with bliss while her muscles tremble against me as she comes undone. I delicately slip my hand from her and stroke her velvety skin, kissing her inner thigh before she pulls me back up to take my mouth with hers. When we break apart, she pushes on my shoulder, pressing me back into the mattress with her soft form.

I spare a glance toward Lennox, still patiently sipping his whiskey as he takes us in. Cupping Delphine's cheek, I ask, "Is it all right if he joins us?"

"I trust him, it's fine," she replies breathily, her eyes half-closed as she presses her cheek into my palm.

"Billy," I murmur, reaching out my free hand to him. I glance at Delphine as he stands, placing his glass on the table.

When Del returns to kissing my neck, then shoulder, I writhe beneath her, soft curves pressing into my own. Lennox strides to the bed, reaching behind to pull his shirt from his waistband and over his head. The bed dips under his weight as he sits on the edge of the mattress, brushing my skin with the tips of his fingers. Delphine kisses down my breastbone, trailing sparks to my navel as she traces where the choker and chain I wear hang to bracket my waist. Lennox stretches out next to me, claiming my mouth with a greedy kiss, rumbling low in his throat at the taste of Delphine on my lips. The feeling of both their mouths and hands floods my senses, making my stomach clench with need. Lennox's hand trails from where it cradled my face to my breast, squeezing it in his palm as our kiss deepens.

When Delphine reaches my waist, she pauses, looking up at me. Desire burns in my core as she runs one hand slowly up my leg, under my thigh, and then behind me to cup my backside, following with the other hand, as if savoring the touch of my skin on hers. I lean my head back and to the side to kiss Lennox as I cradle the back of her head in my hand, fingers gripping her blonde curls, and open my legs to her.

Del dips her head and trails more slick kisses along the

crease between my leg and my hip, and seductively nips my hip bone. Tracing the tip of her tongue downward toward the apex of my thighs she draws a gasp from my lips. Lennox releases a deep rumble in his chest as he watches, while I let out a breathy moan as Delphine's tongue flicks against my core, then swipes through my heated center. At the sound of that tiny exhalation, she grips me more firmly, pulling me against her as I rub against the delicious friction of her mouth, riding the edge of release.

Lennox pinches my nipple, kissing the column of my throat as Delphine circles and sucks at the tender bundle of nerves until I cry out. My teeth press into my lip as I tug her hair with my climax, my hips moving of their own accord, riding the waves of pleasure against her until Lennox captures my mouth with his.

Boneless, I roll to my side, my back pressed against his hot chest as Delphine slides up my body and kisses me, sucking my lower lip into her mouth. I can taste myself on her, and desire courses through me again as our limbs tangle together.

When I turn my attention back to Lennox, Delphine reaches out to him as well, but he catches her wrist. "You don't have to, Del. Just touch her," he rumbles, placing her smaller hand on my waist.

His firm hands settle on my body, shifting me to face him, and I wrap my hand around his neck and draw him close to press my lips to his. Delphine curls behind me, caressing my breasts and kissing my shoulder.

Our shared passion deepens as our tongues dash against one another, sending shivers through me and making my stomach flip with need. With a low sound in his throat, Lennox pulls away and stands to kick out of his boots, then unbuttons his trousers, pushing them off quickly. Standing at the side of the bed he grips my calf and pulls me to the edge of the mattress, posed between my thighs. Delphine reclines next to me, teasing me with kisses along my neck and breasts while I lay across the bed, my legs wrapped around Lennox's waist. His eyes shine in the light of the oil lamps as he looks at my naked body, then at Delphine.

"*Fuck*," he murmurs, slowly running his hand up my leg, across my hip, and then up my stomach to my breastbone. He gently circles my neck with this rough palm, covering the choker I still wear and tilting my mouth up to his, pressing his body against mine. "How did I earn the right to have you like this?"

I keep my legs wrapped around him as he stands once more, thrusting into me as he grips my hips, pulling me toward him so I'm at the edge of the bed. His movements are slow, leaving me panting at the sensation as he pulls out and enters me again, while Delphine claims my mouth and circles the sensitive spot at the apex of my thighs with her delicate fingers. The disparity of their touch on my skin is dizzying — his grip strong and rough, while hers is soft and tender.

"That's right, come again for us," Lennox urges, increasing his speed with eyes focused on where our bodies are joined. The commanding tone and friction make me whimper, my muscles coiling again.

It only takes a few more moments before I can't contain the little noises I've been biting back, giving in to breathy moans as I come around him. He grips my hip in one hand

and the sheets in another as he leans forward, thrusting hard until he groans with his own release. After, he leans down, brushing kisses against my mouth, closed eyelids, and brow, his sweat-covered chest pressed against mine, our ragged breathing leveling out to match one another's.

Delphine curls at my side softly chuckling as she runs her fingers through my loose hair and caresses my skin. Lennox reverently kisses my lips once more before peeling himself off of me and standing. A shiver runs up my spine without his warmth, pebbling my skin, and I pull one of the loose blankets over me, watching him walk to the bathing chamber. It's easy to admire the man I love, the muscles of his broad shoulders and back flexing under a glistening sheen of sweat as he straightens and strides away from the bed. But the scars on his upper body mar the tan flesh with lighter streaks, drawing the eye to the marks of brutality instead of his beauty.

Delphine presses a chaste kiss on my mouth before rising from the soft mattress to gather her clothing as well. She slips the robe over her body and straightens her skirts over her scarred legs, then brushes her wild curls off her brow to gather in a knot at her nape. "Well, this was all very unexpected," she whispers with a wry smile and a wink before she traipses toward the door. "Goodnight, Andromeda."

"Goodnight," I whisper, watching her from where I still lay on the bed.

Glancing over her shoulder, she chuckles once more, calling to the bathing chamber, "Goodnight, William!"

"'Night, Del," Lennox's deep voice rumbles from the bathing chamber as Delphine slips out the door.

I should still be relaxed and sated after our encounter, but instead, the sight of the scars on both of them dims the lingering pleasure. Anger bubbles in my chest at the reminders of the pain they have both endured at the whim of those who serve the King. While the shared passion served its purpose, distracting me from my worry for Erik, Siobhan, and Lyra, my thoughts drift back to somber emotions once more.

Standing from the bed, I grab my cloak from where it lays across our trunk, wrapping it around my bare body. I open the shutters, then the tall glass doors to access the wrought iron balcony, ignoring the chill of the metal under my feet and the sound of people in the street as I step into the bright white radiance of the full moon overhead. Holding the dark wool around me to ward off the breeze, I stare up at the moon to say a silent prayer to the Goddess, willing all of the energy the three of us shared into my appeal.

I want revenge for what has been done to Lennox.

To me.

To all of us.

# CHAPTER 27

Eight days pass, the full moon fading to its last quarter. Each day is the same: lessons with Salome and Delphine, dinner with Lennox, and a neverending worry that eats at me when I wonder when, or if, Erik will return with news of Delosia. The fact that they might have to wait out the season on the island, or that they might be lost at sea in a storm without any way to let us know, is something I refuse to entertain.

Although I was concerned things might feel strained or uncomfortable between Delphine and me after the night of the full moon, I'm relieved to find that it's actually the opposite. She no longer overtly flirts with me, as if her curiosity is sated or a conquest is complete. It's almost as if being together that night has popped the bubble of tension that seemed to surround us, and, although she still teases me, her moods seem more even and her sharp edges smoother.

Celeste has continued to be more sociable, joining us in the evenings for dinner, or going with Lennox when he runs errands in town. But nothing brightens her face and quickens her steps like leaving to check in with Lili and the baby. Lennox insisted that either he or Pike chaperone her visits to the Midnight Magnolia, an order I wholeheartedly agree with. It makes me happy to know someone is taking care of the girls who live there, even if it isn't me directly.

As I sip tea with the other two priestesses one early afternoon, the front door slams. While the sound is not unusual, the laughter and the noisy bustle of people coming from the salon that follows is; it's far too early in the day for there to be customers, and most of the employees sleep late into the day. The three of us look at each other in confusion before Salome leads us from her office.

Joy spreads through me when I recognize the high-pitched voice mixing with Celeste's laughter. "Lyra!" I gasp. In my excitement, I forget all propriety and hurry past Salome, dashing down the hallway to the salon.

Bursting into the bright space, a cheerful scene of reunion awaits — Lyra clings to her mother in a tight embrace. She and Celeste smile broadly with happy tears trailing down their cheeks, while Lennox stands to the side wearing a relieved expression. Erik waits only a few steps past him, a slight tilt to his lips while he watches mother and daughter. Pressed to his side, copper waves flowing loose down her shoulders and back, stands Siobhan. She looks less certain about the surroundings than Lyra. Her blue gaze flickers over the decadent decor, drifting up the stairs, and back, like a cornered hare seeking escape. Her fingers nervously toy with the gold torc that circles her throat, a smaller version of the one Erik wears. But when our eyes meet across the room, she lights up with a grin in greeting.

"Siobhan! Lyra!" I exclaim, skirting around the bar and hurrying to them, pulling each into an embrace. I scan each of them and look over at Erik, noticing that he has several healing bruises and scrapes on his face and neck, as I ask, "Are you well?"

"We are now, Sister," Siobhan answers quietly, grasping Erik's large hand again when I release her from my arms. Her eyes are wary as she observes Delphine and Salome in the background where they wait, allowing us space for our greetings.

"Ladies, welcome. I'm Madame Salome. This is Delphine. We are delighted to have you here at the Den, safe from your journey." The Madame smiles brightly when she steps forward, and I find myself mirroring her expression. "I'm certain you are weary from your travels, but you are both very welcome — and safe — here. May I offer refreshments while we discuss your ordeal? Or would you prefer to be shown to a room first?"

I'm in awe at Salome's ability to shift her tone and manner depending on the situation. Today she is neither the brash Madame, the seductive siren, nor the gentle creature that explained about my mother. She's a confident hostess, her strength flowing throughout the room to envelop and support the newcomers in their new environment.

Siobhan clutches Erik's arm, but Salome senses her distress, reading my friend correctly. "Captain Varangr is welcome to join us, of course." At that, Siobhan visibly relaxes and nods once looking toward the large man.

"Then let's lay it all out now while it's fresh," Siobhan announces, her light brogue rough in the silence of the room.

Needing no further instruction, Delphine ducks out of the salon, heading toward the kitchen, while Salome instructs us all to follow her into her office. It takes less than ten minutes for Delphine to bring a variety of items from the kitchen to serve to the newcomers. Cold chicken, a loaf of dark bread, dried fruit, cakes, tea, and coffee. Salome places a decanter of brandy in the center of the table in case anyone needs more fortification than the tea provides.

We all take our seats, Siobhan sitting between Erik and me on the couch, while Lyra and Celeste take the two armchairs. Salome has pulled her chair in front of her desk to join us, while Lennox and Delphine recline in extra wooden chairs pulled from one of the tables in the main salon. The room feels cramped, but having all of these women near me makes my skin tingle — the air feels charged with power.

Siobhan nibbles at the bread and fruit, sipping on tea laced with brandy, while Lyra delights in the sweets and the novel taste of the coffee with milk I've come to enjoy so much. The room is silent except for the sounds of dishes while the women quietly sate their appetite, the rest of us offering a reprieve before they begin talking.

Once they seem settled, Salome turns to Lyra. "Now my dear, it is evident from Captain Varangr's visage and Siobhan's behavior that this was not a simple retrieval." Her eyes dance over my nervous friend at my side, then back to Lyra. "Can one of you tell us what happened?"

Siobhan and Lyra look at one another, then at Erik briefly. "Grandmama heard word from the captain of the *Island Queen* that the King's Navy was on the move and appeared to be heading toward the island. It was Captain Morel — you know him, Uncle?" Lyra pauses and looks toward Lennox.

"I do. Morel frequently trades with Delosia. His family is from there if I'm not mistaken," he responds.

"Yes. Grandmama heard similar reports from other merchants. Captain Trevino stopped on Delosia again to resupply before embarking for the winter season specifically to tell her that the King's ships were getting closer," she continues, sipping from her coffee. "Morel stayed on the island with his men and helped her rally the militia before the first ship showed up. She said it was just a precaution, but I could tell she was worried, and that she didn't think it was just a rumor that they were heading for us.

"It was shortly after you departed that the first ship showed in the harbor with Blackwell's flag raised. A few soldiers came ashore and acted as if they were just there to trade and refresh supplies, but it made the entire island uneasy. People were reserved, no one laughed, and everyone was wary of them. Grandmama had already warned Siobhan of what to do if they did come, to lock up and stay inside and out of their sight." Lyra's hazel eyes cut to Siobhan and I feel her body tense next to me. I gently place my hand on her knee to calm her, but like a nervous horse, she quivers under my touch.

"Soon, another ship showed up with more men. Then

another. They rented rooms around the island and seemed to be everywhere. No one spoke freely anymore, even though the King doesn't rule Delosia. Grandmama met with their captain and answered his questions — he was looking for a dark-haired priestess that was rumored to be fleeing Selennia on the *Bartered Soul*. Had anyone seen her?"

I swallow at the description. I knew the reason they were there but still wonder what prompted them to start tracking me now.

"Of course, Grandmama said no, that she had only met with the other leaders of the Republic recently for a regular gathering; no one of interest. Their captain also asked about the apothecary in town, saying he had heard she was a priestess, and that strange magic had been happening on the island." Her eyes flick to Siobhan once more, and I study my friend, noticing how white her knuckles are as she grips her cup. "Grandmama told him she didn't know what he spoke of. The apothecary was simply a peaceful refugee woman who grew vegetables and herbs. They didn't believe her though and decided they needed to *investigate further*." Lyra's gentle eyes turn flinty and her young face hardens at the memory. With her tight, dark curls worn unbound around her face, she looks like a vengeful angel instead of the naive young woman who departed Selennia with me.

Siobhan takes a deep breath, steadying herself, then begins her portion of the tale as Erik runs a soothing hand over her back. "They came to my door a week after they arrived on the island, visiting each day. I kept the shop closed the whole time, feigning illness. My neighbors protected me, tended the garden, brought me supplies, and took orders to other islanders who couldn't wait out the King's Navy. Lyra visited, pretending to check on my health. But they wouldn't leave, wouldn't believe I was ill. They finally broke the locks and came in." Her eyes drop, hands shaking as she reaches to put the cup back on the table in front of her.

"They destroyed it all — the shop, my home, everything. Looking for evidence that I was still following the Old Ways. To prove that I was a witch, harboring demons, communing with their Devil. They saw my sigil and insisted that I was practicing illegally, as if their legality had any bearing on Delosian soil in the first place."

Siobhan grimaces as anger fills her voice. "They captured me, and planned to take me back to the ship for questioning," she pauses, looking up at Erik before a cruel smile, so at odds with her normally soft demeanor, spreads across her pretty mouth. "But Erik met us on the shore."

Erik's lips quirk up as he looks down at Siobhan, his adoration for her plain across his handsome face. "When we arrived, Morel's ship was hidden in the secret harbor," he explains, looking at Lennox who nods in understanding.

"We approached and found Morel and his men readying their guns and cannons for a battle. He explained that the militia was waiting on the island for their cue. The Crown's sailors had almost all ventured from their ships onto the island, looking for a dark-haired priestess. I knew if they were seeking women of the Goddess that they would find their way to the apothecary, and I worried we would be too late." He stops, resting his hand on Siobhan's knee, running his fingers over her skirts. "Morel explained that no one had been arrested yet, but that Blackwell's men were throwing their weight around like they ruled the island, and the islanders and captains weren't going to let that stand. So, I agreed to fight with them. I prepared a small crew to scout the situation, and we worked our way onto the beach, ready to give the signal to the waiting forces. When I arrived, I found them hauling Siobhan to a boat to take to the ships. I couldn't let that happen."

Erik's hand shifts from Siobhan's leg to her hand, squeezing it. He reaches up to gently touch her cheek with his other palm, the sweet gesture so at odds with the violence his tale promises. The memory of him swinging his axe against the crew of the *Archangel* on our way across the sea flickers in my brain. Imagining the hulking man doing so again sends a chill down my spine.

"When we landed our boat, the men and I attacked the soldiers on the beach. I was able to get the signal out to Morel and his men, and the militia took care of the rest of the curs plaguing the island. I got Siobhan away, and took her to Lyra and Marie to wait it out." His eyes swing to Lennox, and a cocky arrogance glitters in his eyes. "You and Morel now each have another ship to your name, Captain." Lennox's brows raise at the proclamation, but he smiles at the Northman. "I left it with the shipwright on Delosia until you can return and take control."

"I had to come with Erik. Even if the men hadn't arrived and destroyed my shop, I can't bear to be without him any longer," Siobhan interjects, her eyes swinging to me. "When I saw you leave with Lennox, I realized that perhaps Erik and I *could* have a life together. Not just bits and pieces of one." She smiles up at Erik, a pretty flush on her cheeks. "And, once he explained that Blackwell was looking for you, I needed to see you again. To help you however I could."

"And I was ready to see Mama," Lyra chimes in, smiling at Celeste. "When Erik told me you were here now, I had to come see you." Lyra shifts to focus on me before continuing, "And to help you too, Andromeda. Grandmama wanted me to remind you of what she said when you left. You have her full support. The island will follow her lead should you need them."

A look of understanding passes between Lennox and me. Everyone in this room is at risk because of my identity, but they will all shoulder that burden to protect me. With everyone's eyes on me, pressure sinks in to have all of the answers, but I am unsure what the proper next steps are.

Do we flee? We could move inland from New Aphros easily, even though settlements are few and far between. Disappearing into the new continent is appealing, I could shed my true identity for good and start over with Lennox. But then, would that be fair to everyone I leave in my wake? And these men are sailors, dependent on the sea for their way of life. Even if we follow that route temporarily, it can't be forever. I don't even know if it's a sacrifice I could ask of Lennox, let alone his crew.

Or do I face the future Marie's words hint at? One where I claim my birthright and fight back against Blackwell to reclaim Selennia for my own, and for those who sail with me? Although my desire for revenge is strong, fear slicks my skin at the thought of making that declaration and taking a formal stand. I have no idea how to lead an army, even if it is a rough group of pirates. This is a decision I've been avoiding, but with each passing day, it becomes clear I won't be able to circumvent it much longer.

Only two weeks remain between now and the Winter Solstice. I know no one will willingly travel the open ocean until after that date, so I have that time to make my decision. But in the meantime, my focus shifts back to the priestess at my side. I won't allow Siobhan to be left defenseless again, but noticing the way her hands still tremble in her lap, I decide to wait to bring up the idea of training alongside me until she's had time to settle in.

"Once again, you are both very welcome and safe here," Salome states after the conversation dwindles. "I can make up two additional rooms for you that I think will be comfortable. Lyra, yours will be near your mother. Captain Varangr, will you be staying with Siobhan?"

Erik looks mildly abashed at the question and glances down at Siobhan for an answer, allowing her to make the decision. She blushes, her cheeks reddening to make her freckles stand out boldly, but her eyes don't falter as she nods eagerly.

Lennox scoffs quietly, "As if they haven't shared more than a room before now."

Ignoring his jest, Salome stands, clapping her hands together. "Wonderful. Then I will make sure one of the large suites is made ready for you. How lovely to have so many talented women in this house together." She smiles at me and Siobhan, then steps aside with Delphine to go over tasks to prepare the spaces.

"Ladies, if you will excuse us, Erik and I need to have a word," Lennox says, rising from his hard-backed chair. He bows slightly to us in goodbye and turns toward the door. Erik kisses Siobhan's cheek before walking toward the door behind Lennox, leaving Celeste, Lyra, Siobhan, and myself quietly seated around the table of half-eaten food and drink.

# CHAPTER 28
## LENNOX

"We need to bring Pike up to speed. Do you want to call in any other crewmembers?" I ask Erik as we walk down the hallway away from Salome's office. Pike, once the boatswain on the *Bartered Soul*, has stepped in as quartermaster for me now that Erik captains *Andromeda's Vengeance.* I usually seek the older man's wisdom, and I'm certain he will appreciate an update on the situation in Delosia now that Erik has returned. He has friends in the militia there and, even though he hasn't said anything to me, I know he worries about Marie, too.

"No one else, yet. Let's see what Pike thinks first," Erik replies as he turns his head once more to look toward the door we retreat from.

"Erik, she'll be safe. I wouldn't leave Nerissa here if it wasn't secure."

I'm all too familiar with the sense of dread and worry that no doubt eats at him, but Salome is powerful, both due to her innate power to manipulate the elements and the *glow*, as well as her standing as a business owner in the

Entertainment District. With Del and Nerissa at her side, she should almost be unstoppable should they combine their powers in defense.

Escaping the sumptuous confines of the Den, Erik and I stride down the cobbled street to the modest boarding house where Pike has taken up winter residence. The older man has never been extravagant with his spending, always choosing the same location for its low rates and sense of anonymity. The idea of sleeping on the hard cot they provide and listening to the arguments of the other tenants through the walls has never been something I would entertain, but Pike never selects any other location, no matter the amount of coin he might have in his pocket when we dock in New Aphros.

The shabby two-story brick and weatherboard building is on the far end of the Entertainment District, where it borders the edge of the working-class residential portion of the city. The doors to the courtyard are flung open, and boarders sit at tables dotting the open-air space used for drinking and dining, all enjoying the cool air and flowing ale. Pike lounges at one of the tables with several members of the crew, both men and women, from the *Bartered Soul*, sipping a cup of coffee, and joking with his companions. Many other residents are already in their cups, but Pike seems to have kept his head clear, noting our presence immediately as we step through the entry — not that it's difficult to miss a six-and-a-half-foot tall Northman on the streets of New Aphros.

"Captain! Erik!" the others at the table greet me with dips of their head and glasses raised as we approach.

"Erik! Good to see you're back in the city!" Hadley

greets, returning to the table with a fresh ale. Her long hair is hidden under a cap and she's once again dressed in her breeches and tunic instead of the dress we saw her in last. She pats the big man on the shoulder once before retaking the vacant seat next to Pike.

Pike nods to me in greeting, the watery sunlight glinting off his gold nose ring and the hoops that line his ear as he turns to Erik. "Varangr, you've made it back. Mostly in one piece it seems. What happened?"

"We need to speak with you, Pike. Is it safe to use your room, or should we go back to the ship?" I ask, looking around at the other patrons in the courtyard. Surprisingly, none of them have paid much attention to us, but I can't be certain if it's because they fear our attention or if they are genuinely wrapped up in their own affairs.

"How serious is the conversation?" Pike asks, his brow furrowing under his brick-red headscarf. His dark brown eyes, so close in color to his lightly lined face, study my expression as he stands from the table, leaving our other crew to their ale.

"Serious enough to come down here to seek you out," I reply sternly. The older man's full lips thin at my tone, realizing this is no casual visit to celebrate Erik's recent return.

"I know where we can go. Come on," Pike's deep voice rumbles as he turns to head toward the small stable and carriage house behind the courtyard. Erik and I follow the shorter man past the few horses tied outside the stable.

"Going to need your room for a bit, Georgie. No interruptions, aye?" Pike says to the groom, causing him to pause with the brush hovering over a bay's wither.

"No problem, Mister Pike. No one will enter until you

come back through." The groom gives a curt nod before returning to his task. Erik and I exchange a curious glance, narrowing our eyes at Pike, but continue through the entry and up to the coachman's quarters behind our older friend, our boots rattling the wooden steps underfoot as we climb.

"Mister Pike, is it?" I quirk a brow as Pike takes a seat at the small dining table in the coachman's quarters. He crosses his thick arms over his equally muscled chest and looks at me in anticipation, rather than answer my jest. There are only two other wooden chairs, one at the table and one in the corner by a small bed, or the bed itself to sit on, so I opt to drag the chair from the corner to join my men at the table before speaking.

"The boy knows how to show proper respect to his elders, unlike *some* men in this room," Pike goads, receiving rolled eyes and vulgar gestures in response from both Erik and me. He chuckles at our reaction, but leans forward, placing his elbows on the small table. "What is it we need to speak about? This is a safe place."

I motion for Erik to recount his story from Delosia. "We made it to the island more quickly than I expected, as if the Goddess was pressing us forward with haste. When we reached the cove and I met with Morel, he told me exactly what Lyra recounted. The beach and town were filled with soldiers, restless after Marie's delays and excuses, and the residents were tired of Delosia being occupied."

Pike listens, his wide mouth tilting down at the edges, and I watch the boatswain's reactions attempting to glean his thoughts while Erik speaks.

"When Tom and I made it up the backside of the dunes, I heard Siobhan. Four of them were dragging her to the boats. I cut through the camp to reach her and end them. The crews followed, and, between us, the cannons, and the militia, none of that portion of Blackwell's fleet will return to Selennia."

The older man focuses his eyes on me when Erik's tale is complete. "But it's only a matter of time until they come here as well, then? Follow us to each port looking for her?"

"It seems likely," I sigh. "It sounds as if someone either told the King's soldiers about our usual haunts, or they made educated assumptions. New Aphros is known for being amicable to pirates and others looking to skirt the law. If I were one of their commanders, I would have already added it to the list of ports to search."

I run my hand through my hair; it has already faded to a light brown and needs to be darkened again if I'm to keep up my false appearance while we remain here. I push that reminder to the back of my mind, but at least the nervous gesture expels some of the tension building in my chest.

"The question now is what do we plan to do about it? That's why we needed to talk."

"Do we have enough men to fight if they come here?" Pike asks, head shifting to the side in thought. "Do you wish to return to Delosia to retrieve the newest ship and rendezvous with Morel?"

"I would wait until the season dies down," Erik interjects. "We were hit by a squall on the way back. It only lasted half a day, but we almost lost some of the crew, and I think Siobhan is still shaken." His eyes meet mine, and I briefly remember the storm we weathered on the trip we made to Delosia after we first rescued Siobhan. The priestess had not handled the storm well then; I can't imagine things have changed.

"If the King's Navy comes here, I don't think it will matter how many *men* we have. I think the women we have with us will add more might to our numbers than the crew could. I just don't know if that's a position we can put them in," I respond.

I know firsthand what power lays in wait in the Den of Sinful Delights, and so does Erik, even if many others only think the power of the Goddess is legend or cheap tricks. We both saw what Salome did on her own years ago when we helped rescue Delphine, and have witnessed her fury during a few small scraps throughout the years when reason or threats failed to deter bad behavior from unruly patrons or enemies. Controlling flames and dealing death with a wave of her hand has kept her and her girls safe for years now. I know, too, that Delphine can slip through shadows, her gifts have made her a valuable asset as a spy for all these years, even if she rarely demonstrates her abilities for an audience.

Since Nerissa's lessons have progressed, she's shown me her mastery of the elements, even if she still hasn't learned to use the *glow* itself as a weapon. I can't imagine what it would look like if Salome combined with Nerissa, Delphine, and now Siobhan to challenge the soldiers with their might.

"Will your woman run?" Erik asks under his breath.

"I don't know," I admit uneasily.

Once Lyra and Siobhan are settled, I need to speak with Nerissa about the new information Erik brought back, to find out what our next steps will be so we can all prepare.

"Will *you* run with her if she does?" Pike adds, drawing a harsh glance from me.

"Have I *ever* abandoned my men, Pike? Have I *ever* betrayed my crew?" Anger flares at the insinuation that I would leave them without a captain.

"No. But you've also never had a lover to protect." Pike's gaze turns to Erik, and the Northman crosses his arms over his chest, expression clearing of all emotion under the scrutiny. "Neither have you, Erik. Not really. I know what that does to a man, and I know you're both going to be more focused on keeping them safe than on keeping your wits." He shrugs, and as much as I want to deny his words, I can't. "That's why we tell the crew to not get involved with one another, why we don't want them to bring their partners on the ships, even if the separation is painful. It makes you unfocused and influences your decisions. It's what happened to Charlie."

I hold in a hiss at the cruel words Pike ends on; the memory of Charlie cut down aboard the *Archangel* is like a knife to my heart, but I consider his words.

Was Lyra the distraction that caused Charlie's death?

I shake my head at the silent conversation in my head, refusing to lay that blame at my niece's feet. If anything, it was *my* mistake for missing the weapons the sailors had stored away. Another piece of guilt I harbor along with all the rest.

Before I can say anything, Pike whispers in a softer tone, "It's what happened to Henri."

My irritation fades as I take in the pained expression Pike wears, speaking from his own experiences. His own heartbreak. Henri, Marie's twin brother, sailed with him before we ever joined the same crew. Marie told me once that Henri was mortally wounded during a skirmish, defending Pike from an enemy's blade.

Erik drops his gaze from the older man, clenching his jaw. "He's right." My head snaps to him, shocked to hear what sounds like shame in his voice. "It happened on the beach. I completely forgot the orders I gave the men when I saw Siobhan in harm's way. I charged into battle without them, without a second thought."

"But you fought, and you won. You used that feeling to your advantage and saved Siobhan at the same time," I counter. "Plus, aren't we all in agreement that Blackwell's reign has to end? Even if he wasn't looking for us, for *her*, are we going to spend the rest of our days battling his men, his laws? Are we never going to return home, or sail in peace?"

"I don't think peace is in the cards for any of us anymore, Billy," Pike sighs. His eyes droop as he glances at me, and, for the first time, I'm forced to acknowledge his age. He sailed for years before he ever met me, and the time seems to finally be catching up with him. While he's always been cautious, he's never been one to run from a fight, yet today he seems more distressed at the proposal than usual.

"We ask the crews. Take a vote, like always. Let me talk to Nerissa first, to find out what she wants to do, but I think it's time she lets them know who she really is. If they agree that she's the rightful queen, that they're loyal to the both of us and want to stand against Blackwell if he comes for her, then we do it. If anyone is opposed, they can take any wages I owe them and leave."

"I agree," Erik nods, dropping his hands back down to

his sides. "I will ask the crew of the *Vengeance* the same. Even if they say no, I will stand beside you."

We both look to Pike, seeking his wisdom and confidence in our choices as we've done so many times before, even though we both outrank him by vote. Always the voice of reason, Pike has been the steady calm to keep us all on an even keel. He bows his head slightly, resigned to our decision before looking us both in the eyes with a resolute stare.

"All right, then," Pike says after a moment, pushing back from the table. "No one should come or go for a long voyage between now and Solstice. Erik, you're lucky you didn't get caught in a more severe storm on your return. So, we have time for you to speak with your woman, Lennox. See if she's ready to claim her title. But, I agree. If the vote passes, we all sail against the bastard." He looks between us and his fatherly smile returns, finally. "I hope your priestesses are ready by then, men. Blackwell won't know what's coming for him."

# CHAPTER 29

L ennox and Erik stay somewhat cloistered during the next few days, discussing plans for the new ship Erik left behind, crew information, inventory, and the other details that pertain to whatever voyage awaits us in the spring. I remain preoccupied with trying to welcome Siobhan to the city and maintain my training without pushing her into joining yet, even though I desperately want her to. On the fourth morning after her arrival, I'm surprised to see her finally emerge, stopping me as I head to Salome's office.

"Andromeda?" Her gentle voice stops me as I walk through the velvet-lined room. My heart warms with excitement at seeing my friend once more. She has her hair bound tightly and is dressed in men's clothing, similar to those I currently wear. Fitted breeches tucked into leather boots and a loose tunic tucked in at the waist accentuate her slim curves where she stands framed by the velvet-curtained entrance to the salon.

"Good morning, Siobhan!" Excitement bubbles in my

chest, pleased to have someone I consider a true friend with me here in the city. I don't blame her for taking the last several days to rest, recovering from the anxiety of the storm they passed through on their way to New Aphros, but I'm delighted to see her up and about. "Are you feeling better this morning? I see you decided to have some more rugged attire created, too?"

"I'm feeling much better, and yes, I did. I realized when I said goodbye to you on the island that having a shirt and breeches would make work in the garden much easier. So, I sought out the tailor immediately." She smiles warmly at me, and I revel in the sight of her grin. "I thought perhaps I could wear them today while I join you. Most of my dresses are being laundered," she explains, looking around me toward the hallway Salome's office is in, silently questioning if she can come with me for my lesson.

"Of course, I know Salome will welcome you to our lessons. We can show you how to cloak your sigil first, and go from there," I smile, linking my arm with hers as we walk down the hallway. "It's good to have you back, Siobhan."

<hr>

"WELL, YOU ARE A MUCH FASTER LEARNER THAN SHE WAS, that's for sure," Delphine laughs at my expense as she compliments Siobhan's skills.

After only a couple of hours, Siobhan has already been able to fully cloak her sigil and rustle paperwork on Salome's desk with conjured air. Since she is a few years older than I am, Siobhan spent more years in the temple than I did, and her high priestess allowed them to dabble with the elements, although it was treated as a novelty. I'm proud of my friend, but shoot a glare at Delphine, rolling my eyes to hide the sinking feeling in my stomach. Had these things been purposely kept from me? Del simply laughs in response and pours a glass of wine for each of us. She waters it down slightly since it's still early in the day, but the sweet liquid is a welcome refreshment after our practice.

Just like Salome thought, I *am* stronger in Siobhan's presence, comforted by her gentle nature. Her warmth helps me to relax and enables me to ignore Delphine's distractions, even if I know there is no malice behind Delphine's taunts.

"Now that Siobhan has cloaked her sigil, perhaps you can show her around the city, Delphine? I think you and Andromeda could safely take Lyra and Siobhan to some of your favorite haunts," Salome suggests.

"I'd like that," Siobhan chimes in, her cheeks pink with happiness. It's a relief that the troubled look has faded from her eyes, and I hope the ability to cloak her sigil will aid her in feeling more comfortable in her new surroundings.

"Let's meet in an hour in the salon, then we can go," Delphine agrees, brushing stray curls from her eyes. For once, she looks excited instead of inconvenienced.

"I'll look in on Lyra and let her know. See you both in an hour. Good afternoon, Salome," I dip my head slightly in respect to the older woman, then let myself out of the office while Siobhan and Delphine chat about the city.

Lyra's room stands next to Celeste's, closer to the stairs than my own. I tap lightly on the door but receive no answer, after a second try without a response, I determine she's left her quarters. Thinking she might be with her mother, I move to Celeste's door next and hear hushed voices behind the wood. It sounds like a heated discussion between mother and daughter, and I hesitate to knock, but take a breath and rap my knuckles against the surface once more. The voices stop abruptly as quick footsteps click closer until the door swings open. Celeste stands at the door in a dressing gown, while Lyra is seated on the settee at the end of the bed, her tawny cheeks pink with fury.

"Sorry to interrupt." My eyes dart between mother and daughter, tension radiating out into the hall. "But Delphine is taking Siobhan and me into the city later. She wanted to know if Lyra would like to come with us."

Celeste's lips tighten, and she straightens, meeting my eyes with no sign of the uncertainty she's shown in the past few weeks. The traces of her former identity from the House of Starlight seem to have knitted back together since Lyra's return, and she answers, "I don't thi—"

"I would like that very much," Lyra interrupts. "Thank you, Andromeda," she says before her mother can finish her statement.

"We'll meet in the salon in an hour," I instruct, turning on my heel and scurrying to my room before Celeste can protest. Celeste may be the girl's mother, but it's clear that Lyra is not the same young woman who left the shore in Selennia. She's spent too much time with Marie to quietly follow her mother's overprotective rules any longer. I struggle to fight the smile that tugs at my lips at the change, even as I hope it hasn't made her reckless — pride and worry both flaring in response to her boldness.

Lennox is still out with Erik, so I quietly tidy my hair and wash my face before changing into one of my simple dresses edged in decorative embroidery for our trip into the city. I haven't tried any of the more structured ensembles the women of New Aphros seem to favor, preferring my comfortable body skimming wools to the tight waists and bust-enhancing silks Salome wears. I don't wish to draw attention to our group by wearing my masculine attire, even if the ease of movement it offers would make me feel more secure. I make sure I discreetly attach my dagger so it will remain hidden, but within reach, under my cloak. Since I still have time to spare, I sit in one of the soft chairs and pick up one of Lennox's books to pass the time. Here in the city, with fewer tasks weighing on him, I notice he has been lost in novels more often, at least before we knew for certain Blackwell's soldiers were on the move. The thought of his daydreaming warms my heart as I relax into the seat and start reading.

***

My three companions already wait in the salon when I descend the mahogany steps. Each is a beauty in her own right, even if they are all vastly different in demeanor — Delphine radiates cold ferocity, Lyra is a beam of warm sunlight, and Siobhan is a gentle flame. They are each attired in fine simple dresses suitable for daytime in the city, ready to blend in with the ladies who stroll the avenues.

Lyra makes her way toward the red front doors, but halts when Delphine announces, "Out the back, ladies!" Turning toward the salon and hallway beyond, Delphine gestures for us to follow. "There are still people in the streets, even at this early hour. We don't want anyone thinking we are for sale." Delphine casually smirks, holding the curtain back for us to pass through. Siobhan shudders at the statement, but I smile and grip her hand in comfort as we hastily depart into the streets from the rear exit of the Den of Sinful Delights.

We begin by visiting the market near the riverfront — Delphine introduces us to a confectioner she has befriended who shares a delectable treat of caramel and pecans that is unlike anything I've tasted before, melting on my tongue with sugary joy. Afterward, we stroll down the riverfront while Delphine points out sailors she knows from merchant and pirate vessels alike, waving at a few as she tells stories about the riverboat men that she considers friends.

"How are you on a first-name basis with so many of the rivermen?" I question, remembering the leers of the rough sailors who greeted us on the muddy shores of the gulf. They seem to be the antithesis of the wealthy merchants and businessmen who frequent Salome's salon.

"Haven't you figured out that secrets are a commodity that can't be valued? No one pays attention to servants, whether they be rivermen, whores, or bartenders. We always know the latest gossip before anyone else." I'm impressed by her shrewd street smarts, even though I know she had to learn them to survive. "I run most of Salome's errands, the men know that Salome will pay a bit more for goods if they come with a bonus of hidden knowledge or juicy rumors. In exchange, she gets the first choice of new shipments. Plus, the men get to spend time with me and my sparkling personality," Del explains without prompting, winking at her final words as she preens.

When I cut my eyes at her she shakes her head. "No, never like that. Salome doesn't make me sell myself unless I choose the partner." I understand. The arrangement was similar between Celeste and me, although I never knew the inside workings of Celeste's House or mind like Delphine does with Salome. A tendril of regret curls in my mind as I wonder what things might have been like if I had been more open with Celeste sooner, could we have had a sisterly relationship? Would Lennox and I have shared happy years together? But the past can't be changed. It has forged us all, bringing us to this city, this moment, for a reason, even if I don't know what that reason might be.

"I also *might* do a little blending in to gather my information from time to time, it's funny what people will do when they don't think anyone's watching," Del whispers, chuckling to herself without explanation before peeling away from my side to walk with Lyra.

Lyra seems delighted with the bright and lively city, inspecting each building she passes and dancing freely to the music that is just beginning to drift from the open windows and doors of various taverns and dance halls. Her tight curls bob each time she pivots her head to look at another storefront or street vendor.

Several times I catch Delphine's eyes cast in the younger woman's direction. There is no hint of the usual storm behind the grey shade though, only thoughtfulness and intrigue. The corners of Del's full pout edge upwards in genuine amusement as if Lyra's glee infects even her, and for the first time, her youth is obvious; even though she's lived a harsher life, she is only a few years older than Lennox's niece. She tilts closer to Lyra, her pale curls a stark contrast to Lyra's dark ones as she whispers and points out something as we walk. I smile to myself and store the happy sight away to share with Lennox later. Could it be that Lyra, our beam of sunshine, might burn through Delphine's cloudy disposition?

Shifting my focus to Siobhan, I'm pleased to see her enjoy herself as well. While she's more reserved, as is her way, the tension seems to have flowed out of her as she observes the various people moving through the cobblestone streets with curiosity, her blue eyes raking over each person and new sight we pass.

"Siobhan," I say, walking next to her while Delphine and Lyra lead us through the streets. "How are you really feeling now that you're here?"

She smiles at me before focusing back on the direction we stroll. "I'm well. Now that I had some time to rest, have been able to spend time with all of you, and finally feel my *glow* again, I can tell things will only get better. It's been so long since I even dreamed of being able to actually *be* with Erik for more than a week or two, or to be with my sister priestesses again; I keep thinking it's all going to get pulled away from me. Like I've been in a dream the last few weeks, and I'll wake up to find I'm alone again."

"It's not a dream, Siobhan." I link my arm through hers, pulling her in close so she can feel my physical presence and not just my words. "But I understand. This all seems so surreal. I'm so glad you came back with him."

"I've..." Siobhan starts, biting her lip as if she's searching for the right words. "I've been having visions again. Far more frequently since you came to Delosia as if you awakened my true abilities again after the ceremony. It brings me joy to see you doing so well, to see such joy in you and Lennox. I've thought of you often."

"I've thought of you too, Siobhan." I squeeze her hand once more in comfort. "Have the visions shown you anything new?" I ask, thinking of the one she told me about in her garden, but not sure if I truly wish to know if they hold dark omens. Her mysterious dream of blood, a dagger, and a crown frequently tease my mind, if even I can't comprehend the meaning or whether the vision reflects the future or my past.

"Not that I can tell just yet. It's just…Well, *something* is coming."

Before I can pry further, Lyra falls back to join us, standing on my other side and clasping my hand in hers.

"I'm so happy we are all together!" the younger woman exclaims, a cheerful grin gracing her full lips. "This city is fantastic!"

Lyra's joy is contagious, and I find myself relaxing along with her and Siobhan as we follow Delphine through the Merchant District to window shop and view the latest goods for sale.

---

As the afternoon wanes, Delphine pulls us into one of the taverns, the Gilded Rooster, a few streets away from the Den. Siobhan and I both still as we take in the surroundings. While the room is elegant and comfortable, with polished wood tables and a mercury glass mirror spanning the back wall behind the bar, it's completely occupied by male patrons. No other women are to be found in any portion of the space, and Siobhan grabs my hand in the entry, gripping it tightly.

Delphine already drags Lyra through the room, holding her hand as she smiles and flirts with the men she brushes against. Unease grips me as I stare out at the room with no way for me to stop Delphine or get her attention without shouting. Setting my jaw, I pull Siobhan along behind me, mildly surprised as the men standing in our way politely step from our path without a word. No one touches or speaks to us as we follow Delphine to the highly polished bar in the back of the room.

"Delphine, what are we doing here?" I hiss at Del, who is smiling openly at the handsomely bearded blond bartender with an elaborately styled mustache. He seems strangely familiar, but I can't quite place him as I glare at her.

"What's the matter?" she replies with irritation coloring her words, looking at me sharply. Her brow creases momentarily before she really looks at me and then at Siobhan, noting the fear on my friend's face.

"Oh!" she says, her eyes widening and brows raising. "You don't have to worry about the men here. They don't like women if you understand my meaning. Not *that* way, at least. We're safe within these walls. And Johnny here makes the best rum punch in the city."

She smiles indulgently at the man behind the counter who dips dark red liquid from a crock behind the bar. He smiles back at Delphine, revealing a silver tooth in the lantern light, his brown eyes crinkling with merriment, as

328

he hands each of us a mug of the punch. The drink is sweet and strong with a slight spice to it and reminds me instantly of tropical Delosia. Taking another sip, I allow myself to relax again.

Delphine draws us to an empty table, and it surprises me to see how at ease and friendly she is in this space. She knows several of the patrons by name, laughing and cracking jokes across the tables with them as we sip our drinks. Lyra cuts her eyes to watch Delphine glowing in the candlelight, and it lightens my heart to see Lyra smile and blush at Del's words. I hope this means her heart has healed a bit after losing Charlie on the voyage from Selennia.

"Delphine, why do I feel like I recognize the bartender? Johnny, you said?" I question, taking another drink of the spiced punch.

"He frequently stops in at the Den. I'm sure you've seen him in the salon," she replies casually.

"For what purpose?" I ask, slightly confused if he runs his own establishment and doesn't seek to bed women. Then it hits me; he's the man I saw Delphine fawning over and pulling into the hallway the first night we dined in the salon. "Are you and he…?" I question, trailing off with a raised brow.

Delphine barks a laugh, but lowers her voice to a whisper, "We all have secrets to share in this town, they're as good a currency as coin. Johnny is a purveyor of them as much as I am, and we occasionally share them in private to throw curious patrons off. He always has excellent insight into some of the crews that dock."

Siobhan has relaxed into the booth, inspecting the other patrons while she sips her drink. Lyra stays close to

Delphine but laughs and chats with Siobhan and me as easily as she always has, seemingly unfazed in nearly all situations.

After a refill of our drinks, the four of us chat quietly at our table. Delphine details the various districts of the city. She has lived in New Aphros for several years now and, despite the horrific experience she faced with the priests, loves it here.

"It's like nowhere else I've ever been. Not that I've been to a lot of places, mind you, but it's most certainly home," she explains, contentment evident in her words. She sips her drink as she speaks, tipping the cup to empty it. When she stands to get another, I stop her.

"I hate to end this fun, but it's getting late. Should we be out alone after dark?" I ask. I hate feeling like I can't walk alone at night, but unfortunately, I know what happens in port cities in the dark. Knowing Delphine could hide us, and that I have my dagger close at hand, still doesn't make me willing to risk unwanted attention from men who have spent their afternoon drinking, especially on the edge of the Entertainment District so close to the Houses.

"You're right. Salome will expect me in the salon tonight," Delphine agrees, glancing toward the door to judge the fading daylight. "Let me tip Johnny while you finish your drinks."

I'm still shocked at her easy nature here, so different from the sharp-tongued, haughty woman I'm used to. Siobhan and Lyra finish their drinks, both a bit more tipsy than Del and me, while I leave mine partially full. I want to be alert on the walk back more than I want to savor the last of the delicious drink. When Delphine returns, we make our way back to the front of the Gilded Rooster, waving our goodbye to Johnny as we step through the door.

Twilight has settled over the city and the true noise of the nightlife has begun. Horns and fiddles play lively songs, punctuated by the beat of drums and the laughter and cheers of people enjoying themselves. The celebratory atmosphere is so ingrained into New Aphros that it seems like it bleeds from the very bricks and cobbles that surround us. As if each open door or window we pass calls with its own language, beckoning visitors and permanent residents alike to sample its unique flavor.

As we walk the few blocks back toward the Den, my skin tingles with apprehension when I notice a dark figure in my periphery. They stay in the shadows, darting between buildings or beneath awnings, but someone is most assuredly following us. Not wishing to worry Siobhan and Lyra, I mask my unease, my pulse hammering despite my steady breaths. Allowing Delphine to lead the way, I slow my steps so I walk at the rear of our group to better observe the mysterious figure.

Turning the corner to the row of brothels, the person steps into the lantern light. Without waiting, I spin, palming my dagger, and lunge. Pushing them against the brick of the closest building, just inside a darkened alley, I hold the blade to their throat.

Halting at my sudden movement, Siobhan and Lyra stand together clutching each other's arms as Delphine rushes to my side. The light of the lantern from the nearest building is dim, but, this close, I can see the face of a young man.

"What do you want?" I snarl, pressing the sharp metal

firmly to the man's neck. Even though he stands several inches taller than I do, he's slim, almost skeletal under my hands, and his eyes grow wide with fear.

"Andromeda, it's all right," Delphine whispers, her hand settling on my shoulder.

"He was following us," I retort, looking down at his clothing. I note the black robes the man is wearing, a chill slithering down my body. "And he's a priest."

"It's all right. Let him go," Delphine states firmly. I look at her once, still holding the shocked priest by the front of his robe, and she nods to emphasize her insistence. "His name is Daniel — he's a friend."

Releasing the young man, I step back while Delphine approaches him. "What is it Danny?" she asks carefully as if she's approaching a wounded animal. The young man takes several breaths before reaching out and hugging Delphine tightly. She returns the embrace just as firmly while the rest of us look on in confusion.

"They're planning something," Daniel whispers roughly. He clears his throat as he steps away from Delphine, farther into the shadows. Del closes her eyes briefly, pulling the darkness closer to shield us. Lyra and Siobhan's startled gasps drift through the shadows as Daniel continues, "I heard them talking while I was serving meals this week. They're planning something against Salome on Winter Solstice."

"What are you talking about?" I whisper, stepping closer to Delphine's side.

"At the cathedral, I serve meals to the priests. I'm not officially one, just a novice, so they don't pay any attention to me."

"Perfect for gathering information." Delphine smiles at me.

"I don't know what they're going to do yet, but I wanted you to warn Salome to be on alert. I have to get back; I'll find you if I get more details, Del." Daniel squeezes Delphine's hand once and then retreats into the street, fading into the bustling crowds heading toward the square.

"We need to get back to see Salome, now," Delphine says, watching the young man disappear into the crowd along the main thoroughfare, all sense of merriment from our time in the city vanishing with the wisps of her shadows.

She and I rejoin Lyra and Siobhan to dart down the sidewalk back to the Den, the sobering warning from Daniel echoing in our ears and hastening our steps.

# CHAPTER 30
## LENNOX

"Have you spoken with her about it yet?" Erik asks as we stroll from the docks toward the Entertainment District.

Sighing, I frown and look up at the taller man as we walk. "No. Not yet."

We spent the morning split between the *Bartered Soul* and *Andromeda's Vengeance* with Pike, Tom, and several other crewmembers reviewing recently completed repairs. Satisfied with the progress, the two of us left Pike with the crew to return to the city, trusting him to assign any remaining duties as he deems necessary while I address another task.

"What is it you fear she will say? Has she indicated that she wishes to retake her throne, or does she enjoy life at sea?" Erik prods, always catching my true meaning without me ever having to put it into words.

"I... *Fuck*. I don't know, Erik." I grip the back of my neck as if rubbing my nape will dispel the worry that has eaten at me the past weeks. "I don't know if I'm more afraid that she'll say she wants to flee, or that she wants to take a stand against Blackwell. I can't lose her, but my duty to her is at odds with my duty to you and the crew."

The thought that she might leave me, or that she could be captured or killed by Blackwell's soldiers, are both too painful to even consider. Shame burns in my chest at the idea that I would so easily consider abandoning my promise to my crew. But, deep down, I know that if it comes to it I would abandon them for her. Even if honor says I shouldn't. I've spent so much time building this life and reputation, but if I had the opportunity to lead a peaceful one at her side, I wouldn't look back. The only problem is that whatever life she chooses, I suspect it will never be peaceful.

"I've been putting it off since she's been preoccupied with training and helping to get Lyra and Siobhan settled, but I know I have to speak with her about her wishes soon. And about revealing who she is to the rest of the crew. How is Siobhan settling in?" I change the subject, thrusting the focus onto Erik instead as we head toward one of the taverns we frequent in the city.

It's Erik's turn to frown. He replies, "She is… different. More timid, more preoccupied than I have seen her in a very long time. I catch her staring at nothing, unfocused. But when I draw her back, she shakes it off as if there is nothing to worry about. I have not seen her act this way since we first found her."

"Has she mentioned whether it's due to the soldiers?" I ask, worry coloring my quiet words as we walk through the open door to the worn brick and stucco-clad tavern. Siobhan has always been a gentle woman and the thought

336

of her, or any other woman for that matter, being mistreated makes me clench my fists with wrath. As usual, the windows are swung open, allowing light from the street in. The cool, late autumn breeze catches the flames of the oil lamps that dot the walls and the candles on the tables, sending flickering light around the room.

"She said they did not harm her, not really. She had some bruises on her arms from them dragging her, but other than that, they did not abuse her. I am not sure if the fear of them has taken root, or if it is just the storm we passed through," he confides as we approach the bar. "I get the sense that she is having visions again, but she has not shared them with me. I worry for her, but I do not know what else to do to offer comfort."

The elderly owner of the Forgotten Fortune looks us over once, frowning at Erik's tattooed scalp and long hair with gold braided in the strands. Even though we frequent the town and its taverns often enough, some residents are still wary of his appearance. Old prejudices about violent raiders from the north still invoke unease, even if the wild-looking men rarely drift this far south to trade. Some of the older people from Selennia and the continent remember a time when Northmen would attack coastal villages in the night, burning towns and stealing everything they could. But those days are long past, most of the people who live on the Northern Isles now earn their coin by fishing, whaling, or other honest trades. Or, if they don't, their actions are no different from any of the rest of us on the account.

Regardless of his bias, the lure of full pockets silences any comment the old man might think to utter. Biting his tongue, he brings our tankards of ale and waves away our coin. We frequent his establishment enough, and give him a good deal on imported liquors, so a few mugs of cheap ale won't hurt his profits. He knows to keep his opinions to himself. Should he offend me, or my second, we could easily sell his portion of our stores to another tavern, leaving him stuck with inferior quality, yet higher priced, ales and spirits.

I lean my back against the bar as I scan the room. Men from the *Selkie's Tears* gamble in one corner, locals dine quietly in another, but one table is empty without many people surrounding it. I jerk my chin toward it to indicate Erik and I should take a seat there.

"Has she allowed you to...," I trail off once we are settled, raising my eyebrows.

Erik huffs, his blue eyes sparkling as he takes another drink before answering. "Yes, no concerns there. She nearly tore my shirt off as soon as we made it onto the ship leaving Delosia. I am only concerned because she will not tell me what is truly wrong."

"I'll tell Nerissa. Maybe she can coax it out of her. Has Siobhan shown any interest in working with Salome?"

"Yes, she told me when she was getting dressed this morning that she planned on joining them today. She was wearing breeches." Erik laughs heartily. "I almost did not make it to meet you this morning seeing her dressed like that with her curves on display. I blame your woman's influence, but I am not complaining."

"It *is* a pleasing sight, isn't it?" I grin at the memory of the night Nerissa had me on my knees to pull said breeches down. Chuckling, I down the last of my ale and wait for Erik to finish his.

"Now, friend. Are you ready to address our next task?" I ask when he empties his cup. Neither of us is remotely drunk from the single ales, but I have business to tend to at the Midnight Magnolia before we return to the Den.

"Aye, let's go."

———

WHEN WE STEP INTO THE FOYER OF THE DINGY BROTHEL, A few of the ladies who work there scurry out of our path. It's too early for most customers to be entering, so the women are still in their day dresses and shifts. One of the braver ones dips her head as she whispers, "Afternoon, Captain."

She disappears up the stairs as quickly as the others, looking back over her shoulder before entering one of the closed doors. The cry of a baby drifts down from the upstairs quarters, and I assume it must be the one that Salome and Nerissa helped deliver, the one that Celeste has been tending to.

"Where are the stupid—" Rolfe's voice grumbles before it's cut off at the sight of me leaning against the door frame of his establishment with Erik at my side. "Lennox. What are you doing here? I thought you only gave your coin to the bitches at Salome's." Rolfe's eyes flit nervously from me to Erik and back.

"Now, Rolfe. You should know by now that I'm a man of eclectic tastes; I always vary where I seek my amusement. It's just that nothing about your establishment has ever piqued my interest." The man is almost as tall as I am, but with a lanky frame. While he meets my eyes with distaste, I can see the hint of fear behind them as I smirk at him.

"Until now," I trail off, pushing away from the door frame and strolling around the foyer. "No, this will never do. Far too dark and cheap for my taste." I tear down one of the faded black curtains covering the front window, leaving the rod hanging haphazardly where it pulls free from the plaster, while Erik continues to block the entry. Rolfe stiffens but holds his tongue as I do the same to the identical curtain on the other side. "Oh, I'm sorry. I didn't tell you the little rumor I heard." I toss the curtain into the center of the floor, casually dusting my hands together as I cock my head to the side.

"What the fuck are you talking about, Lennox?" Rolfe asks, swallowing and licking his lips. His eyes track my movements as I stalk in a circle around him, casually examining the room.

"*I heard* that you are not the owner of this building. You just rent it and run your business out of it. I *also* heard that the actual owner is a high-ranking member of the Merchant Council." I stop my circling in the middle of the sun-brightened foyer, dust motes drifting around where they puffed from the ancient curtains, and turn to face Rolfe. "Seems like business has been bad with all the priests running around the city and he was looking for a higher return on his investment, or to shed some bad ones altogether. You have fifteen minutes to vacate the building, Rolfe. I own it now. Get the fuck out."

"You can't do that!" Rolfe sputters, red in the face. "Alexandre signed a contract with me allowing me to rent until—"

"Oh, this contract?" I pull the paper from my inside coat pocket, raising my brows in surprise, then hold it over the flame of one of the sconces that line the wall. "Consider it null and void."

"You fucking thief! You can't do this, I'll—" He makes a move to approach me, forgetting himself momentarily.

"Please, continue to tell me what I can't do," I say, my voice as cold as the steel I wear at my hip. My hand moves faster than he can register and my fingers wrap around his skinny neck as I catch him moving toward me. "The signed contract in Jean Alexandre's possession says that I purchased this building, and all other contracts are now void. Your time is waning, so unless you would like to be in the streets with only the clothing on your back, I suggest you pack your shit and get the fuck out of my building." I roughly push him away by the throat and he stumbles back. "The girls will remain here. I shall do as I please with them, and I expect you to stay away from this street from now on."

I pull my cutlass from its sheath and take a step toward Rolfe, herding him backward toward Erik, who now holds the short axe he wears at his lower back.

After a few stumbling steps, Rolfe's back bumps into Erik's chest, and he spins to look up into the Northman's icy blue eyes. In a panic, he stumbles back toward me, then trips over the faded carpet runner as he rushes to what I assume are his quarters. Within ten minutes, he departs the front door, still spitting empty threats as he hustles down the street.

"Ladies!" I call up the stairs. Slowly, doors creak open, feminine faces hovering in the openings as they slowly step into the hall. One girl holds a bundle against her chest, the grizzling of a baby coming from the blanket.

"Please come downstairs. The Midnight Magnolia is under new management."

---

AFTER EXPLAINING THE CHANGE OF OWNERSHIP TO THE WOMEN, I tell them to expect Celeste to visit them in the next few days to set up the new residence. I'll leave it up to her how she wishes to run the building, or if she wants to entrust it to one of the women to manage; whether it becomes a brothel or boarding house depends on the women and their needs now. It will give Celeste somewhere to work, somewhere to find herself again — a place that is truly hers away from the painful past in Selennia.

Erik and I wait until the evening doorman arrives — the girls told me they trust him — and I explain that, for the next few days, his job is to keep the front door locked against Rolfe and any customers until a determination is made about the status of the business. I hand him a gold coin for his trouble, trusting that the women's instincts and the language of money and power will hold him to his word.

Finally, we step into the streets to head back to the Den, ready to find our women to have a quiet evening over drinks and dinner. The sun is only beginning to sink and the sounds of the city envelop us as we walk. Street vendors sell handheld meal options and alcoholic drinks. Music escapes the music halls and entertainment venues as musicians warm up for their evening performances. The scent of the muddy river, fresh fish, and manure from the horse-drawn carriages drift on the cool river breeze, mixing with the spices and seafood being prepared for evening meals. Even though I miss Selennia's snowy mountains and deep forests, New Aphros brings joy to my heart. Seeing people laugh and dance to the jaunty music inside the taverns and spilling out onto the streets outside, makes me want to shed the hard disguise I wear to join them. Tonight, the cloud of uneasiness cast by the priests seems to have thinned, and it almost feels like the city I expected to find when we docked. One I've grown to love like a second home.

"A successful day, I'd say, Erik," I murmur, taking a deep, satisfying breath. He silently nods before he gives me a half smile.

The sweet herbal aroma of Salome's smoke engulfs us when we enter the Den of Sinful Delights. The salon is only just opening, the early evening serving girl stands bored against the bar chatting with the barkeep as we stroll in, while the other girls lounge against the booths in their sheer attire.

"Evening, Captain Lennox. I hear it's Captain Varangr, now, too, is it?" Juliet greets us with a wink and a sultry smile as we pass. She was a handful on our trip from Selennia but is always in high spirits and good for a laugh. I offer her a wink in greeting, but nothing more to draw her to us. Erik acknowledges her with a nod and makes his way through the tables that litter the central space, folding himself into one of the darkened private booths while I approach the bar.

"Good evening, Captain," the blonde girl greets me with a blush as she brushes her fingers down my arm. I almost roll my eyes at her blatant flirting, but I know it's how she earns her coin, so I can't fault her. "What can I help you with today?"

"A bottle of whiskey. The good kind," I reply with a hint of a growl, giving the barkeep a sideways look. He's new, and I won't be drinking anything watered down tonight. "Is the Madame still with Andromeda?"

"Oh, no sir," the girl answers, disappointment clouding her voice at my interest in another woman. "Andromeda and Delphine took the new girls out — the ones Captain Varangr brought in. They've been gone for several hours now, sir."

Her news causes my worry to spike; the last time Del and Nerissa went out in the city they almost got swept up in a mob. Before I can brood for long, the barkeep hands me a bottle of expensive whiskey and two glasses. I dip my head in thanks to both of them and return to Erik, placing one of the glasses in front of him.

"Seems as though the women went on their own adventure today. The serving girl said they're out with Lyra and Delphine. Maybe this is what Siobhan needs to clear her head," I rattle off, popping the cork from the neck of the bottle and pouring a heavy serving into both of our glasses. My words are much lighter than how I feel, masking my emotion to keep Erik from storming out the door to search for them.

The distraction didn't seem to work, though. Erik's dark brows knit together with the news, and I feel the same unease fizzing through me. I remind myself that, no matter how much I desire to keep her safe, Nerissa can hold her own, and that Delphine is well known in these streets.

*They'll be safe*, I try to reassure myself to keep from marching back out the door to find them.

"Do you think Pike is right?" Erik asks after a tense silence, his gaze switching between the door and then the back hallway every few minutes. Customers have begun to trickle in, and I watch the girls work their own brand of magic on the men. His words snatch me from my inspection and draw my eyes to his.

"About?"

"About the women distracting us? Causing us to make poor decisions?"

"I don't give a fuck what Pike thinks about it. Whether he's right or not." The worrying and whiskey have made my tongue sharp, and my true feelings spill out before I can dull them with tact. "He's welcome to stay behind with anyone who doesn't choose to follow me. To follow *her*. I won't hold it against those who wish to stay behind. But if she chooses it, I will sail against that bastard. It's time Blackwell answered for his crimes."

Erik merely grunts in response before saying, "Yes. I believe it is, too." He downs the rest of his whiskey and I follow his lead, pouring us each another, and changing the subject as we both anxiously watch the entrances.

# CHAPTER 31

Delphine, Lyra, Siobhan, and I return to the Den of Sinful Delights through the back entrance, just as we departed. Delphine immediately peels off from our group and heads toward Salome's office to report Daniel's warning. The little I garnered from Del on our walk back has me intrigued to know more about the young man and their seemingly close relationship, but I allow her the time to speak with her boss without prying.

Lyra, Siobhan, and I stroll into the main salon with plans to go to our rooms, but we spy Erik and Lennox tucked into one of the corner booths when we reach the bar. Celeste stands at the edge of the booth, dressed more modestly than the other women in the salon, looking polished and refined. Both men seem to light up when we enter the room, causing Siobhan and me to exchange an amused glance in response.

We approach the booth, trailing through the other tables. The seats are beginning to fill, and the volume in the salon rises with the deep murmurs from men, flirtatious giggles from the ladies, and soft music from the band as they continue warming up in the corner. An almost empty bottle of whiskey rests between Erik and Lennox on the table, and I glance between the two men with my lips quirked in amusement. Neither of them can hide their intoxication as they admire us from the corner of their eyes, dark heads tilted toward one another as if they are hatching a scheme. Celeste smiles at Lyra's return, and they excuse themselves from the group, parting the heavy curtains to enter the foyer and retreat to their rooms, leaving Siobhan and me to our men.

"What happened to the fierce men we know? You two look entirely too tame for notorious pirates," I chide half-heartedly.

"Join us, ladies — let's see how tame we really are." Lennox's eyes sparkle in the light of the candle flame as they settle on me. He sweeps his hand to gesture for us to sit down and I roll my eyes, but both Siobhan and I acquiesce and join the men. Siobhan snuggles up against Erik's side as he wraps a large arm around her slender shoulders, tucking her under his arm protectively. Lennox, on the other hand, pulls me close as I scoot into the booth and slants his lips across mine, a passionately claiming kiss in the dim light of the salon for all to see. I sigh against him and allow my body to loosen under his hands as he kisses me with abandon, despite our company.

When we break apart, my cheeks feel heated as I breathe, "Goodness. Not tame at all, I see." He chuckles and tucks me against his side, toying with a loose strand of my hair that has escaped its pins. His soothing touch distracts me from the unsettling meeting with the young priest, and I decide to wait to share the warning until Lennox is sober and Salome can weigh in. She knows this city and its threats better than I do, and I trust her judgment.

"We thought we would dine together here tonight if that is all right with you two?" he whispers against my hair but directs the question to both Siobhan and me. We both nod in assent and Erik beckons to one of the serving girls to call her over. She soon brings out plates of warm food and, for a brief moment, it almost feels like we are two anonymous couples enjoying a pleasant evening together, not pirates and priestesses dining in the salon of a brothel so far from our homelands.

"How was your trip into the city?" Lennox finally asks.

"Well, it was fine until—" I begin. But, before I can reveal our meeting with Daniel, any illusion of normalcy is dashed as Salome charges from her office in a swirl of burgundy silk to stand at our table.

"We need to talk," she announces, then turns on her heel and strides back to her office, knowing we will all follow without question.

Lennox and Erik sway slightly as they lead the way to Salome's office, the empty bottle of whiskey making itself apparent. Siobhan and I trail behind, cutting our eyes to one another, already knowing the reason for this summons. As we enter the office, the mood is notably somber, Delphine is perched on the edge of one of the armchairs with a glass of brandy in her hand, eyes focused on the liquid as she swirls it. Salome sits behind her desk with a freshly lit cigarette hanging between her fingers. Lennox takes the other armchair and pulls me onto his lap; while Siobhan and Erik exercise more propriety, sitting side by side on the couch.

"Delphine has come to me with news of the priests. They apparently plan on moving against us in some manner on Solstice," Salome states plainly without preamble, taking a drag of her cigarette. Lennox tenses under me and straightens in the chair as her words sink in.

"What are you talking about?" he asks, his arm wrapped protectively around my waist. When I meet his gaze, he cocks his head, brow furrowed as if asking why I did not mention this already.

"Delphine, explain," Salome urges, gesturing with her free hand.

"I have a friend — someone I trust implicitly — who is a servant in the cathedral. He came to us tonight," Delphine begins, pausing to down her brandy before placing the empty glass on the table. "He told me that he heard the priests talking about moving against us at Solstice. That's all he knows so far, but he'll find me again when he can gather more."

"And you are certain you can trust this informant?" Erik asks, all hint of drunkenness erased from his speech.

"With my life. I've trusted him with that and more for many years," Delphine replies. "Daniel traveled here with me from Selennia. He grew up with me in my village and protected me on the voyage here. He ended up being taken in by the priests when we arrived at the river. They pretended it was for his own good, but they wouldn't allow me to join him. When he protested, they refused to let him back out into the streets with me," she recounts. "He's been kept by them for years now, acting as a servant, pretending to believe in their God. Being beaten and starved as *atonement* for his previous belief in the Goddess." Delphine's eyes turn cold and dark as she explains her relationship with the young man I held at the point of my dagger, any glimpse of joy and youth she showed earlier erased by her memories.

"The boy's information has always been good in the past," Salome interjects, lending credence to Delphine's words. "The only reason he wasn't the one to tell me about Delphine being strapped to the pyre that day was because they had beaten him senseless for trying to save her." Salome's eyes soften as she looks sadly at Delphine.

"Then we need to prepare," Lennox snarls, all sense of the pleasantly drunk lover has faded from him, replaced by radiating anger.

"Stay calm, William. Let's see what other information we can get from Daniel. We have a week and a half until Solstice; we can't allow it to look like we suspect anything. All preparations will continue as planned, but Siobhan and Andromeda will need to practice with me and Delphine more. Do you think we should bring Lyra in for training, too?" Salome asks Lennox.

"I'm not sure Celeste will approve, but it's worth asking. She should know how to protect herself at least," he concedes.

I already know Celeste will not be happy about this. She barely wanted to allow Lyra out to explore the city — teaching her the ways of a priestess will be much riskier and will potentially add a target to her back. Hopefully, the pressure from her brother will convince Celeste that this is a necessary action; he would never put Lyra in unnecessary danger any more than she would, 'nor would I. We sit in Salome's office for a few more minutes, the news that danger is closer than expected sobering the mood and the men at our sides.

Finally, Salome rises from her desk, stubbing out her cigarette in a crystal tray sitting on the surface. "Life goes on. We will prepare. We will defeat them. But tonight, we must continue as though everything is normal. I have customers to see."

With that, she squares her shoulders, checks her hair and makeup in a gilded mirror by the exit, and then saunters out the door to greet the waiting crowd in the salon, crimson skirt rustling with the swish of her lush hips. Delphine takes her empty glass, along with the ashtray from the desk, and walks out the door closely behind Salome, leaving the four of us in silence.

"I—" Siobhan starts, but quiets again, eyes downcast.

"Speak Siobhan. What's on your mind?" Lennox urges gently.

"I'm afraid," she admits, twisting her skirt in her long freckled fingers. They still when Erik reaches over to take her hand.

"Remember my promise to you, Siobhan, I will not allow anyone to harm you," Erik states simply, even though his face is uneasy.

"We'll work with Salome and Delphine, to learn defensive power. Between that and the force of our crews, we'll be all right," I comfort her, offering pretty words despite the fear which now coats my skin.

"Tomorrow, Erik and I will speak with the crews and work out a plan for them for the Solstice. You should bring Lyra in for training immediately. Let me deal with Celeste," Lennox orders, the brazen captain at work again. I turn slightly where I perch on his lap to see the anger in his eyes. But before I can say anything, he pulls me in for a kiss, sparks licking at my skin where we touch. He whispers against my mouth, "Tonight, let's try to have a good time. Tomorrow we can plan our victory."

WE MAKE OUR WAY BACK INTO THE SALON AND TAKE OUR spot in the booth we vacated. Tension surrounds us like one of the storms that keep battering the city, turning the cooled meal to ash in my mouth as I try to choke it down. The band seems muted, the usually lively atmosphere lusterless, and I find no solace in the fine wine that accompanies our dinner. The knowledge of plots against Salome and the Den looms over us, but while Lennox and I are well versed in pretending to be what we are not, no amount of alcohol will dull our apprehension.

I assume Lennox is finally tired of silently pushing his food around his plate when he stands abruptly from the table and extends a hand to me. "Let's go up."

Nodding my agreement, I turn to our friends, Siobhan has consumed more wine than I, and her cheeks are flushed from the alcohol as she curls against Erik. "Goodnight," I murmur, then place my hand in Lennox's to allow him to pull me from the booth, leaving Erik and Siobhan in the dim corner.

Our fingers remain entwined as we silently climb the stairs and return to our room. As soon as the door clicks shut, I turn to Lennox, wrapping my arms around him and finally exhaling my worries into the fabric of his shirt as I implore, "What are we going to do?"

"We'll figure it out," he murmurs, his lips moving against the top of my head, but his tone is far more troubled than his words. "Whatever happens, I won't be separated from you. I won't let them hurt any of the ones I care about. Not again," he promises, both to me and to himself. I pull back to look into his eyes, finding the emotion there as strained as the ones that hold me in their grip.

He presses his lips to my brow, then places a rough palm on my cheek as he leans to capture my mouth. What begins as a gentle, comforting kiss grows more urgent as I open to him, brushing my tongue against his. It seems he's as eager to mask our shared worries and doubts with physical release as I am when he spins me and presses my back against the closed door. His movements are slow and sure as he caresses my breasts, running his large hands down my body to grab my waist, slipping his thigh between my legs.

"You taste so good, Nerissa," he breathes against my lips. His tongue running against mine sets my blood alight, causing me to gasp with pleasure as I twist my fingers in the front of his shirt. As our passion flames, the desperation in our movements increases and I grind against him before we hastily wrest our clothing off, tossing it wherever it might land between kisses.

"Billy," I breathe, as he runs his tongue up my neck. "I need you."

At that, he carries me to the bed, sitting me on the edge of the mattress. I untie my underskirt and push it off my hips while he removes his pants. But, when I move to unlace the garters holding my wool stockings above my knees, he stops me.

"Leave them," Lennox's voice is husky as he smiles and rakes his eyes over my stockings, then the bare skin above them, smiling sinfully the whole time and raising a blush over my exposed flesh as I lay before him.

He runs his palms up the sides of my thighs, then grips my hips and pulls me closer to the edge of the mattress. I reach up to kiss across his inked chest, sucking one nipple into my mouth and lightly nipping it as I watch his reaction through my lashes. Running a hand down my side and across my hip, he slides it between us, teasing the wetness between my thighs so I open to him. A groan escapes my lips as he teases the sensitive bundle of nerves at the apex of my thighs.

With a low rumble of satisfaction in the back of his throat, he leans forward to take my mouth again, still working between my legs. "So fucking wet for me, my pretty priestess."

I whimper in response, arching against his palm. He pulls his fingers away, then flips me over so I lay face down on the mattress, bent over the edge of the bed. A moan escapes my lips, muffled in the soft bedding, as he runs his mouth up the back of my thigh and licks up my center, while I rub against the bed. When I arch my back, he sucks in a breath through his teeth, then grasps one cheek firmly in his rough palm before placing kisses on my lower back, trailing them up my spine until his warm breath reaches the side of my neck as he covers my body.

As Lennox teases my entrance, I can't hold back my groan, raising onto my forearms and arching into him again, my body seeking the release of our joining. He obliges moments later by sliding into me in one stroke, stilling as I gasp and settle around him. As he moves, I press back against him, matching his rhythm as he stands behind me.

"Oh, *fuck*," he growls, gripping my hip with one hand and wrapping the other in my loose hair, increasing the tempo. The friction of the bed pressing against my body while he fills me threatens to overwhelm my senses as my climax coils in my core.

"Don't stop," I beg into the downy coverlet as he continues to move, my release rippling through my muscles as I come around him.

Lennox pauses for a moment, then slides from my body, tucking a strong forearm under my thigh and flipping me onto my back before lifting me higher onto the mattress. He joins me on the bed, slipping one of my thighs over his shoulder as he thrusts into me again with a shuddering breath.

"Nerissa," he breathes, as our hips rock together, sliding deeper into me. "Look at me," he commands, drawing my eyes open to meet his. With one hand above me to grip the headboard, I reach the other to cup his cheek, then run it through his hair, gripping it as he increases his motion. Our gazes stay focused on one another until he dips his chin to his chest, closing his eyes as he finishes.

He untangles himself from my leg, rolling to the side and pulling me close, kissing my cheeks and forehead before pressing his lips gently to mine.

"I love you," he whispers his own prayer to me.

"I love you, too," I reply, curling against him with my head resting on his tattooed chest.

We lay together in the dim glow of the sconces, catching our breath. Lennox absentmindedly strokes my hair as it fans around me, a gentle comfort I've come to crave. But soon, my worry over the young priest's warning returns.

This is the bargain I made when I joined him on the docks of Delosia. I knew we would likely face dangers and hardships, but the knowledge we would face them together made it seem worth it. Now, I wonder if I should have stayed behind and saved him from all of this. Even if neither of our minds would have rested easily if we were parted, and I know he would have blamed himself if anything happened to me in his absence.

No matter what I do, there doesn't seem to be an escape from what I've been fleeing.

# CHAPTER 32

The next week is filled with intense training, tears of frustration, and careful planning.

After an initial argument with Lennox, heard by myself and anyone else walking through the upper hallways, Celeste relented and agreed that Lyra should work with us. Lyra's insistence and Lennox's reasoning eventually wearing down her protests.

This evening Salome will perform a poor excuse for an initiation on the girl, at least in comparison to the formal ceremonies that Siobhan and I experienced — without the support of a sacred grove or the light of the moon. It's the best option we have though, so we plan to make do as best as we can. I haven't witnessed an initiation since the final one held at the Western Temple the year before Blackwell arrived, so the event dawns bittersweet for me.

Salome cleared the Den for the evening, a rare thing for her to do. Locking the doors to patrons, and banishing her girls to the upper levels of the building, only our immediate group — Salome, Delphine, Celeste, Lennox, Siobhan, Erik, plus Pike — stands in attendance in the salon to witness Lyra's initiation. With such a short time frame, Lyra wasn't able to have a robe of her own made in time for the ceremony, even though the seamstress is working to create something for her. So, I insisted she wear mine — the one that belonged to her grandmother, Anise — for the night. It seemed only fitting for her to do so.

When Lyra steps from her room, tears threaten to fall at the sight of her shimmering in the silver fabric. She asked me to stand with her for the ritual, an honor as her teacher and elder, once again gifting me something I never thought I would experience since I left my old life. The same way she honored me by asking me to train her in the surgery on the *Bartered Soul*.

"Are you ready?" I ask, squeezing her hand in mine when she reaches where I wait at the top of the stairs.

"Yes. I already told mama this is in my blood. I know it will work," she replies, her words colored with excitement even if her slim hand trembles slightly in mine. Smiling through the emotions choking me, I walk by her side down the stairs and into the salon where our friends wait.

Salome stands near the bar, flanked by Delphine and Siobhan. Del and Salome wear their robes, while Siobhan is dressed in the gold gown I saw her wear on the beach. The scene is so similar to the way we stood the night of the full moon ceremony only two weeks past. For a breath, I allow myself to admire the women I've grown so close with, a sisterhood I quietly cherish. Standing in the center of the sigil-chalked floor with Lyra, my dark blue gown is like the twilight sky against the moonlight of Lyra's robe. Salome approaches, circling us while wafting smoke over us in blessing, her sigil and my own illuminating the close space.

"Priestess Nerissa," Salome addresses me. All of the people in this room know my identity now, there's no use hiding behind the alias Andromeda any longer in their presence.

"Yes, High Priestess," I answer, using the proper title in hopes that it will strengthen the ceremony, even if Salome assured me that our intention should be enough.

"Will you guide this initiate in her studies and teach her the ways of the Goddess?"

"Yes." The word rings truer than I could anticipate. The desire to share the knowledge I have learned, to rebuild what was lost, and to protect my sisters and the home we left behind, or whatever we build in the future, burns in my chest. For a moment my eyes drift from Lyra, even as I squeeze her hands. My gaze finds Celeste and Lennox where they stand on the edge of the room, promising in one look that their beloved Lyra means as much to me as she does to them.

"Initiate," Salome says, turning to Lyra. "Will you heed your Sister's teachings, learning from her our ways and use the power you're gifted by the Goddess to protect the people and spirit of the land sacred to Her?"

"Yes," Lyra's reply is a mere breath, her excitement almost palpable as she looks between Salome and me.

"Then let it be done." Salome gestures for Siobhan and Delphine to join her, grasping hands to make a triangle around the two of us. In unison, we all speak the ancient words of initiation. The power of the chant, and the priestesses themselves, illuminate our hands as we complete the ceremony. As the *glow* fades from our fingertips, an upturned crescent shines brightly on Lyra's brow. She grins with excitement, her hazel eyes sparkling in the *glow* of her new sigil.

The symbol officially marks her as a priestess now — a novice, but still one capable of accessing power on par with the rest of us. She can now call on the *glow* on her own, not needing to be physically linked to a priestess like on the beach of Delosia, and can begin training with the other gifts from the Goddess.

I knew Salome performed the ritual for Delphine years ago, on her own, without the help of any additional priestesses, so it shouldn't be a surprise to me to see the sigil upon Lyra's face. Even so, a ripple of dread skates over my skin, taking root in my stomach and raising gooseflesh on my arms as I take in her warm tan skin washed out by the silvery light of the sigil.

"Celeste!" Lennox's voice cuts through the silent salon, as he reaches out to his sister's retreating form. She turns once, smiling at Lyra before pushing through the velvet curtain, but in that one look anguish shows in her teary eyes. My heart sinks, wondering if the sight of her only child in the silver robe with the sigil on her brow reminds Celeste of her mother's fate. After the loss of her mother and husband, and the threats she's faced since, it wouldn't surprise me if she resents the mark of the Goddess that now rests on her daughter's brow.

---

CELESTE HAS HIDDEN ANY RESIDUAL DISCONTENT SINCE LYRA'S initiation, acting as a supportive force for Lyra and the rest of us over the following days as Solstice nears. Each morning, we dine quickly together in one of the larger rooms on the upper level of the Den. The men have cleared all furniture from the space and put us through training to effectively use a knife and dagger, pairing us against each of them to prepare for the possibility of a physical attack. Watching from a stool in the corner, my stomach knots as Siobhan is caught unawares by Lennox, his large hand twisting her wrist so she drops the knife she wields. Each time one of my friends is caught or disarmed the worry that has taken residence in my chest grows, wondering what fate lies before us.

Sequestered in Salome's office, I've managed to fully match Delphine in power, while Delphine has been more open with her shadow work and channeling. Now that it might be useful, she not only demonstrates how she can pull the coiled shadows from the corners of the room for temporary stealth, she also practices shifting each of our strengths to one another, acting as a conduit for the power to travel through in case one of us is weakened or injured. Del's shadows seem so at odds with the bright *glow* I'm used to and sends little shivers skittering over me each time I take her hand to experience shifts of power or the caress of her shadows.

Siobhan is close behind me in her mastery of the elements, but in addition to practicing with them, she and Salome spend time alone with black mirrors, crystals, and cards to see if they can divine more information about what we might face, leaving the rest of us in the dark as to the results of their divination.

Lyra remains mostly untrained, sitting in on our lessons and attempting to manipulate elements when she can. With the short amount of time we have, we can't ensure she will be able to master them by Solstice, but it seems I helped unlock her true talents when I taught her about healing and herblore on the *Bartered Soul*. She has taken to these crafts much quicker than anyone I've ever seen, myself included.

While I sometimes still get lost in my worries, second-guessing a choice, or struggling to offer a soothing word, I find that Lyra's empathy and intuition are unmatched within our small circle. Each time she successfully comforts someone in need, treats a wound, or creates a remedy, pride swells in my breast. With a bit more practice her gifts should allow her to heal with the *glow* itself if Salome is to be believed. It's something I've never seen, but would be an asset should we end up in battle.

Lennox and Erik ordered the crewmembers to frequent taverns and blend in with the crowds in the square, listening for any clues of the priests' plans. They also keep watch at sea, ferrying back and forth down the murky river to meet with the ships that wait for us in the gulf, still left manned by skeleton crews. But, to my frustration, even between the divination and our crew, no one has been able to gather any specific information; all we know is that *some-thing* is coming on Solstice, and the looming threat weighs heavily on everyone.

"About your plan," Salome says as Delphine passes cups out to those of us gathered in the office one afternoon, drawing my weary gaze. "I will not wait here to be attacked, cowering behind the walls of the Den."

Lennox sets his teacup down hard on the table, clattering against the wood as he leans forward in his seat. Dark circles bloom under his eyes, his lack of sleep on par with my own. "Salome, it has been a long time since you've been involved in a battle. We're better —"

Anger flashes across Salome's face, her eyes focused intently on Lennox at my side, and even I sit straighter at the look. "I will hear none of it, William. We will be hosting our Solstice ritual at a bonfire on the riverbank. Like all ceremonies once were before the priests started disrupting them over the last few years, and we will wait for what may come. No matter how many years it has been since I last saw a battle, you know full well what I'm capable of, boy. And now, with these four at my side," she waves her hand towards Siobhan, Delphine, Lyra, and myself, "I have even more power at my disposal."

My eyes shift between the two, watching how Lennox will react to her power plays, and I notice that Erik, Siobhan, and Delphine do the same. I want to share in her confidence, but dread curls itself around my heart, haunting me throughout the days and into my dreams, even as I pretend to be calm for the sake of my friends. Charged silence hangs heavy in the air, but Lennox's jaw works, and then he nods in acquiescence.

A satisfied smile takes over Salome's face as she lights her cigarette, blowing smoke out into the room. "Delphine, what of Daniel?"

"I can't find him," she answers quietly, eyes wide with worry. "I've been scouring the streets near the square and the alleys of the Entertainment District, but he hasn't slipped from the cathedral since the night we saw him."

"Hm," Salome purses her lips, cigarette held loosely in her hand. "That is disconcerting."

Taking a sip of my tea, I study Delphine over my cup. More withdrawn and moodier than usual, her eyes are also circled with darkness from lack of rest, but Lyra sits at her side, patting her arm in comfort. It hasn't escaped my notice that Delphine has become increasingly close with Lyra since she's settled in, spending time together in the salon chatting and taking most meals together when we aren't training.

Lyra confided to me that Delphine fears her friend has been found out or punished in some way, and I can't help but quietly share in that concern. The way the young man's bones jutted from his skin when I held him against the wall tells me he's suffered greatly already; I shudder at the thought of how little might be required to break him.

THE DAYS MOVE QUICKLY, WRAPPED IN A DARK HAZE OF foreboding, and I find myself seated once again in Salome's luxurious office sipping brandy with our growing group of companions on the eve of the Winter Solstice. Siobhan and Erik, Celeste and Lyra, Delphine and Salome, and Lennox and I all gather around the low table to finalize plans for the following evening.

"The crew will have the bonfire built and ready to light before dusk," Erik says. I focus on his steady words and lilting voice while trying to force down the nerves that are trying to overpower me as sweat prickles under my arms, nearly driving me to distraction.

"Perfect," Salome nods confidently, tapping the cigarette holder on her desk. "The priestesses and I will walk down to the river shortly after twilight to light the blaze. We will perform the ceremony, then I anticipate celebrations will carry on into the night. Solstice is still a large event in New Aphros since it's a free city — we all know money and debauchery are the true rulers here. Blackwell and his religion haven't been able to sink their claws in to dampen a good time, no matter what they may think. We can only hope that the city's support of the celebration will subdue any of the plans the priests have made, and this worry will all be for naught." Even with her voice steady, I sense the uneasiness in her, my eyes narrowing as I notice how her fingers twitch over the box of cigarettes, the nervous movement matching how we all feel.

Lennox opens his mouth to speak but is interrupted when one of the guards opens Salome's door. He walks to his madame's side and whispers something to her too low for any of us to hear.

"Bring him here immediately," Salome demands, standing to clear the items from the desk's surface, tossing them in drawers haphazardly in her rush. "Delphine, grab bandages and clean water, *now*."

Delphine jumps to her feet to obey, but the door swings inward and another guard carries in a limp body. At first glance, it's hard to tell if they're male or female — alive or dead — but Delphine's sob is enough for me to know that Daniel has been found.

"*Delphine, now!*" Salome commands and Lyra rises to

grab Delphine by the arm, pulling her down the hallway to help gather supplies. Siobhan and I move to join Salome, but she waves us off as the guard lays the boy across the cleared desktop. I exhale in relief when I approach, Daniel's chest rises and falls with shallow breaths — he is still alive. For now.

Lyra and Delphine return quickly and Salome grabs one of the clean towels and water to wipe the boy's face, then cuts the shirt from his thin chest with the sharp blade of her decorative letter opener to reveal the multitude of lash marks covering him. Most are on his back, revealed when we roll him on his side to pull the dirty fabric away from the wounds, but some cover his ribs and chest. I suck in a breath, hissing through my teeth at the viciousness of his injuries, trembling with rage and disgust at the suffering Daniel has endured. Several partially healed marks show signs of inflammation, evident from the redness spreading from them. Newer sores leak blood onto the surface of the desk.

"I will fucking kill them," Delphine breathes, her eyes dark with fury at the condition of her friend. The corners of the room seem to tremble with the tempo of her hands shaking, darkening at her words.

"Del," Daniel croaks through cracked lips. "I'm all right. I think they thought I would die in the street. I think… I'm finally free."

"What happened?" Lennox asks, his breath shallow. My chest hollows when I turn toward him to find his eyes glassy and his mouth twisted with loathing as he stares at Daniel. I remember the day he told me about the repeated lashings he endured when he was pressed into service by the King's Navy. The fevers and infections he survived. The deep scars he will forever bear from that time. I reach out to stroke his arm, trying to comfort him and keep him focused on the present instead of the misery of the past.

"They caught me… sneaking out." Daniel's voice is a hoarse whisper as he struggles to speak, shivering under the damp towel. "They thought I was coming to the brothel… to be with Del. They always thought it was for *baser needs*. They don't know I warned you."

Salome finishes wiping him down quickly, Delphine gripping his hand the entire time, and then they tuck a woolen blanket over him.

"It will be all right, Danny. You're safe now," Delphine whispers to him, caressing his dark hair, as he continues to shiver.

"I just want you to be safe, Del. That's all I've ever wanted," he croaks, closes his dark eyes, and fades into a restless sleep.

# CHAPTER 33

Winter Solstice dawns crisp and clear. Laying awake next to Lennox, I focus on his steady breath, just like I have for hours. Sounds of life rustle outside our door as the rest of the brothel wakes and starts their day earlier than usual for the holiday, but I'm loath to move. It feels as if getting out of bed will make the events of this coming evening real instead of a gnawing nightmare, and I'm not ready to face the dread that lurks beyond the door to our room yet.

I know it's too much to hope for an uneventful day, but I still send a silent prayer to the Goddess as I watch the light get brighter through the shutters. If my friends can stay safe, and my love protected, then I can maintain the strength I've found since I fled in terror all those years ago. My biggest fear is losing any of these pieces of me that I've been collecting — if I lose them, will I be able to continue on my own?

Lennox pulls me from my dark musings when he rolls toward me and props up on one elbow. His hair is light brown now, the color fading more and more with each wash, and is adorably rumpled from sleep. He smiles sleepily at me as if he has no care in the world except to greet me. I can't contain a small smirk as I lean over to brush a chaste kiss against his lips, his golden stubble tickling my skin.

Before I can retreat from him completely, he pulls me against his chest so that my back is pressed against him and I curl up, savoring his embrace as he tucks himself around me. At least for a few hours, I have this. I giggle breathlessly and wiggle my backside when I feel a nudge against me, earning a deep chuckle in response.

"That's not polite behavior is it, my pretty priestess?" he whispers against my hair, wrapping his arm around me to grasp my breast in his palm.

"Whoever said either of us was polite, Captain?" I retort, grinding against him again. We don't emerge from our chambers for another hour.

WHEN WE ARRIVE IN THE SALON, THE OTHER RESIDENTS OF THE brothel are in high spirits. Many of them ignore us and continue decorating for the impending Solstice party they expect that evening, blissfully oblivious to our tension and worries. Juliet is the only one who wears a serious expression when she dips her strawberry-blonde head in greeting.

Garlands of cypress and pine decorated with shimmering crushed glass and red berries stretch across the entry to the salon, and mistletoe dangles from various, strategically placed, locations so guests will be forced to kiss beneath them often. The aroma of melting sugar and chocolate wafts from the back of the salon where the cook must be preparing traditional cakes and sweets for the evening celebration. Despite my nerves, my mouth waters at the pleasant scent, and I wish I was able to feel the same joy that radiates from the space.

The plan, as outlined for public consumption, is that Madame Salome and her priestesses will perform a traditional Winter Solstice ceremony and bonfire on the river's edge in the style of the Old Ways. Anyone from town who wishes to join may do so. Afterward, a more erotic, invite-only celebration will continue at the Den of Sinful Delights. Rumor has it that people are clamoring to obtain an invite, even offering to buy them from those who received their invitation from the Madame personally.

The only difference between previous years and this one is there are more priestesses present, allowing for a larger, more public, bonfire at last. Part of me wonders if we are only provoking the priests with our actions, but I remind myself that New Aphros prides itself on its tolerance of different beliefs. If there was no vendetta against Madame Salome, a celebration of this type wouldn't be unheard of. Other residents enjoy the Solstice in peace — why should we not be allowed to as well?

Lennox pulls me from the salon and past the bar to Salome's office where we find a makeshift sick bay with a mattress lying in the corner where Daniel rests. Delphine lays curled on a thick quilt on the floor next to him, still asleep as well. Lyra opens her eyes, sitting up on the small couch where she must have spent the night in solidarity with her friend. She wipes the sleep from her hazel eyes and looks over to where Delphine stirs at our entrance.

Since Salome is absent, and we don't wish to disturb Delphine, we retreat back to the salon where Erik and Siobhan have entered, also seeking the rest of our group. We take a seat together at one of the tables that's free from stacks of shimmering Solstice decorations, while Lennox strides into the kitchen to tell the cook that we need breakfast. Lyra sneaks from the office to join us, and Celeste appears from the stairway soon after. It feels like a last supper of sorts, even if it's only a late breakfast.

"Is there anything Siobhan or I can do for the boy?" I ask Lyra as she settles into a chair at my side. We are both healers and have stores in our rooms for treating illness and injuries, but Salome has handled all of those tasks for Daniel so far, and neither of us was allowed to assist last night beyond moving him so she could tend to his injuries.

"No. Salome has done all that she can for him and his wounds look much better. The inflammation has receded almost completely," Lyra says as she calmly sips her tea. "Delphine won't leave his side. I think she feels guilty over what was done to him."

Her composure is startling. Although she has only been in New Aphros for two weeks, she's settled in far more quickly than I could have hoped, endearing herself to the residents just as easily as she did on the *Bartered Soul*. Even managing to break through Delphine's inscrutable moods with her compassion and kindness. The time we shared on the voyage from Selennia was trying for her, especially after the loss of Charlie, and yet I see that none of these challenges have dimmed her warmth or weakened her sweet spirit. I catch Celeste's eye as she observes her daughter in the same light, and we share a proud smile over the table.

As we are finishing our meal, Salome walks from far back in the hallway and bypasses her office completely when she spots our full table. I note with worry that she's pale: her usually rich, tan skin is sallow, and her lips are untinted. Ordinarily, she's coiffed and perfumed the moment she steps from her chambers, but this morning she almost appears unkempt — dark waves trailing down her back and circles showing under her eyes. Since my arrival weeks ago, I've never once seen her in such a state and my concern is registered when she meets my eyes.

Before I can greet her, she states, "We need to review everything once more before Captain Varangr goes to rally the crews." Then she raises her voice to the other people in the room decorating, "Everyone out! Now! You can finish decorating later."

The other inhabitants flee through the open curtain into the foyer and distribute themselves into their quarters before she begins reviewing the plans again. Once she's finished, and everyone is clear on their roles, she stands and moves toward her office. She stops once, looks back at me, then shifts her eyes to Siobhan. "Siobhan, please come to speak with me for a while. Since Erik will be leaving soon, you can come by once he has left." Siobhan nods once, understanding flickering across her face momentarily before her expression smooths out.

Curiosity and unease trouble me as Lennox and I enter our room, twisting uncomfortably in my stomach. We have all drifted back to our quarters to spend the remainder of the day in preparation, but now I find I can't focus on anything beyond doubt over the upcoming celebration. Salome and Siobhan have been exceedingly withdrawn. The exchange downstairs has done nothing to soothe my nerves which are tender and frayed at the possibility of an attack from the priests. Swallowing down my concerns I refrain from discussing my thoughts with Lennox, not wishing to distract him as he sharpens his blades. Instead, I ring for water for a bath and begin laying out my attire for tonight, hoping my worry is unfounded.

I READY MYSELF FOR THE EVENING CELEBRATION BY MEMORY, my muscles automatically moving through the actions of dressing, braiding my hair into its crown, and dusting myself with the final remains of my golden powder. It pains me that this is the last of my connection to the temple in Athene. I could have traded or sold it numerous times, but could never bear to do so, to say goodbye to that part of myself completely. And now, the jar I hold is empty. All I have left from my previous life is the dagger I still wear, an ugly reminder of what forged this new version of myself. Even if it isn't beautiful, and still bears the mark of Black-well's army, it's mine now and has served me well.

Lennox is quiet tonight, as lost in his thoughts as I am in mine. He sits in one of the chairs checking his pistols and polishing his cutlass. The worn leather coat he reserves for battle has been repaired and is laid across the foot of the bed ready for him to don it, the first time I've seen him do so since his injury on the *Archangel*. I watch his reflection in the mirror as his hands move confidently over the weapons;

they don't tremble as mine do at the thought of what could go wrong. After observing him for a few minutes, he raises his mossy eyes to meet my blue ones in the glass, a ghost of a smile on his lips. I return the look with a tight smile of my own, swallowing and inspecting my reflection once again. When I'm satisfied with what I see, I stand and walk over to him. He does the same, tucking one pistol at his waist, another at his back, and sheaths the cutlass on his left hip. Once I reach him, he wraps his arms around me and holds me close to his chest for a few moments while I take the moment to breathe in his scent.

"Are you ready?" he asks, pulling back to look me in the eyes.

"I don't think we have much of a choice, do we?" I answer, my voice sounding more confident than I feel. He smiles at me, a true smile that meets his eyes, and kisses my brow even though my sigil remains cloaked. The familiar action soothes my nerves, even if only for the moment his lips rest on my skin.

"You are the fiercest woman I know, Nerissa. And you are backed tonight by a pack of loyal friends. All will be well, my she-wolf." I look away, unable to fake a smile as his reassurance does nothing to make me feel better. The thought that those loyal friends might be harmed tonight is exactly what I fear, but I swallow down any doubts and allow him to help me into my cloak. He then shrugs into his coat, weapons hidden completely beneath its panels.

We walk hand in hand down the stairs, just like any other night, and are met in the foyer by our companions. Erik and Pike are present and look properly turned out for the holiday, but I know they wear vambraces and leather under their frock coats, prepared for battle like Lennox, just in case. Lyra and Siobhan are outfitted in slim-fitting gowns, similar in shape to the robes the rest of us wear, but without the same low neck or high slit. Siobhan's is gold with navy trim, while Lyra's newly made garment is a deep green with gold embroidery — the colors of a true healer.

Salome and Delphine stand side by side in the entryway of the salon, Salome in midnight blue and Delphine in black so dark it seems to devour the warm light from the oil lamps. Both of them look troubled — Delphine has circles the color of bruises under her eyes from lack of sleep, while Salome still bears the sorrowful expression I saw earlier, even if she's now immaculately styled. Siobhan briefly looks between Lennox and me, then at Salome as we step from the final stair. Her lips part as if she wishes to speak, but she turns to Erik and whispers to him when we make it to the foyer. Celeste descends shortly after we do, but she isn't dressed for the riverbank. She will remain in the Den of Sinful Delights to oversee the preparations for the party afterward and wears a midnight blue velvet dress that must be one of Salome's. Standing close to Lyra, she squeezes her hand.

"Good evening, everyone," Salome greets us when we are standing together. "We all know our parts to play tonight. I hope things will be uneventful and pleasant. However, I know we are all prepared should that not be the case." She looks between each of us with a clenched jaw, lips tight with worry, her attitude at odds with her next words. "Let's celebrate!"

With that, we turn toward the door and whatever awaits.

# CHAPTER 34

The two muscular guards who usually work the front door wait under the carved sign of the Den holding torches to lead us down to the riverfront. When the door opens to reveal Salome, cheers rise from the crowd of revelers that wait along the sides of the streets. She beams a smile to them and waves, the bold madame replacing the haggard version of herself I have witnessed today. Followed closely by Delphine, then Lennox and myself, Siobhan and Erik, Lyra and Pike, she proceeds down the steps and into the street.

What a strange sight we must be to those in the crowd — elegant priestesses accompanied by fierce pirates. But then, the new religion paints us as all the same — wild beasts with no souls — so perhaps we are well-matched. Celeste stands in the doorway and watches us stroll down the center of the street until we reach the next corner to turn toward the river. By the time I glance over my shoulder, the red door is already closed behind us.

The atmosphere on the streets is exhilarating — music

from fiddles, horns, and hand-held percussion instruments surrounds us. As we stroll toward the river, people dressed in finery join our procession, the crowd pressing closer to the dark water and the huge unlit bonfire awaiting our torches. It seems as though the entire city has shown up, no matter their beliefs, to celebrate the longest night of the year and to ask the sun to return for longer days ahead. Small packages are tossed from balconies with little candles and trinkets hidden inside, and people drink warm spiced wine, rum punch, and fragrant mulled cider from vendors' carts along the way.

I do my best to keep my thoughts focused, but the energy of the crowd is intoxicating as it swirls around us. I relax slightly as we continue our walk wrapped in their joyful merrymaking, unable to resist the music and songs even though my chest is still tight with nervousness. When we enter the square, the oil lanterns lining the intersecting streets flicker, lighting the group with an amber hue as we parade past the ancient oak tree. There is only silence from the cathedral. The priests don't hold festivities on this day and preach that the raucous behavior is unbecoming. If I wasn't so worried about what their absence meant, I would be relieved by the respite from their scolding.

When we reach the riverbank, the two guards each hand a torch to Salome and Delphine, who walk to either side of the bonfire and thrust the torches in between the logs, igniting the oil-drenched kindling. Flames begin to lick at the wood as they return the torches to the guards who take up posts nearby. Salome's eyes roam over the growing crowd, inspecting each person for any threats before slowly coming back to meet mine. With a tight smile, she nods to the rest of us. At her gesture, Lyra, Siobhan, and I peel away from our escorts to join Salome and Delphine around the fire. My heart hammers in my chest, almost as loud as the drums we passed in the streets as the heat warms my skin.

Our men form a loose perimeter around us, keeping the crowd at a safe distance. Firelight dances on their stern faces, hollowing their cheeks and gleaming in their watchful eyes. The flames glint off the gold in Pike's nose and ears and the pieces that are woven in Erik's hair. Salome lifts her hands and we follow suit as she begins to chant a blessing for brighter days ahead to follow the longest night of the year.

Our sigils shine bright in the darkness, the crowd cheering at the sight — whether they believe in the Old Ways, or think this is a parlor trick, I don't know, but the sound is one I haven't heard in years. Emotions war in my chest — joy at celebrating the Solstice with friends and firelight clashing with the anxiety that causes my stomach to knot. We continue the chant and sing celebratory songs to the Goddess with the crowd joining in, sharing in the merriment of the evening. When our songs end, we each take a sip of wine from a bottle we brought, then pour some into the flames along with silent prayers for the new year waiting just around the corner.

Under normal circumstances, this is a night of wishes and dreams, and many of the partygoers hold offerings and slips of paper with hopes for the next cycle of the seasons to burn in the fire. The energy of the gathered crowd mirrors that hopeful feeling, rather than the tightness in my chest. My own prayer, however, is one of protection, even if just for tonight. Finished with our ceremony, we step away and allow them to approach the heat of the blaze.

I stand with the other women, huddled against the wind whipping off the river in my cloak. I feel safer in the dark fabric rather than being fully exposed with my silver robe glowing in the scant moonlight. So far, there has been no sign of treachery, and I desperately want to believe that Daniel's warning was false. Maybe the priests mean to attack in a different manner, maybe they decided against it altogether since the majority of the city has joined us. But instinct and experience have told me that being too optimistic usually leads to failure and disappointment, so I scan the crowd once again, refusing to let my guard down.

Lyra shivers as a breeze picks up off the water and Siobhan leans into Erik, using him as a shield against the wind. Even with the fire, we all grow more chilled as we wait, and I'm relieved when Salome indicates it's time to head back to the Den. Most of the crowd remains behind, but our guards with their torches lead us back toward the city's dim glow. Those with invites may join us at the Den later, while the rest will continue to their own personal parties at home or in other taverns and brothels.

As we approach the square, an unusual silence envelops us. The sound of the crowd at the bonfire is still at our backs, music and cheering carrying on the wind, and I know the row of brothels and music halls, and the other residential portions of the city, are alive with people celebrating. But the square itself is eerie in the darkness. My eyes drift up to the oil lamps that usually illuminate the square, noticing they are unlit, even though they glowed warmly on our way to the river, and my pulse increases as sweat coats my palms despite the chill breeze. Our footsteps echo off the cobblestones, and the hair on my arms stands on end with my uneasiness.

"Siobhan, what is it?" Erik whispers furiously, halting my steps as I whirl to check on my friend.

Clutching Erik's arm, Siobhan scans our surroundings, her gaze flitting around in a panic. Pike steps in front of Lyra to shield her, resting his hand on whatever weapon he hides inside his coat when Siobhan murmurs, "It's happening."

"They're here," Delphine whispers seconds later, and a chill that has nothing to do with the weather wraps around me, my heart stuttering at her words as my stomach drops. Delphine remains solidly at Salome's side as the former high priestess stops in front of us. Her guards raise the torches to illuminate the space around us, scrutinizing the darkened alleys and balconies.

"Douse the torches!" Lennox hisses. "Now, you idiots!"

We are beacons in the center of the square, easy targets for whatever might be lurking, and panic seizes in my chest sending my heart into a frantic rhythm. The men look around for a way to extinguish the torches, but with a sweep of her hand, Salome plunges us into full darkness. The city glows amber from the oil lanterns that line the streets behind the cathedral, and the bonfire rages far at our backs, but we remain surrounded by gloom without the ones in the square.

The door of the cathedral opens with an ominous creak, the handles clanking against the wood as the iron rings bounce on the surface, and a dark figure emerges. Several more follow behind until a row of priests stands before us. I fight the urge to clutch at Lennox, reaching instead for my dagger with trembling fingers as he places a hand on the hilt of his cutlass. Erik and Pike fan behind us, blocking Siobhan and Lyra, while Salome and Delphine remain in front.

"I see that you whores couldn't be contained tonight. You have to spread your lies and debauchery through the city no matter the cost," the priest standing in front of us snaps. A few of the men in the line hold lanterns and I can make out that he's older, perhaps Salome's age, with grey thinning hair covering his wrinkled brow. His eyes leech hatred toward our group and I recognize him as the man who preached from the steps that first day in the square.

"This is a free city, Father. You are welcome to preach on the streets, just as I am welcome to honor my Goddess. Why don't you and your *brothers* go back inside and repent some more while we continue on our way?" Salome mocks, disdain dripping from her painted lips.

"King Dargan begs to differ, witch. He will rule this city before long and you and your kind will burn as you deserve," another younger priest sneers from the line.

"Dargan Blackwell has no power here. Go back inside and learn how to speak to your elders, whelp," Lennox snarls at the man, stepping forward to stand with Salome and Delphine. Hatred radiates from him and the priest has the intelligence to take a step back at the sight of his wild eyes and clenched jaw.

"That remains to be seen, whoremonger," the first priest replies, no fear present on his face. I know his type — zealots who think they can't be harmed due to their God's protection or who welcome martyrdom in honor of their cause. They are often the most dangerous. A shiver skates down my back as I grip my dagger more firmly to ward off the fear that tries to creep over me, gritting my teeth with my contempt for this man and those like him.

Siobhan stands at my side now that Lennox has stepped forward, her hand gripped tightly in mine, as we help shield Lyra, still too young and too green to be out here if we are attacked. Guilt sinks in my breast — Celeste was right, we shouldn't have involved her. The large clock at the top of the cathedral chimes, drawing my attention.

As my eyes flick upwards to its face, my breath catches in my throat, my heart throbbing in my breast at what I find. Men line the unfinished roof of the cathedral. In the darkness, it's impossible to make out the details of their faces, but the outline of crossbows is easy to define. I swallow, trying to mask the recognition in case one of the men noticed my glance, then whisper harshly, "There are men on the roof. We need to leave. Now."

Lennox spins, locking eyes with me in the darkness, fear evident in their depths. Then chaos unfolds.

# CHAPTER 35

Torches ignite rapidly along the roofline, revealing uniforms emblazoned with the griffin of Dargan Blackwell. The click of crossbows being nocked hurry my steps as Pike and I herd Lyra and Siobhan toward the half-constructed wall surrounding the massive oak tree in the center of the square, hoping it can shelter them. There isn't much we can do against a well-aimed crossbow bolt except force it away on a wishful breeze, and I won't risk them being injured. Hopefully, the thick limbs full of leaves and fluttering ribbons will help shield them if the short wall fails to do so. The first bolts sing through the darkness, drawing my gaze. Panic lurches in my chest at the sound, and my blood turns to ice when the old priest orders, "Take the women."

One of his minions breaks free from the group as the others begin to fan out.

Glancing at Siobhan and Lyra one more time, I dash to the open portion of the square where Salome and Delphine stand together, sigils glowing, blocking the flurry of quarrels with gusts of wind. The priests lined in front of the cathedral steps have pulled a variety of weapons, from flintlock pistols to staffs, and set themselves against the men in our group. Thankfully, the priests are untrained and are no match to the brutes we side with.

As one of the priests steps from the line to approach her and Delphine, Salome slices a hand through the air, sending a burst of her *glow* toward him. My breath catches and my eyes grow wide as the young priest begins to scream, his severed hand flopping to the ground still holding the blade he clutched. Some of the other priests pause in their advance, staring at Salome as if she is a demon, but she never falters as she continues to lash out, preventing the soldiers' arrows from reaching us. The injured priest cradles his arm, retreating toward the cathedral before he can be struck down fully.

Joining Delphine and Salome, I grab Del's hand and together we project our *glow* to blind the men on the roof to impede their aim. My mind races as quickly as my pulse, wondering how long Salome's power will last, and whether she can strike at the men on the roof from this distance. Lennox's insistence we barricade ourselves in the Den to have a defensible structure rings in my ears, but it's too late for that now. Silently, I grip Delphine's hand harder, hoping we can buy enough time to make it back to the safety of the Den where a portion of our crew awaits us.

A cry to my right distracts me momentarily, snapping my gaze to where Erik drops his axe, clutching his shoulder where he's taken a wound from one of the priest's swords. "No!" Siobhan shouts, leaving Lyra behind the wall as she rushes to his aid. I break from Delphine's grip to lunge behind the retreating priest, stabbing him in the back with my dagger while Lennox twists and slashes across the priest's chest with his cutlass. When I pull my blade free, the priest sinks to the cobblestones where a growing puddle of his blood surrounds his limp figure.

Lennox and I lock eyes before lashing out at another priest who approaches Siobhan and Erik as they retreat to where Lyra still waits. Erik has retrieved his axe and shields Siobhan and Lyra behind him, motioning for Pike to join us in his place, while Lennox and I block the shaking priest in front of us. He drops his cudgel, holding his hands up in surrender.

"Please, have mercy," the priest pleads, but Lennox merely sneers before running his blade through the man's stomach. My ears ring with adrenaline as I extend the only mercy I can manage for a creature who would happily see me burn on a pyre — slitting his throat with my dagger rather than leaving him to bleed out or die of infection. Lennox and I share a breathless look, ignoring the blood that coats each of our hands.

Our victory is brief as a wail rends the air behind me.

Delphine.

I turn and stumble at the sight before me, heart dropping and feet faltering along with my breath in disbelief. Delphine crouches on the cobbles holding Salome's dark head from the ground. The young woman keens as shadows coalesce around her, swirling in a maelstrom of grief. In my distress, it takes a few moments before my shock fades enough to realize she is screaming my name. My *true* name.

"Nerissa! *Nerissa!*" Delphine sobs.

I stagger toward them on shaking legs, tears escaping my eyes as I spy a bolt through Salome's chest, blood surrounding her on the ground. It bubbles from her full lips, like thickened wine as I approach, and all other actions around me seem to fade. The memory of my high priestess in Athene bleeding amongst the sigils on the white marble floor as I was dragged through our temple rises to my thoughts and threatens to paralyze me when I reach the two women. I drop to my knees on the side opposite Delphine, and Salome smiles in my direction, but her eyes are already glassy. She gives a small nod and clutches Delphine's hand tightly.

"It's time, Del," Salome murmurs through the life force seeping from her lips. She then turns her pale green eyes to me and whispers, "Step into your power, child. Remember to *use* your emotions, not run from them."

Suddenly, Delphine snatches my hand in her free one and grips tightly, so tightly I feel my bones rub together and try to pull back. Delphine's eyes shoot to mine and the dark grey depths are fierce as she holds on. Within moments the shadows curl around us.

"Wait," she whispers harshly, voice trembling as she grips me tighter. Tears run down her cheeks, falling onto Salome below her, but her fingers never shake or loosen.

Both of Delphine's hands light with the *glow*, followed by Salome's and my own. It's like when we practiced channeling energy in our lessons, but I don't understand how this could be helpful now, not when Salome is so gravely wounded. After a few moments, Salome's hand begins to dim. A surge of power and heat ripples through my flesh as my skin shines so brightly I have to clench my eyes against the light. Surprise wars with the knot of sorrow in my breast as realization flows alongside the power burning through my body.

Delphine's connection isn't just to temporarily channel energy — she can siphon it *permanently*. At Salome's signal, Delphine began channeling all of Salome's remaining power into *me*.

Never have I felt such intensity. Salome's power envelops me in a comforting embrace and dampens my grief. My head swims with the sensation pulsing through my veins as the full amount of Salome's strength is poured into my body. The sadness of her loss fades, replaced by a deep calm that settles over me like armor — a control that rivals what I already thought I possessed over my emotions. Knowledge that her wisdom and strength now reside with me at all times engulfs me, as if Salome has granted me this peace herself by gifting me her remaining power. After what feels like an eternity, Delphine gasps and releases my hand.

"It's done," Delphine says, her voice shaking before she collapses in racking sobs to cover her mentor's lifeless body with her own. "End it now, Nerissa."

When I rise to my feet, angry tears drip down my cheeks. Stepping from the shadows that curl around Delphine and Salome, I find Lennox, anguished pride burning in his eyes. I didn't notice his approach, but he stands at our side, just outside the small shield Delphine conjured, with both pistols ready for anyone who might disturb us. The men on the roofline stand still, mouths agape with their crossbows pointed downward, eyes focused on the bundle of shadow I rose from. Bodies lay around us on the ground, but some of the priests still stand, hesitantly holding their weapons. Lyra huddles with Erik and Pike, holding a cloth against Erik's bloody shoulder while Siobhan stands ready to aid me if needed.

I meet their eyes as devastation and rage burn in my chest — light radiates off of me, illuminating the center of the square, as I calmly focus my gaze on the man on the roof.

Then, I unleash my fury.

The lamps in the square ignite, the glass coverings bursting with the flames that I conjure. Fire engulfs the torches on the roofline, growing until the soldiers flinch away to avoid being burned. As I slice my hand through the air, soldiers on the roof drop to the ground far below, cut down by the power I wield. Those who avoided the slicing light scream in terror and retreat farther from the edge of the roof.

With this power surging through my veins, I finally understand what Lennox meant when he said Salome used the *glow* as a weapon. What Salome meant about stepping into my power and channeling my emotions.

All my rage and pain is channeled into ruining the men who did this to us tonight. With this power at my fingertips, it's easy to understand the fear people once felt in the presence of priestesses, and the quaking respect we demanded. I slice through these men with a thought and a wave of my hand — *what chance do any of them have against* me?

As I watch the bodies of those I've slain fall to the cobblestones, the remainder drop their crossbows to flee. I stand just beyond Del's shadows, waiting for those who escaped the burning roof to burst through the doors of the cathedral when motion in the side streets draws my attention. From the corner of my eye, I glimpse men running, but they are not dressed like soldiers. Many of the remaining priests have dropped their weapons, screaming as they attempt to retreat to the safety of their cathedral, scrabbling with the soldiers trying to escape the burning interior. The newcomers filing down the streets stop all of them, pushing into the group as they swing their weapons and throw punches. Violence surrounds us once again, this time illuminated by the raging oil lanterns and my *glow*.

One of the men in the newly arrived group peels himself from the melee to rush toward us. He's stopped briefly by Lennox's raised hand, and, although I can't hear their words, I see the man gesturing wildly at Delphine until Lennox relents. I recognize his curled mustache, thick sandy beard, and gentle brown eyes. Johnny, the bartender from the Gilded Rooster, wraps his arms around Delphine who still clings to Salome's hand, tears staining her cheeks. These reinforcements must be his companions.

The firelight flickers over the bloody square, its pulsing matching an ache in my head that I try to ignore as I continue to scan the area, searching for my friends. Lennox remains at my side, alert to any possible threats as the fighting slows. I recognize some of the crew from our ships fighting as well, those who attended the bonfire catching up and those left behind must have come looking for us when we did not arrive at the Den.

For a moment, the shouts and moans of pain are muted, the only sound reaching me is the dull *whoosh* of my heartbeat as my head pulses again and the fury and angst running through the people around me matches my own.

Then, I sway on my feet, trying to clear the haze creeping over my vision with slow blinks before everything goes dark.

# CHAPTER 36
## LENNOX

We run through the dark alley away from the square in a tight group of shadows toward Johnny's tavern. I cradle Nerissa's limp form against my chest, trying to avoid jostling her as much as possible. When she collapsed next to Salome in the square, I thought she had died with her, and my heart nearly stopped with theirs. But the steady thrum of her pulse under my hand tells me she's just exhausted. Knowing she's merely unconscious doesn't soothe the fear burning in my chest, though.

Johnny, Delphine's friend and owner of a tavern a few streets over from the Den, jogs at my side. He holds a dagger in each hand in case of any trouble, but it seems we left all the violence behind us in the square. Although I'm relieved they haven't shown, I find it strange that no patrols have descended on the public area after the short-lived battle. But then, in a city fueled by profits and back alley deals, it wouldn't surprise me if the priests or their support on the Merchant Council had paid them to turn a blind eye.

"You can come to the tavern. There are rooms above it

that are empty. I don't think the Den is safe for her or the others tonight. My men can keep you all guarded until morning," Johnny says as we round the corner to the street where the Gilded Rooster rests. The other buildings are shuttered for the night, unusual for the Solstice. When I look at the closed bars, suspicion clear on my face, Johnny explains, "They're all with us. The entire street rallied when Delphine came to warn us this afternoon."

Delphine, always a wild card, surprises me again. She's never been one to flaunt her connections, but here I see she has cultivated many. Glancing over my shoulder, I see Del's pale curls bobbing through the shadows, Lyra close by her side as we move through the streets.

"I need to send word to my sister," my voice is harsh as I pant from our run. "She needs to know where we are. And Captain Jackson needs to be notified about Salome."

Johnny unlocks the front door of the tavern as the men who have returned with us from the square create a circle of protection in case we were followed. Part of the crews from the *Bartered Soul* and *Andromeda's Vengeance* still monitor the streets leading to the Den, where I placed them in case an attack was coming directly to its doorstep. The rest I left to clean up and head back to the ship or their boarding houses to await further instructions. Only a few of my crew mingle with the locals in Johnny's group at my back, along with Erik, Pike, Siobhan, Delphine, and Lyra.

"I can have an errand boy take it. You can either write it down, or he can memorize it and take word to them," Johnny answers, holding the door of the tavern open wide for me to enter.

Nerissa's head lolls to the side briefly when we stand

under the lantern hanging above the door. For a moment I think she is awake, but when I tilt her back up to look into her eyes, they're closed and she remains limp in my arms.

"Have you ever seen anything like that?" Johnny whispers to me, indicating her brow with a thrust of his chin.

"No. Not even when my mother was still practicing. Even when she was at full strength alongside Salome," I confide.

"Incredible. What we saw her do when we got there was fucking terrifying, mate. But it's still incredible," Johnny murmurs. He gestures toward the stairway hiding behind the bar, sheathing the two daggers and continuing to hold the front door for the others to file in behind us. "You can take her up to the last room at the end. It's one of the larger ones, not as big as you're probably used to, but it's better than nothing. Let us know what you might need to make her comfortable."

Lyra slips from where she stands between Delphine and Pike, her green gown tattered at the hem. Her eyes are steely and her jaw is set as she approaches my side. "I can come to help you, Uncle." I nod once as she takes the key Johnny offers, then leads the way up the stairs.

"Is she injured, or only exhausted?" Lyra asks as she unlocks the door and steps inside the room. Johnny wasn't being modest — it *is* small, with only a single bed and a vanity with a mirror, but it's clean and comfortable.

"I don't think she's injured, but I haven't had a chance to check," I reply, hoping I'm right. I wasn't able to keep my eyes on her the entire time, but I haven't seen any injuries. The blood and dirt that stains her robe and skin seem to only be that which she claimed from others, not her own.

"Go down and get some water and a clean shirt. I can get her undressed and check for injuries." Lyra takes charge like she's been caring for the sick her entire life. Despite the worry I feel over Nerissa, pride blooms in my chest when I take a step back to look at my niece, just as strong and wise as the women she descends from.

"I'll be right back. Here." I reach to my boot to remove the blade I keep tucked there, but she holds up a hand to stop me.

"No need. I have this." She pulls a slim knife from where she had it tucked in her boot, grinning at me. I return the smile — she takes a little bit after her uncle, too, it seems.

Downstairs is a somber affair, but the number of people who have returned with us makes it crowded and noisy. I scan the group, easily locating Erik and Siobhan. Erik sits scanning the crowd, always alert, even as blood still seeps from the wound at his untended shoulder. Pike stands guard at the door with one of Johnny's men and he inclines his head sadly to me when our eyes meet. He predicted violence, that one of us might lose our composure defending the women we love, but not the massacre we left behind us in the square.

"Johnny," I address the bartender when I find him in one corner. "We need water and a clean shirt, and I need to send that errand boy to Celeste and Jackson."

"Of course," Johnny responds. "Lucius!" he calls to one of the men near the bar. "Go get one of my clean shirts from our room and a basin of water. Send Sam over, too." A slim, red-haired man nods in understanding and disappears into the back of the building. While he's gone, a lanky boy just on the edge of manhood runs to our side.

"Yessir, you needed me?" he questions, looking between the two of us.

"Sam, this is Captain Lennox," Johnny introduces me. The boy flinches at my name, taking a small step backward, but then stands tall, looking up at Johnny. "Don't fear him, son. He needs you to run an errand for him. Listen to him closely and do as he asks."

"Yessir," Sam replies, giving me a wary glance.

"Sam, I need you to be swift and carry a message to my sister. Madame Celeste at the Den of Sinful Delights. Do you know where that is?" Sam's eyes grow wide at the location, but he nods and listens attentively to my message. Once he has Celeste's description and has repeated my words back to me three times without mistakes, I have him repeat a message for Jackson and give him an address where I know my old friend can be found tonight, waiting in case we need him. Then, I hand him a gold coin and he scurries out the back door of the tavern. By the time his knit cap is out of sight, Lucius has returned holding a linen shirt and a pitcher of water with clean washcloths. I gather them from him quickly, inclining my head in thanks, and rush back up the stairs.

When I enter the room, Lyra sits on the edge of the bed, watching over Nerissa as she sleeps. Somehow, the girl has removed Nerissa's cloak and robe and has covered her with a sheet and wool blanket. "She doesn't have any injuries that I can see. I think the use of power just exhausted her. Would you like my help to rinse her off and get her in that shirt?"

"No, Lyra. Thank you. I think Delphine may need you, this loss will hit her hard." Lyra nods, taking the pitcher from my hands to place on the vanity, then wraps me in a hug. Her thin arms hold me tight as she lets out a small, shuddering sob. Wrapping her tight, I squeeze her to me and smooth her wild curls as best as I can.

"Uncle Billy, I was so scared. I'm so glad you're both safe," she sniffles into my chest before stepping back to wipe her glistening hazel eyes. "I'm sorry about Madame Salome, though."

"I know. I'm sorry, too. Are you all right, Lyra? Do you need a moment before you go down?"

"No. They need me. I'll be fine." She wipes her eyes again, gathering the blood-stained silver robe she pulled from Nerissa's body. "I'll be sure to soak this, too. I don't want Granny's robe to be stained," she says, then swishes out the door in a whisper of green skirts.

Once she departs, I sit beside Nerissa, pulling her up to dress her in the oversized linen shirt. Then, I carefully wipe her hands and brow, removing any traces of blood and dirt from the square. When she's clean, I tuck her back into the warm bed and lay curled behind her over the coverlet, so similar to how we rested the day Crewes attacked her on the *Bartered Soul*. I thought she was fierce then, but tonight she was a force of nature. The Goddess made flesh.

That day, I would have murdered the entire crew if they had so much as touched her. Now, I'm willing to take on a kingdom to protect her. Not that she needs my protection any longer.

As I stroke her long hair, I wonder how this power will affect her — what darkness will she face? What steps will she want to take now? I will do whatever she asks, as long as I don't have to part from her again.

I lay curled around Nerissa until a light tap at the door pulls me from my thoughts. Carefully, I rise to answer, finding Siobhan standing outside, her normally bright blue eyes sorrowful when they meet mine.

"William, I'm sorry to bother you, but I think Lyra may need some help calming Delphine."

I am loath to leave Nerissa alone, but I understand Siobhan wouldn't have come to me without cause. We have a quiet friendship, and she knows I won't leave Nerissa unless it's completely necessary. Closing the door quietly behind me, I follow her down the stairs. When we reach the bottom, I can hear keening from one of the rooms farther back, and I understand why Siobhan sought me out. Delphine has spent so much time pretending she doesn't care about anyone or anything, that she forgot she, in fact, does.

Salome.

I gesture for Siobhan to return to the tavern while I follow the sounds to the main office. Lyra wrings her hands just outside the open doorway, standing near Jackson and some of his crewmen. Young Sam has done his job well if Jackson has already arrived. Captain Jackson clasps my shoulder when I reach him, tears leaving quiet trails down his ruddy cheeks.

"The girl is inconsolable, Lennox. She tried to scratch my eyes out when I went in, and she screamed at Lyra," Jackson tells me as I watch Delphine through the open doorway.

"You can go out with Siobhan, Lyra. I'll handle Del," I tell my niece quietly before stepping into the office.

When I approach Delphine, my chest hollows and I have to swallow the emotions that threaten to choke me. Salome's body rests on a trestle top, all vivaciousness and life drained from her. Memories of finding my mother's lifeless body tumble through my thoughts causing me to grip the edge of a hutch to steady myself. Delphine wails, kneeling at Salome's side, clutching the older woman's hand to her breast as tears pour from her eyes. Red streaks mingle in her pale blonde hair, but her black robe hides all signs of blood and death from her body; a mourning phantom shaking at Salome's side.

As I kneel beside her, she shoots me a violent look. But, when I take one of her hands, she collapses against me, sobbing into my chest and clinging to me as if I can stave off further pain, or at least share her grief. Comforting Delphine, I allow my own tears to fall. My body shakes, as I mourn Salome and my last connection to my mother and the life she led before Celeste and I were born.

# CHAPTER 37

I blink my eyes, trying to clear my foggy vision, and breathe deeply as I wait for them to focus. Pain surges in my skull when I attempt to sit up, so I lay back and cast my eyes around the unfamiliar space. An oil lamp sits on the side table and a wooden chair stands empty beside my bed in the tiny room. Lennox's worn leather greatcoat is draped over a hook by the door. His pistols and my circlet and choker rest on a small table next to the ewer of water, but I'm alone. Glancing down, I find I'm dressed in only a man's shirt and my hair is a tangled mess around me, but other than my unexpected attire and blistering headache, I seem to be whole.

Voices drift through the closed door from the hallway beyond and faint noise from the city floats through the cracked window, the thin curtain waving in the chilly breeze. It seems as though some part of New Aphros is still enjoying the Solstice holiday, oblivious to the violence in the square, as the indistinct hints of distant laughter and celebration find their way to me. I run through my memories of the evening — *has it all happened tonight?* — and tears sting my eyes at the loss of Salome. Yet another name added to the growing list of those I mourn.

This time, when I try to rise from the bed, I move more slowly, allowing myself time to get my bearings. I pause, waiting for the pain in my head to abate enough for me to stand, gripping the edge of the footboard to steady myself. I start to move toward the door to seek out my friends when the sight of my reflection in the vanity mirror across the room stops me in my tracks. My sigil burns dark at my brow, not cloaked after the stress of the square. But, instead of just the single upturned crescent mark of the Goddess, an intricate circlet of knotwork scrolls out from the sides of the sigil, across my forehead, and into the edges of the dark hair at my temples.

I remain motionless at the foot of the bed, caught in my reflection, when the door cracks open, hinges squeaking in the silence of the room. Lennox and Lyra speak in whispers in the hall until they see me on my feet, white knuckles clutching the end of the bed frame.

"You're awake." Lennox rushes to my side, running his hand over my cheek carefully, eyes darting over me as if inspecting me for damage that might have just surfaced.

"Are you feeling well?" Lyra asks quietly.

"I… I don't know. What is this?" I breathe, still looking at the mark on my brow, sinking to sit on the mattress while still holding onto the footboard.

"I'm not quite sure," Lennox starts, sitting at my side to take my hand in his. He traces soothing circles on the back of my hand with his thumb, as I continue to study my reflection. "It appeared once Delphine started channeling Salome's powers to you. I think Siobhan knows more than she's telling us, but we couldn't wake you, and I thought it would be better if we asked her together."

"Where are we? Is she here?" I ask, finally tearing my eyes away from the mirror. His clothing is covered in dirt and dark smears of what I assume is dried blood from the square. Lyra's dress has stains on the skirts and she looks exhausted, but recalling her actions when Lennox was injured on the voyage to Delosia, I gather she has refused rest, choosing to help those who might need care instead.

"We're at the Gilded Rooster, the tavern Delphine brought us to. She snuck off earlier today to warn them, so Johnny and his friends knew we might need help. But they didn't get there in time," Lyra explains. "Siobhan is downstairs with the rest."

"I want to go see them." I stand again, more steady this time. Lennox clears his throat and scans my body with his brows raised, reminding me I only wear a thin shirt. "Bring me something to wear, please Lyra," I order.

She opens the door quietly and slips out while Lennox takes a seat in the chair next to the bed. He runs his fingers through his hair several times before looking up at me, resting his elbows on his knees as he steeples his fingers under his chin.

"You were fucking magnificent, my she-wolf," he whispers. "But you scared the shit out of me tonight."

I walk to stand in front of him and pull his face up to look at me. His eyes are tired and red, likely from mourning

Salome while I slept, and his face has unwashed scrapes and bruises from the square. I sink down to kneel in front of him and pull his face closer to mine, gently brushing my lips against his.

"I thought I'd lost you, too." His breath shudders as he presses his forehead to mine.

"You have nothing to fear," I murmur as he pulls me against his chest. "I'm not planning on leaving you any time soon." With his arms wrapped around me, a soothing comfort takes root in my chest, and I can't bring myself to let go until Lyra reenters the room holding a pair of men's trousers for me.

Once I'm more suitably attired, we slip down the hallway and take a set of stairs to the open tavern below. I hadn't realized it was a public house when I visited with Delphine and the others, but various rooms line the hallway above the bar at the top of the private stairwell. This late, the tavern is empty except for our group and a few of the men who came with Johnny to our aid. The bearded barkeep stands in his usual place behind the bar, sandy hair pulled into a knot at the back of his head. Siobhan sits with Delphine in a corner booth, the younger woman clutching a mug. Erik and Pike guard the front door, quiet sentries observing everything. Erik's shirt is missing, but a bandage wraps around his chest and shoulder, covering his injury from the square. All talk ceases when we step into the room. Siobhan is on her feet immediately and comes to wrap her arms around me. She trembles and looks with wide eyes at my face, inspecting the new sigil up close.

"We were right," she says quietly in her soft brogue.

"What?" I ask, holding her at arm's length as confusion clouds my mind.

"Salome and I… We were right. We *saw* it, and it came true." Her eyes are unfocused as she speaks as if she's not fully present in the moment.

"Siobhan, what are you talking about?" I shake her gently, gripping her arms as firmly as my worry and frustration grip me. She blinks several times before refocusing on my face and taking a deep breath. I follow her lead, inhaling deeply to clear my emotions as I look to her for answers.

"We need to sit. There is much to discuss," she says finally, louder and more clearly than before.

"Johnny," Lennox calls to the familiar bartender. "Clear the room."

Johnny nods once, then gestures for anyone not in our group to retire. "Upstairs, everyone. Leave the Captain and his friends to their business." The few who are unfamiliar make a hasty retreat, but Lennox snags Johnny's arm as he walks past, heading toward the hallway and stairs we descended.

"Not you. We may need you." Johnny looks at Lennox's grip on his bicep once, but purses his lips and nods his acceptance of the order, returning to his place behind the bar.

I allow Siobhan to lead me to the table where Delphine sits, but Del doesn't meet my gaze as we take our seats, focusing on the contents of her mug. Lyra takes the last empty chair, and Siobhan draws in a steadying breath. "I told you when I met you on Delosia that I read for you. I mentioned the dagger and crown. I thought perhaps it was a vision of your past. But, when I came here and met Salome, we talked about my visions and what I had divined. She had *seen* the same images. When we scried together Salome was never able to see past Solstice. I kept seeing crowns and wolves, but she only saw you with the *mark*." Her eyes settle on my face again, drifting up to where the new sigil feels burned into my brow.

"When we met this morning she told me her final vision. She knew she wouldn't survive the night, but that *you* would. That you would take up the mantle of the queens of legend — High Priestess and Queen united once again. But she needed our help to make sure of it." Siobhan cuts her eyes to Delphine, making it clear that Del knew this information, as well.

"Now you…," she pauses, glancing at the others in the room. "*We* can all go against Blackwell. Now, we have a chance at taking back what belongs to all of us, and of keeping him and his fanatics from causing any more damage," Siobhan whispers as if saying the words might bring ruin upon us sitting here. The news of my true identity sits heavy in the air, the truth finally laid bare for anyone who might not have already known.

"The new priests that arrived in the city recently weren't priests at all," Lennox adds, walking up behind me, his voice cutting the tension in the booth. "They were soldiers in disguise to fortify the King's interest in New Aphros. It was coincidental that they were here at the same time we were. Based on one of the priest's accounts, it seems Blackwell is looking to expand territory now that he thinks he has a hold over Selennia. Pike got it out of one of them."

I look over my shoulder to where Pike stands with his

jaw tense as he dips his chin to me. Dark stains mar his breeches and the edges of his rolled-up sleeves, giving the only explanation I need for how the older man succeeded in drawing out the information.

"He doesn't have as strong a grip as he thinks, though," a familiar gruff voice chimes in, drawing my gaze to meet the bold blue stare of Captain Jackson. Ever since the full moon ceremony, I gathered that he and Salome had a more intimate relationship than they presented to the public. His grief is evident tonight, red-rimmed eyes glistening in his weathered face, confirming my suspicions.

"Most of the people back in Selennia are too afraid to challenge him at this point, but the majority don't approve of his methods or his priests pushing through the countryside. You would have support there should you seek to take back your land, Mistress. You have my support, and that of my crew."

Jackson bends one knee, kneeling before me and crossing his arm across his chest so his fist rests on his heart. The action sucks the air from my lungs and makes my knees weak. It seems that even if I don't wish to embrace my heritage, others are already willing to lay their lives down for me, and I struggle to mask the disbelief that pierces my pounding heart as I gaze upon the man before me.

"Please stand, Captain," I whisper to Captain Jackson. He inclines his head once, then returns to his feet. "Before we make any pledges or plans, we need to take care of the people here," I reply, my voice strained but firm, as I look at the friends gathered in the room. "We need to be sure Salome receives the respectful burial she deserves."

I fight to hold in the tears that burn behind my eyes, biting the inside of my cheek to steady myself. I need to be strong now, even if I wish to mourn the woman I've grown to look up to these past weeks. The added pressure of possibly starting a war presses down on me, threatening to suffocate me where I sit, but I can't simply run from the room anymore as I might wish. There are too many eyes waiting to see how I'll behave.

"She's been brought in for preparation already," Delphine finally speaks, her voice rasping as if she has strained it screaming. Her heart-shaped face is streaked with tears and her eyes are puffy from crying. She was the closest to Salome out of any of us, except maybe Lennox and Celeste. If I didn't think she would rebuff me, I would wrap my arms around her to offer comfort, but the anger in her eyes tells me all I need to know about how that gesture would be received. "I'll see to the final preparations and we will send her to the Afterlife tomorrow."

Lennox nods once to Delphine and says, "My crew will have the burial pyre ready by midday. I expect the city will come out to celebrate her."

"As do I," Delphine replies before she turns her hard stare back on me. "I didn't want to like you, but Salome believed in you." She takes a shaky breath, swallowing thickly before she continues, "Don't waste it. Her power. She guarded it when she left Selennia because she knew she would need it. She *saw* you and knew you would come to her. She trusted that you would show her the way to reunite the power of the priestesses and the queen once again. Prove you're worth losing her for. Don't make me regret passing her gifts to you."

Delphine stands, drinking the remainder of her mug before abandoning it on the table. Before she turns to walk toward the stairs, she points a slender finger at my brow. Any hint of affection she may have once held for me is gone from her face as she looks at me, leaning her other hand on the table to steady herself. "And figure out how to fucking cloak that before you get us all killed." Then she disappears into the hallway to prepare her mentor for her pyre.

"I think we should all get some rest," Siobhan suggests, watching Delphine disappear through the doorway. "We can say goodbye tomorrow. Then you can tell us what to do."

I start to speak but pause when Lennox places his hand gently on my arm, silently urging me to hold my tongue, to concede to rest, at least for tonight.

"You are all welcome to stay here tonight. The doors are locked and I don't suppose anyone will think to seek you here," Johnny's voice carries through the tavern from where he leans at the bar. Siobhan seeks refuge in Erik's arms and Pike leads Lyra to her chambers before returning to the bar to share a drink with Johnny and Jackson. Lennox grabs a bottle of wine from behind the counter as we walk past to climb the stairs and return to the small room overhead.

"Is Celeste all right? Did they get word to her?" I ask him once we are behind the closed door. He sinks into the chair, exhaustion written in the slant of his shoulders, and takes a swig directly from the bottle, once, then twice, before answering.

"She is. They closed and barred the doors before anyone could show up to the celebration. Some of the women of the crew are inside and others still guard the streets. No one has been allowed to enter. Messages were passed through the door once the errand boy confirmed Celeste's identity," he sighs, dropping the bottle down to the ground at his feet. "She has it under control; she's handled these situations before."

"Are you all right?" I ask him gently. He'd known Salome since he was a child, and he's already lost so many people. When he looks up at me after taking another sip from the bottle his eyes are lined with silver and a tear escapes to run down his face. It breaks my heart to see him troubled, even if my own heart aches for the same loss, and I quickly step to his side to take him in my arms.

"I'm fine," he says with a shuddering breath. "But I need you to tell me what you're thinking. What do you want to do next?"

I sit on the edge of the bed facing him, his question washing over me as I place my head in my hands. "I don't know."

"We can go. You don't have to stand against him if you don't want to. We can flee this city and disappear if that's what you want. But know, if you want to go back to Selennia, if you want to claim your birthright, I will be by your side. No one will harm you again as long as I live, Nerissa. The choice is yours, but I *will* be with you, whatever that choice may be. Forever, if you'll have me." At this, he takes another drink from the bottle and slips from the chair onto his knees in front of me. His arms wrap around my waist as he lays his cheek against my lap.

"Of course, I'll have you," I whisper back to him, emotions clogging my throat as I run my trembling fingers through his hair. "Forever."

"Then the decision is yours. Think about it tonight. We can make our plans tomorrow," he says gazing up at me. I pull him up to kiss me, soft and comforting after the pain of the past hours. Curling together on the small bed, our tears quietly cleanse the pain from our souls.

# CHAPTER 38

The next morning we slip out the back of the tavern as a small group, leaving Delphine and Lyra behind to finish Salome's preparations. When I checked in on them this morning, I promised to send clothing back for them for the processional later that day. Death has always been a natural part of the cycle of life for priestesses and those who follow the Old Ways, but today is still somber and painful. An unnatural or unexpected death is never easy to make peace with.

My chest aches with woe when I walk through the door of the Den of Sinful Delights. The entire building feels small and dull without Salome's bold presence and soothing smoke filling the space. It's almost as if the very walls of the Den mourn her with us. The glittering Solstice decorations are still hanging, waiting for the celebration that never came, at odds with the sorrow that suffuses the empty rooms. Erik and Siobhan head to their quarters immediately, while Pike takes up guard at the doorway even though his eyes are bloodshot from lack of sleep. Lennox and I walk into the salon and down the hall to Salome's office where Celeste sleeps on the small couch, a sharp knife and a bottle of brandy laying on the floor next to her.

Celeste starts when Lennox shakes her awake, but she hugs him tightly when she sees who rouses her. Standing from the couch, she pulls me into a warm embrace as well. While I tense at first, I quickly relax against her soft body, allowing her to offer comfort whether I'm deserving of it or not.

"We are the last ones left now, brother," Celeste says sadly to Lennox. Salome was the last semblance of family they still had from Selennia, all that remains is one another and Lyra's shining smile to offer memories of the past. At least Celeste still has her mother-in-law on Delosia, should she decide to venture away from New Aphros.

I made peace with the loss of my family years ago, even if the ache in my heart never truly ceases. But now, I've found a new family: Lennox, Celeste, Lyra, and the rest of our friends. We may not share blood or lineage, but we share the same relentless spirit, the same fierce desire to survive, and the dream that one day we might be able to live in peace, free of the tyrant who sits on my mother's throne.

"We won't let this go unpunished," I murmur, surprising both of them, their eyes wide when they take me in. After laying awake most of the night, I've made my decision. I know what I want to do next. Watching Lennox and Celeste mourn only further steels me, but this is not the time to address my plans. This is the time to celebrate Salome and send her to the Afterlife.

Lennox and I wearily climb the mahogany stairs and

enter our room to dress. I long for a hot bath, but can't bear to bother any of the mourning servants to request hot water. Instead, I make do with the cold water in the ewer, rinsing my arms and face in an attempt to look refreshed. Lennox follows suit and combs his hair back. We both dress in finery — this is a celebration of Salome, after all — and could be mistaken for preparing for a ball or other celebratory engagement. I select the black and midnight blue gown with constellations of metallic embroidery covering the skirts that Lennox gifted me on Delosia, packed in case of a special occasion, but suitable for today's mourning. He matches me, wearing his black coat with silver embroidery. My chest tightens as I admire him so handsomely turned out, wishing it was for the festivities we should have celebrated last night instead of mourning our friend.

Is this what we will face now? Endless days wishing we were celebrating instead of continually mourning?

For a moment, my resolve falters, and my heart stumbles in my breast as a wave of panic washes over me. My palms grow sweaty as my hands tremble, and I almost blurt that I want to flee, to leave now and never look back, just the two of us. The heavy air in my lungs seems to suffocate me as I try to push down the thought of what losses we may still face.

But I owe him more.

I owe my friends more.

I owe *myself* more.

So, I blink my fear away along with my tears, brushing my palms down my skirt and breathing deeply before I take Lennox's arm to walk down the stairs to where the wagon awaits.

The entire staff of the Den of Sinful Delights follows us into the hazy late morning sunlight to walk behind the wagon that stands out front. The driver wears a mask and a fine suit, and his matching bay horses gleam in the sunlight while they stand with their legs cocked, waiting for the procession to begin. Lennox and I take our place directly behind the wagon, followed by Celeste, Siobhan, and Erik. Pike shores up the rear of our small party and then the rest of those who live and work in the Den fill in, sprinkled with members of our combined crews. Daniel limps into the line, recovered enough to make the stroll now that he has been partially healed. I assume he wishes to offer support to Delphine once we retrieve her from the Gilded Rooster.

The other Houses on the row open their windows and doors, some of the madames joining us, while the girls stand on the balconies to observe the procession. As we make our way the few streets over to collect Salome's prepared body, other windows and doors swing open to honor us. At the tavern, Johnny and a red-headed man carry a trestle top between them, Salome's prepared figure wrapped in red cloth from head to toe resting on the surface. Delphine steps from the doorway behind them, her gown the darkest black to match the gloom that hangs over us all. Lyra holds her hand and leads her to join our party. Daniel breaks from the back of the group, limping to take Delphine's other hand regardless of the pain that he surely must still be feeling in his beaten body.

Once Salome is loaded on the wagon, the entire procession moves out, slowly walking behind the horses. New Aphros celebrates funerals more elaborately than we did in Selennia, merging the traditions of the islands and other cultures to create a beautiful send-off for the deceased. As we walk to the beat of a slow dirge, the cathedral looms ahead. Since we must pass the square to reach the pyre on the riverbank, I can only hope that any priests or soldiers who still live will stay inside.

As we approach, my stomach flips, and my muscles tremble at the destruction. The roof of the nearly completed building is charred, the supports hanging into the now open interior, but the surrounding brick buildings stand unscathed by the fire that raged around the square from my anger last night. Glass from the lantern covers glitter in the afternoon sunlight, stuck between the cobbles like ice. Standing before the open cathedral doors wait several young men.

My pulse climbs, panic gripping me at the sight of another line of men on the threshold of the ruined building. I clutch at Lennox's hand, carefully schooling my expression to hide my fear, but he squeezes it once to settle me. Once we are closer, I note that these men are not wearing black robes, but instead hold them in their outstretched hands. As Salome's wagon passes, our footsteps slow to watch as they drop the robes to the ground and kneel, dropping their heads in respect as they cross a hand over their chest.

My eyes grow wide and my breath catches with surprise at their act of reverence, halting my steps. A gasp echoes through the procession as the men then rise and join at the end of the line, evidently renouncing their new religion to return to the Old Ways. Tears threaten to fall, but I force myself to remain poised, holding them back for now as a glimmer of hope threads through my sorrow. I fear if I allow them to escape I won't be able to stop them again, and I'm not willing to share my emotions with the growing crowd if I can help it.

No one creates any further disturbance as we continue to the murky riverfront, where all trading has paused and the sailors and riverboat men hold their hats in respect for the fallen madame. Salome was a force in this city. I knew it before, but this show of love and respect in a city driven by commerce proves it.

Standing with their backs to the river, familiar faces greet us. The remainder of the crews of the *Bartered Soul* and *Andromeda's Vengeance* are almost all present, save for the few who stayed behind to keep an eye on the ships at anchor. Captain Jackson stands in the crowd with most of the crew of the *Selkie's Tears*, standing out in his bright patchwork coat. Several other men that I recognize by sight, if not by name, from my time on Delosia are also there to pay their respects, alluding to other ships seeking calmer shores and the comfort of the city of New Aphros for the winter storm season. Even the portly merchant Lennox spoke to at the full moon ceremony stands in the crowd in a black suit.

Lennox and Erik lift the trestle top holding Salome and carry it up the makeshift steps to the pyre. Delphine, Siobhan, and I all ascend once they have placed her in the center and returned to the ground. My hands tremble as we sprinkle herbs and flowers over the red cloth, whispering prayers and blessings with shaking voices to say farewell to our friend, our teacher, our High Priestess. I expect Delphine to light the pyre, but when Lennox hands her the torch from the ground, she turns and places it in my hands, bowing her head slightly before taking Siobhan's hand and walking back down the steps. For a moment I'm unable to hide the shock that she would allow me the honor of lighting the pyre, my lips parting in surprise as I watch their retreating forms.

I stand alone on the pyre with one of my last links to my mother, my past, my truth. My chest aches and the flame of the torch shivers in the wind as my hands shake with the feelings I restrain.

"Goodbye, Salome. Thank you for everything, " I whisper, my voice cracking with the tears I refuse to shed, quickly adding the final words to send someone to the Afterlife. I fear if I begin crying now, I won't be able to finish the ritual.

Looking between the torch in my right hand and the waiting pyre I close my eyes, reaching within to the emotions that crash through me — despair, regret, outrage. Pulling on each feeling, I hear the gathered crowd suck in a breath as I push my power through my empty hand, igniting the oiled kindling without using the torch. Opening my eyes I stare into the flames for a moment, dropping the unnecessary torch on the pyre in finality before stepping down the wooden stairs to return to Lennox's side.

Ignoring whispers and glances from the crowd, I grip the front of Lennox's coat and rest my cheek against his chest, finally allowing the tears I've reined in to slip from my eyes. Nothing reaches my ears beyond the lap of the river as it splashes on the shore and the snap of twigs burning in the oil-soaked pyre. The voice of nature drowns out the mournful songs of the gathered crowd as Lennox wraps his arms around me and holds me tight to protect against the sorrow in my heart.

Opening my eyes while holding tight to Lennox, my gaze flicks between those closest to us. Resolve in what I must do, and who I must protect, washes over me. I can no longer allow fear to rule my decisions. The haughty confidence I wore as a mask at the House of Starlight is no longer enough to protect me, or them.

As the last embers burn, glowing a deep orange to match the setting sun, the music that surrounds us becomes upbeat and my tears dry. Turning to make our way back toward the city, we pause, allowing the merchant who hails Lennox to approach as people start to laugh and cheer, milling around us back toward the city — the mourning has ended and the celebration of life begins. The merchant addresses me first with a sad smile. "My sincerest apologies for your loss, Mistress."

I swallow and dip my head in thanks.

Then, he turns to Lennox and says quietly, "Caldwell has been removed from the Council. The munitions you delivered to me last month will be returned to your ship this evening. The city of New Aphros stands behind you, Captain. Whatever you may need. Whatever *you both* may need."

Lennox's jaw tightens as a flicker of surprise flashes in his eyes, but he nods once in understanding, shaking the man's hand before placing his palm on my lower back to guide me back into the procession. "Thank you, Jean."

We all file back to the Den of Sinful Delights, the streets cheering and singing along with the bright music. As tears return to slip down my cheeks, I allow myself this time to smile and dance with Lennox and my friends by my side.

For today, we can celebrate Salome and life.

In this moment, I can be happy. Just a nameless face in the streets of a welcoming city.

Tomorrow, we will plan our attack and plot our vengeance.

Tomorrow, I will claim my birthright.

Tomorrow, I will become a queen.

# EPILOGUE

Over a month and a half has passed since we bid farewell to Salome, the time since spent mourning and preparing before we departed New Aphros. Another week has dissolved since the final supplies were balanced between the *Bartered Soul* and *Andromeda's Vengeance* and we returned to the sea. Erik still captains the *Vengeance*, but this time Siobhan stands firmly at his side. Lyra and Delphine are with us on the *Bartered Soul,* taking the cabin Lyra and I shared on our trip from Selennia. Daniel, fiercely loyal, refused to leave Delphine's side, so he and the other young reformed priests joined the crew to aid us in our endeavors.

A stack of ancient texts, bound with a thick length of ribbon waited for me on Salome's desk when we returned after that fateful night. I haven't had the heart to open them yet, but I know I must review the knowledge within them soon if I hope to fully embrace my new title, even if I can't fathom what I might glean that Salome could not.

Salome also left a journal outlining her visions for how to help the people in New Aphros and a letter of last requests, bequeathing the Den of Sinful Delights to Delphine. Since Del decided to come with us, Celeste has taken up the helm in New Aphros. She agreed to remain in the city and manage our interests until we know the outcome of our return to Selennia, both running the Den and installing Juliet to manage the former Midnight Magnolia after turning it into a boarding house for women in the city who need a safe place to stay.

Celeste said farewell on the riverfront, her newly colored auburn hair shimmering in the misty late winter sunlight. This time, she hugged Lennox and me as tightly as she did Lyra, no longer hiding her affection like when she bid farewell to me outside the House of Starlight.

"Make them all pay," she whispered holding me close. Tears glistened in her hazel eyes when we parted and I stepped onto the deck of the flat-bottomed boat.

LENNOX STANDS AT MY SIDE ON THE QUARTER DECK, WRAPPED in the night sky and starlight. The decks are quiet except for the few crewmembers who keep watch through the dark hours, only the stars providing light since the moon is in her dark phase. The sea is calm and the sky is cloudless, so much so that it's difficult to distinguish the horizon line where the water ends and the sky begins. My eyes scan the black water where the reflection of the stars blends with swaths of glowing ripples. We have reached a part of the sea I missed before, where the ocean shines with tiny glowing creatures who make the waves their own shimmering galaxy in the depths.

"Are you ready, my pretty priestess?" Lennox murmurs against my ear, pulling me close to his chest and smoothing the tendrils of hair from my cheeks where the gentle, briny breeze has blown them.

"Are you?" I tease, pulling my attention from the water to smile back, taking his hands in mine.

"Since I first saw you," he replies, his eyes soft as he brushes a gentle kiss against my lips.

Stepping back, I pull a golden ribbon from the pocket of my cloak and, together, we wrap it once around our clasped left hands.

"I, Nerissa Faelan, bind myself in love to you — tonight, and all nights we may have together," I begin, wrapping the ribbon around further, my actions binding us as much as my words. "By the moon in the sky and the fire in my soul, I will love you until the Goddess parts us and we meet again in the Afterlife."

Lennox clasps my hand tighter in his as he takes the ribbon and begins to wrap his portion. "I, William Lennox, bind myself in love to you — tonight and all nights we may have together. By the blood in my veins and the ocean I sail, I will love you until the Goddess parts us and we meet again in the Afterlife."

Once our wrists are bound, and our vows are spoken, we drink sweet wine from a goblet perched on the railing, pouring some into the sea to share with the Goddess. When the goblet is empty, I smile, looking up at Lennox through my lashes. His expression is soft, his eyes studying my face before he pulls me closer with his free hand.

He tilts my face up to his, pressing a gentle kiss to my lips to seal our handfasting. When he steps back, he reaches into his pocket and pulls out the gold ring he usually wears on his little finger, and I glance at the hand that is tied to mine, spotting a white line where it normally rests. Lennox slips the thick band on the middle finger of my free hand. Then, smiling wickedly he grips me tighter and deepens our kiss, sending fire licking through my veins at his urgency.

I pant when I pull back, desire coursing through me along with the love that swells in my chest. "Well, husband. Do you feel any different?"

"I feel whole, my love. Shall we consummate our union now, wife?" he asks with a rakish grin.

I allow a laugh to pour from my lips at his glittering eyes and bright smile.

"You rogue!" I tease, gently smacking his hard chest with my free hand, where he covers it with his own, holding it over his heart.

Although we have handfasted in private, it isn't to hide our union; the crew knows we are one. It's merely a tradition we decided to uphold together while we still have peace to do so, the way we celebrated the rites alone in the grove years ago surrounded by the trees and stars. I allow myself this night of happiness, one I never anticipated having after the life I've led so far.

Pushing my sadness from the past back down to join my worries for the future, all things I can focus on another day, I pull the ribbon from our arms. Wrapping it around

Lennox, I tug him close, flashing a broad smile as he presses against me. Then, we seal our union with another kiss under the glittering starlight.


TO BE CONTINUED
in *Andromeda's Vengeance*

# AFTERWORD

Thank you so much for following the next installment in Andromeda and Lennox's story! I can't wait to share the next part of their journey with you in *Andromeda's Vengeance*.

If you enjoyed this book or any of the others in the series, please consider leaving a review on Amazon or Goodreads (or any of your other favorite review spots!)

Reviews and word of mouth are the best ways you can support your favorite indie authors, and I appreciate every review! The more people who read my stories, the more I can continue to write and share them with the world!

xo,

LB

# ACKNOWLEDGMENTS

Oh my goodness, friends, we made it to the end of Book Two! I never imagined that I would be writing acknowledgments for a single book, let alone a second one.

First, I have to give credit to my darling husband, Matt. The one who supports my nonsense, even if he doesn't know what I'm rambling on about most of the time. Thank you for giving me the space to devote this much time to fictional people and for taking such good care of the real people in our world. Also, to little E — who I hope will one day look at what I've created and be inspired to follow her dreams and embrace her creative side. I'll always support your nonsense, too, little one!

To Kyle, Renee, and Michelle: The IRL BFFs. Y'all have been amazing in supporting my weirdness and creativity. I love you all, and even though we are all busy living these crazy lives I appreciate your friendship and support.

To my alphas, Elle, B., and Brit: The alpha doc for this was *rough*. Thank you for giving me the feedback and insight I needed to push through and move it along.

To my Betas: Kaitie, Rhiannon, Caity, Meg, Danielle, Lauren, and Bex: Y'all gave me the extra boost and feedback that I needed to keep going when things were tough. Thank you so much for being excited for Lennox and Andi and keeping me motivated with your excitement.

To Aimee: This book would not exist without your help. From your support with *TBS* to the amazing developmental insights and editing of this book, you have been invaluable. Thank you for knowing how to deliver the important messages without me wanting to burn the whole draft and thank you for helping me to grow into a better writer every time.

To *The Daily Discord*: Ladies, your friendships and insights have uplifted my spirits and kept me laughing throughout this process. Thank you for letting me be part of your little circle, I can't wait to see where we all go and what stories we create.

To every single ARC Reader, Hypewoman, and Booksta-Besties: There are far too many of you to list, but please know that every sweet message, every like/share/review/tag, means the world to me. I never in my life thought I would find so much support from people I have never met, but I am so happy that Andromeda and Lennox's story has meant something to each of you, I can't wait for you to see where they go next.

Finally, Mom: Thanks for all of your support and the peddling of my book to all of your friends, whether they want to read it or not. I love you!

# About the Author

L.B. Benson is a native Texan and a lifelong reader. She formally immortalized her love of books by earning a Bachelor of Arts in English from the University of Texas. While she primarily writes romance, you can find her engrossed in almost any genre.

L.B. spends her spare time dreaming up stories in the Texas countryside where she lives with her family.

Stay up to date by following along at https://lbtheauthor.com or on social media (@lb_the_author).

instagram.com/lb_the_author